VICIOUS KNIGHT

PROLOGUE

Thorne

One year ago

LIFE IS WHAT YOU MAKE IT.

There is no such thing as good luck or bad.

There is only giving and taking.

Conquering and defeat. War and the peace you allow.

I learned from an age too young for most that you have to know when to choose your battles.

Sometimes you have to wait for the perfect moment to strike. Or for the right opportunity to come along to get what you want.

Like now.

Tonight is my initiation. The moment I've been waiting for my whole life.

In just a handful of minutes I'll become a member of the Knights, one of the most powerful secret societies in the world.

Becoming a Knight will define everything I do next with my life.

It will be the foundation of my success.

Pushing my shoulders back, I walk through the large oak doors of the ceremonial hall. The instant I'm inside the scent of power wraps around me and sinks beneath my skin.

That potent scent is everywhere—in the ceiling above, the stone floor beneath my feet, and it ripples through the members of the Knights Council standing on either side of the room watching me.

Like me, they're wearing the black Knight's tunic with the blue-silver Raventhorn Crest embossed in the center.

In another world we could be mistaken for Templar Knights, but we couldn't be more opposite. Ours is a society borne from darkness and danger.

Aleksander Ivanov, my uncle and leader of the Knights, stands at the head of the hall.

He is the sovereign of our beginning and our end. The man tasked with ensuring we live by the Oath, and die by it.

I focus on him and, like always, my thoughts collide. We're family, but it's in name only.

If my dear uncle truly had things his way I'd be long dead and just as much a ghostly memory as my father, mother, and sister.

After their massacre my uncle took me in and raised me along with his sons, but he's grown to despise me.

I bow my head respectfully when I reach him. He does the same with that emotionless stare he always gives me.

"Raise your right hand." His voice rumbles through the hall.

I obey, lifting my hand.

"Thorne Nicholai Ivanov. Do you swear your life and allegiance to our cause?"

"I do." Those simple words reflect my deepest desires and all the hard work I've put in to get to this point in my life.

"Then please take the Oath." His unwavering gaze scrutinizes me, finally showing some emotion.

In his eyes I see dread laced with the undertone of fear. He doesn't know I can see the latter, but it's as clear as his presence before me.

In his eyes I see his fear of the threat he thinks I'll become to him some day.

He's scared I'll be just like my father. A man who could unearth the deepest of secrets. People say that's what got him killed. People also say that's why no one to this day has been able to find out who was responsible for killing my family.

Since I'm a literal chip off the old block, my uncle thinks I'm death. A disaster waiting to happen.

That's why he didn't want me to make it this far. But that's too fucking bad because I'm here.

"*Iuramentum est vita nostra et mors nostra*," I say in Latin, which translates to: The oath is our life and our death.

Aleksander picks up the ceremonial blade from the stand next to him and slices a thin line across my palm. Blood seeps from the wound and I turn my hand over, allowing it to drop into the fountain between us.

My blood blends with the water and he nods his agreement with my

VICIOUS KNIGHT

SINS OR SAINT SERIES

BOOK ONE

USA *TODAY* BESTSELLING AUTHOR

FAITH SUMMERS

vow, displaying acceptance so the members can see. However, we both know this is just for show.

The Oath dictates that my uncle now owns my ass. Except he doesn't really.

You can't own death. It's a bitter truth for him. At the same time, I won't be a fool and take comfort in that notion.

To get what I want, or have any part of my family's legacy, I'll have to play by my uncle's rules for a little longer.

He will make everything harder for me from tonight onwards.

Tonight is round one, and *I* won.

Now I just have to keep on winning by doing what I do best—being the conqueror.

Failure is not an option. To fail is to die.

I would never give my uncle such a pleasure.

I'm Thorne Ivanov. I always get what I want.

This path will be no different.

I'll make sure of it.

CHAPTER 1

Present Day

I'M SUPPOSED TO BE DEAD...

I promised myself I would never think about that cold, callous truth. That secret part of my life is supposed to stay locked away in Pandora's box, but for the last few months the wretched thought is all that's been living inside my head. *Along with the past.*

My hands glide over the keys of the piano, summoning each note to life with the grace of a renowned concert pianist.

Music fills every corner of the living room, flowing from my heart in a dark melody of Wagner meets Debussy. That's my style. I marry Wagner's deep emotion to Debussy's atonal structural pattern.

The tune rises with the sounds of the oncoming storm outside my parents' manor. My fingers dance across the ebony and alabaster keys and a fierce gust of wind sends a shiver through the windows. Thunder rumbles across the skies and lightning strikes in the distance, piercing through the blanket of night.

The weather has been like this all week. Unsettled, unstable, unhinged. *And so have I...*

I can't help it. No matter what I do, I can't seem to breathe past the taut ropes wrapping around my soul. Everything feels like a bad omen to me.

Me, the girl with the borrowed life.

Tomorrow I'll be making the journey from L.A. to Raventhorn University in Boston. There I'll pursue my dreams to study and compose music.

Like most eighteen-year-olds starting their freshman year, I've worried about leaving my home, friends, and family. And I've obsessed about fitting into the place where I'll be spending the next four years of my life.

I'm sure anyone would tell me it's completely normal to feel this way. But what's not normal is me.

For the last nine years I've lived a secret life. One where my mother and I have assumed new identities to keep us safe from the past.

This will be the first time I'll be on my own and expected to be mindful of all those parts of my life that *need* to stay secret.

As if sensing the heightened shift in my mood, another flash of lightning crackles across the sky.

With a deep breath I school my thoughts and lean forward, allowing the platinum ends of my ponytail to drift over my shoulder as I play the quick-tempo bridge of my composition.

The sudden sound of footsteps in the corridor makes me lift my head. Moments later my mother and Levgen, my stepfather, appear at the door.

They'd gone out to dinner earlier with their friends. Because it's my last night at home they wanted me to join them, but I wasn't in the mood to socialize.

When I get worked up like this the only thing that can calm me is my music.

Mom hits me with one of her I'm-worried-about-you smiles, while Levgen gives me a hope-filled stare.

With his loose wavy hair and neatly-trimmed beard, he's always reminded me of a blond version of Sirius Black from the *Harry Potter* movies.

Next to his tall, muscular stature my mother looks like a little fairy.

I look like her. I got everything from her long platinum hair to her silver-gray eyes, and her five-foot-four willowy figure.

The moment people see me they know straight away that I'm Oksana Yegorov's daughter.

I stop playing to greet my parents and try to look like I've controlled my freakout.

"Hey, sweetheart, just checking on you." Mom's light Russian accent is a welcome sound.

She walks ahead of Levgen to give me a little hug, then keeps her gaze trained on me as if she's trying to unlock the worries from my mind.

"You've been in here since before we left." Levgen rests his hands on top of the piano and sighs.

"I'm just trying to get in some quality time. I won't have my own piano on campus. It's going to be strange scheduling practice time when I'm used to playing whenever I want."

"That's understandable, but you have a long day tomorrow. Flying across the country is exhausting enough, but you're also going to college."

"I promise I'll head up to bed in a little while."

"Alright." A warm smile grazes his lips. "I'm going to miss you like crazy, sweet girl. The house won't be the same without you and your beautiful music."

I smile back at him, appreciating his love even more than I already do.

"I'll miss you, too." I truly mean that. Levgen has been a great stepfather to me.

My father might have taught me how to play the piano, but Levgen nurtured my musical talents. He took me to all my classes, sent me to music camp every summer, and attended every single concert with my mother at his side.

More importantly, it was Levgen who saved Mom and me in Russia when my father went to prison and became a disgraced Knight.

He was Dad's best friend. So when Dad was found guilty of being an accomplice to a murder plot of a group of political and mafia leaders, Levgen took care of us. He gave us this new life in L.A. where we could be safe and he could provide for us.

"Knowing you're going to study music at one of the best colleges in this world makes up for us missing each other." Levgen taps my head the same way he used to when I was little. "I know you're going to do amazing at Raventhorn."

"Thank you."

"My God, I'm going to cry again." Mom chuckles, but her eyes hold a sheen of tears.

"I know just the thing we need." Levgen looks from Mom to me with a spark in his eyes. "How about I fix us some hot fudge sundaes?"

"I would love that." I grin back at him.

"Anything for you, sweet girl." Levgen dips his head and leaves us.

Mom pulls up a chair and plants herself beside me.

"Talk to me, Ivy." She scans my face, looking at me again with a poignant stare. "How are you really feeling? I'm already missing you and I can't believe my little girl is going off to college, but at least I have Levgen to comfort me."

"I'm just nervous, but I'll be okay."

"And you're worrying about Raventhorn again?" She raises her brows inquisitively.

There's no point lying even if I want to because my mother can always see straight through me. "I'm trying not to."

"I know you wanted to go to Juilliard or Berklee, but you understand why you have to attend Raventhorn, right?" She holds my gaze with the same intensity she's shown me over the million times we've spoken about Raventhorn.

"I understand."

Raventhorn is an elite college all the heirs of the Knights are required to attend. Heirs like me.

The Knights are a secret society that has always governed our lives. As Levgen is a senior member, it's mandatory that I study at Raventhorn.

Although they accept students whose families are allies with the Knights, like those in the Bratva and Italian mafia, the majority of students there come from Knight families like mine.

"Raventhorn is just as good as Juilliard or Berklee." Mom leans forward and takes my hands into hers.

"I know, but it's the Knights who worry me. Going to Raventhorn means being around the same people we've tried to keep our secrets from all these years."

Mom stares back at me, wordless. She knows I'm right. And that I have every reason to be worried.

If anyone were to find out that the two of us are alive when we're supposed to be dead, and that my real father is a convicted Knight, it would be the end of all of us.

"Levgen has put his life on the line to make sure that neither of us have to worry about the past ever again. You don't even need to think about it."

"It's on my mind because I've never been around these people without you."

She looks me over with understanding and gives my hands a gentle squeeze. "Just remember everything we told you and you'll be absolutely fine."

"The three warnings." I speak with reflection, showing her I remember. "Yes."

When Mom and Levgen got married they gave me the 'safety talk'. The talk I will need to remember for the rest of my life. From time to time Mom gives me a reminder of those warnings when she thinks I need it. Like now.

Number one: Stay focused.

Number two: Never mention my father to *anyone* and keep the old life I had as *Annika Bershov* buried with the past.

Number three: Avoid anyone with the surname Ivanov.

That's the one that worries me most.

"Up until now I didn't have to worry about the Ivanovs." I bring my hands together in my lap.

"And you still don't."

"Really, Mom? Aleksander Ivanov will be on campus *all* the time. Raventhorn is the Knights' headquarters and Aleksander is the leader of the Knights."

Most of all, he's the man who put my father behind bars for life. He also linked Dad to an attack years before where Aleksander's brother and family were butchered. He pinned that on Dad because there were striking similarities between the two incidents that made it seem like he was involved in both attacks.

Aleksander is a nasty piece of work who wouldn't hesitate to skin me alive and unearth my secrets if I drew the wrong kind of attention to myself, so of course I'm worried.

Mom has gone silent so I continue speaking.

"When I went to Raventhorn over the summer for registration, I was told Aleksander's son, and his nephew—as in the guy whose father, Dad is in prison for killing—would be attending the college for the next two years. I'm likely to see them and I don't even know what they look like."

Caspian—the son, and Thorne—the nephew were talked about like celebrities. Most of the students went to high school together in New York, so they all know each other. "I tried to Google the Ivanovs, but other than details of their *billion dollar technology* company nothing else came up. It wasn't surprising given who they are. So I guess I'll meet them when I see them."

I've spilled all my worries and Mom is still just staring at me.

"I hate that your father put us in this position." She eventually speaks after another minute passes. Her voice is whisper soft, as if she's scared the very walls will hear us. Her eyes are glassy too, full of regret, disappointment and the deepest sorrow.

"Mom. Dad didn't—"

"No. Don't say it." The finality in her tone severs everything I want to say in my father's defense.

That what happened wasn't Dad's fault.

That he didn't mean to hurt us.

That he's innocent.

Mom doesn't want to hear any of those things because she believes he's guilty.

My father was set up to take the fall for a crime he didn't commit, but no one can prove it and no one believes him but me.

I was there on that night when disaster struck. I just didn't see enough to help him.

I couldn't help anyway because Mom and I had to flee for our lives by pretending to be dead. If Mom hadn't gone to Levgen we would have been executed as punishment for my father's crimes. In the Knights, part of the punishment for unauthorized killing is death for your family.

The worst thing is, like everyone else we once knew in Russia, Dad believes that my mother and I are dead.

"If not for what he did you wouldn't be worried now. You'd be excited to go to college and study music like you should be. You'd see the value of attending Raventhorn instead of fearing it."

There's no point arguing. One, because she is technically right, and two, I'd only end up sounding like the lost little girl again. The lost little girl who continues to hold onto her belief in her father's innocence.

"I want you to stop worrying." Mom's voice is firmer now, reflecting the determination in her expression. "Worrying is only going to hurt your success. We've been through too much for that to happen, and I just want you to live your dreams."

She presses her finger on the middle C key on the piano twice and guilt washes over me. I think of what she's had to do to keep me safe and make this moment possible for me. She married my father's best friend, moved across the world and literally became someone else, for me.

"I'm sorry. You're right. So I'll get my head together." I drag in a deep breath to clear my mind. "I have too many dreams to allow fear to stand in my way."

"Exactly, my dear girl. *Exactly.* You're going to be absolutely fine. I promise. Okay?"

"Okay." I try to sound more sure of myself and give her a small smile.

"Come on, let's go help Levgen. You know he's going to whip up the best sundaes ever."

"He always does."

She smiles back at me and lowers to plant a kiss on my forehead, then we make our way to the kitchen.

As we walk down the corridor I balance my mind with the reminder of my dream to become a classical concert pianist. I want the world to love me as much as they love the great composers and pianists of all time. That starts now.

So I have to shove my worries about omens, the Knights, and the Ivanovs to the back of my mind.

One thing my father told me that I'll never forget is this:

When you walk in the dark you have to take one step at a time. If you don't, you'll get lost and never find your way back to the light.

That's what I have to do now.

Take one step at a time, so I don't lose my way.

If I do, I'll lose myself too.

I can't let that happen.

CHAPTER 2

SHIT. I'M LOST.

I'm actually lost.

I'm already late as fuck because my flight was delayed by several hours and now I'm… I don't know where the hell I am.

After the day from hell, I arrived at Raventhorn about an hour ago.

I missed orientation and the campus tour, so I don't know where to find my dorm, Myrrdin House.

When I pulled up on the campus grounds I went straight to security, where I was issued a map and given directions to follow the red route.

I thought I was doing exactly that, but here I am again, in the same spot I stood not ten minutes ago.

Frantically I look around the dark surroundings of the campus. At the vast expanse of the Science Building and the cluster of oak trees on its left. Next to that is the river with a bridge going over it and more trees.

I've circled this area five times and followed the map exactly as it directs, so why the hell am I still lost?

I glance at the tiny silver face of the watch around my wrist and frown when I see it's nearly one in the morning.

Damn it. This is not how I imagined spending my first day.

Things started off so well with Mom and Levgen taking me to the airport. We even had time for breakfast together in our favorite café.

Everything was so nice, and the quality time gave my nerves a much-needed break. Then things went straight to hell the moment they left me. That was when the announcement came up that my flight was delayed.

It was only by forty minutes, which was bad but not so bad. But then forty minutes turned into an hour, which swiftly became two, then finally four.

It was nearly four p.m. when I eventually boarded the plane, then the flight from L.A. to Boston took just over five hours.

When I got out of Boston Logan International I was thrust into the gridlock of traffic in my town car. There was simply no hope of getting here any sooner than I did.

Now I have no one I can call and nowhere to turn to.

And where the hell is everyone? The campus holds the silence of a mausoleum.

With over eight thousand eighteen to twenty-four-year-old residents on this campus there's no way I can be the only person wandering the grounds at this hour of the night. Yet it seems I am.

The only sign of life I've seen so far was the guard at the gates, who was actually rude and barely wanted to help me.

A haggard sigh falls from my lips as I turn to my left, directly into the cold wind as it blows my way. It lifts the ends of my hair and rushes up into the trees, making the leaves rattle.

Hopelessly I stare at Raventhorn Hall sitting on the hill in the distance.

With the elegance of a medieval castle and the expanse of a fortress, it takes up most of the space on that side of the campus.

Many of the buildings around me have similar Gothic architecture, but with its stone walls, lancet windows, and stained glass, Raventhorn Hall looks like it was pulled straight out of the fifth century.

When I visited the campus weeks ago Raventhorn Hall was the first thing that fascinated me. The building the registration was held in is just across from there, so I got a good view of it.

In the daylight it looked like something from a fairytale or the paintings I love by John William Waterhouse. Even though I'm pissed as hell that I'm lost and late, I can appreciate its beauty against the moonlight. The building holds a different sort of magic and fascination.

Knights become Knights in that building, and that is the place where they do *everything*.

The building is completely off limits to me and those who aren't either married to a Knight or a fully-fledged member of their Brotherhood.

Attempting to go inside without either of those criteria will land you in the kind of trouble I don't even want to think about.

It is curious though—the things they do inside there.

I imagine all sorts of scenarios and I know I wouldn't be the first person to wish they could get a peek in. Even for a second.

The secret affairs of the Knights weren't discussed in my household. I was only ever told things on a need-to-know basis. When I was growing up Levgen made life for Mom and me as normal as any other family, but there were times when I was forced to acknowledge what we weren't, and what we are.

I imagine it would have been the same way if Dad were around.

Maybe even more so because my father was one of the senior guards to the previous leader of the Knights.

Dad came here, too, after completing his earlier education in Russia.

This was where he would have taken his vows and where he met Levgen.

They were as close as brothers. It was while they were on vacation in Russia that my mother and father met. Again, thanks to Levgen.

I'm sure he never saw it in the cards that he'd end up taking care of his best friend's wife and daughter to keep them safe from certain death.

"A word of advice. It's never a good idea to roam around campus at this time of night by yourself." A cold, chilling voice speaks from the shadows behind me, stealing the breath from my lungs.

I whirl around, nearly jumping out of my skin from the fright that clutches my nerves with long, sharp talons.

I grab my chest, feeling my heart pounding as I come face to face with a tall, *tall*, muscular man.

Standing paces away from me, he looks me up and down while he takes a drag on his cigarette. The silver moonlight is bright enough to highlight the handsome Viking-warrior features of his chiseled face and sharp jawline, along with the vicious-looking dragon tattooed down the length of his neck.

His dark hair is styled in a sexy, trendy undercut with the sides short and the top long and swoopy in the wind.

He looks young enough to be a student here, but the five-o'clock shadow darkening his chin makes him appear older in a forbidden way. And those eyes...

People always stare at mine because the silver-gray color looks like frosted glass. He has the opposite effect because his are a blue so bright they almost have their own light.

The fright has momentarily paralyzed me, but so has the unmistakable menacing vibe emanating from him.

It has nothing to do with the fact that he's dressed in full black—black jeans, black shirt, black biker jacket. The menace is directly coming from *him.*

The curious look in his eyes suggests he's been watching me for a while.

But I never even heard him come up. The path where he stands is a mixture of pebbles, leaves, and twigs, so I should have heard *something.*

Either I was so engrossed in my thoughts that I didn't hear him, or he's good at sneaking up on people. Something tells me it's the latter.

"Is that all you do? *Stare?*" He tilts his head, gives me a lopsided grin, and blows out a ring of smoke that surrounds him in a misty haze.

I swallow the discomfort and strange fascination slithering up my throat, then take a breath to clear my head so I can speak. "You scared me."

Most people would give some form of apology or something along those lines, but the full-blown wicked smile that spreads across his face tells me that this guy isn't like most people.

Puffing on the cigarette, he comes closer. So close we're almost sharing the same airspace, and I have to admit I'm not ready to be that close to someone so striking they don't look real.

He towers over me and I peg him to be about six foot four because he seems to be the same height as Levgen.

His lips part but another bout of seconds passes before he speaks again. "What are you doing in the Hollows out here by yourself, *Bambi*?"

Bambi?

And Hollows?

That sounds like the Knights' prison, the *Hallows.* The place where my father rots.

"I'm lost. Is this place off-limits, too? I didn't see a sign." I look around again, just in case I missed something.

He laughs, deep and smoky, as if the smoke from the cigarette obeys his command to amplify the power behind his amusement.

Since I'm not sure what part of what I said is funny, I remain silent and hope he'll tell me.

"There is no sign. We call it the Hollows because a student was murdered here many years ago. The killer remains a ghost. No one comes here at night, and certainly not by themselves."

Goosebumps rush over my skin and my body heats like I've just broken out in a fever. "They were murdered?"

"Yes."

"And no one found the killer?"

"You weren't listening to me, little deer." His grin becomes more animated. "I said the killer remains a *ghost*. Urban legend has it that the killer matched the description of the caretaker who died a year before the murder in the same spot you're standing now."

While my stomach plummets past my feet he takes another lazy drag on his cigarette, looking pleased that he's managed to scare the absolute shit out of me.

Then something happens. I'm not sure what it is exactly. A shift in the air. A shift in the tension between us. A shift in my being.

It's not clear but whatever it is changes the way he's looking at me.

The look he's giving me now is more predatory, animalistic and hellish.

"People and their urban legends." I speak only because he's looking at me like he expects an answer.

"Had to come from somewhere, though, right? There's always some truth to these *urban legends*."

"Maybe."

"The moral of the story is you never can tell when someone crazy might decide to rip your little body to pieces. Bad things happen to the lost on this campus." He smiles as if captivated by the idea of watching me being ripped apart. "Some guy with a fucked-up mind and a bad attitude might get the wrong idea."

My breath stalls in the cage of my chest, turning to ice, and suddenly I can't breathe.

The ounce of my brain that's working presents me with two options.

Run like hell. Or tolerate this…*creep* for a little longer to get some directions to my dorm.

Running from a guy who's giving predatory vibes when I don't know where I'm going might not be the smartest idea. After all, what do all predators do when you run?

Chase until they catch you.

Chase until they kill you.

Chase until they consume you.

With that reasoning I decide to go with option two.

"I'm trying to find Myrrdin House." I nod as if the action can change the subject to a safer topic. I hope it can.

He observes me silently for what feels like years before he lifts his hand and points to my right.

I turn to look and frown. There's nothing there but darkness through the thicket of trees. "I went past there several times."

"There's a path through the trees." His voice returns to that low rumble. "You can't see it from here because of the overgrowth of honeysuckle, but it's there. You'll see Myrrdin House once you reach the end of the path."

The tension in my body unravels and I feel some semblance of relief for finally having directions. "Thank you."

"You're welcome."

"I should get going. I'm already late as it is." Now that I have directions, instinct is telling me to wrap things up as quickly as possible with this guy.

"What's your name, Bambi?"

"It's not Bambi." I smirk.

That grin comes back, but this time it reveals dimples that should be made illegal. "What's your name, *new girl*?"

I want to counter the new girl comment, too, but decide against it. "It's Ivy. Ivy Yegorov."

"Hello, Ivy Yegorov."

"Hi."

When he holds out his right hand to shake mine, I take note of the tattoos on the underside of his wrist peeking from under the sleeve of his jacket.

One is the Elder Futhark rune for defense. Although I can barely see the other I know what it is. It's the Greek symbol for Sigma. Levgen has both of those tattoos, and so did my father.

This guy is a Knight. The realization throws me because he's the first I've come across in nearly a decade.

Since they get that Sigma tattoo after initiation, and that takes place at the start of sophomore year, I know he's not a freshman. From his confidence I also don't think he's a sophomore. I guess him to be a junior or senior here.

I shake his hand briefly and take the opportunity when he releases me to move a step back, out of the unwanted close proximity.

"You might do well to remember you're not in Kansas anymore." He holds my gaze, and the blue of his eyes seems brighter with a sheen of interest.

"Sure. I'll try to remember that…" I drop my voice purposely in a suggestive manner that gives him a chance to tell me his name. I'm just being polite. The last thing I want to do on my first day is make an enemy out of a Knight.

"My name's Thorne. Thorne Ivanov."

The moment his name falls from his lips the air evaporates from my body and my lungs compress into nothing. If it were possible for me to fade into the air with the breeze, I would.

Avoid anyone with the surname Ivanov.

Sorry, Mom. Everything has gone wrong since I left you, and this has to be the cherry taking its place on the top of my shitty day.

What in the ever-loving hell are the chances of the first person I meet being *Thorne Ivanov*?

This is him. This is what he looks like. Deadly handsome with a deadly presence and a deadly smile as potent as poison.

This is the guy. And my father is in prison for plotting to kill his.

Jesus. This is so much harder than I could have ever imagined.

Stay calm, Ivy. Breathe slowly so you don't have a panic attack.

He doesn't know who I am, so there's no need to give *Thorne Ivanov* something to be suspicious about.

"It's nice to meet you." That's the best version of calm I can muster with my insides wrapping into knots. "See you around."

"I hope so." His voice takes on a smooth, silky edge. "Maybe next time I'll show you my dick piercing. Unless you want to see it now."

Heat rushes over me, dancing across my skin, and the sinful smirk on his lips makes me feel like I'm on fire. Then he makes everything a hundred times worse by closing the space between us again.

I already look like the fish out of water, but looking like the inexperienced virgin who's never even seen a dick before is another thing. *And in front of Thorne Ivanov?*

When his smile brightens I swallow past the wedge closing my throat and force my brain to work so I can say something.

Anything.

"No, thank you." My answer shouldn't amuse him, but it seems to.

"Are you sure?" He comes so close his breath tickles my nose and the scent of him, a spicy woodland fragrance laced with smoke, invades my senses.

He stares down at me and I realize he's close enough to kiss me.

His gaze flicks down to my parted lips and I wonder for a fleeting second if he's actually thinking about it.

What if he is?

What if he did?

A kiss from a stranger who's supposed to be forbidden to me.

What the hell am I thinking? I'm supposed to be planning an exit route, not thinking about what the guy I need to avoid tastes like.

"You don't look so sure, Bambi." He doesn't miss a beat.

"Yes, I'm very sure," I answer with more firmness and steady my thoughts. "I'm positive I don't want to see your dick piercing."

He could be pulling my leg about that, but somehow I don't think he is. He looks like the kind of guy who would have a piercing… *like that.*

Regardless, I have no desire to see it—pierced or otherwise.

Thorne narrows his eyes and looks me over with scrutiny before inching away. "Never had a woman refuse my dick before."

"People say there's a first time for everything." I step back again, reclaiming my personal space.

"Maybe we should see about that." He gives me a look that says *I could fuck you right here if I wanted to,* then lifts his chin as if in defiance of the thought that he's anything other than irresistible.

Looking at him, I understand why. He's gorgeous. Greek-god gorgeous. But I'll be the girl who resists him.

"Good night," I mutter, taking another step backward.

"Good night, Bambi."

I'm grateful for the chance to leave, but I remain calm as I turn and walk away.

The weight of his stare rests on my shoulders but I keep going, heading down to the mass of trees.

When I reach it, I spot the paved path straight away. Now that I'm so close, I can also see where I went wrong. It's indeed the overgrowth that's concealing the path. You wouldn't know it was there unless you were told.

Everywhere I've been so far has looked so immaculate that I'm guessing the groundsmen must have left this section like this on purpose because it looks good.

When I'm enveloped by the trees I risk glancing back over my shoulder to see if Thorne is still there.

He is.

I quicken my pace until I'm far enough away and there's no possible way he can see me. But still, I can feel his eyes on me.

Even when I reach the dorm those piercing eyes still burn into my skin.

I know I'm being utterly paranoid. He'd have to be the ghost from his urban legend to see me through the walls of the building.

Except my gut tells me that my slipup tonight in meeting him might have earned me the type of unwanted attention I never wanted.

CHAPTER 3

Thorne

IVY YEGOROV…

Her name in my head sounds like delicious temptation I want to sink my teeth into.

I wonder if she tastes as delicious as she looks.

Her with her lithe little body, full round breasts, those otherworldly eyes, and that long silver-white hair that battled with the moon.

Her hair flowed behind her like a cape in the wind as she made her escape. I watched her flee down the path until I couldn't see her anymore.

I finish my cigarette and light up another.

The whole time she stood before me, I imagined my hands in that hair. I could almost feel my fingers laced through the silky fibers while I wrapped it around my wrist and slid my cock inside her mouth.

When I got close enough to smell her fear and arousal, it wasn't that hard to imagine myself buried deep inside her.

The little deer with her caught-in-the-headlights Bambi eyes is fresh meat for guys like me.

She's beautiful with that hallowed, ethereal beauty you imagine on an angel, and God would I love to have her in my bed, but she's too sweet, too innocent, and not my type.

Virgins also aren't my thing.

She never said anything about that, but I *just* knew.

Despite those details, I'm still staring into the shadows of the empty path as if I can see her. And yes, I *was* going to kiss her.

Then I might have shoved her up against one of those trees and taken the cherry between her legs, just to say I was the first to have her.

I would have fucked her again for the fun of it.

I only restrained myself because I like a chase. And I still like the hunt even though *Ivy Yegorov* might not be my type.

I'd also still like her to see my dick piercing some time. I don't actually have it in tonight. I don't wear it that often anymore because I outgrew it and it's not exactly the safest thing to wear when I'm training. But I'd put it in just for her. Just so I could see that look of shock on her pretty face again.

She's the first girl to fascinate me in a very long time. It's been even longer since anyone managed to pull me out of the convoluted web of uncertainty surrounding my life.

After the fucked-up-as-hell conversation I had earlier with my dearly beloved uncle, I needed the break of a beautiful woman. If only for those few moments when I know I scared the shit out of her.

I was on my way back to my dorm when I spotted her pacing around like a lost little animal. I watched her, stealthily keeping my distance until it got to a point when I had to say something.

The poor little deer would have guessed within seconds of speaking to me that I was deranged and dangerous. When I gave her my name, it creeped her out even more.

I already guessed that she's one of the students we call foreigners here. Those students either come from another state, or they're international, so they had more *normal* lives. Regardless of where they come from, everyone knows the Ivanov name.

And they know me.

Now *she* knows me.

Ivy Yegorov was a pretty little distraction. Now that she's gone, the shit that was on my mind has resurfaced like backed-up sewage that's been building for weeks.

Last year when I stood before my uncle and took my vows, I knew everything would be different, but what I didn't realize was how soon things would change. *For me.*

It was like the asshole couldn't wait to start fucking with me.

I'm twenty years old and in my junior year here at Raventhorn. The year when I'm supposed to start my internship at Ivanov Tech, the family software engineering company.

I'm the only real technologically-minded person in the family, so the process of getting me started should have been easy.

But no.

That motherfucking asshole not only wants to streamline my internship with a *review* at the end to ensure my suitability to join the company, but he wants to lock me in a marriage contract.

Yes, I knew I'd have an arranged marriage someday. My cousin Caspian, who is the same age as me, is already married, so it was a given that I would be next.

Caspian and his wife, Willow, technically had an arranged marriage, but really it wasn't because they'd been in love with each other since they were kids.

Their situation was completely different to what will be forced on me.

Since I'm not a direct heir there wasn't supposed to be any talk about marriage anytime soon, so I never saw this coming.

It certainly wasn't supposed to be a fucking contract term to getting my share of the company. That's something new the old man threw in to piss with me.

And the shitty thing about it is, there's nothing I can do.

I'm in a game of war, and I've landed on a spot where I have to play by the rules. *Again.*

My uncle owns the majority of shares in the company and holds all the decision-making power over my inheritance until I graduate. Meaning that asshole gets to decide every motherfucking thing.

If I didn't stand to lose a billion-dollar fortune, I'd leave the miserable prick to it. But I can't turn my back on a legacy my father helped create.

I also can't turn my back on what's rightfully mine. My father wouldn't want me to.

Since my uncle can't destroy me the way he wants, the asshole is trying to make use of me. I'm sure that's still with the hope that I'll destroy myself one day.

With a shake of my head I step back onto the pebbled path and resume my route to the dorm.

I live in Erebus House, home of the Sigma Alpha fraternity. The place where men become first-class Knights.

Of all the fraternities ours is the strictest, and you must pass all the trials we set to even be considered for initiation as a Knight.

Our freshmen pledges arrived last week, so they could get all the admin out of the way and find their feet before we got down to business with them.

Part of the finding-your-feet stage is partying, so there's been a wild party every night for the last four days with the guys getting wasted, fucked, and shit-faced stoned.

If my mind were more settled I would be right in the midst of the indulgence.

Loud heavy metal music greets me when I approach Erebus.

As there are still some guys chugging beer on the lawn I can see the party is still going with no end in sight.

I walk inside the house and see I'm right. The wildness is still going on.

There are guys and girls all over the living room. Some fully clothed, some naked. Actually, most are naked.

Some are fucking right there in the open, others are doing lines of cocaine off the tables or the topless girls waiting to be fucked.

When I turn down the hallway I find couples molded to the walls either making out or fucking. The sound of flesh slapping against flesh and moaning follows me down the marble path until I reach the end.

Public sex and open drug taking is so commonplace to me now that it seems like part of the furniture or the paint on the walls.

I head into the break room and nod to the group of guys in the corner playing pool, then I spot Caspian sitting with Lucian Sokolov on the second-floor balcony.

They're at the table by the long French windows and seem to be mulling over paperwork. I didn't expect either of them to still be around at this hour.

Caspian lives in one of the special houses for married students, so I thought he would have gone home to Willow, his wife.

Lucian took his vows yesterday, so I thought he'd be celebrating with Eilish, the girl he doesn't realize yet is his girlfriend.

I guess he and Caspian are getting a head start for the week we have planned for our pledges.

All the heirs to the Knights on campus are part of the Sigma unit, but there are separate units. Caspian and I will get to lead our unit until we graduate because we're Ivanovs. Caspian is also the new fraternity president and I am his vice president.

As Raventhorn won't have the pleasure of any other Ivanovs in attendance until the next generation, they're making use of us.

They also know that we're veterans of the type of hazing trials designed to fuck with your mind. When you live through the shit we've seen, you're qualified to do *anything*.

We enlisted Lucian as the third member of our team. He's in the year below us but we grew up together and have been through life together. Despite any difference we had in our younger years, we've become close since attending Raventhorn. It seemed fitting that the three of us lead together.

The pledges we accept will stay in our unit for the rest of their lives and will be classed as an elite group. Almost like a separate brotherhood.

In time to come when the leadership changes hands, Caspian will take the lead of the Knights and become the Pakhan of the Komarovski Bratva, the Brotherhood owned by the Knights. I will be his Sovientrik—second in command—and these will be our men.

Curiosity fills Caspian's expression when he sees me approaching. He knows I spoke with his father and the conversation went to shit.

He has his father's blond hair and stern eyes, but the gentleness of his late mother in his face gives him that touch of humanity that makes him different from his father.

"You look like shit." Lucian smirks, scanning my face.

"Thanks, Sokolov. *Shit* was the exact look I was going for." I flip him off and grab the nearest chair. "You should try it sometime. It's not that bad."

He chuckles and stands. "I'll take that as my cue to leave. We have an early start tomorrow. I need my rest to deal with these guys."

"You're too good." Caspian gives him a clipped nod and smiles.

"Just want to be in top form, *Lord Commander.*"

Caspian's smile widens. "That title does have a nice ring to it."

I roll my eyes at them both but I have to agree that the title does have a good sound; so does being second in command to the Lord Commander. I'm the one who gets to come up with all the wild ideas for the men to prove their loyalty. Like the game maker in the *Hunger Games.*

"See you both tomorrow." Lucian bows his head.

"Have fun with Eilish." He hates when I tease him about her, so I try to do it as often as possible.

"You know it's not like that with us."

"*Yet.*" I don't know what he's waiting for. The fuck if I could have a girl as hot as Eilish hanging on my arm and still call her my *friend.* I don't believe in keeping girls as friends anyway.

"How about we cross that bridge when we get there."

"If you say so." I half-lunge at him.

"I do say so. Night, boys."

Lucian leaves and Caspian gives me his undivided attention. Now his curiosity has morphed into worry.

"What did my father say?" He sits up straighter.

The viper tattooed on his neck looks like it's ready to pounce at me. He got it after high school. I got the dragon on my neck at the same time.

The emblem was as fitting for me as the viper was for him. Both are deadly animals, but when dragons strike and breathe fire they obliterate, leaving nothing behind.

I release a heavy sigh but my lungs still feel tight with pressure.

"Your old man is putting me on an assessment for my internship, and he wants to talk about the marriage contract. He wants one in place so I can say I *do* come graduation day." That doesn't mean I *have* two years to find a wife. It means the wedding itself will be in two years, so that prick could sign my life away tomorrow.

Caspian's face reddens, then he leans forward with balled fists. "What the fuck are you saying to me?"

"You heard me, cousin. Aleksander Ivanov strikes again, showing who's boss."

"You can't let him fuck with you like that."

"*Let* him?" I raise my brows and give him a sharp stare. "You know I would never *let* anyone do shit to me. Even him."

"But it sounds like you're going to do what he wants."

I inch closer to make sure that only he can hear me. "He's getting even with me, Caspian." We've had no end of run-ins with Aleksander, especially recently, as he attempted to keep his secret affairs *secret from me.* "It's clear he wants to exercise more control over me to hide whatever shady shit he might be up to, *again.* Keeping me under his thumb will ensure my allegiance to him."

If anyone were to hear me utter such words about my uncle it would be as bad as treason. And it would be so much worse because of who I am.

"He already has your fucking allegiance."

I tilt my head and shake it. "We both know that's not true, Caspian."

Caspian's chest caves and his shoulders slump. He knows full well what I'm talking about. It's called the *obvious truth.* The type that no one can refute or change.

Although his father might have raised me with his sons and could be said to have raised me like his own, my allegiance is *not* to him.

"You have my allegiance, because I owe you my life. You got my loyalty the night my family was taken and my father's enemies took *you* instead of me." I don't usually speak about the past, or so plainly.

The tension in Caspian's face loosens but it's still there. "You don't owe me, cousin."

"But I do."

We were eight years old. Not old enough to be able to think so fast in the face of danger, but *he* did. Thinking on his feet, he told me to hide and swapped places with me so they would take him.

As close as our fathers were, it was protocol that the direct heirs to the Ivanov line mustn't fall. Meaning priority was always given to Caspian's father as he was the firstborn Ivanov son, and his sons.

At that young age Caspian knew that if those men had taken me, no one would come looking for me. Him, on the other hand… yes.

And that's what happened. It took ten months for his father to find him, but he found him.

"You're the reason I'm here today." I will always acknowledge that. "We became brothers the moment you chose to sacrifice yourself to save me. That was when I decided I would always have your back. Your father knows that and hates me for it."

Aleksander hasn't allowed me to forget how lucky I was to keep my life. Every time shit happens, that motherfucker goes in hard on me.

Years ago, when Zak, Caspian's brother, was killed, Aleksander took out his frustration on me as if it was my fault and even told me that I didn't deserve to be alive. He'd been telling me fucked-up shit like that since I was eight, so by then I was used to it. That's the kind of asshole he is.

"I can't let him screw with your life, Thorne." Caspian lands a fist on the table so hard it shakes. "I'm going to speak to him."

"That will make it worse. And I need to take the reins on this." I'll never allow anyone to fight my battles.

"I have to do something. This is a serious matter. You and I will be running Ivanov Tech one day in the near future. My father can't just suddenly pick his terms and conditions out of thin air."

"Yet he has, and yes, he can. Don't worry. I'll figure it out. Right now we need to focus on the unit." I tap the table. "That's going to take up all our time. We don't want to get in trouble for not doing our jobs, and this is something we've always wanted to do."

With reluctance, he nods. "Promise you'll let me know if I can do anything to help with my father."

"Of course." I sound like I'm truly making a promise, but I'm not. I already decided I won't involve him.

Things are different for Caspian now that he has a wife. I can't let him get involved in the shit with his father.

For now, I'm going to see how my dear uncle wishes to play this game he's unleashed on me, then I'll know what moves to make.

I straighten and rest against the back of the chair.

"So, who do you have in mind to join us?" he asks, changing the subject and glancing at the guys at the pool table. "Those three have been vying for our attention all week."

"I know." I plaster a cunning smile and stare at them.

Kade Gurkovsky, Dmitri Valneko, and Logan Konnikov have practically been crawling up our asses since they stepped on campus.

"I like them and Alek, Lucian's cousin." Caspian sounds certain.

I glance back at him. "Seems like you've already picked."

"Just voicing my thoughts. They're already top-notch with good careers in the making and they come from families who would make good business associates later down the line."

He's right. Kade and Dmitri are star athletes who will be joining the football team here. They have a very good prospect of playing pro in the NFL. Their fathers also own two NFL football teams and are business associates. Logan is going into business and investments. His family owns a hedge fund company. Alek's family owns a weapons and technology company.

"They also all came out with top marks in the Reaping." Caspian continues staring at them.

The Reaping is the rite of passage every boy of sixteen years of age must go through to join the Knights. That's the first step.

Our forefathers who created the Brotherhood of the Knights were originally Vikings, so everything we do is based on the old Viking laws. The Bratva influences are mixed in, because of those who went to Russia and allied with the Vory when they began. That's why the Knights own the Komarovski Bratva.

To become a full member of the Knights, men have to go through the Reckoning. This is the separation of the men from the boys, and that's where I come in.

The group below looks as close as a wolfpack. I can imagine them preparing for this moment for years at the academy because they knew Caspian and I would be in charge.

As if Kade Gurkovsky can hear my thoughts, he glances up at me and we stare at each other, a silent conversation unfolding between us as if we're equals.

I admire any man who can stare at me head on like that as if to challenge me.

He has some balls on him, so I give him a nod of approval. He nods back, then I look at Caspian, who seems fascinated by our exchange.

"Let them get through my challenges, then we can talk." I give him a devious grin.

"Okay. Well, let the games begin. From here to Valhalla."

"From here to Valhalla."

This is all I can do to keep myself sane.

This, and fucking.

The sudden thought of fucking pulls the little deer back to my thoughts and I know I won't forget the platinum-haired beauty as easily as I'd hoped.

Maybe sweet and innocent has become the new flavor of hot.

I'd certainly like to try it and see what she tastes like.

CHAPTER 4

AFTER A HECTIC MORNING OF GETTING MY MUSIC COURSES SORTED out, I'm finally at the English and Arts Building.

I called ahead to find out if I could still sign up for the English literature course and they agreed.

I head over to the registration desk and the assistant hands me the registration clipboard.

My name is already there, so I sign next to it, relief filling me.

I'm doing this course as a minor. Since I missed out on yesterday's events, I worried I wouldn't be able to join, but hope was on my side.

For the first time since arriving at Raventhorn I feel like I can relax.

I may even be able to forget my encounter last night with Thorne Ivanov.

I've been crazy busy so I haven't had time to think about him. But every so often, *like now*, he creeps into my thoughts.

I hand the clipboard back to the course assistant and she smiles at me from beneath her thick-framed glasses.

"This is yours." She gives me a folder with the course materials.

"Thank you."

"Professor Bates is doing an intro workshop tomorrow. Would you like me to sign you up? He has an interesting way of teaching so he likes to give his students a heads-up."

"That sounds like I should be there."

"If I were you I'd definitely go." She gives me an exaggerated nod.

"Then sign me up." I grin back at her, already liking Professor Bates. In high school, my senior year English teacher also taught us drama. She liked to have us act out our novels so every English class felt like we were on stage.

"Do you have any questions I can help with?"

"Not yet, but I'm sure I will. I'm one of those people who will have a million and one things to ask when the course gets going."

"All my details are in the back of the folder. Just send me an email when those questions come up."

"Thank you, I will." I give her a grateful smile before ambling away from the desk.

I head over to the shelves by the entrance and grab the map from the side pocket of my bag. I need directions to the coffee shop. With the day I still have ahead of me, I'm going to need the strongest coffee they can make.

I'm glad I got my courses sorted out, but no way am I out of the woods yet.

My lateness yesterday did not go unnoticed by the Theta Alpha leadership.

The first thing to greet me early this morning before I left my room was an envelope slid under my door. Inside the envelope was a letter from the president, Tiffany Vasilyev, expressing her displeasure that I missed the first day.

She didn't care why I was late, or about the trouble I had getting to campus. She just went in on me for my *insolence.*

The letter ended with informing me that I would be dealt with at the meeting after lunch—which is in two hours.

This is the kind of stupid shit I wasn't looking forward to. I didn't even want to join a sorority, but as an heir I have to.

I pull out the map, locate the nearest coffeehouse, and circle it.

When I look up I find myself staring at a dark-haired girl standing across from me, smiling.

She has the same build as me but is slightly taller and looks like my opposite with her smoky-eyed Goth makeup.

I scan her little puff-sleeved dress edged with lace and quickly realize she looks like a living Lolita doll.

She has the sort of delicate beauty you'd find on a doll anyway, so it suits her.

She walks up to me, her smile brightening. "Hi, I'm Isabelle." She stretches out her hand for me to shake and I take it.

"Hey there, I'm Ivy." I try to sound as confident as she does.

"Good to meet you." She nods with enthusiasm like it really is good to meet me. "I saw you this morning at Myrrdin House. I live there too. I'm also taking English literature as a minor."

"Oh wow, then I'm especially happy to meet you." It's refreshing to meet someone who not only lives in the same dorm as me but will be going to the same classes.

"What are you majoring in?"

"Music. I play the piano."

She looks thoroughly impressed. "I absolutely love the piano. They have the best music degree here so I'm sure you'll enjoy it."

"Thank you. I'm looking forward to it. What's your major?"

A spark of pride comes into her eyes. "Art."

I could have guessed that. She has that artist vibe. "I love art. My mom and I are always going to exhibitions."

"I do that with my Dad too. Did you want to grab coffee together? You looked like you were trying to find the coffeehouse." She glances at the map in my hands.

"I was." I sigh, relaxing my shoulders. "I'm in desperate need of a quadruple shot of espresso. I missed everything yesterday, so I've successfully managed to piss off the Theta Alpha president."

Her smile fades and she bites the inside of her lip. "God, my condolences in advance. Tiffany can be an absolute bitch."

My stomach twists. "Is she really that bad?"

"Yes. I went to high school with her and let's just say we all celebrated when she graduated."

"Damn. That doesn't sound good."

"Try not to worry." She attempts to school her disdain by making her voice sound positive. "Tiffany and her lackeys were born bitches. You just have to know how to maneuver them."

"Here's hoping I can."

"Come on, let's get that coffee then we can head back to Myrrdin for the meeting. Oh, and I'll introduce you to my friends. They're the best bunch ever. We've all known each other since high school, so we've been crazy together for years."

"They sound great." I smile back at her but talk of friends reminds me how alone I am here. At least I'm making friends now.

"You'll love them."

"I'm sure I will."

We head to the coffeehouse and sit at one of the tables outside on the terrace. There we talk and talk and talk, and it's as if we've known each other for years.

Isabelle tells me about her friends, her family, and her art. I learn that she lost her mother when she was young and that her father is the principal of Raventhorn Academy in New York.

She also explains to me that because her mother was of Knight descent and her father from the Bratva, she had a choice of what she did here in regard to where she lived and even in joining the sorority. She chose the Knight route because it would be more prestigious for her and her family.

I have no such choices because Levgen is a senior Knight. Listening to Isabelle talk with such excitement makes me feel like I'm the only student here who would have preferred to attend a normal college, free from the Knights.

After an hour I loosen up enough to tell her about my family—as in the parts I can tell. Then somehow our conversation switches to our favorite foods.

Isabelle is in the middle of telling me about the best restaurants on campus when I spot Thorne walking down the path across from us.

The sudden sight of him makes my nerves scatter, as if little sparks of electricity are dancing beneath my skin.

In the daylight Thorne Ivanov is a million times more handsome and striking than in the moonlight.

He's the kind of handsome and striking that demands the undivided attention of everyone with eyes. And he gets it.

Every girl within my line of sight is looking at him. With the exception of Isabelle because she's so focused on what she's saying to me.

Two other guys walk on either side of Thorne. Both are as tattooed as he is, wearing full black, and exude the same badass vibes that tell you they're worshiped here.

The tall blond one looks like Thorne, so I assume he must be Caspian.

There's too much similarity in their faces for him not to be. The other guy has olive skin and Italian features. He has the same tough guy exterior but there's a touch of humanity in him that makes him look more approachable than either of the Ivanovs.

I'm about to look away when Thorne sees me. His stare is so riveting and commanding I find that I can scarcely breathe, let alone turn my head.

Those piercing eyes bore into me, rooting me to my chair. My nerves become a frazzled mess and my brain turns to gloop.

Isabelle's light laughter breaks the spell. I look at her and realize she's watching the obvious silent exchange between Thorne and me with fascination.

"Looks like you already made friends with the big guys." A sly smirk tips her lips.

"Oh, no." I quickly glance back at Thorne. He's moved past us now and the world has started functioning again.

Isabelle's smile becomes more captivated when I look back at her. "Sure doesn't look that way to me."

"Honestly, I'm not friends with any of them. I ran into Thorne last night when I was trying to find the dorm."

"And what did you think?" Mischief lights up her eyes.

I don't know her well enough to tell her that Thorne reminded me of a cross between the Joker and Hannibal Lecter. Or that I'm not immune to his looks.

Isabelle leans closer and lowers her voice. "Just to clarify, I think the Ivanovs are all hell spawn."

I suck in a breath. "Can you say that about them?"

"I just did. I thought that might help you trust me with your answer." She winks at me and sits back in her chair. "So what did you think, other than the fact that he's hot?"

"I felt the hell spawn vibe."

She laughs. "Glad we're on the same page."

"I take it you know him from high school too."

"I do. He was so much worse than he is now. That's what I hear anyway, I'm not sure I believe it. I think he just has more control and power over the things that interest him. You know, like a psycho when they get a new fixation. It's never the same as what previously got them going."

I laugh, unable to help myself. "How do you know that? Do you know many psychos?"

"Unfortunately I do, and I suppose I can admit to spending all my time watching way too many shows like *The Mentalist, Law and Order* and *NCIS*."

I continue laughing. "I like those shows too."

"Then you'll know what I mean. The Ivanovs are all bad news. It's entirely up to you but I'd give Thorne a miss. They call him the crazy one and he has no end of girls chasing him."

"Believe me I have no desire to get mixed up with a crazy playboy." Not that I'd have a chance, even with his offer to show me his dick piercing.

"Good. I had a friend who was completely in love with him. He did *not* let her down gently. You saw *Carrie*, right?"

My insides squeeze. "The first and the second movie."

"Yeah. He's like all the bullies rolled into one and then some. Caspian has only tamed because he's married to Willow Raventhorn. She's really sweet. We have some English classes with the sophomores so you'll see her then."

"Willow Raventhorn. Wow."

"I know, right. She's the heir to all of this." Isabelle waves her hand around, motioning to everything. The things we can see and the things we can't, which includes anything with the name Raventhorn attached to it. "Her marriage to Caspian quadrupled the Ivanov name in wealth and power. I can't imagine what it must be like to be so rich."

"Me too. My stepdad is wealthy, but nothing like the Ivanovs."

"There's *no one* like them on campus at the moment and there are some pretty powerful families here."

She's talking about people who come from families with billion dollar wealth, so I can only imagine how much the Ivanovs have.

"What's Aleksander Ivanov like?" I need to know. We have a welcome meeting with him on Friday. I just want an idea of who he is before I see him.

Isabelle shakes her head slowly. "Not good. You don't ever want a run-in with him. I've met him a few times because my father has to report to him and he runs the fundraisers. Each time I saw him I liked him less and less. But you didn't hear that from me. I'm sure he'd have my head on a spike *Game of Thrones* style just for saying that."

I gulp past the lump in my throat as I'm pulled into her grotesque vision. "Wow, I guess I have a lot to learn."

"You'll be fine. Most of us have the advantage of knowing each other from high school. Once you get used to the place you'll fit right in. And you'll see there's more fish on campus than Thorne Ivanov." She looks toward the entrance of the café, watching a group of guys walk in.

I saw them earlier. They're freshmen too and of course they're all good looking.

"Like them?" I grin.

"Yes. But the tall dark-haired guy with the snake on his neck is mine."

The guy she's referring to looks like he should be a Hemsworth brother. "Is that your boyfriend?"

I'm surprised when her cheeks color fiercely. "I wish. I just meant I want dibs on him. That's Kade Gurkovsky. I've known him since forever, but he's never said a word to me."

He must feel her eyes on him because he looks around, takes note of her and looks away again.

"Like that." Her smile is small and playful but there's notable disappointment in her eyes.

"You should speak to him." I'm the last person to give any kind of relationship advice but I feel she needs the encouragement.

"I promised myself I would. That this year would be the year."

I smile back at her. "Good. That sounds exciting."

"Oh crap. We need to go." She glances at her phone. "If we don't leave now we'll be late for the meeting."

"That's the last thing I want." The rush of nerves I previously had returns, making me feel queasy like I might throw up.

"We can finish our coffee on the way over."

That's what we do and we even reach Myrrdin with ten minutes to spare.

We head into the meeting lounge which looks like it was plucked from the set of *Legally Blonde* with its pink and gold décor. There Isabelle makes use of the time by introducing me to her friends.

There's Mackenzie, a slender redhead who's studying dance and the performing arts. Billie, who Isabelle introduced as her best friend, and Sawyer and Savannah who are identical twins.

As they have near enough the same hair color as me they made the joke that I was their missing sister.

Everyone is nice and seem genuinely interested in knowing about me.

Billie had just asked me about my life in L.A. when someone clears their throat loudly and in an overly exaggerated manner.

We all turn to see a pretty black-haired girl standing at the door who could be a dead ringer for Megan Fox. In fact she looks more like Megan Fox than she does.

Joining her are a group of the girls who follow her as she glides in, her Jimmy Choos clicking against the floor.

"Well look at this." Her tone in those few words is condescending as hell. "You'd think that the *latecomer* would have at least had the sense to keep her voice down in *our* room, but here she is stealing the show."

One guess; this must be Tiffany.

Everyone is silent. Not the kind of silent when people stop talking to show respect. But the other kind. The kind you witness when they're protecting themselves.

"I'm Tiffany, latecomer, your president."

I already can't stand a bone in her Dior-clad body, but I know better than to show her how I feel.

"It's good to meet you. Sorry about yesterday and for just now. I was just—"

"I don't care. Listen to me and listen well." Her eyes grow large with contempt. It's strange to see someone look at me like that when we've only just met. "Don't you ever be late for anything again. Not while I'm president of this sorority. As punishment you can clean the kitchen and do the dishes for the rest of this month. The dishwasher broke yesterday, so there's plenty of work to do."

"You want me to clean?" Who told me to ask her that? And in that are-you-serious tone?

Tiffany glares at me as if I'm dog shit she's trying to avoid stepping in. "Yes, *latecomer* I want you to clean. You can add cleaning the toilets and bathrooms to the kitchen for your insolence. I want it done by midnight and everything must be spotless every single day for the rest of the month. Go. Now." She points at the door.

I look back at Isabelle and the girls who watch in absolute horror, but no one is saying anything. Of course not. They don't want the same fate as me, or worse.

Embarrassed, I leave the room and head to the kitchen with my legs trembling. Not because I'm scared of Tiffany—*hell no*—but because I loathe being bullied and unable to stand up for myself.

I can't believe Tiffany is allowed to treat me like this, but why am I even surprised. This is how the Knights treat people. Like they're nothing.

Right now I have to be nothing to fit in and not draw even more attention to myself.

CHAPTER 5

"Need some help?"

I lift my head and look at the lilac-haired girl standing at the door, watching me. She's holding a mop and bucket. Two things that look completely out of place against her cute little jumpsuit and ballerina pumps.

I'm still in the kitchen. I've been in here for an hour already and it looks like I've barely done anything.

"I won't say no." I set the cleaning sponge on the side and smile at her. "I don't want you to get in trouble though."

"I won't." She walks in and sets the mop and bucket to the side. "I'm beyond the reach of Tiffany's bitchiness. I would have defended you earlier but we're not allowed to challenge our superiors in front of the others."

"Oh. Thanks for coming to help me."

"No worries. I'm Eilish."

"That's a nice name. I've never heard it before."

"It's Irish."

"It's very pretty."

"So is Ivy."

"Thank you." When people compliment my name I always think of my real name—*Annika.* That was a pretty name. My father gave it to me.

Mom called me Ivy after her great grandmother when we had to take new names.

"I'm a sophomore here and the sorority's student counselor. Basically you come to me with your grievances."

Given my situation, I half smile, half frown at the irony in that. On seeing my reaction, Eilish gives me a sheepish grin.

"Believe me I've noted this unfortunate event. That's why I'm here." She nods. "But if you have any other grievances, like with your room, classes, or you just need to talk, I'm your girl."

"I appreciate that." I look around at the mess and dirty everything still left to be done. I frown when I think of simply touching it. "What happened in here? It was completely trashed."

"We had a party last night."

"I'm sorry I missed it."

"Don't be. Tiffany should have been more understanding because your flight was delayed but she loves being queen bitch. By the same token, you need to watch your back now. She'll make life hell for you until she finds something more interesting to do."

"Oh God. I really don't need this."

"Once you get past the trials and you're in the fold she won't be able to screw with you as much, so just tread softly."

"Okay. Tread softly." I attempt to smile and resume cleaning the counter. "Like, *just keep swimming*."

She giggles at my Finding Nemo reference. "Yes. Just keep swimming."

"Come on, let's get to work. I have an hour before I have to go."

"Thanks again for helping me."

"No worries."

We manage to get most of the kitchen done by the time Eilish has to leave.

To my surprise the guy who was with Thorne and Caspian picked her up. Eilish introduced him as Lucian.

Without the company of the Ivanovs he seemed even more approachable and the fact that he knew Eilish made me like him. She said he was her childhood best friend but I saw something more than that when they looked at each other.

Now I'm alone.

There's movement outside the kitchen but no one is coming in. Since our rooms are like mini apartments equipped with a state-of-the-art kitchenette and state-of-the-art everything no one needs to come in here.

I work for several more hours, cleaning until the damn kitchen is spotless. I move on to the bathrooms, where I mess up my nails and bruise my knees.

It's ten p.m. when I finish. I don't want to think of how much later I could have been if Eilish hadn't come to my aid.

When I go up to my room, I find a little pink pastry box outside my door.

I pick it up. It's from Isabelle and the girls.

Inside the box is a delicious cupcake from the pastry shop on campus everyone is talking about. There's a note next to the napkin with Isabelle's phone number on it along with the other girls.

Under Mackenzie's number are the words:

Sorry for what happened to you. Let's hang out for lunch tomorrow xx

It's really nice of them to do this for me. As horrible as my punishment was—*and Tiffany*—the incident helped me make progress in the friend department.

I open the door and go inside my room, which is stunning.

With its baby blue and rose gold color scheme, French Provençale furniture and décor, the room looks like it was made for a princess. And I feel like one, even after hours of cleaning like a hopeless Cinderella.

Levgen and Mom had the room decorated for me. As these are the rooms you get to keep for the duration of your stay at Raventhorn you're allowed to decorate to your taste.

Last night I was so tired and freaked from meeting with Thorne that I didn't get to appreciate the beauty until I woke this morning.

Taking in the stunning beauty, I appreciate it again now, allowing it to calm me.

I head to the ensuite to shower and get ready for bed, then I eat the cake which tastes like a slice of heaven. I make a mental note to get the same cupcake tomorrow when I'm done with Professor Bates workshop.

To wrap up the evening I call Mom and Levgen and then Millicent, my friend from high school. She went to study at Cambridge in England.

We have a circle of four friends but I haven't heard from the others. Honestly, I was closest to Millicent, so it's okay that I've only been in touch with her.

The fact that she's in England is the only easy thing about being at Raventhorn. It would have been harder to part ways if we'd planned to go to the same college and couldn't.

At least I didn't have to explain the Knights to my friends because people on the outside consider Raventhorn on par with the Ivy league colleges.

I get in my bed and find I can't sleep. I just lie there thinking for hours.

I'm tired, but I can't seem to summon sleep.

It's a good thing classes don't officially begin until next week or I'd be in trouble. There's nothing worse than having a zombified mind when you're trying to concentrate in class.

My thoughts drift to my father and I wonder how he is. I always think of him, especially in these quiet moments.

Moments when I see his face with that smile and the wealth of love in his eyes.

He loved me so much. But now he believes I'm dead.

It's not the first time I've wondered how he took that news. I know it would have broken him.

Memories of that night I will never forget drift into my mind and I allow them to come.

I see myself as the little nine-year-old girl with her teddy bear. My father took me to work that night because Mom was working late.

She was a cardiothoracic surgeon in Russia. She got called in for an emergency.

I was only too happy to go to work with my father because he was at the palace in Moscow. Because of his role he'd move around a lot and I got to see some of the wonderful places he'd work at. The palace was my favorite.

I felt like a princess then too, roaming the halls with the tapestry on the walls and the crystal chandeliers hanging from the high ornate ceilings covered in paintings.

Dad put me to rest in one of the guest rooms.

"Off to bed with you now, little one." He spoke to me in English sometimes because he wanted me to learn the language.

That's why he also allowed me to call him Dad or Papa.

I begged for a story but he told me it was too late.

The last thing he said to me was he'd wake me up when Mom came to pick me up.

I fell asleep but the sound of gunfire that woke me. It sounded like a war zone. There were people screaming amongst the rattle of bullets firing.

I knew to hide if ever I heard anything like that. My father drilled it into my head. So I jumped off the bed and hid behind the secret wall behind the bookcase.

It had a little frosted window, so I was able to see what was going on.

I was just in time getting myself to safety. Not a minute later the door smashed open and two men came in, throwing punches at each other.

One was Michael, another guard who worked with my father. The other man was one I'd never seen before. He had a scar entrenched so deep across his face he looked monstrous.

He also had tattoos on his wrist. The tattoos of the Knights.

The man shot Michael in the head twice and killed him. But it didn't end there. When Michael fell on the ground, the man pulled out a knife and stabbed Michael through the heart. Then he carved out his heart and held it up to the light with blood dripping from it.

I heard him say 'I will kill all of you. Every last guard here', then he uttered a chant in a language that sounded old and creepy.

"*Valin mortilum dohaliues.*" That's what it sounded like.

He placed the heart in a black bag and hurried out of the room after, looking hideous with his knife in the air.

I didn't know what to do. I just wanted to find my father but I was so terrified I couldn't even move. I'd never seen a man die before, and it was someone I knew.

Michael was always so kind to me and looked after me when my father was busy. Now he was dead.

An eternity might have passed before my father came into the room, but he was covered in blood from head to toe. I was so happy to see him that I rushed out of my hiding place.

He grabbed me and picked me up, but I made the mistake of looking at Michael's bloodied, heartless body. His eyes were wide open, the bullet hole in his head was oozing blood, and blood gushed from the place his heart used to be like a river.

"Papa," I screamed and Dad held me closer.

"Don't look, *moya lyubov.* Don't look," he'd mumbled in my ear, but it was too late. I couldn't unsee what I saw.

Dad ran out of the room with me straight into more dead bodies of people I knew. They littered the path.

The sight of death, blood and gore only ended when we reached the door to the underground tunnels.

We went down there and met Mom on the other side where she waited in hysterics.

Dad had managed to tell her about the attack and got her to meet us somewhere safe.

As he handed me over to her, we begged him to come with us but duty sent him running back into the arms of danger. My father was the senior guard, and he took that responsibility to heart.

That was the last time I saw him.

After that night I only knew what had happened to my father from what I heard by eavesdropping or Mom actually sitting me down to tell me.

Dad was found unconscious on the palace grounds. Even though he was injured there was evidence that suggested he was involved in the attack. The targets were the Russian Syndicate of Bratva leaders and senior Knights.

Dad saw the man with the scarred face too, but no one believed him.

No one could identify anyone who fit that description, and since the cameras at the palace were all down they had no footage of the incident or the man.

Eventually people thought my father was lying and when I told Mom I saw the man she thought I was lying too to save Dad. Because mom was worried for our lives she forbade me to mention him again.

She wouldn't even allow me to talk to Levgen about the scar-faced man, so he never knew that the man was a Knight or about the mysterious words he spoke.

My mother was disgusted with Dad for putting me in danger. The thing was I wasn't meant to be there that night. My presence there was solely because Mom had an emergency at work, but she felt my father risked my life anyway to kill the Syndicate members.

Apart from me, Dad was the only person in the palace who survived. That was suspicious enough.

We weren't allowed to see him, but Mom knew what was coming next— our deaths.

That's when she got Levgen's help. The only thing he could do to save us was stage our deaths by blowing up our home. Then he arranged for us to go to L.A. under the pseudonyms of Ivy and Oksana.

He made it seem like my father's enemies had killed us in retaliation for what had happened at the palace.

Levgen married Mom to add a further layer of protection. It was expected of him as a Knight of his caliber to take a wife. His previous wife had died years before from an illness.

We started our lives in the States with the vow to forget my father.

Except I can't forget him as easily as Mom did.

My body feels heavy after that trip down memory lane, and tears well in my eyes.

I get off the bed and pull out my storage box from under it. I have a little trinket box I took from home. Inside is something that should have stayed in L.A. but I couldn't part with it.

I pull out the little ring my father had made for me. He was going to give it to me on my sixteenth birthday.

At least Mom still honored him by giving it to me, but she gave it to me when we'd just gone to live with Levgen. It didn't matter if she was doing so because she was trying to rid my father from her mind. I was happy to have it.

The ring has my father's family crest embossed in the center, but on the inside is the inscription in Russian: *To my daughter Annika, love you forever.*

This is the only thing I have left of my father. I always feel close to him when I look at it. Always, even at two in the morning when I should be asleep in bed.

Who am I kidding? I won't be able to sleep tonight. Not even the Sandman can help me.

Feeling frustrated, I sit on the fluffy white rug and stare at the ring.

I usually don't keep it on me—or anywhere anyone can find it—but I feel like I need it now. Just for tonight.

I push to my feet and set the ring on the nightstand. Then I pull on a sweatshirt and yoga pants, and slip the ring into the inside pocket.

I'm going to do what I always do when I get like this —write music.

The library here is open twenty four seven and they have sections there for people like me who like to vocalize when they're writing music.

They also have a café that's open at this hour too, but that closes in fifteen minutes. If I hurry I can catch them open and grab a cappuccino.

It's going to be a long night, so I need it.

Half an hour later I'm seated in a comfortable spot in the library.

There's no one around but me, and it's so quiet I can hear my heart beat and myself breathe.

I grab one of the worktables by the window. It offers a great view of the moonlight kissing the surface of the river. The trees in the backdrop look like an army of shadows.

I sip my cappuccino and lose myself in the scenery while musical notes bounce around in my mind.

There's a stillness about the campus tonight with anticipation heavy in the air, like time is waiting for something to happen. It feels like a macabre precipice between worlds, between life and death.

I love it.

And I love being able to admire my surroundings when I'm working. My pieces are inspired by landscapes, moods, and atmosphere.

There was a melody teasing me on the flight from L.A. I wrote down the first verse in my notebook while I was on the plane. The melody came back to me yesterday when I was talking to Isabelle in the café.

I can hear it again now, but within the still silence and the dark beauty before me the melody deepens and grows the longer I stare.

I decide to write down what I can hear so I don't lose it, but when I turn around I find Thorne Ivanov sitting right in front of me.

The fright that shoots through my body at the sudden sight of him devastates my nerves worse than the first night we met. It rips through me like a hurricane, sending a wild shudder over my skin.

It's the type of fright that would make you scream, but I just about manage to stop myself.

Nevertheless, my coffee has slushed over the desk—thank God it was a small cup.

My free hand clutches my rapid beating heart, holding it in and my breath is lodged in my throat.

"Oh my God." The words tumble out of my mouth through my panting.

"Jesus, Bambi, you really need to be careful. I'd bet someone could kill you and you wouldn't even know you were dead *until* you were dead."

If that's not a fucked up thing to say, then I don't know what is. "What the hell is wrong with you?"

I know my tone is way harsh, but I don't care who he is. He frightened the living daylights out of me. *Again.*

I'm still trying to catch my breath and assure my heart I'm not under attack while he just watches me with that unhinged calm. And of course, even at this ungodly hour he looks as shockingly handsome as ever, with that dark, dangerous edge that both warns and, regrettably, entices me.

"It's funny how we keep meeting like this." He sits back and sharpens his stare. "In these strange places."

I grab some tissues from the holder on the table and clean up the spilled coffee. "This is the library. It's not a strange place. Also, last time I was lost."

"But that wasn't the last time we saw each other. Was it now, little deer?" His lips curl into a slow predatory smile.

At first I'm stumped about what he's talking about, then I remember. I saw him yesterday when I was with Isabelle.

"That was hardly a meeting. And must you scare me every single time you see me?" Once again I didn't hear him come up.

"You need to be more aware of your surroundings."

"I am, but you snuck up on me."

"What are you doing up at this hour?" He taps the table and lifts a skeptical brow.

"Studying."

"There's no way you have shit to study yet. And not at this hour."

"Maybe I want to get ahead of myself. What are you doing up?"

"Taking a walk."

He seemed to be out for a walk the other night too. "*Here*?"

He pulls out a slim cigarette from his pocket and allows it to dangle between his fingers. "You don't think I use the library?"

I choose not to answer because, no, I don't think the library is his scene.

"No comment, huh?" He chuckles and lights up, completely ignoring the no smoking sign across from us.

"Is there something you want?"

"Of course. There are many things I want."

"I mean specifically from me."

"Like I said. There are *many* things." The way his gaze moves over my face, slow and unhurried, makes my temperature rise, but I try to keep my head screwed on.

His cryptic words are the least of my worries. The problem is that he's talking to me again. *Why?*

I'm not the kind of girl who attracts guys like him. And it's nothing to do with looks. I'm just different, and in this instance he's off limits to me.

"It might not be such a good idea to want anything from me."

My answer seems to amuse him. "What if I like you? Are you telling me I can't?"

My eyes widen and my breath stills. I don't know if that was a joke or a trick. Something to rattle my brain or jar me like the urban legend.

I wait for him to say something more like he's joking, but he looks serious. I don't know him, but I think I know enough from our brief encounters to figure out that he's not a guy who wastes words. No matter, I already know the answer to give him.

"Yes. I am saying that you can't like me."

Thorne leans forward, resting an elbow on the desk. "What if it's too late and I've already decided you're mine?"

My lips part and my mouth goes dry as all the moisture drains from my body. When the moisture returns it beads between my thighs, sending ripples of heat through me like liquid fire.

I try to school my thoughts but my damn traitorous body likes the way he said that word—*mine*.

"I'm not your type." I have to rein this in. Diffuse the situation before it gets worse. Things feel like they've already gone south, so I need to change course and hope he does too.

"Interesting, first she refuses my dick, then she refuses me." He gives me a maddening smile. Then he tilts his head to assess me, the way you would when you're trying to figure something out like a puzzle. "How do you know what my type is?"

"I just know it's not me."

"Why'd you say that?"

"You don't know me." *And he can't.*

"I know enough. Ivy Yegorov, age eighteen, daughter of Oksana Yegorov and step daughter to Levgen Yegorov. You're doing music here with a minor in English literature because you love classical literature and post-romantic poetry. Favorite color is lilac, favorite artist is William Waterhouse, favorite bands are The Cranberries and Heilung, favorite movies are the Lord of the Rings and the Hobbit trilogies, favorite food is cannelloni. And you hate graveyards, which is interesting because your compositions all sound like death to me."

My lips tremble. I stare at him, utterly taken aback. Unlike him I can have social media because my relatives aren't part of the Knights leadership, but since I still have to be careful I don't post a lot of personal stuff. He knew a lot of *personal stuff* I don't think I've ever shared with anyone.

He looked me up. No. It's more than that. He knew about my music. You'd have to look deep to find that because I only have my collection uploaded to SoundCloud.

"You looked me up?" Saying the words outside my head sounds incredulous in relation to him.

"I make it my duty to know who I need to know. Should I tell you some more things I know about you?" He flutters his fingers over the table as if playing the piano.

"Tell me." A cold tremor lances through me. I don't think he knows my secrets or we wouldn't be here talking like this. But curiosity pushes me to find out what he knows.

"Fear looks good on you, little deer. So does innocence. Maybe that's why I want your V-card."

Shock slams into my chest and stays there, shackled to my heart. My nerves erupt in tremors and I know I've turned several shades of red, each one deeper than the shade before it.

How in the hell does he know I'm a virgin? *How?* It's not like I have the word virgin stamped on my forehead. And that's not usually something you can tell just from looking at someone. *Is it?*

Thorne stares back at me with expectancy. I want to tell him he couldn't possibly know that about me and he needs to leave me alone, but my mind can't compute an answer.

"So you see, I do know you." His menacing voice pulls me from my stupor.

"How… how did you know I still have my v-card?" It's silly, I know. I should have chosen to tell him I'm not a virgin, but I'm so stunned that he would know something like that I want to find out how.

"I just told you, I make it my duty to know who I need to know."

"But that's personal."

"Not to me, Bambi." A lopsided grin slides across his face, then it disappears as if it was never there.

"Now I'm left with the question of what will happen next." Thorne keeps his gaze trained on me.

"What will happen next for what?"

"You. Do you give me your V-card? Or do I take it?"

The seriousness that creeps into his expression makes my heart stagger in an offbeat symphony. My skin crawls as if a million ants are beneath it and I try to calm my breathing. But I fail.

Thorne is an absolute psycho. I suspected it before, but now I know.

"I'm not giving you my V-card and you're not taking it."

"That's debatable."

"You need to leave me alone." I summon courage, hoping like hell he'll listen, but when that sly smile returns to his face my hopes die.

"No."

"Why?"

"You got my attention, little deer. And remember, there are *many* things I want from you. Your V-card is just one of them. Those lips around my cock are another. I always get what I want, so…" He taps the table again and then stands, looking colossal, like a giant.

It's not until he leans over the table to stare at my notebook that I realize I'm not breathing. And I'm still *not* breathing. It's like I've forgotten how.

"G sharp, F sharp, C sharp. Try that. It will give you the atonal structure you're going for. You might also want to get a better look at the river in the moonlight. See what's beneath the surface."

I simply stare back at him, my mind a chaotic mess of thoughts and emotions.

He straightens, then walks away.

I actually hear his footsteps against the concrete floor which makes me think he really did sneak up on me. Or like he said, I wasn't aware of my surroundings.

I'm aware now. Aware of him.

What the hell just happened?

He wants my V-card, my lips around his cock and God knows what else.

How in the hell did this happen to me?

That whole encounter felt like I just stepped into some alternate fucked up dimension.

I might be new but I know most girls would kill to get Thorne Ivanov's attention. I'm the only one who doesn't want it, but I have it.

Now that I do, I fear what else I might get.

Thorne dug for information on me. He knows me and my music. He knows my music enough to decipher the algorithms of my mind just from looking at the few notations in my book. I picked up the fact that he must play the piano too, but what he said to me was more than that. He figured out what fascinated and inspired me.

What else will he figure out?

CHAPTER 6

IVY YEGOROV…

I wonder how much more freaked out she would be if she knew I'd been smoking outside her dorm for several hours.

I saw her leave at this crazy hour and decided to follow.

Earlier when I went out for a walk I didn't intend to end up at Ivy's dorm, but my mind drifted to her and that's where I went.

I was near her the whole time and she didn't even know. Not until I was sitting right in front of her, gazing into those silver eyes.

Silence can be a man's best friend when you know how to use it properly.

It's as subtle as breathing air and deadly as a lethal poison.

I've been able to hide in plain sight since I was five, and walk into a room like a ghost—unseen and unheard.

It was a trick my father taught me, while my mother appealed to what could pass for my softer side with music.

I'm not entirely sure if I ever really had such a thing as a 'soft side' or if I just made my mother believe I did to please her. I think it's the latter.

There was never anything soft about me. I was always fucked up, but my mother was the exception to every rule in the book. So was my sister Anushka, who was five years older than me. Our mother gave us piano lessons together because it was the thing we bonded over.

Having them—all of them, my father, mother and Anushka—ripped out of my world turned me into the soulless creature I am today.

That's why I don't play the piano anymore. It reminded me too much of them. Of how they went. They were all good people who never deserved to die the way they did.

The last time I saw my mother and father, the house was under attack and they were telling Caspian and I to hide. I saw my sister several hours before when we sat in the kitchen eating ice cream. We were staying at one of our safe houses, but neither of us would have known that was because my father was protecting us.

Sometimes I'm grateful I never saw their deaths, then like now, I feel like a coward for admitting that. Because Caspian saw. At eight-years-old he was forced to watch them die. Their deaths were so horrific it took him years to tell me how it happened.

They beat my father to death with a metal pole, but before he died, the men made him watch them rape my mother and sister. They'd gouged out my mother's eyes, so at least she didn't get to see what happened to Anushka.

The devils then left the remains of my family to rot in the bottom of a well with Caspian, who they tortured daily until he was rescued nearly a year later.

That is the horror I was spared from. I will always be grateful to Caspian for what he did for me, but I hate that I wasn't with my family in their final moments.

For a time I tried to keep them alive in music but all that did was make my grief and loss worse. So I stopped.

From time to time the music calls to me. It did tonight when I saw the little deer's composition. And I guess I can still read music and put notes together well enough to surprise people like little Miss I'm-not-your-type.

Despite the dark memories of my family, thinking of the shock on her face makes me smile to myself as I step onto the cobbled path leading back to my dorm.

She's actually right. She's not my usual type.

So why am I jonesing for this girl?

What the fuck is so interesting about her when I have a sea of women at my beck and call?

She's beautiful with a kind of beauty I haven't seen before. And yes, I'd love to get a taste of that body of hers, and I meant what I said. But that's not it.

None of those things is what has my interest.

Maybe it's because she's actually scared of me. People know to fear me and they're wary enough of the Ivanov name to know not to fuck with me. But she… she's genuinely terrified.

Even when she's trying to mask her fear by throwing her snippy remarks, the scent of it is as rich and potent as fresh blood. I'm like the shark when I smell that, and I still want a taste of the girl.

When I reach Erebus I go up to my room and stare at the computer, at the email from my uncle that sent me outside.

Aleksander wants to meet first thing in the morning, before I start my training.

Motherfucker. He would want to meet then, wouldn't he?

This year I'll be spending Wednesdays and Thursdays at Ivanov Tech and the rest of time on campus. Over the summer I was counting down. I couldn't wait. Now I'm dreading it.

Today is my official start and my uncle has already ruined it. The prick wants to go over the *matters* he discussed on the phone the other night and the unit Caspian and I will be selecting this year.

What pisses me off is I'm still in that mindfuck limbo where I'm not sure what to do. Nothing may come to me until my uncle makes his move.

I guess I'll know more in a few hours.

Until then I'll occupy myself with something a little more entertaining.

Using my tracker pad I flick back to Ivy Yegorov's high school records and scroll through the details on my little deer.

Music, music, music. That's all she seemed to love.

But there must be something darker in that pretty little soul of hers.

She portrays the sweet little angel but her music says otherwise.

It speaks of darkness.

Darkness like mine.

Aleksander's office door is already open so I walk in.

He's standing by the floor-to-ceiling glass windows talking with his new secretary. Another young pretty toy for him to bang.

He leans forward to rest his hand on her ass and the sun makes his white hair look like a ball of light.

Watching him squeeze his secretary's ass and licking his lips makes me sick.

He's only fifty-two but he looks like he's in his seventies. That hasn't stopped the women.

The prick keeps a steady supply of young women around, so he can fuck when he feels like it. There's never a shortage because of the money and power attached to his name.

I grew up watching him and his harem of women.

But, if I'm being honest, his one redeeming quality was that he loved his wife, Caspian's mother.

He never remarried after she was killed and it broke him when he found out she cheated on him throughout their entire marriage.

Aleksander glances my way when he hears my footsteps, so does the secretary who composes herself. She was smiling before at something he said.

As he's not a funny guy I can only assume he's paying her the same kind of money to laugh at his jokes as he is to suck his dick.

"Wonderful, you're here." His cold voice takes on that authoritative tone I loathe.

"Bright and early at your request." I summon a fake-as-fuck smile I know he can see through but I don't care.

New toy smiles at me and makes her way out. Aleksander stares at her ass until she goes through the door.

It makes me sick that he doesn't even have the decency to hide his disgusting habits. Should I even bother to tell him that new toy left lipstick on his collar?

No. He can fuck off and look stupid all day for putting me through this bullshit.

"Take a seat." He points to the chair in front of his desk.

I go over and sit, while he lowers into the winged leather chair behind the desk.

Steepling his fingers he sets his elbows on the arms of the chair and stares at me as if he finally has me exactly where he wants me. I suppose he has, but it won't last forever.

"You didn't reply to the email to confirm." His jaw clenches.

"I didn't think I needed to."

"In future you will be required to respond with your confirmation to all my emails, and act in a professional manner. Is that understood?"

"Loud and clear, *my Lord*." That's what we have to call him when we're at Raventhorn Hall—my Lord. He's anything other. Usually the title doesn't extend to Caspian and me when we're in a setting like this, but I wanted to rile him up. The twitch of his lips suggests I have.

"I can see you're still upset about the changes."

"No offense, but wouldn't you be? I prepared all my life for this. I am my father's heir. His *only* heir, and you're essentially telling me that if I don't do what you tell me to do I get nothing."

"But you *will* do what I tell you to do because you're not the kind of person to end up with *nothing.*" He gives me a wide satisfied smile, and again I think he looks pleased that he has me where he wants me. "The company is changing, Thorne. We have to appease the investors and the board. You are part of the future of the company. I want people to see that you worked hard to get your share of the business."

I don't know who he thinks he's fooling but it's not me. The things he's saying all make sense, but it's all bullshit. I know because he won't do this to Caspian.

"What do you want me to do?" Better to cut to the chase.

"You will be training with Aiden Sabioni."

A fist clamps around my stomach. "Aiden Sabioni as in your vice president's son who's currently at M.I.T?" *And hates my guts.*

"Yes."

"Why? Why does he have to train with me?"

"He'll be working here after graduation just like you. You'll be in the same department and have the same role."

Fuck. This is it. The first heads-up. And now I know he's trying to get rid of me. Aiden would make a fine replacement for me. M.I.T is exactly where I would have gone if I didn't have to go to Raventhorn. I was offered a place when I was fucking sixteen but the old man raised hell, asking me if I wanted to throw away my legacy in the Knights.

"How the hell is he supposed to have the same role as me?"

"That is what I would like. Of course if you make it that far."

"What's that supposed to mean?"

"The two of you have to complete various challenges that I will personally judge. If either of you fail to impress me… well, I think you know what will happen then."

"I get nothing," I fill in, keeping my tone measured.

"I'm sure you won't let that happen."

But *he* will. Then Aiden will take my place. What a fucking joke.

Aiden will take my legacy and my uncle will allow this because he's threatened by me.

"This year will be about learning everything you can about Ivanov Tech, so you'll both begin training next week. Of course you'll have the unit to look after as well, so I expect you to organize your time efficiently."

"Sure." *Asshole.*

"A word on the unit: I need you to be highly selective on who you choose. In other words don't pick shit. I don't think I have to remind you that these people will form the next generation of the Knights leadership."

"No, you don't."

"I don't like Lucian Sokolov or his family. You know this, but I see you and Caspian have him and his cousin at Erebus house all the time. They are not fit for the elite."

This is where I draw the line and take back the reins of control. He's not allowed to tell me who to choose. It's against the Knights' law.

"Yes they are." My voice is firm and I take pleasure in hearing it.

"You dare defy me on this?" His brows knit.

"Uncle, you know damn well you can't sway my decision on the unit."

He looks me over with distaste. "You need to remember who the fuck you're talking to. Your future is in my hands, boy."

"Maybe so, but you won't choose my men for me."

He looks taken aback and I'm actually surprised when he appears to back down. "You better make damn sure you pick the best."

"Let me worry about that. What else do you have to talk to me about?" It's time to change the subject before I say something I can't take back.

"Your marriage prospects." It's he who claims back control now.

As he's the head of the family and all things that have power over me, the fucking marriage is one topic I definitely can't fight. It would be like trying to put out an infernal fire with a bucket of water.

"What about it?"

"I'll have some marriage prospects for you within the next few weeks."

"Weeks?" This is so much worse than I thought. I sensed he may do shit like this to me but I never thought it would be as soon as *weeks.*

"Yes. I want you engaged by the end of the year. I have my eye on a few potentials."

"Like who?"

"You'll find out soon enough. In the meantime try to keep your dick under control. Wouldn't want you to father any bastard children."

"Don't worry about my dick." I should spite his ass by fucking every woman within my sight, including his new toy. "Anything else?"

"Not right now. I think that's enough for the day don't you?"

I don't answer. I just stand and march out. Not looking back.

I'm screwed to fuck and I can't see a way around it.

When I get down the hallway and I'm sure I'm alone I throw a fist in the wall. It's concrete so I feel the pain shooting through my knuckles.

It hurts like a motherfucker. But that was the idea. I needed to feel something other than fury.

I have to figure out this shit. Somehow, some fucking way.

I can't let Aleksander shepherd in Aiden to boot me out. No doubt he's getting him in to learn my tech skills and anything else he'll pick up from me when we work together.

And as for being engaged by the end of the year…

Fuck.

Fuck him.

My phone buzzes in my pocket with a text. I pull it out and look at the message. It's from Lucian. He's sent his guest list for the Lords and Ladies party Erebus and Lapetus house are hosting. It's on Saturday night and it's an invite-only party.

I'm supposed to approve all guests because it's going to be one of those wild risqué events that everyone will remember for time to come. The idea behind it is a dark fantasy version of a speed-dating session where you can do *anything*. The girls who are invited agree to be tributes to the Knights who pick them. Everyone gets seven minutes in heaven.

Lucian has sent me eight names of girls who live at Myrrdin house. Eilish is at the top of the list as his plus one—as expected. And beneath her name is Ivy's.

Something I can't quite describe pulls on my insides. It feels like rage. I've been feeling that asshole emotion all week, so I'm not surprised it's eating me alive again. What's surprising is I'm feeling it for a girl I haven't even fucked yet.

When I imagine her going from guy to guy to play seven minutes in heaven doing fuck knows what, a rush of primal possession charges through my blood.

They'd get to touch her before me. Or do other things.

There's a lot you can do in seven minutes, including taking someone's V-card.

Ivy would have to put her name forward for this party knowing what it was. Even though this is clearly Eilish's doing. She's the student counselor for the Thetas, so I can imagine her rallying the girls who need to get a life. The other girls on the list are freshmen.

Tiffany already sent a list to me of who she wanted to attend. But I know what that bitch is like. She would have excluded anyone she didn't like. Eilish gets special privileges because of Lucian.

So, Ivy wants to be a tribute?

Yeah she will be. She'll be mine.

It's time to have some fun.

With her.

CHAPTER 7

"Are you serious? They were having actual sex? In front of *everyone*?" Isabelle's face is a bright crimson and her eyes display the same wealth of shock I feel.

Mackenzie giggles mischievously and flicks her wrist, flaunting her just-done coffin shaped nails. "Yes they were. *Everyone* was. It's a sex club."

The girls all gasp and look at each other. Sawyer and Billie exchange curious glances. Savannah and Isabelle look like their interests are peaked. I'm somewhere in between curious and dumbfounded.

Everyone decided to assemble in my room to get their hair and makeup done for the Lords and Ladies party tonight.

The six of us are all sitting together in my living room. I've been on hair duty, while Sawyer and Savannah have been doing our makeup.

I've gone from Ivy, new girl on campus with no friends, to this little gathering which has happened every day for the last few days.

It started with me inviting them to watch a movie the other night. When they saw my room they fell in love with it.

It was so exciting to have them around that I dropped my guard and allowed them to talk me into going to this crazy party that has bad news written all over it.

Tiffany made a point of not inviting us but Eilish got us in.

We got on to the topic of sex clubs because the party is being organized by the same people who own the Dark Odyssey—*a sex club*.

I've never heard of the club before. Of course I knew that places like that existed but I didn't know just how popular they were. Mackenzie on the other hand is a well versed and very satisfied patron.

She turned eighteen nine months ago, *but* has been going since she was seventeen. I get the feeling though that she might have been younger. She's the girl with the wild streak. Sawyer is a runner up.

"And you do this?" Billie asks, looking at Mackenzie as if she's checking she's really telling us the truth. "I mean you go there and have sex?"

"Yeah." Mackenzie answers as if she's talking about the weather. "But I was with my boyfriend at the time. I've never been by myself."

The said boyfriend was five years older. They broke up just before she came to Raventhorn because she caught him cheating on her with her cousin. Mackenzie is also the girl with the kind of outlandish drama you'd see on Jerry Springer.

"Would you go by yourself?" Isabelle cuts in.

With a guilty look in her eyes Mackenzie bites the inside of her lip. "Yes. I love the excitement and thrill of doing something totally wild. Something you'd never do in real life. The club allows you to step into a fantasy. Knowing the Dark Odyssey guys and the frat guys at Erebus and Lapetus, tonight is going to be one hell of a party."

And that's what worries me. Along with the fact that I'm very likely to see Thorne.

I haven't seen him at all in the last three days but I'm sure he'll be there tonight.

I haven't been able to get his words/threats out of my head. Or the worry of him and this weird fascination he seems to have with me.

Because I haven't seen him I've been hoping that maybe he's forgotten me. It's wishful thinking but I'm wishing anyway. Maybe he found another girl to haunt.

With his looks and status it wouldn't be that difficult to replace me.

"You're super quiet, Miss lady." Isabelle looks at me and chuckles. She knows I'm nervous and that I'd prefer not to go to the party.

"I just don't know what to expect from tonight."

"Think speed dating meets seven minutes in heaven." Mackenzie flashes me a wicked grin. "But we're considered tributes to the guy you end up with."

"And we have to agree to do anything he wants?" I fill in because she's totally missing that part.

"Yes. That's the fun part. Come on Ivy, where is your sense of adventure. This is college, the place where you're supposed to live a little and experience life."

Live a little and experience life. It sounds… normal. I've lived this secret life so long that I don't know what normal feels like. I've never known and this—being here at Raventhorn and going to a crazy party—might be as close as I get.

"There's nothing to worry about. It's just a little fun." Isabelle nods and Sawyer joins her.

"Wild, sexy fun with hot blooded *hot* guys," Mackenzie cuts in and they all laugh.

I join them, but it's not funny. Apart from Isabelle and me, they've all had boyfriends. And they've all had sex.

Billie is even engaged to her boyfriend, Chad. They're going to the party together.

"It'll be alright." Isabelle reaches across and taps my hand. "It's going to be great to go and meet more people."

"Exactly," Savannah chimes in, beaming with anticipation.

"And hopefully, I get Kade." Isabelle rubs her dainty hands together. "This party is the perfect opportunity to speak to him."

"Speak? Girl, there's no way that's all you want to do with that boy." Savannah giggles, swatting Isabelle's leg.

Isabelle gives her a sheepish grin. "Of course I want to do so much more, but this is a start. Seven minutes in heaven for the three years I've known him. Maybe he'll want to speak to me for longer than seven minutes."

I smile back at her. It's nice to see her so excited. Isabelle has spoken about Kade more than anything over the last three days.

"I hope tonight goes well for you." I give her a positive nod.

"Me toooo."

She's praying for a kiss. But I just want to make it through the night without seeing Thorne, or doing anything completely insane with anyone else.

"Okay ladies, we have to get dressed now." Sawyer glances at her watch and stands.

"Yayy. I can't wait to get there." Isabelle bounces to her feet.

"Easy tiger." Billie giggles. "Remember to play it cool."

"Of course. I wouldn't dream of doing anything else." Isabelle tosses her hair over her shoulder and does her best rendition of a runway walk. She does great until she stumbles over Savannah's makeup bag.

We all laugh and I catch her when she stumbles again.

"Oh my gosh. Tonight is going to be very interesting if nothing else." Mackenzie rolls her eyes and chuckles.

The girls leave but Isabelle hangs back, laughing at herself.

"I'm so silly." She shakes her head. "I pray I don't fall over again in front of everyone, especially Kade."

"You'll be fine."

"Are you worrying about Thorne?" She raises one perfectly arched brow and gives me a questioning stare.

"A little?"

Against my better judgment I find myself telling her about what happened with Thorne at the library. He's been on my mind so much that I had to talk to someone.

"Okay a lot," I amend. "It's not like I can ignore him if I end up with him."

"I know, but that's no reason to miss out on our first party, or worry yourself. If you end up with him, then it's just for seven minutes. You'll live."

"I guess so. And I'm still hoping he's forgotten me."

"No offense, you're absolutely beautiful, but I know what he's like with girls. He probably *has* forgotten you. You haven't seen him in days, right?"

"I have not."

"That's a good sign. Now suck it up and get ready. Let's go party." She gives me a tap on my shoulder and makes her way out the door.

Suck it up.

Okay. Maybe I can. I've been doing well here so far even though I've still had to clean the kitchen. I've just tried not to let it get to me.

The best thing was speaking with the music teacher about my lesson plan. I found out that each student actually has allocated study and practice times in the music room and if we need extra time we can get it. The room is also open twenty four seven. Meaning I can play the piano whenever I want.

Yesterday I went there at four in the morning. I played for several hours.

It was just the medicine I needed.

So I can do tonight and live a little. The last date I had was just before graduation. I'm here now at Raventhorn and I don't intend to spend the rest of my time here living like some kind of social recluse.

I've been so hard on myself over the last few months, worrying myself sick. This could be medicine my soul needs too.

And who knows, I just might surprise myself and actually have fun.

So far so good.

We arrived at the Verge, the campus club, ten minutes ago. Billie left with Chad, leaving the rest of us to look around.

My mind is totally blown. I've never seen a club that looked like this in real life. It has multiple levels and wide arches on each floor, decorated with a contemporary meets Renaissance vibe.

There are aerial acrobats floating around the ceiling and pyro artists, juggling and breathing fire.

On top of that, all the girls are wearing elegant dresses and the guys are in full dress suits with black button down shirts and pants. I wondered if they'd be dressed in their Knights' tunics or some sort of period wear, but this suits them more.

The girls who are taking part in the activities are wearing gold bracelets, so each of us—except Billie—was given ours at the door.

The bracelet is symbolic of the token of a favor given to a knight at a tournament like jousting. For this game, if a Knight requests your favor it means he wants to spend more time with you, or do *more* with you.

My bracelet matches the gold, Grecian-style dress I'm wearing.

Isabelle and I went to Nordstrom yesterday to get our dresses.

"Oh my God, this is fantabulous." Isabelle twirls around, taking in all the awesome things around us.

She's swapped her usual Lolita style for a blue sleeveless cocktail dress. It's the most colorful thing I've seen her in since I met her.

"It certainly is amazing." I look around too.

"Hey let's get some cocktails before we join the games." Mackenzie points over to the bar where they're making colorful cocktails and other drinks that are in keeping with the Renaissance theme.

We head to the bar and get our drinks, then we sit in the little lounge nearby and absorb the atmosphere.

Everything seems run of the mill so far, and no one is having public sex. But that could be because the section we're in is just the beginning.

The club owners have created a labyrinth for tonight's game, which you have to go through to get to your guy or guys. That's where all the wildness will take place.

Apparently all the girls who've agreed to take part have already been selected by the guys they're supposed to see.

When we go over to the entrance of the labyrinth the organizers will split us up, so I won't see Isabelle or the other girls until we get back to Myrrdin.

Now that I'm here I fully realize that coming to this party was truly a bold move for me.

As we're all underage our drinks are non-alcoholic but Mackenzie had a flask of brandy. She gave us each a little drop to give our drinks a kick.

Usually I'd say no but I needed a little something to take the edge off. It worked. I have a gentle buzz going that's sated my nerves.

When we finish drinking we head to the labyrinth.

Isabelle was already bouncing with excitement, but her drink has given her additional energy.

"This is it," she bubbles, walking ahead of us. "Have fun, girls. I know I will."

Mackenzie glances at me and we giggle.

"Have fun and do something wild," she whispers to me.

I nod, although I've already decided against anything wild.

We walk through the entrance to the labyrinth where we find four guys dressed as knights in full silver and gold armor.

Once again I'm fascinated by how much effort was put into this party.

"Your hand please," the Knight closest to me says.

I put out my hand and he scans my bracelet.

"That way." He points down the dimly-lit path.

I glance back at Mackenzie and Isabelle who are nodding at me, silently telling me I'll be okay. I hope I will.

With a wave I leave and proceed down the path with my nerves rolling into a ball of heat in my stomach.

What on earth am I getting myself into?

And what if I see Thorne?

I rehearsed a speech to give him where I sounded confident in my mind, but every time I've seen him the guy has left me tongue tied.

The things he says to me… well, no one I know speaks like that. And not because there's that much difference between guys here and guys in L.A.

He's just… *him.*

At the same time I've become increasingly aware that something happens to me when I'm around him. Something different from fear and apprehension.

I'll be honest. It's attraction. I hate that I can even admit that, but deep down, I know it's true. And that's why I mustn't lose my mind when I'm around him.

Thorne Ivanov is no ordinary guy, so no matter how persuasive or gorgeous he is, he will always be off limits to me.

Suddenly the path becomes darker and the music changes. The wall becomes glass and I realize I can see a bed behind it. A fog of mist surrounds it.

When the fog clears I see four people on the bed having sex—three guys and a girl.

My mouth falls open and if it were possible to hit the floor and smash it would.

I'm so stunned I'm frozen to the spot.

Two guys pound into the girl at the same time—one in her pussy, the other in her ass—while the other feeds her his cock.

They take her like they own her inside and out. And she looks like she wants to be owned.

Suddenly I understand everything that Mackenzie said about being wild and doing something you'd never do in real life.

I've seen some porn before but I'm the kind of girl who can't watch for too long. A minute or two at the most before I feel all weird. This is different.

Would I do this?

Could I allow myself to be taken in such a way, by not just one guy but three? It seems inconceivable but unnervingly fascinating.

Mom and Levgen have encouraged me to fit in, but I *knowwww* they would never class *this* as fitting in.

The spell is broken when the fog comes back, covering the glass so I can't see the group anymore. But that doesn't mean the show is over.

I notice the rest of the wall on this side has more to see. More that lures me away from my shock.

The next window shows only one couple. An older man and a younger woman who doesn't seem that much older than me.

I'm captivated by the sensual way they touch.

It's like they're satisfying a thirst for each other. The group before had a savagery about them.

I realize both impressions were right and designed to come across that way on purpose.

"I'm trying to figure out which you like more," comes a deep voice I've come to recognize awake and asleep. It's the voice of the man I prayed I would avoid tonight.

I turn around to find Thorne leaning against the wall opposite me.

Although I've seen him wearing nothing but black since we met, tonight he has an elegance about him in his smart-casual clothes.

An elegance that seems too refined for him yet enhances his masculinity in a way that makes him look as irresistible as a Hollywood heartthrob.

"What do you mean?" Like always when I'm around him, I try to imbue my voice with confidence.

"The group or the couple." His eyes roam over me, taking in my dress, my hair, my lips. "You wouldn't like being shared."

"Wouldn't I?" He's right but I don't want to give him the satisfaction. "Maybe I'd like that."

"No. You wouldn't. You can't divide your attention between two men."

"How do you know? Maybe I could."

A muscle twitches in his jaw, but he keeps that cool edge about him that's as dangerous as it is alluring.

"You're the kind of girl who will be satisfied with the attention of one man *only*. But that man has to worship you like you're the only woman in this world, and fuck you like a savage. Like he can't get enough of you and he'll die if he doesn't touch you."

I didn't realize I was biting down hard on my back teeth until the tightness in my throat begged me to swallow. And I'm parched. Parched as if I haven't drunk water in decades.

Thorne watches me, his face stern and stony, but amusement dances in his blue gaze.

"Looks like I'm right, little deer." His voice forces away the awkward silence between us.

"I don't know. Maybe I'll experiment." I decide to rile him up and throw him off his game.

"Come here." The possession in his tenor hits me low in my core, grabbing at my insides with the savagery he spoke of moments ago.

My breath stills but I try to think of all the things I need to say to stop this craziness in its tracks. He's clearly guy number one, so I'll use our seven minutes to set him straight.

"I like over here, thank you very much."

His lips curl into an award-winning grin. "With the people fucking behind you?"

I frown and move a few paces down the wall where the glass stops and it's concrete again. It puts some distance between us, but not enough.

"We have seven minutes so let's just get to the point." I set my shoulders back and lift my chin.

"What point would that be?"

"You need to leave me alone. Even you can see how closely you're bordering on stalking. It's creepy as fuck and not a good look for anyone, least of all you. An Ivanov."

The humor in his expression intensifies as if I just added to a running joke we've had going for years.

Thorne stares back at me for a few heartbeats while I wait with expectancy for an answer. Another stretch of time passes before he pushes away from the wall and my breath falters when he comes closer, taking slow, methodical steps.

I move back, pressing right into the wall as he invades my personal space, making it non-existent.

Using his body he presses into mine and I swear I can feel every hard muscle of his wide torso molded against me.

Leaning in, he brushes his nose against mine and inhales me, then he moves to my ear and lingers there. I'm numb with trepidation and a potent dose of apprehension that has my stomach fluttering with electric butterflies.

"I'll bet you practiced that little speech every day since I last saw you." The scruff of his jaw grazes my cheek and the heat of his breath tickles my skin.

"It doesn't matter how much I practiced it. I mean it." I try to shove him away but he grabs my hand and presses it against the wall, holding me captive. "Let me go, I'm sure your seven minutes are up."

He laughs, cold and twisted. "Really, now? Did you seriously believe I was going to allow you to come to *my* party and only give me seven minutes?"

I struggle against his grasp. "Your party?"

"My party. You seem to forget who I am, little deer. Pretty much everything that happens on this campus is mine." He presses his lips to my cheek, and a finger to my already-leaping pulse. "Nothing happens here unless I agree to it. So you're certainly not going to give me seven minutes, and you won't be seeing anyone else."

"You're insane. You need to leave me alone."

"No." He clutches my throat. His large hand wrapping around me is terrifying and I'm wildly aware of the fact that he could snap my neck if he wanted to.

Thorne moves closer so we're eye to eye, and the demented expression on his face scares and excites me at the same time. That shouldn't make sense, yet it does in my head and I hate it.

I hate it because it means I'm accepting that I'm attracted to him.

My nerves frazzle at the acknowledgement in my mind. Then my heart triple beats when he holds up my gold bracelet before me, showing he's taken my favor.

"My lady."

"You asshole."

"Finally, you see who I am."

Before I can comment his mouth crashes down on mine, stealing my senses as he pins my body and soul to his. Thorne captures my head and soul kisses me, leaving me numb and aroused in a way I can't describe.

Nothing makes sense to me but his lips on mine and the important parts of my mind that should be working are frozen. Frozen like a fossil captured in amber, waiting to be discovered.

The kiss turns greedy and needy and desperate.

I lose my mind.

I lose myself.

I lose sight of every single warning my mother gave me and in those moments I don't care about anything.

I don't come back to earth until he lifts the hem of my dress and cups my sex through the lace of my panties.

Thorne presses his fingers into my clit and I gasp against his kiss. No one has ever touched me there before. The foreign sensation of his fingers fluttering over my mound makes my head spin and my breath go short.

He stops kissing me, just so he can look at me and smile at what suddenly feels like my defeat—me unraveling in his arms.

"You're wet, *malen'kiy olen'*." He calls me little deer in Russian sounding sexier for speaking the language I haven't heard in far too long.

I've barely paid attention to the fact that he's telling me I'm wet.

"No," I pant.

"Yes. You want me to fuck you and take the cherry between your legs."

"No."

"Liar." This time he slips his finger into my panties so he's touching my bare pussy. He flicks his thick thumb over my aching clit and I moan out so loud the sound echoes around us.

"Thorne—"

He answers by pushing my dress up my hips and spreading my legs wider, then he adds another finger into my pussy and pumps hard, in and out, finger fucking me.

"Let's play this game tonight." His sinful smile adds to my delirium.

I can't think anymore and my body has taken over control of my mind.

Lost in rapture, I press my fingers into the wall and surrender to him.

Vicious waves of pleasure sweep through me, up and down my body. Once. Twice. And all over again. I'm so hot my skin feels like it might fall off.

Finally the deadly combo of Thorne's ruthless fingers and the insatiable pleasure splits me apart and I come. A sharp cry leaves my lips and the waves of my orgasm leave me trembling against him.

I grab on to his shirt, squeezing tight as if he can stop me from falling off the face of the earth, and he smiles.

Thorne holds my gaze, his piercing stare intensifying with every passing second of me trying to regain my composure.

Damn him for doing this to me. And damn me too.

I didn't stop him. I didn't try hard enough.

I'm better than this.

He withdraws his hand and I slump against the wall, my chest heaving, my soul shaking. Then the devil shocks me even more by holding up his fingers, showing me the glistening juices of my arousal. He places his fingers in his mouth making a show of licking it off with a satisfied smile.

And then he looks at me as if he's only just getting started.

CHAPTER 8

Thorne

Finally I tasted her.

I continue licking my fingers.

The beautiful silver-haired siren watches me, mortified that I'm savoring the sweet nectar from her pussy.

The color of our sexy encounter drains the blood from her already Snow White-skin, leaving it a deadly shade of alabaster.

Like the bastard I am, I've enjoyed every second of watching her squirm in my arms. Nothing was sweeter than seeing her fight then fail when she realized she wanted me. She wanted everything I had to give her and more.

"You taste like you want me to fuck you, little deer."

"Fuck you."

"That's the idea, *malen'kiy olen'.*" I lean forward and laugh, infuriating her further. "Was that a request?"

"You know it wasn't." The color returns to her cheeks and she tries to move, but I restrain her.

With the weight of my body I push her harder into the wall, allowing her to feel the bulge of my cock.

I'm hard as fuck and I know there's only one thing that will satisfy me—being inside her.

"Let me go."

"No. I'm not done with you yet."

"What are you going to do to me now? You're such an ass—"

I silence her again with another kiss.

She puts up a fight and I realize that fire is another reason I like her. Ivy fears me but at least she tries to unsnare herself from my grasp.

It's commendable, but just like before she loses. She loses to that thing that's screwing with both of us—*desire.*

My dick grows harder and I know I have to be inside her, right here and now. Up against this wall.

I grab her ass to pull her closer, but the sound of footsteps pulls me back from the wild sexual spell that's seized my mind.

No one is supposed to come down here but us. I sealed off this section of the labyrinth so I could finally fuck this girl out of my system and move the hell on.

I tear myself away from her lips and look across to find Lucian coming down the path.

Ivy pulls out of my arms when she sees him and quickly fixes her clothes. I only released her because her dress is up around her waist and I don't want anyone to see any part of her body except me.

On seeing that I'm clearly in what was nearly a compromised position, Lucian grins.

I glare back at him, wanting to rip the smile off his face.

The instant Ivy is decent she rushes away from me without looking back at either of us.

I watch her go, fleeing again. This time is worse and now I have a major case of blue balls.

I snap back to face Lucian when he reaches me and I stare him down.

"Not like you to go for a freshman." Lucian smirks.

"Fuck you, Sokolov. You better have a fucking good excuse for disturbing me."

"I do. Kade locked James Valmik in your pressure chamber."

Oh, fuck. I'm already moving. Lucian falls in step with me.

"I thought they were at the party."

"They were, but shit went down and they started fighting." Lucian quirks a brow. "Kade beat James to a bloody pulp before he shoved him in the chamber."

My pressure chamber is not like the ordinary ones people use for altitude testing. It's deadly and meant for torture. When used the wrong way, like I'm guessing it has been, it could mean death.

I designed it for the trials this week and kept it hidden at the boathouse. I never taught anyone how to use it because of how dangerous it is. You can only open the chamber with my fingerprints.

"What the hell happened?"

"James called Kade's mom a whore and his father a cocksucker."

Nothing further of explanation needs to be given.

Kade's parents are both dead. Just like mine and, like Kade I'd want to kill anyone who spoke about my parents in a derogatory way.

We leave the club and head across to the boathouse, but I take one last look at the sea of partygoers outside, looking for Ivy.

I didn't expect to see her, so I shouldn't be disappointed.

Knowing Ivy she will have rushed back to her dorm.

That's okay.

Tonight was just the beginning.

A taste of her.

The next night, we gather outside the boathouse for the first big trial.

This event is the only thing that's successfully occupied my mind enough to keep me from seeking out Ivy Yegorov.

I've been working with Caspian and Lucian all day. Now we're here for the big moment.

Caspian, Lucian and I stand before the twenty pledges who are competing to be selected for our elite group.

"*Haec nox est nox, quam vitam tuam effundis vetus ac de novo incipis,*" Caspian speaks first as our leader, reminding them of the first paragraph of our Creed.

It's in Latin, like the Oath. It translates to: *Tonight is the night you shed your old life and start anew.*

"*Ego spondee,*" they all reply in unison, confirming their pledge to us.

"I hope you'll all remember that." Caspian scans over the guys, focusing mainly on Kade, who stares back with a stern face.

Caspian switches his gaze to James next, who still looks like he was ravaged by wolves. James is lucky Kade didn't kill his ass. The fool would have died in that chamber last night if Lucian hadn't come to find me when he did.

"Tonight is the beginning of the rest of your lives." Like a war commander, Caspian walks down the line of the first row of pledges and stops. "Each of you here was assured a place at Raventhorn, but it is not guaranteed that you will become a Knight. The same as it's not a guarantee that you will become part of my elite. Tonight, eight men will be chosen to continue the trials for the elite group. In the weeks to come, only four will remain."

I focus on the four I've been drawn to since the semester began. They're standing together now. Kade, Dmitri, Logan and Alek, Lucian's cousin. I predicted Alek would join the trio, which he did.

They were accepting of him joining their pack for two reasons.

The first is, he's Lucian's cousin. As Lucian is already in with us, they believe Alek has a sure spot and want to make use of him. It's human nature to use others. Part of the survival of the fittest.

The other reason is he's just as unhinged as they are.

"Over to you, Thorne." Caspian looks at me.

I give the pledges a wicked smile. A sign I'm about to fuck with them all six ways to Sunday. "This trial will take place in the river."

The puzzled look on each of their faces is exactly what I expected to see.

Except for the moonlight and the light from the boathouse, it's pitch black. Since I gave no indication that there would be any water activities, they're wearing T-shirts and jeans.

"You will work in groups of four. There's something at the bottom of the river I need your group to retrieve for me. The item holds some specific meaning to each of you in the group. I will hand your team leader a number. First, you must locate that number along the riverbank to know what part of the water to enter." This idea was one of my best. Inspired by my love for *Raiders of the Lost Ark* and the *Resident Evil* movies.

"The first two groups to bring their item to me will win tonight's round. There's a box of waterproof flashlights over by the boats. Use whatever you can find around the docks to help you." I smile wider when I think of the twist in this trial. "Oh, and beware of my friends at the bottom of the river that bite. They're particularly fond of human flesh."

With that declaration, even the guys acting like they're hardcore motherfuckers look like they're about to shit themselves.

"What's down there?" James stutters. The little prick has the audacity to look scared in front of me.

"Crocs."

The silence that descends on the group is like death. Still, unmoving and cold. It lasts for a full minute before James takes a quick breath. Or maybe it's more like a gulp. Or he heaved.

"How did crocs get in the water?"

"I put them there. The river has been sectioned off, so the crocodiles won't escape. But you have to deal with them."

"And all we get is a flashlight?" He stares at me wide-eyed.

I answer with my trademark smile.

This is hazing like no other. But I expect some of these guys will be so terrified they won't get in the water. The others with common sense will actually seek out the danger first and eliminate it.

"How many?" Kade asks, glancing at Dmitri.

"Five. One for each group. Any more questions?"

They're quiet. What more can they ask me though?

Either they accept the trial or they don't.

I divide the pledges into groups, choose their leaders, and hand them their numbers from one to five. Even though Kade deserves punishment for last night I chose him to lead his pack for group four.

"Ready, set, go." I wave my hand and they all rush to the riverbank.

"You are one crazy motherfucker." Caspian nudges my side. "Crocs?"

"This is a walk in the park. Remember our Reaping?" That stops him in his tracks from saying anything more.

To this day, I don't know how we survived. His asshole father set things up, so it was like the fucking *Hunger Games* meets hell. We were thrown into a deathtrap in the forest and pitted against the Bratva assassins, men trained to kill on sight.

"My Reaping wasn't that much different, nor my trials here last year." Lucian smirks with a nod. "I know why you added the crocs."

"I knew you'd appreciate my stroke of genius." I grin back at him.

The three of us watch the chaos unfold.

Team Three is the first to find their number on the riverbank, but one of the crocs surfaces and none of the guys get in. They stand there, waiting, wondering, then accepting defeat when they walk back to us and keep going, eliminating themselves.

The same thing happens with Team One, leaving Teams Two, Four and Five, who are now in the water.

Here's where things get interesting, and as Teams Two and Five look like they're already failing I focus on Kade and his group.

They understood the assignment.

Logan and Alek lure the crocs away while Kade and Dmitri dive in beneath the dark depths of the river.

They're all good swimmers, so that's a plus. And they're all clever. Another plus.

Moments later Kade and Dmitri surface with the wooden coffin I left for their group at the bottom of the riverbed.

Each group has one. A symbol of the death of their old lives.

They swim to the riverbank and pull out the coffin, free of the crocodiles.

The whole diversion gives Team Two the chance to get their coffin and follow suit.

Logan and Alek split up, swimming separate ways, and so do the crocodiles. That messes with Team Five's chance, and they end up swimming back toward the riverbank empty-handed.

The chaos they cause creates a stir among the crocodiles, something they hate, but that gives Logan and Alek a chance to escape and swim back to land.

They join Kade and Dmitri, and the four bring their coffin to me.

The rest of the guys try to make it back in a state of panic. They're nearly back when one smooth-swimming croc catches up to Blakeley, the slowest swimmer.

He shouts for help as the croc opens its giant maw revealing a million teeth.

No one is dying on my watch today, including my animals, so I pull out my gun with the idea to scare off the crocodile.

I'm about to shoot when Kade runs forward and throws his knife. It sails through the air and lands in the crocodile's head. Seconds later, my croc flaps around the water until it goes still, dead.

Blakeley and the others climb out of the water then Kade looks back at me, taking note of the gun in my hand.

"You killed my pet." I raise my brows at Kade.

"I thought it was going to eat him."

I don't bother to answer since he passed the test, which was teamwork and bravery. "Team Two and Four stay. The rest of you can go."

With sour expressions, Team Five leaves.

I look back at Team Four and Two, Kade and James specifically. James knows he's only standing there because he and his group piggybacked off Kade's group effort.

"Well done, men." I nod at them. "You made it this far. As you gathered, the test was to see how well you can work in a team and how brave you can be. Also, I saw just how much you want to be part of our elite. You may open your coffins now."

They open them, and the looks on their faces when they see what's inside are memorable. But not in a good way.

It's my job to know these guys inside out so I'm aware of their deepest emotional wounds. Each of the items in the coffin represents a nightmare that would fuck with these guys for years.

I pay attention to Kade the most as he looks at the picture of his parents.

Feeling my gaze, he locks his eyes with mine and it's the first time I've seen any emotion in him apart from that stern, unreadable expression.

"Tonight, you banish the memory of your old lives and move forward. To be a Knight you must be fearless and sometimes you have to be heartless. Is that understood?" I look around at the faces of the eight left behind. All of them nod their understanding. "Then here endeth the lesson. Place your items back in the coffins and close them, then you may go. Everyone except Kade."

I focus on Kade while the groups do as I instructed. He does it, too. Caspian and Lucian lead the rest of the group away, leaving me with Kade.

He looks nervous. Another emotion I haven't seen him display since knowing him. And I make him more nervous on purpose by prolonging the stretch of silence between us.

He's figuring me out while I'm doing the same to him. People say it takes one to know one and that like minds are drawn together. I sense that's what's happening between us.

My problem is I always clash with people who are like me. One could argue that Caspian and I are so similar that we have the same personality, but that's not true. He has a heart. I don't. It makes the difference. It means you don't easily allow your emotions to get in your way and hinder you.

Looking at Kade, I see he's as heartless as I am.

Maybe just a little more. The kind my particular blend of fucked up calls a challenge.

"If you pull a stunt like last night again, you're out of Raventhorn." My tone is as sharp as a slap in the face. It slashes Kade's bravado down by another few notches.

"I'm sorry for what I did. I know James could have died." He looks like he means that apology well enough, but I know he's not sorry in the least. It was his intention to kill James.

"If you're going to be in my unit let's agree not to lie to each other. You don't give two shits if James lives or dies. Is that correct?"

His jaw tenses and he looks uneasy at being called out. "Yes. It's true."

"My problem with what you did is that you used my shit. My modified, illegal, deadly shit that has my name written all over it. If he'd died they would have blamed me, and I would have been stripped of my Knighthood."

Realization forms in the press of his lips and in the wideness of his stare. "I never considered that."

"No shit. Don't fuck with me like that again. If you do, I will fuck you up and make you wish you'd never been born. Is that clear?" I stare at him hard, but with the cool calculated mask of malice.

"I hear you."

"Good, because you don't get any more chances with me. Now get out of my sight."

He takes a few steps but stops and turns back to me, his face contorted with the combination of trouble and the moonlight.

"What?" I stare him down but the instant he glances at the closed coffin that contains the picture of his family, I know he's going to ask me something to do with it.

"Have you banished the memories of your family? Have you moved on?" He searches my face, giving me a frosty stare. "I'm not in your unit yet but I still don't think we should lie to each other."

This guy has some balls on him. I've had to kill men for less than questioning me. This guy is putting me on the spot and I sense he already knows my answer.

"No. I've neither banished the memories of my family, nor have I moved on."

"Then how must I?" He balls his hand into a tight fist at his side.

"Consider the guidance a favor, *Pledge*. It's what you need to hear to be on my unit. If I didn't want you on *my unit*, you wouldn't be here."

He straightens, his fist loosens, and the tension in his shoulders subsides. He gives me a curt nod and glances at the coffin again. "They were murdered, and I wasn't there."

"Neither was I. For mine."

"Sorry."

I dip my head and he leaves.

It doesn't take much for me to think about what happened to my family.

Especially when I'm reminded about it. My memories of them are a dark mixture of pain, sadness, and grief. I hardly remember the good things.

The pain from losing them will be forever engraved in my soul.

It's late when I get back to Erebus.

I walk into my apartment, close the door and leave the past outside, behind me.

The automatic lights snap on and the four Prussian blue walls of my living room greet me, along with the silent glare of the flatscreen TV taking up most of the wall to my left.

I left the TV on earlier by accident and I see that the computer is on, too, *unlocked*. Anyone could have broken in and had a field day with my secrets and the ones I keep of others. I have enough shit on there that could put me and said *others* away in a federal prison for life.

My fucking brain has become scanty since a certain virgin stepped into my sphere of existence.

And now that I'm alone with my thoughts and my rock-hard dick, Ivy Yegorov is dancing around in my head again.

She didn't really leave. She and her music, her glossy pink lips, smooth skin, and that silver-blonde hair.

It's getting worse. This obsession of mine.

The unsatisfied part of me that didn't get what I wanted from her last night is pushing me to the edge.

I know I'm supposed to control myself, but I only do that when I want to. Not because I must.

That's why I purposely walked by Ivy's dorm on the way here. The lights were out in her room so I assumed she'd gone out.

My little deer is not asleep. It's eleven, so it's late enough to assume she could be. But I know she's not. Especially not after last night.

Ivy is a night owl anyway and there's something about the darkness that soothes her when she's troubled. At the same time, she fails to factor in that monsters like me love the darkness, too. It's where we can be who we are without restraint.

Where did she go tonight?

The library? The coffeehouse? The auditorium? They're all still open.

Or maybe she's with someone.

A guy?

If she is, he's dead.

There were several eyes all over her body last night when she arrived at the party with her friends. Twelve guys signed up to have her for seven minutes in dark fantasy heaven before I stepped in and took them off the list.

She was supposed to be mine.

My dick is on the verge of explosion by the time I walk into my bedroom and I know I'm not going to be able to sleep until I find some relief.

So I strip off my clothes, head to the shower in the ensuite and grab my cock.

I turn on the water so it sprays over me with a cool but not cold temperature.

I rest one hand against the granite wall in front of me then, just like last night, I clamp a fist around my shaft and stroke.

Closing my eyes, I imagine Ivy naked on her knees before me. I've never seen her fully naked but what I conjure seems to fit. I already know what her legs and hips look like, so I add large, bouncy breasts, a curvy waist and the flat stomach I felt when I shoved her against the wall.

Now that I have a good visual I imagine her hot little mouth sliding up and down my length, then she takes me deeper, deeper, deeper.

The sight of her in my mind is so prominent and visceral it sends a rush of blood straight to my dick.

Moments later I'm pumping like a madman on crack and like I've lost my shit.

It gets worse when I imagine what her face would look like if she were really here with me.

I see those magical, seductive gray eyes staring up at me as if she worships my dick and that's when I blow my load.

A guttural roar pours out of me as virulent as the cum flowing out of the aching head of my cock.

I'm fucked. Fucking fucked.

Whatever the fuck it is that's captivated me with this girl has possessed me.

And I'm worse than those creepy fuckers in *The Exorcist* movies because I'm more than aware of what I want.

Her.

I want her.

I actually fucking want her.

The darkness inside my head that usually whispers its evil plans to me is now shouting to take what I want.

This is a new strain of greed. Something I crave and can't control.

And I don't want to control it.

I want it to consume me. I want it to erase the notions of right and wrong from my mind, along with honor and duty to who I am.

I want to break her, break down all her walls of resistance, and truly make her mine.

Only then will I be satisfied.

Because I'm obsessed.

CHAPTER 9

NIGHT FELL HOURS AGO BUT I WANTED TO STAY OUT AS LONG AS possible to hide myself from my new tormentor.

I'm nearly back at the dorm.

Glancing cautiously around my surroundings, I make my way down the path.

There's no one around but I keep thinking Thorne is going to jump out from the shadows, or I'll turn the corner and crash right into him.

It's been two days since I last saw him. Two full days as of one hour ago.

That should be good. It might even suggest that he's had his fill of me and I might not have to worry about him anymore.

But I made the mistake of thinking that before and look what happened to me. I was so wrong.

After our last encounter, I know there's no way I'm off his radar. And Thorne said he wasn't done with me.

As today was the first day of classes I managed to stretch out my practice time with Francois, my music tutor.

I had a great day making more friends, pairing up with two other students with a similar style to me, and I got my schedule nailed for the week.

Dare I say it, things felt like they were coming together here at Raventhorn. I even felt that sense of comfort you experience when you're exactly where you should be.

When Francois and I got talking after class to set up my sessions with him, I instantly became wildly fascinated when I learned he'd trained under the great Martha Argerich, one of the best classical pianists of all time.

He went on to tell me about his musical career where he traveled worldwide, and he even set up a meeting for me with a contact from the New York Philharmonic Orchestra.

If he thinks I'm good enough by the end of freshman year he promised to put my name forward for the spring internship in my sophomore year. That is the kind of benefit you receive when you attend a college like this.

Francois already likes my music, so I can only hope to earn such an opportunity when the time comes.

We stayed in the auditorium for five hours. I was so engrossed by what he was teaching me that I hardly noticed the time pass.

More importantly, during that time I wasn't thinking about Thorne.

It wasn't until I left that he reentered my mind like a ghost, so I went to the ice cream parlor—a place he hasn't seen me before. I stayed there until they were closing.

Twigs crunch beneath my feet when I take the shortcut across the garden.

The wind rustles through the trees. It's subtle but my senses are so heightened that to me it sounds like banshees howling through the clouds as they sweep across the sky.

Any moment now I expect the gargoyles sitting on top of Raventhorn Hall to come to life and join my host of mythical creatures.

God… I must be more tired than I thought.

My wild imagination is totally spurred on by lack of sleep, stress on stress, and the worry over keeping my sanity.

I don't know what I'm going to do about Thorne but I have to do something. I just don't know what yet. It would be easier if he weren't an Ivanov.

No one is exactly going to come to my aid if I tell them he's harassing me. I thought of talking to Eilish but that idea died in the water when I remembered how Lucian caught me with Thorne in the labyrinth.

He would have heard my stupid moans of pleasure, which didn't exactly sound like I wasn't having a good time.

You can't explain natural bodily reactions to guys like that. Especially when I'm not entirely sure if it really was a natural bodily reaction or just me.

I allowed Thorne to touch me. I can't lie about that.

I actually allowed him to touch me. And I kissed him. Twice.

Shit. I didn't even remember that.

Surely, if I didn't want his touch or his lips anywhere near mine I would have kicked and screamed and tried to save myself.

It bothers me that I didn't.

It bothers me more because I know I can't get involved with this boy—*man.*

Thorne is not a boy.

Boys are the male creatures I left back in high school who pulled pranks and got up to all sorts of immature shit. I don't think Thorne was ever anything like them. He seems to have been a man for a long time.

I cross the bridge, and my steps quicken when I see Myrrdin House ahead.

I can't get inside quickly enough, then I rush up the stairs to my room just as fast. I'm not in the mood to socialize tonight and I'm not in the mood to deal with Tiffany or her lackeys.

I make it to my room safe and unseen, then I set my bag down, feeling the weight of the day drain from my shoulders.

I grab a quick bite to eat and check my messages. Mom and Levgen always message at this time. Sure enough, there's a message from each of them.

I update them on my day, telling them all the good things that happened with Francois. They text back with encouragement and excitement, making me miss them so much more than I already did.

I'd love a little slice of home right about now, so I can bury my head in the sand and come up with a way to deal with Thorne.

Since I can't have that I settle for the next best thing—a hot bath.

I do the whole scented oils and muscle soak ritual that usually calms me.

It works to some degree but when I head back into the bedroom, there's a weird feeling about the place. A strange presence.

The air is thick with it.

It's as if…someone else is in here with me.

Thorne?

No.

But what if he is?

I didn't hear him. *Really, Ivy?* The man has snuck up on me twice in the same week without me knowing. He was sitting right in front of me at the café and I didn't even know.

A shiver runs down my spine at the unsettling thought that he could be here and I stop in the middle of the bedroom to look around.

The tension wrapping itself around my nerves is so tight I'm forced to walk around the apartment to check out everything.

I search the apartment from top to bottom and find nothing. I'm alone, paranoid, and frustrated at myself.

Why the hell am I letting this guy screw with me?

It's okay. It will be okay. I just have to get to bed.

I head back to the bedroom, lock the door and take off my robe.

As it's hot I turn up the AC and crawl into bed just wearing my panties. I've been sleeping with the window open but I think it's best if I don't tonight.

I turn out the lights and lay my head down on the stack of pillows. A sense of safety drifts over me, lulling me to sleep.

I slip into a dream. One where I see my father. We're in the park I used to play in when I was little.

He's pushing me on a swing.

I go up and down, slicing through the air. Dad is laughing as he pushes me.

I go up again, higher, higher, higher, and when I come down a warm finger trails over my leg.

The sudden feeling pulls me from the dream. Dad and the playground disappear.

I expect the weird touching sensation to fade along with them but it returns, sliding down, down, down my leg.

Still half-asleep I reach out to feel what it is but when I hear a deep, low chuckle my entire body goes rigid with dread and fear.

My eyes snap open and I see him.

Thorne.

Thorne standing over me.

Thorne standing over me lying *naked* in the bed.

"Was this for me?" He traces his finger over the flat of my stomach and my heart wedges in my throat. "Thanks for the visual. It was driving me crazy wondering what you looked like naked."

"What the hell are you doing in my room? Get out."

Thorne gives me a wolfish grin that suits him. "I told you I wasn't done with you yet."

I try to cover myself and sit up at the same time so I can escape but he catches my leg and yanks me to the edge of the bed.

"You crazy bastard. What are you going to—"

In one swift movement he crouches and pulls me toward him, spreading my legs wide so he can bury his face between my thighs.

The next thing I know his mouth is covering my pussy and he's sucking down on my clit through the cotton barrier of my panties. I cry out from the impact of his hot mouth on my sensitive skin. And from the raw dose of pleasure.

Like a floundering idiot, I buck and thrash against him like I can't make up my mind.

I hate to love what he's doing to me and love to hate him.

Suddenly recalling my prior embarrassment from the other night of not *trying* hard enough to get away, I try now.

I give it my all. But damn it, when the devil moves my panties aside with his teeth and his tongue laps against my bare pussy, I arch my back and moan as if I've been starving for him.

I totally skip past the *what the fuck is wrong with me?* moment I had the other night and soak up the brutal way he thrusts his tongue into my pussy.

And those sounds… the purely erotic sounds of moaning and groaning, they belong to me.

Thorne doesn't relent. It's like he's starving for me, too.

The wild thought of him, one of the most desired men on campus, wanting me makes me throw my head to loll back and yield as he eats me out.

The rhythm of his tongue thrusting in and out of me, faster and deeper, makes me wonder what his cock would feel like inside me. The forbidden thought sends me further down the rabbit hole of lust, whimpering like a wounded animal with every thrust of his tongue.

Thorne pauses for a moment to look at me. The wild smile dancing on his lips is as devilish as his touch.

Satisfied that he's unraveled me again, he takes my hard nipples into his mouth and sucks briefly on each while his fingers play with my pussy.

He bites on my tight, taut nipples and swirls his tongue around them before returning to my pussy to feast.

Feeling the violent tug of an orgasm stirring in my soul, I grasp the sheets on either side of me and grind on his face as I come.

Shit, I come so hard my head aches from back to front.

My arousal flows into his mouth and he drinks me, lapping up my juices until they're gone and his tongue is teasing me for more.

I close my eyes and lose myself in the sensation, feeling nothing but him and this moment.

But then he releases me and I climb down from the high.

Raw humiliation weighs down on me. Humiliation over his knowledge that I wanted him.

Thorne rises, keeping his gaze on me, and I pull up the sheets to cover myself.

He wipes his mouth with the back of his hand and continues staring, watching my heaving chest.

"See why I can't leave you alone, Bambi? We have unfinished business." He smirks and licks his lips.

"No, we don't."

"Your greedy pussy says different."

"You broke into my room and violated me."

He laughs. "*Did I?* You didn't sound violated to me, but maybe I should do it again. We can check this time to see just how violated you feel."

"No."

"You sure? You don't look sure."

"I'm sure."

My skin is so hot I'm finding it difficult to breathe let alone find words to defend my dignity. And I'm watching him. Watching him to see what he'll do next.

He leans close. Too close again.

He looms before my lips and brushes his nose over mine.

"I'm sure, too. I'm sure that I want to fuck you." A sadistic grin creeps over his face. "But let's play."

He inches back, straightens, and walks out of the room through the door I closed and out of my apartment that I locked.

I stay right where I am, shaking to the core of my soul.

It hits me moments later what's happening here.

It's a game.

This is all a game to him. He's mentioned playing twice now, and right from the moment I met him I felt like I've been in some kind of arena where I'm being hunted.

Hunted by him.

When I first thought of him as a predator, I was right.

And I'm his prey.

CHAPTER 10

SEVERAL HOURS PASSED BEFORE I FINALLY FELL ASLEEP LAST NIGHT, but I still woke up early. Thankfully not crack-of-dawn early, but still early enough to feel like I needed to go back to sleep.

It's eight in the morning.

The Thetas have a meeting after breakfast so I get up.

After the last meeting, I need to be prepared. This is the week where we start our trials to get fully accepted into the sorority.

I need strong coffee and I need to take a walk to cool off.

I realize I'm in serious trouble and this thing with Thorne is only going to get worse.

For some damn reason unknown to me he has this fascination with me that I can't control.

I thought I could do something about it, but now I know I can't.

So what do I do?

The question rings through my mind like a church bell calling its parishioners to service on Easter morning.

I get dressed, make my coffee, and head outside with my mug for that walk.

The air outside is cold, which is strange considering how hot it was last night.

I still can't believe what happened. I've only known Thorne Ivanov for a week, and look where we are now.

I walk down to the rose garden. There hasn't been anyone down here at this time over the last few days so I'm hoping for the same sort of luck today.

When I reach the garden my spirits lift when I find myself alone, but then I look over to the river and spot Isabelle sitting on a bench by herself.

Guilt suddenly tugs at my insides when I realize I haven't seen or checked on her since the party. The last time I saw her was just before we all went into the labyrinth.

As everyone has been busy getting ready to start classes this week, and I've been hiding from Thorne, I got lost in my problems.

Isabelle looks lost, too, and I get a bad feeling it has something to do with Kade.

I haven't known her for any length of time but I feel that if things had gone well—even if she'd gathered the courage to say two words to him—I would have known about it by now.

Instead of wallowing in my own sorrows I decide to make my way over to her.

She hears my footsteps when I get closer and looks around at me.

Although she smiles I can see something's not right.

"Hey, there." I return the smile and even add a bounce in my step.

"Hi."

Yup. Something is definitely wrong. Isabelle is sunshine but she looks at me as if someone has stolen her light.

"Are you okay?" I sit next to her.

"Yeah. How are you doing? I hope classes are going well."

"Yes. They've been… amazing."

"Wow. That's brilliant." She looks genuinely happy for me, but there's a dullness in her aura. "I know you were worried about being here so I'm thrilled you've had a good start."

"Thanks. What about you?"

She shakes her head the way people do when they don't want to talk. "It's been shit. Everything's completely shitty."

I look her over, taking note of the sourness of her mood. "What happened, Isabelle? I haven't seen you since the party. Did you see Kade?"

"Yeah. I saw him."

"He picked you?" I give her a half smile, deciding to stay on the side of caution.

"He did."

"And?"

She looks away, staring off into the distance, but I can see the tears glistening in her eyes. "He was the first guy. I was so excited to see him. There were a million things I wanted to say. I started out by talking to him about high school but all he did was look at me."

I give her a narrowed stare. "He didn't talk at all?"

"We basically stayed in that dreadful silence the whole time then seconds before the end he said to me…" She pauses for a moment and catches her breath. "He said I didn't deserve to be at Raventhorn, and I barely deserved to have the miserable life I have. He told me to stop watching him like a dog and find someone else to obsess over."

My mouth drops open. I'm so stunned I can scarcely breathe. "What the hell? That's what he said?"

"Yes." The faraway tenor of her voice displays the wealth of her hurt.

I hurt for her, too. It's bad enough to be rejected. That would have been awful and I could have made her feel better by calling Kade an asshole, but what he said was worse than bad. It was obscene and threatening. Vile.

Isabelle is such a happy person that I can't begin to imagine anyone being mean to her. But seriously, what can anyone expect from the guys at Erebus?

Thorne and Caspian are their leaders.

"Why the hell did he say that to you? It makes no sense. You've known him for what…?"

"Three years. I waited three years to have him speak to me like shit. Probably because I really don't belong."

"Don't say that."

"It's true. My mother was of Knight descent and my father not. He's hardly part of the Bratva. We're what people call lower class, and we're not rich."

"Why does that matter?"

"It matters here, especially amongst the students who have parents who are both of Knight descent. People like Kade. His lineage traces right back to the forefathers."

Like Thorne and the Ivanovs. Their forefather was one of the original Knights of Raventhorn during the Viking age. That's why they have so much power.

"I didn't know that was such an issue."

"You wouldn't have experienced it because you're from L.A. and your stepfather is well known amongst the Knights. Sadly, you might get some backlash because you're a stepchild." Isabelle swallows hard, then looks back at me. "My story is a little different because it's not common for women to marry outside of the Knights. My mom was only able to marry my father because she was pregnant with me. Because of that she was considered an outcast. And so am I."

"This is unbelievable."

"It's their way."

"And you think that's why Kade was so mean?"

"I don't know any other reason. I've never done anything to him. We've never spoken until the other night. The words he said were so hateful I can only assume he did it because of who I am."

We stare at each other in contemplation for a few moments before she looks away, back to the fish pond.

I hate to think she's right, but there's so much I don't know about the Knights. This is another thing. Another thing that's not good.

"I'm sorry, Isabelle. That's horrible."

"I know." More sadness fills her features, making her look completely unlike herself. "My mother was killed when I was twelve."

My breathing slows. "*Killed*?" When she told me the other day that her mother died when she was young I assumed it might have been an illness.

"Killed. Murdered. It's all the same to me." She takes a quick breath and her chest caves. "My mother was in the wrong place at the wrong time and saw too much. I was there when she died. A man shot her."

I clutch my chest. "Oh my God. Isabelle."

She faces me again. "That man went to prison, but there was someone else there with them. Someone I didn't see properly, but I know they're linked to the Knights."

"What?"

"The Knights refused to investigate because my mother was an outcast."

My lips part and there's a tremor in my soul. My heart goes out to her but hearing her story makes me think of mine. Of my father and the injustice he faced and continues to face, because it was someone in the Knights who set him up.

Isabelle has bared her soul to me. I wish with all my heart that I could do the same. It would be so freeing to speak to someone. But I can't.

"Saying sorry doesn't feel like it's enough," I mumble, reaching out to tap her hand.

"It's okay." She gives me a small smile of appreciation but I can still read the dullness in her expression. "I wouldn't know what to say to me either. I've tried to move on and live my life."

"How do you feel about the Knights?" Although I shouldn't ask her such a thing, I'm interested to know.

"Like everything, some are good, some are bad. I honor my mother and my grandparents by being here at Raventhorn, but I know I have to watch my back."

I nod slowly, heeding the advice for myself. "Don't worry about Kade. He's a complete ass."

"Yeah. I know that now. I feel like such an idiot, though."

"He's the idiot. He doesn't know what he missed out on."

"Thank you. I appreciate the *Kade is an asshole* talk." She nods at my coffee cup. "That must be cold now."

"It's okay. I think I might have consumed way too much coffee over the last few days."

"Join the club." She giggles then sits straighter, looking like she just remembered something. "Did you see Thorne at the party?"

"Oh… yeah." At the mention of Thorne I remember my *situation*.

"Sorry, I totally forgot to ask you about him. Did something happen?"

I don't really want to talk about Thorne but I know I have to tell her something. "Things just got more complicated."

She's about to say something when we hear our names called.

It's Eilish. She's standing on the path across from us, tapping her watch.

"The meeting starts in three minutes. Don't be late," she calls out, looking worried.

That damn meeting. I forgot it. "We're on our way," I answer.

Eilish nods and heads to the dorm.

"I'm totally not in the mood for this meeting." Isabelle rolls her eyes.

"Me neither."

We stand and make our way back to the dorm.

"Promise me you'll tell me about Thorne later."

"Sure." I feel like I was saved by the meeting because I don't know what to tell her about Thorne.

We make it back just as the meeting is about to start.

Tiffany begins with a haughty speech about herself and the pride she takes in being president of the Thetas. We get the history lesson of all the women in her family who were presidents before her and how well they did for themselves.

Then she moves on to the challenges she has planned for us and the threat that if we don't pass, we won't make it. As if we didn't know.

"The first challenge will take place tonight. We're going with a simple get-together at Erebus House." Tiffany infuses her voice with pride and looks at each of us. My insides twist the moment I hear *Erebus House*. She might as well have said Thorne's house. "My mother has kindly agreed to supply us with her delectable cakes and catering for the event. You will all be serving."

She picks up a little cupcake costume that looks fit for a child. "Isabelle, you will wear this and you will be responsible for taking care of the guys who won the Ivanov Elite's recent challenge."

Everyone looks at Isabelle who has turned ghost-white pale. "Me?"

"You're Isabelle, aren't you?"

"Yes. I just don't want to do it."

Tiffany's expression shifts from lighthearted to hellish. "Excuse me, are you actually questioning a direct order?"

"Those guys are a bunch of mean assholes."

The moment she says that, I know Kade must be one of the bunch of mean assholes. The problem is Tiffany wouldn't have understood that even if Isabelle told her what happened. That aside, everyone in the room is shocked to hear sweet, usually quiet Isabelle speaking with such fire.

"I don't care what you think. You will do this, and I'm deducting points from you for your insolence." Tiffany stamps her foot.

"I don't want to do it. Why have I been singled out to wear that stupid costume? You know the guys are going to make fun of me."

"Oh, I see what's happening here." Tiffany flashes Isabelle an evil smile and taps a finger to her temple. "Isabelle is sad because Kade shot her down at the party. He reminded her that she's a joke. Really now, girl, did you seriously think a guy like that would go for someone like you, let alone someone who thinks it's cool to look like a Lolita doll?"

Tiffany and her lackeys all laugh like they're at a standup comedy show.

Watching them, I feel even sicker to my stomach that Kade must have spread the word about what happened with Isabelle. So when I spot the defeated tear sliding down Isabelle's cheek, I snap.

"Stop it," I speak up, cutting through the laughter which stops instantly, as if someone switched them off.

"What did you just say?" Tiffany makes her way over to me.

"I said stop it. Stop laughing at her and talking shit." I don't know what stroke of madness has taken over me but I've had enough of people like her. Because of Tiffany and her arrogance I've had to clean all manner of filth for reasons beyond my control all week. I can't stand by and watch her bully Isabelle. Especially not after our conversation and the whole thing with Kade, which she's clearly still upset about. "Isabelle is not a joke and when last I checked, the Lolita doll look actually has a huge following. It's cool. Look it up."

"Who the hell do you think you are speaking to me like that? You're lucky to even be at Raventhorn. If not for your *stepfather,* who knows where you'd end up."

"I actually got into Juilliard *and* Berklee." I use my best matter-of-fact tone to inform this bitch that I'm worth more than she believes and have my own talent. I want to add that I have every right to be here at Raventhorn because my father is a Knight. I'm not just a stepchild with a privilege up my ass. But I know I can't say any of that.

To my surprise, Tiffany looks me up and down and delivers that evil smile again. "Maybe you should go to Juilliard or Berklee."

"I—"

Mackenzie, who's standing next to me, grabs my hand and stops me from pursuing the argument with a firm shake of her head. The look of dread in her eyes warns me that if I dare speak another word, it will be my last at Raventhorn.

I think of Mom and Levgen. How they would feel if I got kicked out. *And how I'd feel.*

The unsettling dread of failure shoots me down.

"A wise choice to listen to your friend." Tiffany folds her arms across her chest, keeping her gaze trained on me. "However, it's too late to backpedal. I'll be sure to contact your mother and stepfather to let them know what little value you place on being here at Raventhorn. I also have something extra special for you tonight. Something that will teach you the meaning of respect."

The vindictive look in her eyes tells me it still may be my last moments at Raventhorn.

Great.

Just fucking great.

CHAPTER 11

"I FEEL SO AWFUL," ISABELLE MUTTERS. HER VOICE JOINS THE CHORUS of crickets around us, hopping in the grass.

"Don't feel bad. Tiffany was bullying you. I had to say something."

Isabelle, Mackenzie and I are walking through the murky woodland area way, way, way on the other side of campus. Our flashlights and the faint moonlight are our only sources of light.

This is the extra special thing Tiffany had planned for me. The *way* to it. I won't know what the actual thing is until I reach the hollowed-out willow tree.

"It's just a shame it had to come to this." Mackenzie waves her flashlight around.

We're following a pebbled path but it's clear that no one has used it in a long time. Unlike the rest of the campus, this area is unkempt, unruly and creepy.

"Thank you for coming with me for this part." They can only accompany me to my destination. They have to head to Erebus after.

"Of course." Isabelle glances at me. In the faint moonlight I can just about pick her black hair from the shadows.

"My advice is do what you have to do and get the hell out." Mackenzie waves the flashlight again. "Call us once you're done."

"I will. What's down here anyway?"

"Tunnels and all kinds of shit. My dad has always told me to keep away from this place. The frat boys love it because there are no cameras past a certain point, so if anything happened to you no one would know."

Mackenzie's father is one of the judges. "I feel even worse that you guys are here." And I'm even more creeped out.

"As if we'd allow you to come down here by yourself." Mackenzie shakes her head at me. "I'm sure Tiffany knows about the cameras. That's why she chose this place."

"It makes me wonder what she's planned." Isabelle winces. "I should have kept my big mouth shut and just worn the stupid costume. Given that I have to wear it anyway."

"Tiffany's a bitch. You were both right to stand up to her. Despite the punishment you have to put people like her in their place sometimes," Mackenzie says with conviction. "She still won today but I know she'll be worried about other people standing up to her in the future."

She's right, but I can't help but feel like I made things worse. Isabelle still has to wear this costume, I have to do this shit, and both Isabelle and I have to clean Myrddin House for the next two months.

"We're here." Mackenzie shines her flashlight ahead, lighting up the willow tree.

My God in heaven, it looks like the demented hell tree from *Sleepy Hollow* where the headless horseman's body was buried. The only difference between that one and this is the hollowed-out trunk of the tree.

Even with my fascination for dark, edgy things, my skin still crawls at the sight of it.

Isabelle looks like how I feel—totally creeped out.

Mackenzie keeps going and after a moment we follow.

She walks up to the tree and shines her light over a white envelope pinned to one of the low-hanging branches with my name scrawled across it.

I take it and open it. Inside there's a note which says:

I left something in a blue bag in the tunnel ahead of you.

Bring it to me.

Tiffany.

I show the note to Mackenzie and Isabelle, and they both exchange worried glances.

"Don't do it." Isabelle grabs my arm. "It feels like a trap to me. She hasn't given you any directions or anything."

"I don't want any more problems with Tiffany. Or to embarrass my parents." I haven't heard from Mom or Levgen yet today, so I don't know when Tiffany plans to contact them.

"It's so irritating that this is supposed to be college but feels like kindergarten." Mackenzie frowns.

"It could be dangerous," Isabelle huffs.

"It *is* dangerous."

"Don't worry about me. My stepdad and I always go hiking and we love exploring in caves. This can't be that much different." I sound sure, like I know I'll be fine, but I know no such thing.

"Okay. Be careful. Please." Isabelle gives me a hug and holds me like it's the last time she'll see me.

"Remember to call us once you're done." Mackenzie nods.

"I will. Be careful on your way back."

"We'll be okay."

I take a deep breath and continue down the path with my nerves nestled in the pit of my stomach churning.

I feel like hell but I keep thinking of the end goal and getting back to my dorm with today behind me.

All I have to do is focus on walking into the tunnel, getting the bag, then heading over to Erebus so I can hand it to Tiffany.

But entering a dark tunnel by yourself in the dead of night is one hell of a twisted form of punishment. I pray that Tiffany has nothing else in store for me or any nasty surprises.

I find the tunnel's entrance and walk in. It's so quiet in here. Too quiet.

I expected to perhaps hear the dripping of water somewhere or tunnel-like echoes.

Shining the light ahead, I pray with every step I take that I'll find Tiffany's bag but I see nothing. I'm heading deeper and deeper, getting further away from the exit. Soon I can't see it at all when I look over my shoulder.

As I keep moving the walls feel like they're getting smaller and tighter, although they aren't. That's just me losing my mind.

I trip over something. It feels like a rock. Suddenly I lose my footing and fall flat on my face, dropping the flashlight, which rolls down the path to my left.

My knees are hurt. So are my elbows and when I touch them I feel blood.

Cursing, I lift myself up and retrieve the flashlight but the sound of scuttling and squeaking makes me freeze.

I hear it again. This time much louder. Then a million furry feet run over mine.

Rats! Lots and lots of them come rushing my way. I scream, then I run, losing sight of where I'm going. The tunnel splits into two paths and since I have no idea which one to take, I choose the nearest.

I just want to get out of here. I don't even care at this point if I find Tiffany's stupid bag.

The rats follow me and there's so many of them I figure out straight away that someone set them loose on me.

This was such a bad idea.

Not just this. *Everything.* Even being here at Raventhorn.

Menacing male laughter fills the air and I realize I'm right. Tiffany set me up to fail.

I run as fast as I can until I feel like my soul might leave my body, then I see light ahead of me. A soft amber glow.

Hope sparks that it might be some kind of exit, so I head there.

The light gets brighter and the rats decrease, so I follow the path. The deeper I go, the wider and brighter the path becomes. I get my hopes up that I'll find an exit soon. This area looks like it might be used more.

Minutes later I'm still walking. I try to figure out where the path might lead but I have no bearings. At least the sounds of the rats have decreased, and I can't hear the laughing anymore.

The rumble of voices suddenly fills the tunnel. It's different from the laughter I left behind. These voices sound like people talking. Men talking in normal conversation.

I follow the sound but stop dead in my tracks when I see runes engraved on the walls ahead of me. Straight away I realize with horror where I am.

The Knights use the old Elder Futhark runes to communicate secret messages.

Levgen taught me how to read the runes. The ones ahead tell me that I'm beneath Raventhorn Hall. As in the place I'm not allowed to be.

And I'm right near the meeting hall where the Knights gather for ceremonies.

If I'm caught down here…

Oh my God, if I'm caught down here I would be in all sorts of trouble. Me and my parents. The male voices I heard just now were Knights. Shit.

What the fuck have you done to me, Tiffany?

What the actual fuck?

I whirl around to go back the way I came—even if it's infested with rats—but I crash into a hard body.

Before me stands a tall and muscular Knight. He's even wearing his tunic. The black Knight's tunic with the blue raven insignia embossed on the front.

His hood is up, so I can't see his face properly.

The voices sound again and the Knight looks behind us, then back at me, his mouth curling into a deep frown. He takes his hood down and I'm almost, almost relieved when I see it's Thorne.

It's him, but for once he looks pissed off to see me. The joviality I usually witness is nowhere to be found in the hard lines of his handsome face.

I open my mouth to tell him why I'm here but when he grasps my throat, I realize my false sense of hope.

"You should never have come down here, Bambi. You really have a death wish."

"I didn't mean to. I—"

"Shhh."

He presses his thumb down on the side of my neck and everything goes dark. The world tilts then fades into nothing, taking his face with it.

Then I go to the land of nowhere.

CHAPTER 12

Thorne

I BROUGHT IVY BACK TO MY PLACE.

Now she's asleep on my bed.

I lean against the doorframe of my bedroom watching her lithe, doll-like body resting peacefully on my king-size bed.

She looks even more delicate and beautiful in this vulnerable state. That hair of hers has spilled across my navy pillows in contrasting waves, making her look like a silver-haired Venus painted against the sheets.

In my fantasies of this moment she was naked instead of wearing the yoga pants painted to her legs and the T-shirt hugging her breasts. The circumstances of her being here were also definitely different from what I'd conjured in my mind.

I never thought I'd run into her in the secret tunnels beneath Raventhorn Hall and have to knock her out.

I had to do it.

It was the quickest and easiest thing I could think of to hide her.

I tossed her over my shoulder and barely managed to escape the Knights who'd gone down there to investigate. They would have found her and they would have punished her.

It was the motion detectors that picked up activity down in the tunnels.

The Knights also heard Ivy scream along with the army of rats that had suddenly taken up residence down there.

I just happened to be at Raventhorn Hall tonight. Lucky for the little deer.

Caspian and I had to attend a Knights' council meeting. Afterwards we were going to head back to Erebus House for the party.

I went down to the ceremony hall to speak to one of my friends and that's when I heard the commotion—aka Ivy. I decided to join the guys who were checking it out but I almost didn't.

There are cameras down there in the tunnels but they were switched off.

It's not the first time that's happened. People like me do that all the time. We also use the secret tunnels when we want to get on and off campus without being seen or recorded.

The moment I saw her, frightened and terrified, I knew exactly what happened—*Tiffany and her pranks.*

The evil bitch set Ivy up to get kicked out of Raventhorn. If Ivy had been found, her stepfather, Levgen, would have been reprimanded, so he would have been restricted from his senior Knight privileges for a year.

He would also be excluded from the annual collective fund award, which can earn you a million dollars in bonuses each year.

I don't know what the hell Ivy did to Tiffany to deserve this sort of punishment but she crossed a line that shouldn't have been crossed.

I'll definitely be having words with her, but I'll admit I'm not too mad that her prank got me the woman I want lying in my bed.

Ivy is sprawled out like a virgin sacrifice.

I should wake her. She's been out for a little over two hours. But the fascinated part of me wants to savor this moment just a little longer. In this quiet, intimate space, she's mine.

Mine to watch however I want.

Mine to dissect from head to toe.

What would she do if she knew all the lewd thoughts running through my head, and all the ways I've fucked her in my mind in just the last five minutes?

I smile at the thought and the memory of her perfect, perfect naked body.

What I'd imagined hadn't done her any justice. The real naked Ivy I saw was a goddess.

Now she's here. The little deer is caught in the hunter's trap, and the only way she's leaving me is if I say so.

I could certainly have some fun with this because no matter what Tiffany did, Ivy now owes me for saving her ass.

The sound of my front door opening pulls me from my wild fascination.

Moments later Lucian finds me. He helped me get Ivy here. He met me at the tunnels in his car and we drove her back here. It's crazy how the two of us have become as thick as thieves.

"She still asleep?" he asks, glancing at Ivy in my room.

"*Yes*. There's no need for you to check." I step in front of him so he can't see her. I don't want him or anyone else looking at her.

He smirks and rolls his eyes at me. "Alright, Thorne. Let's not forget that I was the guy who helped you get her here. And I'll be the same guy who'll keep his mouth shut about where she was."

"And that's why you have the privilege of being called my friend. Otherwise I'd have to kill you. Or at the very least cut out your tongue so you can't speak and chop off your hands so you can't write."

"Jesus. You are one crazy motherfucker."

I smile back at him. "Why are you back here?"

"Two things. I found this in the tunnels. Ivy dropped it." He hands me a little blue pouch with Ivy's name on it. "Two, I had to tell you that Eilish is worried about her. Apparently Ivy got on Tiffany's wrong side when she defended Isabelle."

Isabelle always needs defending. She thinks I'm scary. She's right, but unknown to her, back in high school the bullies stopped bothering her because I kicked the ever-loving shit out of them for teasing her about her mother's death. It was my parting gift before my graduation.

"Eilish doesn't know Ivy is with me. Does she?"

"Of course not. If she did, Eilish would be here, not me. Please send Ivy back to Myrddin in one piece."

"I swear. Scout's honor." I make a show of placing my hand at my heart, but he can still see the horns on my head.

"Thorne, you were never a boy scout."

"Exactly. Run along now, Lucian. We're done here." I raise my brows and he sighs.

He knows not to argue with me so he leaves.

As soon as I hear the door close I go back to looking at my prize, then I open her pouch. It reminds me of one of those little bags a bride would carry on her wedding day.

The pouch has a few things inside. A mini notepad has musical notes written on it, an iPod which probably has all the classical piano music that was ever created, including her own, and there's a ring.

An old-looking platinum ring. It looks like the kind some old Knighting families would make for their children for their sixteenth birthday. I never got one because my family was dead by then.

I hold up the ring and look at it. My interest is drawn to the crest engraved on the front.

It's a family crest. A Knights' family crest. It's not Levgen's, but it's one that looks familiar. So familiar it produces sharp tingles in my nerves. The kind you get when your nerves are amplified by fear.

The design of the crest is a griffin catching a leviathan snake with its mouth.

I don't know all the family insignias of the Knights, but some are as memorable to me as the algorithms in a computer program. This is one of them but I don't remember it as being anything good.

I stare at the crest a little longer until it suddenly hits me. The memory of where I've seen it before.

This is the family crest specific to the Bershov family.

The last surviving member of that family is Gustave Bershov. I remember him and that name because he sits in prison rotting for his part in the mass murder plot of the Russian Syndicate. And for his suspected connections to the attack on my family.

I saw this crest when I was looking through the files on my family and the people Aleksander suspected were involved with the attack.

Why would Ivy have this ring?

It makes no sense to me. How would she even know that family?

The answer comes when I flick on the light and notice an engraving on the inside:

To my daughter Annika, love you forever.

I look at Ivy on the bed again as my mind spins. Something pulls on my heart as I attempt to ask myself what this might mean.

I felt she had secrets.

But… not something like this.

If this ring is what I think it is then her secrets run darker than I thought.

CHAPTER 13

A KALEIDOSCOPE OF COLORS RIPPLES THROUGH MY MIND. THEY DANCE and sing through my soul until they finally settle on the color green.

Green grass in the meadow.

The meadow my mother and father used to take me to when I was little.

I know I'm dreaming. In this listless state I always linger between the edge of asleep and awake. As if my heart wants to hold on to a plane of existence where we can still be those people we used to be.

I see myself running through the meadow and laughing. My father is ahead smiling at me, with his arms outstretched waiting to take me.

Mom is behind me, running too. She's laughing because I'm running so fast she can't catch me.

"Idi ko mne, moy malen'kiy," Dad says. In English it means *Come to me, my little one.*

I run to him, but the moment I touch his hand he disappears from my view and so does everything else.

Darkness fills the void in my mind. It's all I can see for miles and miles, until a sliver of light pierces through and my eyes flutter, opening slowly.

A shadowy figure looms before me. It's blurry, but as my eyes adjust I realize it's someone standing over me.

And not just any someone. It's Thorne.

I blink several times until his face becomes clearer, and with the clarity comes the memory of running into him down in the tunnels. Raventhorn Hall tunnels.

He told me I shouldn't have gone down there, then he… did something to knock me out.

That was him. I'd seen stunts like that in the movies but I didn't know it was real until tonight… or today. I have no idea what the time is or how long I was down for.

When I look away from him I realize I have so much more to worry about than him.

I'm on a bed, and from the look of my surroundings this must be his bedroom. But that's not all.

The crazy psycho has my wrists handcuffed to the rails of his bed.

I swallow hard, blinking again, my mouth going instantly dry.

"Uncuff me," I stutter, thrashing against the cuffs, which are too tight around my wrists.

"No."

Again with that word. This man has told me no more times than anyone has in my life.

"You can't do this. I was in the tunnels by accident. It was Tiffany. She sent me down there. Ask her." The moment I say that I realize how foolish I sound. There's no way Tiffany is going to confess something like that to Thorne. No way.

"Bambi, I truly wish that was all you were in trouble for." His voice is too cool and collected. The almost eerie tone makes my stomach flip-flop.

"What do you mean? I didn't do anything else. You have to let me go. You can't handcuff me to your bed."

"In case you haven't noticed, I already have."

"You fucking asshole. Let me go!" I shout, fruitlessly trying to free myself.

Thorne smiles and moves closer to sit next to me. When he tries to touch my stomach, I flinch and kick out at him.

"Don't touch me. Ever."

"Little deer, it just so happens that my fascination with touching you is the only thing that's saving you right now."

"Stop talking shit. What—"

He holds up my father's ring and all the words I've ever known evaporate like mist from my mind.

Thorne waves the ring in front of me then holds it steady, as if he wants me to get a good look.

"You dropped this in the tunnel. It was in your bag, Ivy. Or is your name *Annika*?"

My heart is beating so fast and loud I'm sure everyone in the world can hear it. Along with the sound of my soul shattering against the floor of reality.

Oh. My. God.

No…

This isn't happening.

I accidentally left the ring in my pouch. I'd taken it out of the box again when I couldn't get to sleep. I put it in the pouch just as a temporary measure and I totally forgot.

I forgot. Now Thorne knows. But does he really?

Maybe I can still turn this around.

"I don't know who that is. You know my name is Ivy."

He gives me a mirthless smile that says *don't fuck with me* then he touches the curve of my waist, tracing the edge with his thumb.

"That's just the thing you want everyone to believe, isn't it. Your birth certificate, passport and other documents are *very* convincing. Just as convincing as the death certificates for you and your mother."

"I don't know what the hell you're talking about."

"That's okay. I wouldn't crack either. You're in some serious trouble. I'd lie like my life depended on it, too, to save my family." He nods with conviction and in his eyes I see truth, like he meant what he said.

He holds the ring up and reads the inscription on the band, "To my daughter Annika, love you forever. This ring is a symbol of Heiðr. The Norse word for honor. Families like the Bershovs would have taken part in the tradition of passing rings to their children. This one is yours from your father, Gustave Bershov."

"No." Tears pull at the backs of my eyes and I try to keep them away. I have to be strong. I have to, even though it's tearing me apart that I'm denying my father.

"I hate lies, little deer, and they don't suit you. They taint you and everything I like about you. So don't lie to me."

"Let me go." My voice is small but brimming with the anguish stirring in my soul. "You are mistaken."

Thorne stares at me as if he can see deep, deep, deep into my soul to the place where my secrets are stored away.

He reaches out and I think he's going to touch me again but instead he picks up something from the nightstand.

It's some documents.

He takes the first one and holds it out for me to see.

"This is from the official Knights report: *Following the sentencing of Gustave Bershov for the murders of the members of the Russian Syndicate, the remains of his wife and daughter's bodies were found in their home following a gas explosion," he reads. "Their bodies were so badly burned they couldn't be conclusively identified using forensic DNA recovery. The evidence, however, is strong enough to suggest the remains are theirs, so we are satisfied to list them as deceased."*

He looks back at me. I keep my poker face. I've never seen this report but Mom filled me in on everything Levgen did to save us.

"Levgen did this. He would have been the only person who could help you in this way. Your father was his best friend. I didn't know that until I checked it out. He helped you and your mother escape from Russia."

"No. Levgen met my mother at work here."

Thorne flicks to the next document, which is a picture of me. Me at nine years old. He places it next to my face.

"Same silver eyes. Same silver hair. Same jawline, nose, mouth and the little mole on your left cheek. The computer generation thinks so, too." He grabs another document, showing a computer-generated image of me next to my nine-year-old self on the right and on the left a picture of me now.

Anyone with eyes could see it's the same person. Just nine years older.

"Do you still want to lie to me?" He searches my face as if he's still checking to see that I'm the girl he shouldn't know about.

"Let me go."

He gives me a steely stare and stands. "Okay. I'll let you go. But if I do so now without hearing the truth, you can deal with my uncle instead. You can lie to him with your parents in the room next to you and tell him you're not Annika Bershov. Rest assured he will not be as *gentle* as me, nor would he hesitate to kill all of you. Considering you should be dead already, it would be no problem for him."

"No! Please." I push against the cuffs, trying to reach for him. "Please don't tell him. Please, Thorne. Please don't."

I hate begging him but I would do it forever if it kept my mother and Levgen safe. I'm not even thinking about myself anymore.

I totally fucked up and allowed the worst person possible to discover our secret.

"Does that mean you confess, little deer?"

With all the reluctance in the world I find myself nodding and I can't believe this is me. All the omens I sensed before leaving L.A. were right.

I shouldn't have come to Raventhorn.

A lone tear tracks down my cheek. More follow even though I do my best to keep them away.

The time for bravado is gone. I don't know where I stand now or what to do.

Thorne sits back on the bed and gazes at me. At what feels like my defeat again.

"What are you going to do to me?" I have to know.

"You're not ready to hear that yet." The sexual spark I've seen several times before flickers in his eyes.

It's out of context to what is happening, and I don't know how to take it or his comment.

"Are you going to keep me locked up in here? Is that what you're going to do? Lock me up and get your uncle, who'll kill me and my parents." More tears come and I feel like such a fool.

Thorne just stares at me, watching me fall apart, then he reaches for my wrist and undoes the first handcuff.

Trembling, I watch him, wondering what he'll do and say next.

He releases my other hand and stands.

"Get up." He motions for me to stand next to him.

My arms hurt from being raised above my head but they are the least of my worries.

I get off the bed and stand next to him on shaky legs.

He seems much taller than usual but that could be because I feel like I'm shrinking away in the darkness of my worries.

He leans forward and I remember what it was like to kiss him. I must really have lost my mind if I can think of such a thing at a time like this.

"Go back to your dorm."

"That's it?" I dare to hope.

"No. That's not it. I'll let you know what I decide to do with you."

"When?" I can't wait indefinitely.

"I don't know yet." The ghost of a smile tugs on the corners of his lips. "Until then, do your best to not get expelled, and if I were you I'd keep this between us. As in, your parents mustn't know that I know your secret. Do you understand me?"

"Yes." I nod fast.

He catches my face and runs his finger along my jaw. Once again that stroke of attraction lights up inside me.

"Don't even think about running away. You can't run from people like me. I love to chase but if I catch you I might destroy you."

My stomach knots into tight loops as I watch the emotions play out on his face.

It's strange to accept that someone so striking could be so utterly terrifying.

He releases me, picks up my little pouch, and hands it to me. I take it, feeling worse when he slips my ring into his back pocket.

"I'll be holding on to that. Go."

I move, focusing on putting one foot in front of the other.

I don't look back at Thorne either.

Better if I don't see his face.

What are the chances he'll keep my secret?

Slim to none.

He wouldn't implicate himself in such a way.

So I'm as good as dead.

Instinct tells me I should be calling Mom and Levgen to tell them what happened so we can flee, but I believe Thorne. I believe him when he says he may destroy me if I run.

It feels like he already has.

CHAPTER 14

Thorne

I STARE AT MY COMPUTER SCREEN LOOKING AT A PICTURE OF GUSTAVE Bershov, Ivy's father.

Ivy—*Annika*—only has a few similarities in her face to him, but she looks exactly like her mother.

Ivy.

Annika. It's strange for me to think of her with that name but then again, I haven't known her long enough to have gotten used to her being Ivy either.

This has been one hell of a ten days.

And now this thing with her real father. The disgraced Knight, Gustave Bershov.

The picture I'm looking at was taken before he went to the Hallows, a prison set up by the Knights to house the criminals they want to keep alive for one reason or another.

The Hallows is situated on an island in a secret location that only the leader of the Knights and his elite know. The laws there are above everything else, so they can keep you there and torture you until you beg for death.

The Knights don't take prisoners unless they need you.

Death is the only way out. When we take the Oath and vow to live and die by it, that is what we agree to. And that agreement extends to those who become our family—like wives and children.

I'm perhaps the only reason Gustave Bershov was allowed to live.

It's because of what I saw on the night my family were attacked. A night I'll never forget as long as I live on this earth.

It was just after Caspian got taken. I was in the coat closet, hiding, and I was so fucking terrified I pissed myself.

On our way to finding a hiding place we'd already passed several members of the house staff who were dead. I thought we were going to die.

I was about to get out of the closet to get help for Caspian when two of our guards came rushing into the hallway. But they were shot. I didn't see who shot them until they fell to the floor in a bloodied heap.

Through the keyhole I watched a man with a deep-set knife scar on his face walk over to them. He was a scary motherfucker. The stuff nightmares are made of. Sometimes that man still haunts me in my sleep.

He pulled out a knife from some old-fashioned sheath and stabbed the guards through the heart. Then the motherfucker carved out their hearts. It was like watching something from a nightmare come to life.

He muttered some strange, foreign words as he effortlessly harvested the hearts. Terror robbed me of everything that night, so I didn't know what the hell he was saying. I couldn't even try to repeat what the words sounded like. I still can't.

At the time I only spoke Russian and barely any English. What he said sounded like Russian, but it wasn't. I always knew, though, that if I heard it again, I'd know it.

The man put the hearts in a bag and walked away, never knowing I was hiding in a closet breaths away from him.

The only person to survive the attack was me.

Anyone else who could have been guilty or witnessed anything died.

When I told my uncle about the man, no one could identify anyone by that description. Aleksander and his men searched the planet to no avail.

The man became a mystery until years later when Gustave Bershov was found guilty of his crimes and reported seeing the same man at the palace he was working at.

My uncle kept Gustave alive because he was the only person to mention that man besides me.

The attack on the palace also mirrored what happened at my family's home with men stabbed through the heart or missing their hearts. There was too much evidence that proved Gustave's guilt, so Aleksander linked him to both attacks. But he was only interested in what happened with my father, which still remains a mystery to this day.

Gustave is alive because Aleksander views him as a link. A lead. Even if that lead is leading nowhere, he's still alive because Aleksander is hoping that one day something will come up. He doesn't want to go down as a leader who couldn't even resolve his own brother's murder. It makes him look weak.

I'd put it all behind me as a dead end, but the revelation about Ivy has taken me back to my nightmares. It's made me wonder if Gustave truly had anything to do with my family's deaths.

He's always maintained his innocence. *Always.*

He was accused of being part of the plot to murder fifteen senior Knights and ten Bratva leaders. Such a massacre carried the death penalty for Gustave and his family.

Even though Gustave is being kept alive, his family would have still been executed without question. I saw the order for their deaths issued by my uncle when I was digging around.

I don't know if Gustave arranged with Levgen to get Ivy and her mom out of Russia. Or if Levgen did that on his own accord. But they're here now.

Their secret was well hidden and safe until the little deer ventured into the dark woods and ran into me. The Big Bad Wolf.

The question is: What do I do now?

The fact that I'm sitting here contemplating that question and haven't called my uncle yet says a lot.

But it's not a simple decision.

They've been in hiding for nine years, and the truth came out tonight.

It could come out again and if it was discovered that I knew, I could be killed, too. And my uncle has always been looking for a reason to eradicate my ass.

I have to think about this.

Two nights later my mind is still a fucking mess. I'm still conflicted and torn on what to do.

If I'm like this, I can just imagine that Ivy must be losing her mind over what I'm going to do with her secret.

For now, I'm putting the shit on pause so I can focus on having dinner with the man I need to keep the secret from.

Caspian and I just arrived at Aleksander's new home for dinner. He lives closer to Raventhorn now. When we were younger he lived in New York, near Raventhorn Academy. It's like he wants to keep tabs on us.

We used to do dinner once a week when Caspian and I came to Boston for college, then it went down to every other week, then once a month. I pray Aleksander doesn't expect us to resume the weekly schedule because I already see him more often than I'd like.

Willow, Caspian's wife, should be here with us, but she hates Aleksander with a vengeance. The feeling is mutual for him, so he's okay with her making appearances only when she absolutely needs to. Like at Christmas.

I wish I could have stayed away tonight. It would have been easier on my mind, but with the added stress of my situation regarding the company I needed to see what's happening with my uncle. His mood shifts like the wind.

Caspian and I head to the dining room where Alexander is already waiting at the table, which is covered with a delicious spread that reminds me of a Thanksgiving feast.

The maids surround Aleksander, organizing the dishes on the table to enhance the presentation. At least the staff here look more like those you'd find on the set of *Downton Abbey* as opposed to the Playboy bunnies he has running around at work.

"Great, you're on time." Alexander motions for us to sit.

We sit on his left and say nothing. The tension is higher than ever now that Aleksander has spoken to Caspian about the new changes in the company regarding me.

Of course, despite my caution, Caspian has tried to argue on my behalf and failed. So I'm still neither here nor there, and I'm forced to play out this shitty game my uncle has set up for me until I find a way around it.

Brigette, the head maid, brings out the wine and pours us each a glass before she leaves, taking the other maids with her.

When they close the door the room feels as enclosed and suffocating as a crypt.

Aleksander is the first to sip on his wine while we help ourselves to the food.

"I heard the elite trials are going well." Aleksander sets his wine glass down and looks from Caspian to me.

"Yes, we do have a good lineup of eight," Caspian replies. "They all have a good shot at making it."

"That's good to hear." Aleksander cuts me a glance and I instantly recall our conversation about the guys he didn't want me to choose. "I hope you choose wisely."

"Rest assured Thorne and I will choose the best."

"Of course. But it's still my job to guide you. You have some good choices amongst the eight. Choices who will be highly beneficial to us. Like James Valmik and Paul Coleus. Their fathers are co-owners of a multibillion-dollar diamond mining company."

"We will take that into consideration."

"Good." His thin lips spread into a smile before he focuses on me. "What's the plan for their Reckoning trial?"

The prick wants to know because he wants to try and gauge who'll make it through what I have planned. He knows neither James nor Paul is particularly strong-minded or strong-bodied. They're businessmen, but to be a Knight you have to be able to fight.

"Something similar to ours," I answer with pride.

His smile fades because he remembers how we barely made it out alive.

"Just be sure to do what is required and don't fuck things up with your crazy stunts."

"Sure."

The Reckoning is hard as fuck but I've always thought that ours was set up by him as another attempt to try and kill me.

"Very well, then." He keeps his gaze trained on me. "In other news, I thought I'd share that Aiden Sabioni will be transferring to Raventhorn next week."

A flash of anger roils deep in my gut, rising to the surface like a tidal wave. I drop my fork and glare at him. "*Aiden Sabioni* is going to Raventhorn?"

"It seemed appropriate if he'll be working at Ivanov Tech."

"Since when has that been a requirement?" Caspian challenges.

"It's not written in stone, son. I'm just ticking all the boxes. His father and I have been friends and allies for a very long time. So I trust that once Aiden starts, you will welcome him on campus as your peer and equal."

"I am a Knight. He is not my equal." I glare back at my uncle. If I were in charge, I would have sliced out his tongue for putting me in the same category as someone like Aiden, then I would slash his neck and watch him bleed out with no hope to survive. "Are you going to make him a Knight, too?"

"Watch your tone, boy." He points his steak knife at me. "This is the second time in a matter of days that I've had to give you the same warning."

"I don't give a fuck how many times you have to give it. That's nothing to do with me. How dare you call Aiden Sabioni my fucking equal?" And this is where Caspian and I differ. Caspian would never speak to his father like this even if he weren't his father. He has that respect for authority that I don't have.

"He will be whatever I say he is. And you will either accept it or suffer my wrath." Aleksander keeps his gaze trained on me. "If I want Aiden to work in a senior position at the company it would be unreasonable to expect him to do so without doing the things we've done at Raventhorn."

"So if I fail to secure my position in the company, you'll have a ready-made replacement for me," I fill in, deciding not to beat around the bush. I'm sick of pussyfooting around shit.

"We all have to have a backup plan, don't we?"

Caspian glances at me, then back at his father. "This is absolute bullshit, you know that. The position is Thorne's. You can't rob him of that. Aiden shouldn't even be in the picture."

Aleksander takes another sip of his wine and stares at Caspian. "The position is Thorne's if he does what I tell him to do."

"If Uncle Nicholai were around—"

"Caspian, don't," I interrupt him and shake my head. It's hard to hear my father's name at the best of times, but it's significantly more difficult to-night. Not because of this, but because of the new shit with Ivy. "It's okay… It's fucking okay. The situation is what it is."

Aleksander smiles at my remark. "Exactly. *It is what it is,* and that is whatever I say it is. When last I checked, I was still your leader."

Caspian closes his hand into a fist but doesn't say anything more. Good.

It's best he's silent because we have nothing. Speaking without ammunition is like waving around a gun full of blanks. It achieves fuck all.

The news about Aiden is his second hit. What will be the third? Or the fourth? Or the fifth?

"My sources tell me you've taken an interest in the Yegorov girl." Aleksander shifts the subject and my stomach tightens. He's talking about Ivy. I've always known that he has his minions watching me, so I shouldn't be surprised to hear about his sources.

"Like you, I take an interest in many girls." I clench my jaw to mask my internal turmoil but this fucker knows me. He knows I've taken a *genuine* interest in Ivy or he wouldn't be mentioning her.

"You know the girl I mean."

"What about her?"

"Fuck her out of your system and get rid of her. I will never allow you to be with someone like that. She is Levgen's stepchild and not of Knight descent. Try to remember that. If it were up to me, people like that would never be allowed to have any claim in the Knights. They wouldn't even be allowed at Raventhorn."

If only he knew whose daughter she is. The hatred in his eyes tells me he'd kill her with a song in his heart. He'd do it to punish her father. And me, too.

I'm not even sure what Ivy Yegorov is to me yet, but obsession must have its claws deep inside my soul because here I sit, *still* keeping her secret.

"You will not entertain anything serious with this girl and embarrass me," Aleksander continues in that patronizing tone I loathe. "And you will not ruin your chances with the potential brides I have lined up for you. Is that understood?"

"Loud and clear." *Motherfucking asshole.*

He shifts his gaze away from me and dismisses any further discussion by tucking into his food.

Conflict returns to haunt me.

I always know what to do but for the first time it seems that I might be way in over my head.

"What was that about with the Yegorov girl?" Caspian asks when we're seated in his car.

Thank God and all the hosts of Valhalla that we're heading back to campus. One more second of being in Aleksander's presence and I would have torn my skin off.

"Nothing." My voice is low and lethargic, as if my soul is being drained of energy.

Caspian starts up the car and drives onto the road, then he glances back at me.

"He wasn't acting like it was nothing."

"Trust me, cousin, it's best I do as he says. She's just a girl. There are plenty others." I'm talking out of my ass. If I truly believed that, I would have forgotten Ivy after that first night I met her. We wouldn't even be having this conversation now.

"Alright, if you say so."

We're silent on the drive back. When I return to my apartment I become more restless and unsettled as fuck.

Then madness takes me and I find myself standing in the shadowy grove of trees outside Ivy's bedroom window smoking a spliff. I needed something stronger than my usual concoction.

I've never watched her from this close before. Up until now I sat by the river, which is several feet away from the dorm.

Tonight I'm in full stalker mode.

On this side of the building the kitchen takes up the entire ground floor, and Ivy has the top. Since hardly anyone has any use for the kitchen at this time of night, no one else would be able to see me out here.

And I'm staring right into her bedroom. The dorm windows all have opaque glass so you can't see inside, but of course that becomes easier when the windows are open. Like hers is now.

Even with the AC on it's too hot tonight to keep the windows closed.

My little lamb is home, and the lights are on. I can see her moving around inside the bedroom, but she can't see me.

She's wearing a camisole pajama top that shows off her gorgeous breasts, and a pair of shorts.

The poor thing has a haggard look on her face, and she looks like she's lost weight in just the few days since I last saw her.

She's still beautiful. Still a one-of-a-kind masterpiece.

And I'm still obsessed.

Since I tasted her, there's something more alluring about her that I can't un-fuck from my mind. And like before, I don't want to.

Ivy stops walking around the room as if she just realized something, then she turns and sees me.

The blood drains from her face and I swear even her lips turn blue.

It's a pretty sight. I meant what I said when I told her fear looked good on her. It does, and I'm conjuring one hell of an idea.

A very bad, twisted-as-fuck idea.

CHAPTER 15

THORNE IS STILL LOOKING AT ME.

Is he here to deliver my fate?

Goosebumps slither across my skin and the spine-tingling sensation of fear creeps into my throat. It slides down to my core and sits there like a nest of poisonous snakes.

I've waited for him for the last two days to get back to me. Every second of the day saw me going insane as I worried about all the horrible things that could happen to me and my family because of my foolish mistake.

All Thorne is doing is staring. Staring at me while he smokes.

Is he waiting for me to go outside to him?

Maybe that's it. Even though he broke into my room the other night, that was super late. The girls are still awake. If he comes in and anyone sees him walking into my room, it's going to look weird.

I break away from the prison of those bright blue eyes and grab my robe, deciding to go out to him, but when I look back through the window, he's gone.

Thorne is gone like he was never there. I can't even see which way he went.

All that greets me is the stillness of nothing and a host of shadows that live in the night.

He's just fucking with me again. Fucking with me and taking pleasure in my distress.

I have no idea what he's thinking and as the days have gone by I've lost perspective on what he might do. From what I know about Thorne Ivanov, I can tell he's volatile, reckless and vicious. To be that way you also have to be heartless, which doesn't bode well for me.

The one thing I'm holding on to is the fact that he saved me from being caught at Raventhorn Hall. That suggests something human resides in him.

I hope I'm right.

More importantly, I hope that Thorne will give me an answer soon.

He warned me not to run, but if he doesn't tell me what he's going to do I'd be a fool to stick around.

I can't put my family at risk. The more days that pass, the more dangerous things become. For all of us.

"Ryan Konilova asked me out. Do you think I should say yes?" Isabelle asks, glancing at Mackenzie and me nervously as we turn down the path.

The three of us are heading to the pizzeria for dinner.

"You waited until now to tell us this?" Mackenzie snaps, nudging Isabelle in her side.

"Ouch. And yes. I waited because I needed to think about it."

"Why? He's hot and he's a Bratva heir. The answer should be yes."

"I don't know. What do you think, Ivy? You've been super quiet. All week."

"Hey, maybe she's still traumatized from that horrible tunnel experience." Mackenzie places an arm around me.

I never told anyone, including Tiffany, about Raventhorn Hall. I made it seem like my encounter with the rats in the tunnels was my punishment.

Tiffany wasn't happy that I'm *still* a student here, and only she and I know what her true intentions were.

She never mentioned anything about it and she never called my parents either. I have a feeling that Thorne spoke to her.

"I'm okay. Just tired."

"I hate rats, so I feel your pain. If you need to talk about it, I'm here to listen."

"Thanks."

God, I wish the fucking rats were the problem. They've served as a good excuse but I can only act traumatized by vermin for so long.

It's night again, and still nothing from Thorne.

"So, what do you think?" Isabelle asks with a little smile.

"About what?" *Crap.* I've lost my focus and can't remember what she was talking about.

"Ryan. He asked me out. He seems nice enough and he's not…"

"Kade," Mackenzie fills in with disgust.

"Yeah. He's not Kade." Isabelle tries to sound like that's a positive thing but I can tell she's still hung up on him.

"I think you should go. It's just a date." I offer her a gentle smile.

"Okay, I'll say yes."

"Wonderful." Mackenzie claps her hands. "Let's talk about what you're going to wear over dinner. You have to wear a killer dress and drop the Wednesday Adams look."

"Not you, too. And I'm not trying to look like Wednesday Adams. I love Japanese street fashion. It suits me and my art."

It does suit her, but I also understand what Mackenzie means.

"You can still be versatile," Mackenzie scoffs. "Even you can agree with that. The dress you wore for the party last week was amazing. If you're going on a date with Ryan you have to change things up a bit. Trust me."

"Okay, fine. Maybe you're right." Again her voice dulls.

We head into the restaurant and they talk about the date, clothes, and makeup while I sink further into my despair.

I hardly speak and when the food arrives I barely touch it, giving the excuse that I don't feel well.

It's not a lie. That's why I gave my mother the same excuse earlier today when we spoke.

I feel sick with worry and I haven't eaten properly in days. Speaking to my mother was hard but I had to do it. I'd been avoiding her calls since the secret broke free.

I'm glad when Isabelle and Mackenzie finish eating and are too full to order dessert.

I just want to get back to my apartment.

Being alone and worrying about my life is awful but right now, it's better if I'm by myself.

When we get back we say our good nights and branch off.

Feeling close to tears, I practically run to my apartment.

I open the door and sink against the hard wood once I've closed it. There I fall apart with my head in my hands and my entire body a shuddering mess.

And that's when I smell the distinct scent of tobacco.

My apartment usually smells like honey and roses, so that smell could only be there for one reason.

One guy.

The guy who's driven me crazy since I first stepped onto this campus.

The guy who holds my future in his hands.

I rush away from the door, look around the living room, then head to the bedroom where I find him.

Thorne is sitting on my bed with his feet up on my sheets looking through my notebooks. He's still smoking and even though he knows I'm standing in the doorway, he hasn't looked up at me yet.

"Why does everything sound like death?" He flicks through the notebook that holds most of my compositions. "You have no variety."

"What if I don't want variety?"

"If you want to play for companies like the Philharmonic Orchestra then you need variety."

"I'll take that into consideration if I live long enough to apply."

He sets the notebook down and makes a show of resting back on the stack of pillows with his arms above his head.

The dragon on his neck looks as vicious as he is, but the display of raw muscle under his short-sleeved T-shirt sends a ripple of heat through me.

"The bed smells like you. The room smells like you. I like it."

This is so freaking awful. He's fucking with me again, and I have to wait and take it.

"Can you just put me out of my misery and let me know what you're going to do? Please. It's not just me I have to worry about."

"Yes, I'm sure your mother and Levgen would be very disappointed to know you've fucked up all their carefully-laid plans to keep you alive."

"That only happens if you tell someone. I will do anything if you keep my secret."

"I know, *malen'kiy olen'*. I know you'll do *anything*. So here's what I've decided to do…" He pauses and stares at me, his eyes roaming over my body carefully and leisurely. It feels like centuries pass between us and all the ages of the earth before his lips part to speak again. "I won't tell anyone."

The tension prickling my scalp loosens and hope fills my heart at this possibility. Until Thorne straightens and gives me a devious smile.

Malice and mischief come alive in his eyes and my little spark of hope flatlines faster than a heart with no beat.

"You want something in return." My voice is a hushed whisper.

"You learn fast, little deer."

"What do you want?"

"You."

"You want me?" I search the hard lines of his face.

"Yes. I won't tell anyone, but in return for my silence I get you. I get to own you. *Every* single part of you." The smile that dances across his lips makes Hannibal Lecter's look like nothing. "You do whatever I tell you and you belong to me to do with as I wish, for as *long* as I call you mine."

I didn't realize how badly I was trembling until I glanced down and saw the ripple of fear trembling through my hands. The same thing is happening to my legs.

He wants to own me.

I lift my chin and level him a hard stare. "What happens when you stop calling me yours?"

"How about we cross that bridge when we get there? You haven't agreed yet, and I'd say your choices are very limited." He puts out his cigarette on my pencil holder I got from Holland, then he pushes to his feet and comes closer. "What's it going to be, Bambi?"

Like he said, my choices are limited. Thorne knows my secret.

He could tell his uncle at any time. My only chance of staying alive and making sure that Mom and Levgen are safe is to agree. Agree and be his and trust in his word.

Trust in him but be mindful that he could destroy me with the truth.

"Yes. I agree. I'll do what you want me to do." What am I getting myself into? It doesn't matter. Whatever happens next will be better than getting my parents killed.

"Wonderful. Well, I think we should get started straight away." His eyes darken with lust and hot desire.

"What do you want me to do?"

He steps closer and cups my face. His touch is almost gentle and would be if not for the malevolence alive in his expression.

"I want you to take your clothes off, then get on your knees and suck my dick. I want you to take my dick deep into your pretty little mouth. Then I want to fuck your face until you choke on it. Once I'm done, you'll let me come down your pretty throat."

My ears burn from the heat of his dirty words and my mind fills with the wild, sinful image of us in such an erotic state. I've never done anything like what he's demanding of me.

I've been so worked up that I hadn't even realized he's the only person who's ever seen me naked. The most I've done is kiss.

Now I have to be his slut.

"Don't keep me waiting." He taps my cheek and winks at me. "I hate waiting."

Swallowing my pride, I lift the hem of my tank top and pull it over my head. Because I want to save the hardest part for last, I take off my shoes, then jeans.

I'm stuck between my bra and my panties but I go with my bra first, allowing my breasts to spill out.

Thorne keeps his gaze riveted to my body.

The heat from his stare touches me everywhere. It feels like my insides are on fire by the time I take my panties off.

Then I'm naked. Naked again. And the look on his face is like that of a hungry wolf who hasn't eaten in years.

I'm about to go down on my knees but he takes my arm and turns me around in a circle so he can get a good look at my body, then he traces a finger over my stomach and up to my breasts, where he lingers. I go still, holding my breath.

"Mine," he mutters, gliding his finger over the swell of my breasts.

He takes a moment to fondle them and squeeze before he lowers his head to suck my nipples.

I watch his tongue loop around the taut peaks and the sight of him sucking is so hot it makes me wet.

I'm so stupid. Even my body is betraying me at the worst time ever.

He sucks on me for a while before stepping away to unzip his pants.

Thorne pushes his pants and boxers down, and I stare with anticipation remembering his taunt about his dick piercing.

When he frees his thick, very hard cock, I stare at it, shell-shocked. There's no piercing but…

He's *huge*. Like really huge and his cock is so long and hard that it looks like it's straining.

Thorne flexes his hand around his length, fisting it. I'm shocked to see his cock grow even harder. "Don't worry, I'll be sure to wear my piercing next time, just for you."

I can't look away from his cock. This is the first time I've seen one of those in real life and the first time I'll have one in my mouth. I don't even know what the hell to do first.

"Come on, Bambi, let me teach you how to please me," he says, reading my mind. I suppose it wouldn't be that hard since I know I look like the terrified virgin. "Get on your knees and open your mouth."

I lower to my knees, then with his free hand he digs his fingers into my hair and directs his cock to my mouth, which now has precum beading at the tip.

I open my mouth and take him in, eliciting a deep groan from his lips.

The sound makes me clench my thighs together to try and control my wetness. I don't even know if that will work, but it seems to calm my arousal.

Thorne pushes me down on his cock and suddenly he's pumping into my mouth, in and out. He slides deeper until he hits the back of my throat. I gag but he holds me in place so I take what he's giving me.

He starts fucking my face like he said he would and his groans of pleasure increase.

His thrusting becomes relentless and savage and, damn me, it feels good.

Everything feels good. The way he's owning my mouth with his cock, the way his pleasure-filled groans sound, the way he's touching me.

I hate that I find myself sinking into his dominance, even though tears stream from my eyes.

Thorne pounds into my mouth, continuing his savagery until his cock jerks and the hot flow of cum hits the back of my throat.

Threading his fingers through my hair, he guides me to drink his cum, and I do. I swallow it all, feeling it slide down my throat. It feels like a mark of ownership inside me.

Thorne loosens my hair, then releases me and pulls his cock out of my mouth.

I watch him tuck himself back into his pants and smooth his hair back.

"Lesson one complete. You did well, little deer."

He's already talking to me like I'm a whore. I have to bite down hard on my back teeth to keep my rage from spilling out.

"You will come to my place tomorrow. You're spending the night." He smiles down at me.

"You want me to spend the night?" *Translation*: he's going to fuck me.

"Yes. Get there at six and let yourself in. I'll leave something out for you to cook."

"You want me to cook?"

"Are you going to repeat everything I say? This is what being owned means, Bambi. Get used to it. You and I are just getting started."

To piss me off further he leans forward and plants a kiss on my forehead, then he leaves me kneeling there, naked on the floor.

I listen for his footsteps until I hear him open the door and let himself out.

My life is a nightmare.

An absolute shitshow of a nightmare.

Thorne is just getting started, and now that I've signed my life away to him there's nothing I can do but obey.

CHAPTER 16

Thorne

I VY IS MINE NOW.

All fucking mine.

Last night I went to bed with the memory of her mouth around my dick and her perfect naked body before me on her knees.

She was better than any fantasy.

I make my way to the computer science building with the little deer in my head and all the filthy things I plan to do to her virgin body.

It's only been one night and I'm fucking addicted to her.

I can't wait to get my hands on her again tonight at my place, in my bed, on my time.

I wouldn't be the first man in history to lose his head over a woman. I know I certainly won't be the last.

Hades stole Persephone.

Ares obsessed over Aphrodite.

Eros lost himself to Psyche.

The list goes on and on and past Greek mythology.

I accept that doesn't make my decision okay and my arrangement with Ivy is still crazy.

I'm in breach of all I vowed to uphold, but I couldn't allow my uncle to kill her.

That motherfucker has far worse secrets than me. He has so many skeletons in his closet they're fighting for space.

This is *my* little secret.

I'm aware I still need to talk to Ivy about the things I don't know.

Last night was the verbal signing of our unwritten contract. But I need to caution her. There's no way I'm saving her ass and putting myself at risk because I was thinking with my dick.

The only physical thing we have to worry about is that ring.

I only knew it belonged to Ivy because it was in her pouch. Discovering it led me to dig deeper and put two and two together to come up with the truth.

If I keep that ring hidden away in my closet in hell, no one will find out who it belongs to.

I'll also look into everything Levgen did to conceal Ivy and her mother's true identities, and make sure there are no gaping holes. I have a penchant for finding things, and you'd have to be above board genius to find whatever I choose to hide.

I don't have to feel bad about this. Not when I've finally found a way to own the girl who's driven me crazy with lust and obsession.

Ivy Yegorov is a sweet distraction and payment for shit Aleksander has dumped on me.

I own her now, and I'll have her again all to myself in a matter of hours.

I have a class in twenty minutes. I wanted to stop by my workspace to get my notes.

I'm creating a new-age antivirus software I want to patent when I graduate. It needs a lot of work and testing, but my theories are sound so far. I'm basically trying to devise an unhackable piece of technology that could take Ivanov Tech to the next level.

Everything I need to test is within my grasp here on campus, and what I don't have here I can get from my pals at Harvard. We share the campus with them and have a lot of liaisons.

I've always been testy about sharing my ideas but in recent years I've benefited from working with other like-minded techs.

I reach my workroom and stop short at the doorway when I see Aiden Sabioni sitting on the edge of my desk looking through my stuff.

If it were possible to burn him alive with my stare, it would happen right now.

"What the fuck are you doing in here?"

Aiden lifts his head and simply smiles at me, then he runs a hand through his dark curls and stands.

"Hello, old friend," he says with a dip of his head and makes a show of bowing as if he's on stage.

"Answer the fucking question." I don't know who he's calling friend. The last time we saw each other we nearly fought to the death.

He stabbed my hand with a steak knife and I would have smashed his head to pulp and powder if Caspian hadn't held me back. That was two years ago.

Aiden gives me a thin smile and folds his arms. "I came to say hi and check out my new space."

I give him a narrowed stare. "What the hell are you talking about? This is my room."

"Your uncle said I could share your room. The place looks big enough for two people." He looks around and I see red.

Red lines of angry fire blazing before me.

This is not fucking happening. Once again my uncle has struck and delivered a blow to make me feel insignificant.

"This is *my* room." I speak in a firm tone, so he understands I don't care what my uncle says. "I'm not sharing anything with *you.*"

"Oh, come on, Thorne. Be a good sport. Surely you're not that pernickety."

"It turns out I am."

He laughs, and I wish I could rip out his throat.

"The way I hear it, it doesn't seem like you have a choice. I just thought I owed you a courtesy visit, to let you know I'd be here. My desk will be delivered by Monday morning."

I march up to him and stare him down. He's an inch taller than me but just as wide and muscular. He always gives me a good fight but this time I wouldn't allow him to win. And there's no one to save him from me.

"Listen to me, you little prick. It's bad enough you're going to work at my company. You're not coming in here, too."

"That's just the thing, though. None of it is yours." He inches closer with that vile smile and shakes his head. "Nothing is yours, Thorne. Not a goddamn thing. So suck it up. If your uncle wants me in here, I'll be in here until further notice. Speak to him if you have a problem. However, the way I hear it, things might not be as rosy as you think."

"What did you hear?"

"That your uncle might not be opposed to me taking your spot. Imagine that. You'd end up working for me." He laughs and steps around me. "See you later, *roomie.* I'm off to English class. Maybe I'll experience a better welcome there."

He heads to the door and I stare after him.

That was the next blow. It's one thing to have a suspicion, but hearing your fears voiced by your nemesis is fucking low.

I'm right. Aleksander is working overtime to get rid of me.

It makes me wonder why.

And why this?

Why use the company against me?

Why would he use the only thing I have left from my father *against* me?

I had a fucking horrible day.

It turned sour from the moment I saw Aiden, then the guys got on my nerves.

During training only two of them proved to be ready for the Reckoning. No surprise that the two were Kade and Dmitri.

Alek came in a close third, but Logan got knocked out when he fell off the assault course.

It was a fucking shitshow.

If I only have two guys who are ready for the Reckoning, it means the rest of them are gonna die. And I can't have shit like that happening on my watch.

I'd be the only planner with dead men on his hands.

With the weight of the day on my shoulders, I walk into my apartment, eager to see Ivy.

She's all I want right now. She was the only thing to pacify my mind.

The sweet scent of honey and roses fills my nose when I reach my living room, and I'm like the dragon tamed by the presence of precious jewels. My dick hardens when I see her little pink overnight bag on the sofa.

It's been a while since I had a girl stay the night and I've never invited one to stay with me before. Ivy is the first.

I hear her in the kitchen so I make my way there. I find her standing over the stove. She turns to face me with that deer-caught-in-the-headlights expression of hers.

She straightens, putting her game face on to address me. She'd almost look like the shy wallflower, but that's not what she is. My little deer is as fierce as a fury. She's just been forced into this position because she knows if she pisses me off I'll ruin her.

"Hi," she says in a meek, cautious voice.

"Hello." I look her over.

Tonight she's wearing another tank top and a little mini-skirt.

Both are a baby blue color that brings out the metallic gleam of her eyes.

"I'm not really good with chicken," she confesses, glancing over at the pieces of chicken I left out defrosting in a bowl of water. "I did oven pizza."

"Next time, I'll teach you to make chicken." I grin. "But the pizza works for tonight. Did you eat?"

"No, I waited for you."

"All right, let's eat." I point to the breakfast table.

She takes the pizza out of the oven and sets it on the table. It's a pepperoni pizza. I have a stack in the freezer for times like this when I need something quick to eat.

We sit opposite each other at the table and dive in. I'm not starving, so I eat slowly, but she eats even slower than me, looking like a little bird pecking at her food, piece by piece.

"Are you gonna watch me eat all night?" She lifts her gaze to mine.

I grin back at her again. "I have many things planned for you tonight. Watching you eat isn't one of them."

She'll soon learn that I always have a good comeback.

We continue eating in silence as I watch her, much to her dismay. Soon she has only one slice of pizza left on her plate. I finished eating long ago.

"Eat that and we'll go take a shower." I tap the space near her plate.

She snaps her gaze up to me looking bewildered. "Shower together?"

"I did say *we*."

"I don't bathe with other people." She wrinkles her nose, looking more deerlike.

"You do now. And I'm not *people*. I'm Thorne, and you are my Ivy."

She grinds her teeth, probably trying to bite back her next words. Good. She's not getting out of showering with me. Now that I have her here there's no way I'm going to rob myself of the privilege of having her up against the wall of my shower.

Ivy continues pecking at the pizza until it's gone. Once it is, I stand, signaling it's time to get into the shower.

"Come on, let's go."

She rises and I place my hand to the small of her back. I lead her into the ensuite and the walk-in shower.

"Take off your clothes," I tell her.

Her back goes rigid at my command but she obeys without arguing.

She starts taking her clothes off and I do the same while watching her.

I'll never grow tired of seeing her naked body. It's like being served my favorite drug in an IV drip.

Once I pull off my boxers her eyes go straight to my very erect, pierced dick and her mouth drops.

Despite being in training for most of the day, I wore my piercing for her, just like I promised. I have a Prince Albert-style piercing, so a little barbell goes from the opening of my dick and comes through the underside.

"Just for you, Bambi." My fingers flex over my length, and I tap the tip of my barbell.

"Just for me?" She gives me a narrowed stare.

"I only wear it on special occasions. Like now."

Ivy answers with a deeper frown, and the fear in her eyes triples.

"This should be fun." I almost laugh at her discomfort and trepidation. Not only is she wondering when I'm going to fuck her, but now she's worrying that it's going to hurt even more with my piercing. It won't. Piercings heighten pleasure.

I am going to fuck her, so I'll teach her about pleasure very soon.

I open the shower door and motion for her to get in. She does, and my eyes go straight to her fully-rounded ass.

I touch it, squeezing her cheeks and she winces, looking back at me with disgust.

Ignoring the look, I step in with her and turn on the water to a light, cool spray.

Ivy keeps her back to me and I take advantage again to take in her body while the water runs through her hair, down her back and her ass.

I grab the sponge from the tray on the wall, squirt some shower gel on it and rub it across her back.

She glances over her shoulder at me, uncomfortable as fuck. "I didn't realize you were actually going to bathe me."

"I guess I am."

She turns back to face the wall while I rub the sponge over her shoulders.

Silence fills the space between us and I think of what to say to her. It feels like a million things are competing for attention in my mind, but I need to focus on the most important questions.

"Does your father know you're alive?" The question sounds odd outside my head.

Her back tenses again, showing me how much the subject of her father bothers her.

"He doesn't know." Her voice is small and barely there.

"Hearing you died must have been hard for him."

"I'm sure it was. My father loved me. I was nine when I last saw him and it was…" Her voice trails off and her fingers linger over the smooth surface of the wall, as if she's touching something that's not really there.

"What? What was it like?"

"Emotional. It was very emotional. My mother and I came to the States after he was sentenced. I never saw him again."

I never feel sorrow for anything but the lowliness in her tone triggers compassion I shouldn't feel. Her father was part of a murder plot, and he might have been responsible for my family's deaths, too.

"My father was a good man." She sounds like she's telling herself that more than me. "He didn't mean for what happened to those people."

"Are you saying you believe he's innocent, little deer?"

She glances over her shoulder again, more worry in her eyes. "He didn't do any of it."

Now I pity her. She sounds like a lost little girl holding on to a dream, so I won't tell her that to be in the position her father is in there would have been seriously strong evidence.

"You sound sure." I decide to humor her.

"I believe him."

"Sorry, little deer. Hell is paved with good men who didn't mean to do what they did."

She winces, as if my words physically hurt her. "Are you going to give me my ring back?"

"I'm holding on to it for the moment. I don't want to risk losing it again."

"I won't lose it. That was an accident. I just needed to feel close to my father. It's been hard coming to Raventhorn, with the burden of the secret. I didn't even want to come here in the first place."

I run my fingers through her hair and turn her to face me. Sad eyes stare back at me and for the first time, I feel like I'm looking at the real her. The version without the barriers and the guards keeping me out.

"Which college did you want to go to?"

"Juilliard or Berklee. I got into both."

"You can still realize your dreams by attending Raventhorn. In fact, you might get a lot more than you hoped for."

"Yeah. Maybe."

She stares back at me as if she's trying to see into my mind to figure out if she can trust me.

I know she doesn't. I can't blame her for that when I don't even trust myself.

The only thing I know is we need to be careful from here on out.

"I'll give you your ring back when the time is right. In the meantime, you need to make sure you keep things quiet. As far as anyone is concerned I don't know anything. Do you understand me?"

"Yes. Of course, I understand. No one was supposed to find out, let alone you of all people."

"Except I did." I touch her face and slide my finger to her jaw to lift it. "And now we have our little arrangement."

Her expression darkens, reminding me of the sky before a storm breaks. In her eyes I see fear, distrust, and desperation for hope warring with each other.

I'll fix that.

"Time to stop talking about business, little deer." I lean forward and brush my nose over hers. "Time to play with you."

A delicate flush of rose-pink tickles her cheeks. It makes me want to peel back the layers of her milky skin and take a peek at what lies beneath the smooth, silky surface.

"What are you going to do to me?"

"You know better than to ask me that." I catch her left nipple between my thumb and forefinger and her breath catches.

I savor the staccato rise and fall of her chest and the soft swells of her breasts. The color from her cheeks flushes down her body, turning her nipples a dusty rose.

I want to seal this image of her in my mind and devour her at the same time.

Caught in my grasp, she looks fragile, like she might snap under the weight of her fear. The same fear that continues to fuel my desire.

I accepted long ago that I'm the type of fucked-up psycho who gets off on things like fear and terror. Such emotions are food for my soul and nourish my being.

I crave them from her the way a hungry wolf does meat. But there's something I want more. Something I tasted when I kissed her the other week.

"Come here." I guide her to my lips.

She comes to me and I brush teasing kisses along her mouth.

"Are you on the pill, little deer?"

"Yes," she rasps.

"Good. You came prepared."

"It's for my skin." Frowning, she tries to pull away but I slip my arm around her tiny waistline, holding her still.

"Skin or not, in my eyes you came prepared for me. Ready for *me* to corrupt you and wreck your pussy when I fuck you."

Her lips part with another comeback but I crush my mouth to hers, stealing away her words.

I shove her up against the wall and kiss her hard and cruel, showing her exactly who I am.

Fuck. She tastes like honey and innocence and fear.

And there it is—the thing I'm looking for.

Her desire. There it is, right there in the way she kisses me back. It happens the moment she yields to me. The moment she sheds her resolve and accepts she wants the darkness. She wants me.

She hates to want me. The psycho. The vicious Knight.

She hates to submit to the thing that makes her want me and surrender to this insane chemistry between us. But no one can run away from the truth. Not even her.

I grab her leg and wrap it around my waist, then I push my fingers into her pussy. She's so wet and so tight the walls of her pussy feel like they're about to crush my finger. I salivate at the thought of what my dick will feel like inside her.

But the instant I think that, the sweet taste of desire fades from her lips.

It's gone and I can't find it anywhere.

I realize it's because fear has come back and stolen it from me.

And she's not ready yet. I can feel it in the way her lips have slipped from mine and the tremble in her body.

I could still ram my dick into her and fuck her raw. I've fucked without emotion many times before on one night stands and just-because fucks.

But… that isn't how I want her.

This is fucking crazy, but when I take her, I want everything. I want to her to want me.

I pull my fingers out of her and stop kissing her. When I set her down she stares back at me with disbelief.

Her lips part with a question but it never comes. Good. Because not even I am certain of what I'm doing. I'm just allowing my obsession to guide me.

Right now that demands something Ivy can't give me. *Yet.*

"Get on your knees and stroke me." We can still do other things from the fantasy. Everything we do works together to break her down and make her mine.

Ivy lowers to her knees and strokes my length.

"Harder," I groan.

The good little deer obeys, rubbing my cock up and down.

The sight of her on her knees and my cock straining in her hands, makes me lose control and I come.

My cum sprays all over her chest and splashes in her face, marking her as mine once more.

I cup the back of her head and lace my fingers through her hair. "It's going to be a long night. I hope you're not tired."

She swallows and gazes up at me.

"Open your mouth." I guide my cock to her lips, and she opens her mouth, licking off the cum already on me while she makes me hard again.

CHAPTER 17

TWO WEEKS HAVE PASSED, AND MY VIRGINITY IS STILL INTACT. I don't know if Thorne is screwing with my head or if this is part of some weird ritual where he's trying to drive me insane.

I'm having lunch with Isabelle at the café. She's talking about her dates with Ryan, but my mind is on Jupiter. I'm listening to her but not really paying attention.

Thorne has scrambled my brain worse than eggs and I can't focus on anything else. Since this whole *arrangement* started I've just about managed to get through my classes and do my sorority stuff.

I keep remembering that first night in the shower when I was sure he was going to take my virginity.

Shamefully, I'd wanted him, then I realized that taking my virginity would mean nothing to him. That saddened me deeply, and then, by some stroke of magic he changed things up.

He didn't slam into me with his pierced dick—which totally terrified me when I first saw it.

He's only worn it once since and I've gotten so up close and personal with him and *his dick* that I know he really does just wear his piercing for me. To *shock* me.

He'd be shocked if he knew that I think it suits him and his dick looks good with or without it.

Shit. I have gone crazy and my brain must have turned into a blob if I can admit to liking his *dick.*

I'm supposed to see him tonight. I know we're going to be doing the exact same as every other night.

I'll have his cock shoved down my throat as often as he can manage and he'll have me spread out on his bed where he'll eat me out and feast on my body.

That's what we've been doing, but any day now I know he'll take my innocence. He just wants to make me crazy first. Until then I'll continue to hang off the precipice of sanity, holding on to whatever I can of my dignity.

The question is, do I want him?

During the moments when we're close and intimacy has robbed my brain of thought, I think I do. I know my body does.

Sex was an obvious part of my agreement with him. I geared myself up for it but that doesn't mean I know what I want.

Or maybe it does and I'm finding it hard to accept it.

Then there's the obvious elephant in the room carrying my secret around its neck.

I always feel awkward around Thorne because of my father.

When I'm with him I think about his family and what must have happened to them. I think about how he must blame my father, and what he may think about me.

We haven't spoken about my father since that first night but maybe that's a good thing. I wouldn't know what to say.

I've kept my presence at the palace on the night of the massacre a secret. I also kept it secret that I saw the scar-faced man. Thorne already knows too much as it is and, like he said, we need to be careful.

But I need to be more careful than him. He might be keeping my secret but he's blackmailing me, using my body and making me feel things I didn't even know I could feel for him.

I went into this plan thinking I could keep my mind strong and resist him, but I lose myself every time he touches me. My emotions and body are a mess.

Isabelle taps the table, snapping me from my thoughts. "I think it's best I just put guys on pause for a while," she declares with a huff.

"Really?" Since it's been a while since I spoke my throat feels dry, so I take a

sip of my drink. "It's just been bad, bad, bad since I've come here."

"I'm sorry."

I truly sympathize with her. Her dates with Ryan were going great, until they weren't.

Her first date with him was so good she said it made up for the bad experience with Kade, then last night everything took a nosedive.

"It was like Ryan was a different person." She releases a heavy sigh. "Like someone swapped him for his silent twin. I don't know what I did wrong in the space of a few days."

"Why do you think it's you?"

"It must be. On our previous dates he couldn't wait to see me again and planned another right away. But last night he barely said anything to me and left within the hour. Clearly he doesn't want to see me again. I haven't even heard from him."

My shoulder slumps. "The last thing you want is some guy treating you like that."

"Exactly. So I've decided I'm just going to focus on classes, which are finally going great." She gives me a proud smile.

"I'm glad to hear that. Mine are great, too." At least all my classes are going the way I want. When I'm there I allow myself to get lost in the lessons.

"I also noticed that Thorne seems to have left you alone. So now you can breathe."

"Yes." I nod with conviction, feeling terrible that I have to lie. I've done such a good job at hiding my relationship from everyone that no one suspects I'm seeing Thorne.

He either comes to my room late at night or I spend the night at his place. I'm sure, though, that someone at Erebus must suspect something. I've encountered one or two guys when I've gone to his apartment.

Maybe they have some sort of bro code of silence so they can hide things until they're ready to share with the world who it is they're dating.

It wouldn't matter if people know I'm with him but I'm mindful that my parents could find out. The chances of them knowing are very slim, especially because they're in L.A. and this isn't exactly breaking news, but I'm paranoid because Thorne is an Ivanov.

"I heard some seriously hot seniors are joining us on the Amherst trip." Isabelle perks up, rubbing her delicate hands.

"I heard that, too."

I'm excited about that trip. Amherst is the hometown of Emily Dickinson. We're going to be there for three days to sightsee and learn about her life.

Amherst is in Massachusetts, so not that far, but a trip is a trip and we're going to be away from campus the whole time.

The course leader is also planning a mini-trip to Salem while we're there. I've always wanted to go there to see the famous sites of the witch trials. More importantly, the break will give me some time away from Thorne and the stress of him knowing my secret.

"I've been to Amherst before." Isabelle takes a sip of her coffee. "But I was just passing through."

"Did someone say Amherst?" comes a deep voice from behind us.

We both turn to find a tall guy with curly hair who looks like he just stepped off the cover of *GQ* magazine.

Isabelle and I both stare at him. *Correction*, Isabelle is gawking at him. I expect drool to slide out of her mouth any second now but she saves herself by nodding.

"Yes," she perks, "someone did say that."

The guy smiles. "Then I'm hoping one of you is Ivy Yegorov."

Isabelle nods vigorously. "This is her." She points at me. "And she's single."

I feel my skin pale then go red. And I flash her a withering stare.

"What?" She chuckles.

"Don't *what* me. You know what." I turn back to the guy, who's smiling back at me looking amused. "Forgive my friend. She's had too much sugar."

"That's okay. I have a sweet tooth, too."

This guy looks like he's never consumed sugar in his life, and I'm not sure what to make of him. He's not a Knight by the looks of it. There are no visible tattoos anywhere on him.

"I'm Aiden Sabioni," he introduces himself when he notices me looking at his wrist. "I just transferred from MIT. I'm doing a minor in English, so I'm tutoring on the side. Professor Dane allocated you to me."

"Oh, wow. That's great, and great to meet you. A tutor was the last thing I was waiting for."

"Perfect. Maybe we can catch up over coffee tomorrow."

"I'd like that."

"Are you single?" Isabelle cuts in, craning her neck around me.

"Yes. I just so happen to be."

"Wonderful. Well, Ivy will bear that in mind." Isabelle winks at him while I glare

at her again. "I hope so," Aiden says with a nod. "See you tomorrow, Ivy."

"Sure. See you tomorrow." He leaves, and I return my death stare to Isabelle. "I am going to strangle you."

"Why? That guy was seriously hot, and he's your tutor which means he's probably going on the trip. This is perfect."

In a normal world it *would* be perfect, and she'd be right. Aiden was hot, but while whatever is happening between Thorne and me is happening I can't date anybody.

I'm not even looking to date. I've said that to her a few times and explained that I wanted to get used to living in Boston and settling at Raventhorn before I did any kind of dating, serious or otherwise.

"Just promise me you'll think about it. He clearly liked you. He said he was single. And did you see the way he looked at you? Come on, Ivy, think about it."

I sigh. "Fine. Sure, I will." I'm only saying that to keep her quiet.

"Yay! This week is going to be great. You have this coffee meeting with Aiden, my dad is coming to visit, and then we have the trip."

"Yeah, it's going to be good."

"You should join my dad and I for dinner tomorrow night. I'd love to introduce you."

"Sure. That would be great." I should be able to work something around seeing Thorne.

"Cool. I'll warn you now, though, he'll talk your ears off about work and the stuff he does with the Knights' database."

I laugh. "That's fine. I don't even know what that is."

She sucks in a breath and stares back at me as if I just said something utterly ridiculous. "How can you not know what that is?"

"My stepdad never spoke about anything like that at home."

"Well, it's like the Knight's bible. It also has a listing of every single Knight who takes the Oath."

"Wow, there must be hundreds."

"Thousands," she corrects me. "And you can search for anyone you want by name, country, age. They even have it fine-tuned so you can search for specific physical attributes, like a mole on their face."

As the words fall from her lips something clicks in my mind and my insides go still. Those last words pierce through me and suddenly I think of the man with the scar.

He'd be in the database. If I could check, would I find him?

My God, if I found him, would that mean I could find some way of helping my father?

That man has been mentioned before, and maybe others have checked, but no one believed my father.

But if *I* looked I'd be able to identify him. I'd have a name to put to his horrible face.

It wasn't even the scar that made him horrible. It was the evil in his eyes.

"How do we access the Knights' database?"

Isabelle laughs. "We can't. You have to be a Knight or like my father. He's part of the system's maintenance team."

Damn it. My spirits sink faster than they rose.

"They have a hard copy of the files in the archives department in Raventhorn Hall," Isabelle explains. "But only Alexander Ivanov and his Knights' council have access to that. Sorry."

I try to hide my disappointment. "That's okay. I guess I got excited because there's so much I still don't know."

"There's a ton of stuff I don't know either, but maybe we don't need to know it."

"Yeah, maybe."

Now that this possibility is in my mind it's stuck there. There must be a way for me to search the database. All these months of worrying about coming here, maybe this was just the thing that could help me and help my father.

If I achieve nothing else from coming to Raventhorn I'd love to get anything that could help Dad.

Dare I imagine finding that something and freeing him from the Hollows?

I could see him again.

He'd know I'm alive, and I wouldn't be indebted to Thorne for the rest of my life.

CHAPTER 18

Thorne

"**Y**OU GUYS ARE A FUCKING JOKE."

I glare at each of the guys standing before me. We're in the training hall at the gym doing our combat class.

We had to take things back to basics, so Caspian, Lucian and I joined the training sessions. Combat training is part of the curriculum here at Raventhorn, but the Reckoning training is separate and more intense.

Some of these guys are so unsuitable it makes me wonder how in the hell they passed previous trials and got this far.

It's my job to prepare them but I shouldn't have to do this much work.

At least Kade, Dimitri, Logan and Alek are still my favorites. The others are total shit.

"I'm going to split you up and you'll work in your teams for the next four weeks. It's important you make use of this time. The end will be the real ritual for the Reckoning where only four of you will be chosen. Understood?"

They nod.

"Kade, Dimitri and Logan, you're with me. Alec and James, go to Lucian. The rest of you, go with Caspian."

We split up and I take my group to the far corner of the training room.

"Let's do some jujitsu." That's one of our basic trainings. Watching them will give me the opportunity to see exactly what areas we need to work on.

I pair up Dimitri and Kade first to spar while I watch with Logan from the sidelines.

Kade and Dimitri begin sparring. Now that I have them away from the group I can see how good they are.

Outside of computers, combat training places me in my element. I've had one hell of a week so this is a distraction I need. Especially when the worst is yet to come.

My uncle has been more of an asshole than ever, and since Aiden has been in my workspace he's gotten on my last nerve.

I see him nearly every day, either at Raventhorn or Ivanov Tech. I can't stand him and his snide remarks. I fear I might snap and I won't be able to hold back.

The only thing that's managed to keep the inner beast inside me from ripping him apart is training the guys. *And Ivy*. Even though it feels like we're trapped in a game of emotional tug-of-war.

Kade beats Dimitri, and Logan takes his place. The two are just as good as each other, but Logan isn't as confident with his strikes.

"Logan, watch your footing and keep your chin up," I order.

Logan tries his best but he's still making the same mistakes. I watch them for ten minutes more until Kade wins again, giving Logan a shit-eating grin.

"Fight me now." My command wipes the smile off Kade's face.

Of course, he's not going to want to fight me because people know I'm unbeatable.

I move forward, taking my stance. Kade does the same.

I've been the best in my class for years. I've done boxing, sword fighting, jujitsu, ninjutsu and kung fu. If I were him I wouldn't want to fight me either.

"If you can hit me, all of you can go." I smirk.

"That sounds like I won't be able to hit you." Kade shrugs and glances at the others.

"It's in your best interest that you try."

"All right, boss. Let's go."

Kade lunges forward with a jab. I dodge it. He's fast but not fast enough. He comes at me again with a left hook, then an uppercut. I dodge both and throw a cross punch right in his face. He staggers backwards but catches his footing. Then he tries it all over again.

"Come on, Kade. Stop fucking around. Give me all you got. Convince me you want me to pick you for the unit."

That order seems to wake him up. It's like someone switched on a light in his head and his moves become sharper, stronger, swifter.

We take things up a notch and really fight. Suddenly everyone stops to watch us, because as good as Kade is, he can't touch me.

Minutes pass with us dancing around. Admittedly, the exercise helps me blow off the steam I'm desperate to release. Finally Kade's fist connects with my jaw but I hit him at the same time.

We freeze mid-stride with our fists striking the other's jaw and I smile at him. I take pride that I'm the best but I feel in this instance I'm only the best if I can teach my students to be as good as me. If not better.

"Well done. You got me." I grin back at him, impressed.

Kade smiles and steps back to release me. I release him, too.

"I've never fought anyone as good as you," he says.

"Don't let that get to his head," Caspian calls out.

"Get out of here. Practice, and don't come back tomorrow throwing punches like pussies." I point to the door.

They head out and I move toward Caspian and Lucian to help with the others. We finish half an hour later and discuss the plans for the week.

When it's over I decide I need some air and a break. I have an hour to kill before my last class for the day, where I'll see Aiden.

Things are getting to the point now where I feel like I'm at a crossroads and I don't know which way to go. It's not a good place to be because it means that I'm living my life in uncertainty.

I head to the balcony of the gym and light up a cigarette. Taking a long drag, I hope that some much-needed nicotine will help me collect myself before I have to go.

I rest my hands on the metal rail and look around me. There aren't many people on campus below. It's Tuesday, the busiest day of the week for classes.

At Raventhorn everything is scheduled earlier in the week to allow more free time toward the weekend. I've always liked that about this place.

I'm about to take another drag when I look to my left and spot Ivy sitting outside the café. She's talking to a curly-haired guy and laughing.

A closer fucking look reveals the curly-haired guy isn't any ordinary guy. It's Aiden. My fucking nemesis.

My blood instantly rises to volcanic temperatures and I see red. I keep seeing that color a lot these days. A fuck of a lot more than I want to.

What's he doing talking to her?

I mull over how this coincidence could have come about and two answers slam into my mind.

The first is that Aiden's minor is English literature. But he's a junior; she is a freshman. They don't usually mix in classes unless they're tutoring.

The other glaring answer is my uncle. My dear, dickwad uncle.

It was only the other day that he cautioned me about Ivy. Since he'll do anything to screw with me, despite telling me to get Ivy out of my system this has his name written all over it.

I don't give a flying fuck what the reasoning is. She's mine and Aiden is not getting her in any kind of way.

I put out my cigarette and practically fly down there.

It makes me sick to my stomach to see her laughing at his jokes. I've never seen her laugh before or look so carefree and relaxed.

The only time she's ever looked relaxed was when I snuck up on her in the library weeks ago. She looked content staring at the river as she was lost in her inspiration.

I think I might have seen her smile once. It was when she was with her friends. Never with me.

She and Aiden look like a couple.

A couple flirting with each other who need to get a room.

"In Italy my family owns one of the biggest vineyards," Aiden is telling her. "We make one of the best loved wines in Europe."

"That is amazing. I've always wanted to go to Italy." Ivy laughs again, and this time she flicks her hair over her shoulder. I note the way that asshole's eyes move straight to her breasts.

"You should go. There are some fantastic places to see."

"The Vatican and the Colosseum are top of my mental bucket list."

"Along with my family's vineyard."

Motherfucker, he's inviting her to Italy.

"Yes, that sounds great."

We will see about that.

"I'm taking some wine with me on the trip Friday. Come to my room once we're done sightseeing. We can have our own wine-tasting party."

My lungs burn with fire that I want to unleash on this asshole. Before Ivy can give him an answer I walk up to them as if I've carried the winds of a raging storm on the soles of my feet.

The two stop talking and look at me. The smirk on Aiden's face tells me I'm right about my uncle's influence in this shit.

"Get the fuck away from her." My voice is colder than the grave and of course my obnoxious words make Ivy's mouth drop.

"Thorne. You don't have to be so rude." She stares back at me, red-faced. "Aiden just transferred from—"

"I know who Aiden Sabioni is." The look I flash her way shoots her down.

"Sorry, old friend. Didn't realize she was anything to do with you."

"Yes, you did." I give him a mirthless grin, letting him know that I know how far he lives up my uncle's ass.

"Well, I was told she was single."

I cut Ivy a hard stare. "*Well*, you were mistaken. Now get the fuck away from her."

"We're actually working. I am Ivy's tutor."

Just fucking great. *Well played, Aleksander. Well played.*

My uncle has delivered so many blows at this point that I've lost count.

The shitty thing is that I'm still on square one. I may have been a badass back there in the training hall with Kade and the others but in reality I can't even block my uncle's punches.

"The lesson is over. Ivy, come." I look at her again, finding her seething. I've never seen her angry. I'm getting a lot of firsts today.

"You don't have to listen to him if you don't want to." Aiden stares at Ivy and does that thing therapists do when they're trying to connect with you by reaching out a hand to touch hers. "We were having such a great session."

"Ivy, come with me. Now." The way I look at her this time with that sternness in my face should remind her that I own her and she isn't to defy me.

She gets the message. I see the moment her eyes dull and her spirits fall in defeat.

Like a retreating general who knows he has to tell his men to fall back, she stands and gathers her things.

"Ivy. Don't let this bully tell you what to do." Aiden has the audacity to touch her again. This time latching on to her arm.

It takes very little for me to lose my shit, especially when it comes to him. So when I find myself grabbing my pocket knife from my back pocket and holding it out to his hand, I'm not surprised.

He is, though, and so is she.

"Get your hands off her or I'll slice you up and gut you like a fish. Rest assured this won't be like last time. *Ya ub'yu tebya, zasranets.*" Calling him an asshole in Russian and telling him that I'll kill him should show him how serious I am.

He removes his hand from Ivy and stares me down.

He got lucky when he managed to cut me during our last fight, but I wasn't a Knight back then. I was being careful.

Things have changed drastically since, and this is Raventhorn. My territory. His family is part of the Italian mafia, so as an ally he's considered a guest here. Any further disrespect to me means death, and not even he is foolish enough to test me in such a way.

Even without us being here at Raventhorn, he knows I'll make good on my threat.

I put my knife away and look back at Ivy who is so shaken she looks like the breeze might blow her away.

We just had another first. The first time she's seen me angry. And what she saw was just a taste.

She moves toward me and I slip an arm around her, guiding her away.

She's shaking. Instinct makes me want to pull her closer but I don't. I know she hates me right now.

I wait until we're well out of earshot before I slow down and cut her a hard stare. "You told him you were single."

"I *am* single." Her eyes blaze and I swear I see fire burning in the depths of the smoky hues.

"What part of being mine makes you single?"

"You asshole. You are such an asshole. I wish I'd never met you."

I grab her shoulders and stare her down. "Meeting me was the best fucking thing that could have ever happened to you. Don't let me remind you of all the ways I've saved you."

She doesn't have a good comeback for that one because I'm right.

"I don't want you hanging out with that guy in any shape or form." I release her.

"He's my tutor."

"He wants to fuck you."

Her entire face colors fiercely. "You don't know that."

"Of course I do. He's a guy. I'm a guy, and I want to fuck you."

"So why haven't you?"

As soon as those words leave her lips, I know she regrets every single one. She probably meant to say it in defense of Aiden but the embarrassment in her eyes tells me more. It tells me she's been thinking about it. About me fucking her.

She's mortified, but that desire I crave from her is getting stronger. It's winning and knocking down her walls, brick by brick.

Despite my rage I find myself giving her my usual menacing grin. "Well, look at this. Bambi wants the dragon to fuck her."

"That's not what I meant."

"Yes, it is." I reach out to touch her face but she backs away.

"I don't want you to touch me."

"And yet, if I chose to fuck you right here in front of everyone, you'd let me."

She balls her hands at her sides and glares at me. "You're sick."

"Maybe. But at least I get to be who I am…" I lean close to her ear. *"Annika."*

She flinches at the name, which brings the reminder of my power over her.

"I never told you I like that name." I lick the shell of her ear. "Maybe more than Ivy, but Ivy seems more fitting for us. All ivies have thorns, don't they?"

"Why are you so mean?"

"I'm different. That doesn't mean I'm mean. Your new friend there, on the other hand, *is* mean." I motion back to the café as if we can still see Aiden, and I hold up my hand so she can see the scar the asshole left me. "I haven't cut him yet but look what he did to me."

She takes in the scar then looks back at me. "Maybe you deserved it."

I smile back at her. She's really growing some balls. "Maybe. But guess what?"

"What?"

"You're not going on that trip on Friday."

Her eyes snap wide and her lips part. "You can't tell me not to go. It's just a trip."

"Didn't I just hear Aiden invite you back to his room for wine? Do you really think that's all he has planned for you? You're not going."

"You are unbelievable. This is so unfair. I've been looking forward to that trip for weeks.

"I don't care. You're not going."

"Fuck you, Thorne. Fuck you."

I allow her to walk away. She needs to blow off steam. I do, too.

Ivy was my distraction, but now she hates me more than ever.

CHAPTER 19

"How have things been?" Eilish asks, resting her hands on her desk.

We're sitting opposite each other in her office. The room is a quaint little space, with high-end décor like the rest of the sorority house, and even looks like a therapist's office except for the life-size poster of Aerosmith on the door. That belongs to Eilish.

While I think of how to answer her question, I stare at her perfectly manicured fingernails and get lost in the electric purple color. It's more vibrant than her lilac hair, but the shades complement each other.

"I've been okay." I've never had to lie so much in my life. Definitely not for normal, common-place things like how I'm genuinely feeling.

But I could never tell anyone the truth. At the same time I entertain the words in my mind with the answer I really want to give her:

Life is actually fucked up, Eilish, and I really want to go home. I attracted the attention of a monster who harassed me to no end during the first few weeks of college, then he discovered my darkest secret and decided to blackmail me.

He went apeshit when he saw me talking to another guy and I practically, foolishly, oh-so stupidly asked him why he hadn't fucked me yet. Much to his satisfaction.

I could have withered away when those words came out of my mouth.

The monster then forbade me to go on the trip today. That's why I'm not going. I'm terrified of what will happen if I piss him off.

In the same vein, I think I might have found a way to help my father but right now, getting into the Knights' database is near impossible.

"Are you sure you're okay?" Eilish searches my eyes and I wish powers like telepathy or some mind-reading spell really existed so she could see into my head.

"Yes. I'm fine."

"You've been spending a lot of time with Thorne." She raises a questioning brow.

"Oh, it, um—"

"It's okay. You don't have to explain yourself." She laughs. "I'm not being nosy. I just want to check on you and give you the chance to speak to me about whatever you need to. Even about Thorne."

I stare back at her, still not knowing what to say, but she made that sound like she might have some positive details about him.

"You know him well?"

"I do, so I'm just going to tell you what you've probably heard before, which is to be careful. He can be a little difficult at times."

No, Eilish, *difficult* is not the right word for Thorne Ivanov. Difficult is when your car won't start or you have to solve a quadratic equation.

Thorne is just fucked up.

"You're right. He can be difficult." I decide to agree because it's safer.

"I'm sorry you won't be joining us for the trip. You were so excited about it."

I'm so sad I'm not going I want to scream. "Me too. Emily Dickinson is one of my favorites."

"Mine too, which is why it's such a shame you won't be coming. It's nice to share an experience with people who appreciate it. Are you sure you can't work something out?"

I shake my head. "I wish I could. I just got so delayed with my music project I have to stay back and work on it." *More filthy little lies.*

I finished that project two weeks ago. It was as easy to me as breathing air. We had to write a piece on two composers who inspired our music. I'd had so much information on my idols that I did my project over one afternoon. Now I have to act like I'm behind in my work.

"Okay. I understand. I hear we're going to Amherst again next year, so you can join us then."

"I'll definitely be there." At least I hope I will. Who knows how long Thorne will keep me captive to our arrangement? I'm little more than a princess locked away in a tower, but I have no one to rescue me.

"In the meantime, please do let me know if I can help you with anything." The warmth of concern fills her eyes. "I know how hard it can be to be new here. Also, talking with you will give me the chance to build up my experience. Since I discovered that I wanted to be a therapist, I've been on a roll."

I smile back at her. "I think you'll make a great therapist."

"I hope so. I'm a little obsessed with it. I've become more focused since freshman year. And I've even been practicing my cognitive behavioral skills on Lucian *but* I think he's getting tired of me."

I like the way she talks about Lucian. I might have only known her for a little over a month but it's clear she loves him. They remind me of an old married couple. They've never given me best friend vibes. Definitely not with the way they look at each other.

"I'm sure he won't get tired of you."

"I hope not. I only have him until January before he leaves for his placement in Russia. Then he'll be gone for a year."

"That's sad."

"Yes. It's going to be weird not seeing him. We've always been in each other's lives since we were kids."

"That's a long time. And he's always been your best friend?"

She gives me a knowing laugh. "Yes, Lucian has always been my best friend. It's always been him, Willow and me. Then Willow married Caspian."

"And you and Lucian?" I'm stepping over a line I wouldn't normally cross but hearing about someone else's life is a good diversion from mine.

"At the moment we're just Lucian and me. If it changes, I'll let you know." She gives me a little wink.

"Okay."

"You do realize that we've spoken more about me than you, right?" She raises another hard brow.

"I know. And I am okay. I promise I'll let you know when that changes, too."

"I'll hold you to that promise. Do you want to go to the pastry shop and get some donuts? I have an hour before I have to head off with the others to Amherst."

"I will never say no to sugar."

"Girl after my own heart." She giggles and grabs her things. "You can tell me about the piece you were composing the other day."

"Sure." Finally something I can talk about.

We head to the pastry shop and stay there for the full hour. I'm surprised I'm able to talk so much when I get going.

I feel like myself and like I never had the misfortune of being railroaded by Thorne Ivanov. But then it's time for Eilish to leave. I get to say goodbye to Isabelle, Mackenzie and Sawyer, who are also going on the trip. Then I'm alone again.

There are no classes to fill up my time because I would have been doing English literature for the rest of the day.

I head to the library, where I study for a test I won't have until the end of the semester.

I'm seeing Thorne later and I'm really not looking forward to it. I had two nights off from him, so I haven't seen him since our blow-up. Only God knows what awaits me, after the way we parted.

And still my mind and body are at war with each other.

Because of him.

Something has to change soon. It has to. I just don't know what.

A pool party…

Wonderful.

Just fucking wonderful.

I arrived at Erebus House at eight p.m. to find it brimming with people inside and outside the house. Loud music filled the air and the living room looked like a replay of the sex parts of the Lords and Ladies party.

There were people having actual sex on the sofa in the living room. I didn't know where to put my face. At the Lords and Ladies party they were behind a glass wall and it seemed more like an exhibition.

This is wayyy different, and it doesn't have that fantasy vibe.

Thorne could have given me a heads-up, but it's just so typical of him to make me swim in the deep end to find my way to shallow waters.

I was told he was by the pool, so I make my way through the crowd to find him.

Of course, he would be the one sitting shirtless at the head of the pack with his beer in his hand along with his muscles and tattoos on full display.

I've never come across a twenty-year-old guy with a body like that. But here it's not uncommon.

Most of the guys walking around look like him, but Thorne has an untamed beauty that's unique to him. Like an unrefined diamond that's just been discovered.

The other girls around him see it, too. How could they not?

He's as obvious as the sun rising in the morning and the moon taking its place at night.

When he spots me those blue eyes light up with a lethal concoction of mischief and malice.

It fuels the ball of emotion settling in the pit of my stomach that's always there.

"Bambi, come here."

This is the first time we've been around so many people. Around him are Kade, Dmitri, Logan and Alek. I don't look at them too much even though they're watching me.

I stop before Thorne and glare at him. "You could have told me there was going to be a party."

"I could have. I just chose not to. Here is your uniform for the night." He reaches down for a bag beside him and pulls out a little black bikini. It's pretty but I'm not in the mood to wear anything like that. Especially when I could have been on the trip.

"I'm not wearing that."

The guys chuckle, but one look from Thorne and the snickering dies.

"Yes, you are. Go upstairs and put it on then bring some drinks for us on your way out."

My entire body tightens with the rage of a bull. He wants me to serve them. He stopped me from going on my trip by being his jealous, possessive self so I could be his servant. What a fucking jerk.

"Go on now." The stiffness in his tone carries a warning, so I don't bother to defend myself. What's the point? It's not like I can win here.

I take the bag from him and walk away feeling like my dignity is in pieces around me.

I go upstairs to his room and change into the bikini, which barely covers my body.

Just as I thought, the moment I step outside all the guys are looking at my boobs, which look even bigger in the bikini top.

I grab a tray of drinks from the server in the kitchen and walk back to Thorne with it.

He smiles when he sees me strolling back to him, loving the conundrum I've found myself in where he is my master and I have to do exactly as he says.

Bastard.

He takes another beer, and I set the tray on the little table between the guys.

Thorne then holds up a bottle of massage oil to me. "Make your hands useful. I need a shoulder massage."

Grudgingly I take the oil from him, squirt some into my palms, and rub it onto the wide expanse of his shoulder blades.

The muscles here are so thick they feel as solid and compacted as the ropes on Levgen's sailing yacht back home.

My fingers are no match for them and I actually hurt myself trying to press into them.

"Harder." He throws the word over his shoulder in that commanding voice I hate.

I try my best to rub him harder but it's clear I'm struggling.

The guys start talking about all sorts of nonsense. Women and booze and training for their trials.

My mind drifts to my father and this possibility of finding the scar-faced man.

I haven't stopped thinking about that.

I wanted to tell my mom and even speak to Levgen about it, but I stopped myself.

Mom would go crazy if I mentioned one word to Levgen about my father. The subject of the scar-faced man was explored before but I was never asked to identify him.

I know the description of the man is vague and so many people have scars on their faces, but maybe this is closure for me. Because I didn't get to help my father when he needed it most.

The other day I went to the library and tried to look for the database on their computer. I thought they might have a systems portal where you could access it from certain locations. I was sorely mistaken. Of course, a secret society wasn't going to have a list of its members readily available at the library for someone to hack.

And hacking is all I could do.

Not that I can hack anything. I couldn't even pick a lock if someone taught me.

The only way for me to get anywhere near that database is if a Knight helped me. How crazy is it that I'm surrounded by them and literally rubbing up against the devil, yet I can't ask any of these people for help?

The entire idea is a dead end but I can't allow myself to truly believe that.

"You can stop now, Bambi." Thorne clasps his hand over mine. "Get us another round of drinks. Jack Daniel's this time."

I hate my life. I hate my life. I *hate* my life.

I go back into the kitchen and look for the Jack Daniel's. The server who was in here before isn't around. Maybe she joined the party.

I find one bottle of Jack Daniel's and some beer in the fridge, so I grab those.

When I walk outside my steps slow when I find a girl with a bob massaging Thorne's shoulders and getting ready to pour more oil on him. A blonde girl stands next to him with her surgically-enhanced breasts shoved in his face.

"You know she didn't do it properly, right?" The girl with the bob laughs. The *she* she's referring to is me.

"Everybody learns," Thorne replies.

"Why get a learner when you can have an expert?" The blonde girl coos, taking off her bikini top so she's topless.

My throat goes dry when she then plops herself onto his lap and for the first time since ever, the slithering green claws of jealousy crawl into my soul.

"Get up and put your top back on, Jenna."

"Nope." *Jenna* slips her arms around his neck and kicks her legs like a little girl on Santa's lap. "Please tell me you have no interest in the little freshman."

"Leave my new toy alone."

Toy.

My God. I studied so hard all my life only to end up like this.

Someone's toy.

And the girl is still on his lap with her tits in his face. Thorne told her to get up once, but he hasn't said it again.

She's *still* on his lap and the other girl is *still* rubbing his shoulders.

Something weird comes over me. It feels like falling asleep and slipping into survival mode in a nightmare where you're not really yourself.

My feet move but I divert toward the nearest table and set the tray down, then I open the Jack Daniel's and take it over to Thorne as he requested.

The girls look at me with vicious smiles on their faces as I march up to them. Thorne is watching me, too.

None of them expect me to lift the bottle up, tip it, and pour it all over Thorne's head.

"Here is your drink, my Lord." That's how you're supposed to address a Knight when you're at a formal event. "Hope you enjoy it, Your Grace." That last part is from watching *Game of Thrones*.

Bare-breasted blonde—Jenna—gets up, and bob-head stops massaging Thorne's shoulders as the drink splashes over them.

Thorne glares at me, and everyone around us goes silent.

Most people would stop and take that silence as a warning but I keep going until the bottle is empty.

When it is, I set it down on the table.

Thorne stands, rising like Poseidon in the ocean.

"Wrong move, Bambi. Wrong move."

The same madness is still with me because I raise my hand and slap him across his cheek.

"My name is not *Bambi*. And I am not your fucking toy. How dare you stop me from going on my trip just to insult me like this?" I glance at the girls. "I hate you."

I whirl around and march away, knowing I have to leave. Not just leave the party. Leave Raventhorn.

Leaving Raventhorn is my only escape.

It might still mean death, but I have to try something.

Something different from this.

I race up the stairs to Thorne's room and grab my clothes. The moment I pick them up, he's at the door.

He walks in, slamming it so hard behind him the ornament on a shelf nearby falls to the ground and breaks.

The other day when I was speaking to Aiden and Thorne got mad, he was scary, but now he looks a different kind of scary.

The kind that tells you you should be running and never looking back. Not staying frozen to the spot the way I am.

Thorne advances toward me and grabs the clothes out of my hand with such force my top tears.

"Leave me alone." I try to hit out at him but he catches my wrist and yanks my jeans away from me, tossing them to the side.

"You really must have one hell of a deathwish." In one quick move he picks me up and shoves me against the wall, barricading me with his body.

"Let me go."

"No. It seems like you need a reminder, *Annika*."

"Stop calling me that. You're so cruel." He's hurting my wrist.

"I haven't begun to show you just how cruel I can be, Annika."

"Fuck you."

"Yes, please."

His mouth covers mine hungrily, sending spirals of ecstasy ravaging through me like a river of fire.

I want to push him away but he turns up the heat and the kiss morphs into the carnal sinful kind that robs me of all reasoning. Shivers of desire race across my skin, leaving me breathless and helpless to its potent power.

Thorne is the last man I should allow myself to feel such aching desire for, but here I am again.

"If you wanted me all you had to do was say the word, *Annika*," Thorne speaks through his merciless kisses.

"I don't want you." The sultry tone of my voice gives me away for the liar I am.

"Isn't that why you got jealous?"

He presses his hard body into me, forcing the bulge of his cock into my belly while he cups my sex. "Answer me." He slips his finger into my bikini bottoms and pushes into my pussy.

My heart pounds in my chest. "No…"

"Liar." He pulls away from my lips but holds me in place so he can finger-fuck me. "Your body betrays you again. Your nipples are hard and your greedy little pussy is wet for me."

He's right. I was wet from the moment he touched me and the two distinct points of my nipples are poking against my bikini top.

"Maybe you need to get a better look." He pulls off my top and rips off the bottoms, leaving me naked.

"Let go of me, Thorne."

"I can't. I don't want to. It's all the same thing to me. That's why you have no reason to be jealous. Open your eyes and see. I'm fucking obsessed with you."

My heart skips several beats and then quivers. My breathing turns shallow as my lungs constrict, narrowing to nothing.

I heard him but I wasn't just listening. I heard him. I heard the words he said and they reached that place inside me, that secret place inside me that hungers for him.

His mouth returns to mine in a fiery kiss that leaves me breathless. And I kiss him back, really kissing him with reckless abandon.

The kiss turns into a greedy frenzy of us feeding off each other, but then he pauses and releases me only to shove his shorts down his legs.

His cock juts free; thick, massive and fully erect, ready to fuck me.

He hooks my leg over his hip and rubs his swollen erection over my entrance, his eyes heavy with lust.

I already know this time won't be like last time when we did this, because now he knows I want him, too. There's no hiding anymore.

He kisses the side of my face. "Hold on to me, Bambi. I won't be gentle."

A shudder runs through me but I slip my arms around him and hold on tight.

He trails kisses down my neck and breathes into my hair. The tension inside me rises, pulling at my core. When he pushes into my pussy, it hurts. It hurts even more as he goes deeper and deeper.

"I knew your beautiful cunt was made for me," Thorne groans as he inches his way into my body.

I moan, too, then he thrusts up inside me in one brutal move, tearing his way past my innocence.

I cry out so loud the sound of my own voice ripples through my body, but he holds me down while stretching me wider to take his length.

Soon he's buried deep inside me, moving past the pain until suddenly a flow of intense pleasure takes over.

It's so powerful my entire body feels like it's gone up in flames.

Thorne pulls back to look at me, then he catches my face and wedges me against the wall.

"You're all mine now, Ivy Yegorov. I will fuck you so hard you will never forget who you belong to. You aren't single anymore. Do you hear me?"

His fingers dig into my throat, almost choking me.

"Yes."

I barely catch my breath before he starts pounding into me, fucking me into the wall.

The sounds of our passion and pleasure fill the room, and my heart hammers in my head. Everything about us is intense. Like a hurricane clashing with a tornado.

Tidal waves of pleasure roil through me when I come but he keeps going, and just like he warned me he's not gentle. He fucks me so hard I fear he might rip my body in two.

Time seems to freeze around us, capturing this moment in which we lose ourselves in each other.

I come again. This time harder. My spasms barely slow when his begin. A deep groan rumbles in his chest and his muscles turn as hard as stone, then he comes, too.

His hot cum floods my body, pulsing through my soul. I'm used to that sensation in my mouth. Having it inside my pussy feels different. It's indescribable.

He whispers my name into my ear, then he slows right down to a stop.

Thorne rests his forehead on the door behind me until his breathing slows down, too.

He pulls back far enough to look into my eyes. I'm covered in sweat.

Sweat is dripping down the side of his face, too.

Carefully he eases himself out of me and we both watch the gush of blood run down my thighs mixed with his cum. The remnants of my virginity.

A quiver ripples through me at the sight of it. Like a wakeup call from reality of what I just did. What *we* just did.

I'm so sore the pain is traveling down my legs, but it's a good pain. A sort of bitter-sweet feeling.

Thorne grabs a wad of tissues from the dresser next to us, rolls them together, and cleans me.

It's strange watching him do something so tender. Then he presses his lips to the smooth mound of my pussy and kisses it. He kisses his way across the skin and up to my hip before standing and planting his hands on either side of me.

"You're staying the weekend, and we're staying in here." He keeps his eyes glued to mine. "No arguments, you hear me?"

"Yes."

CHAPTER 20

Thorne

I BLEND INTO THE SHADOWS OF MY ROOM LIKE A CREATURE OF THE night.

It's just past three a.m. so that still silence of the darkness reigns.

The only light around me is the faint moon spilling through the windows and the red glow from the end of my joint.

I take a hit, hold the smoke deep in my lungs, and allow the psychedelic effect of the joint to take me. It's good, but it's nothing like her.

Nothing has ever been as good as the little deer asleep in my bed with her silver hair teasing the moon.

Finally she looks the way I've always wanted her to look. Like I fucked her the way I've always wanted.

She fell asleep an hour ago, after the last time, which was the third time.

I want more, so much more, and that's the problem. I keep wanting more. *From her.*

She's fucking with my system and making me act in ways I never thought possible.

If anyone else had poured a drink over me the way she did at the poolside they would have at best ended up in the ER.

Then to slap me. And in front of everyone?

Fuck, no.

I would have never stood for that, but this girl has been the exception to every rule written in the book.

I never knew I could be as obsessed with anything as much as I am with her, and I slipped up by telling her.

I don't even care. It was obvious. Just not to her. Or maybe it was but she kept resisting the truth.

I know I did, too, to some extent, even though I accepted it. Then I found myself cleaning her blood mixed with my cum, and possession stirred in my soul.

I haven't had sex since I first met her. Before that I'd only gone a few weeks because I was keeping my eye on my uncle.

Now my dick feels like it only wants her.

Like sex isn't sex unless I fuck her.

I take another drag on my joint at the same time she rolls over and the sheets slide from her breasts and down her legs, showing off her puckered pink nipples in the moonlight.

The sight hardens me up again, and when she shuffles onto her side, revealing her pretty pussy, I decide I'm done waiting.

I put out the joint and make my way over to her, my cock hanging heavily between my legs.

I give her ass a squeeze, and her eyes open.

She lifts her head to look at me, her hair falling over her face and her lips pursed in an erotic porn star pout.

"Ready again, little deer. Are you sore?"

Her cheeks flush. "I'm okay."

I grin back at her, knowing that even though I left her raw, she still wants me.

I flip her onto her back, so I can watch her while I pound into her.

She gazes up at me, her eyes searching mine, still trying to figure me out. I want to wish her good luck because no one has ever been able to do anything close.

I never let anyone that close to me. Not even those I claim to trust.

"Spread your legs for me." I could do it myself but I want to watch her obey my every command.

She spreads her legs and I savor the sight of her soaking pussy.

I dive in, my tongue pushing deep inside her, licking and savoring her arousal.

She doesn't taste of innocence anymore. Now she tastes like temptation. Like feminine desire and all the things that could make a man go crazy.

This is the sort of sinful temptation that would compel a devious fucker like me to burn the world to ashes for one kiss from her.

"Thorne," Ivy breathes out my name, which always sounds so glorious on her lips. "I'm coming."

"Then come for me, *malen'kiy olen'*."

She does, and I take pleasure in the fact that I barely touched her and she came. It means she needed me just as much as I needed her.

I drink up her arousal as it flows out of her, then I suck on the hard nub of her clit, making her arch her back and rub her pussy over my face.

I take one last lap of her clit before I guide my cock to her slick opening and slam into her pussy, impaling her.

We both groan out in pleasure and her inner walls clamp down on me, welcoming me home.

I grab her hips so I can pound into her and fuck her the way I want to. Brutal and reckless, rough and restless, cruel and relentless.

The walls of her pussy are thumping against my length, and she's slick and hot around me.

I drive into her. Thrust after thrust. And she's goddamned glorious, writhing against me.

She comes on my dick again moaning her pleasure, making me harder and hungering for her even more.

I pull out of her and flip her onto her hands and knees. We haven't done it like this yet. I've been obsessed with watching her face as she comes for me.

Now I want to see her lush, curvy ass.

I squeeze her ass cheeks and slip back inside her. This position feels better and I know I'll lose control quicker, but it's worth it.

"Does that feel good, little deer?" I groan.

"Yesss."

"Do you want more of my cock?"

"Yes. Give me more."

I hammer into her, tunneling through her broken moans, until I explode inside her and roar out my climax.

And still I want more. Even as her cunt is fucking milking me dry.

I can't get enough of her.

I wonder if I ever will.

CHAPTER 21

"Y OU MISSED ONE HELL OF A TRIP." AIDEN SMILES AT ME, GIVING ME a curious stare as he rests his hands on the table between us.

"I know. My friends have been talking about it all day."

"Mine, too."

We're sitting by the window in the English classroom. This is our first tutorial session.

Around us on the neighboring tables are several other tutors and students, including Isabelle.

This is also the first time I've seen Aiden since his encounter with Thorne.

Thorne hates that I'm meeting Aiden today but he agreed because it's a tutorial session.

I should be more focused on the meeting. If only to be polite and respectful to Aiden, but I can't think past my weekend with Thorne.

We stayed in bed the whole time. There was barely a minute when he wasn't touching me in some way or buried deep inside me.

Thorne owned my body in every way, making me forget there was ever a time when I was a virgin.

Thorne had me in his bed right up until this morning when his alarm went off, signaling that it was time to leave the wild sexual bubble of recklessness and step back into the world.

The world where I'd missed ten calls from my mother, several from Isabelle, and an email I was supposed to respond to from Friday from Professor Grimfrost.

And just when I was leaving Thorne's room he took me again up against his door, making us both late for class.

I've never met anybody like him.

Thorne is wild and reckless and so opposite to me. He lives by his own rules, and I swear he makes up his days as he goes along.

And oh God, Aiden is looking at me and I've completely zoned out.

Did he say something?

"Sorry, I was just thinking. Did you enjoy the trip?" I ask with the hope of saving the conversation and myself from looking like an airhead.

"It was great."

"It's a shame I had to work on my project."

A slow smile spreads across his lips and his stare deepens with curiosity. "Yes, your project. Want to hear some advice?"

"Sure."

"If I were you I wouldn't allow Thorne Ivanov to rule my life and make me miss out on experiences of a lifetime."

My breathing turns shallow and I take a quick breath to clear my head. I expected him to say something about Thorne but I didn't think he'd be so blunt.

Then again, what he said was tame given that Thorne threatened to kill him just for touching me.

"Thorne doesn't rule my life." I try to make my voice sound light, so he doesn't see through my lies.

"Really? Didn't look that way the last time I saw you. He was in full-on touch-my-girl-and-die mode."

"I'm sorry about that."

"Don't apologize for him. Just be careful around that asshole. He's unstable as fuck."

I can't argue with that, so I don't. "I'm always careful."

"I hope so. Anyway, I still have that wine, if you ever want to stop by my place and try it out."

It sounds like an innocent offer but I know it's not. "I don't think that's a good idea, but thanks for offering."

He gives me a deep chuckle. "Not single anymore?"

His question is answered when the door opens and Thorne walks in.

On seeing him I sit up straighter and heat rushes over my skin like someone set me on fire.

My body instantly craves his touch as if he didn't own me hours ago. And I'm wet. I'm so wet I have to clench my thighs together.

Thorne walks right up to us and sits at the table opposite. "Don't mind me. I had some time to kill."

Aiden stares back at Thorne, his face hard and his hand balled into a fist on the table.

"Unbelievable," he mutters under his breath. "Are you going to join us for every tutorial session?"

"Yes, I am." Thorne harsh tone has everyone glancing our way.

I look at him and I don't know if I should be angry that he's clearly here to watch over me, or if I should be happy to see him sooner than tonight.

"So, let's start with *Wuthering Heights,*" Aiden's voice cuts into my thoughts.

I look back at him, and he holds up his copy of the book. He sets it down but he's looking at Thorne.

"Tell me what your thoughts are so far about the characters in this book."

My thoughts…

Thorne is like Heathcliff. Brooding, arrogant, and hyper aware of himself.

I'm not exactly like Catherine in the book, but I'm just as conflicted. I don't tell Aiden any of that, though. I give a standard literary answer Miss Bailey, my high school teacher, would be so proud of.

Surprisingly, Aiden and I get through the hour, even under Thorne's scrutinizing stare. But the moment the hour is up Thorne walks over to our table.

"Come on, Bambi, let's go."

Aiden and I both look at him.

He's getting on my nerves again, and I wish he would stop calling me Bambi in front of people. Or at all.

"We were just finishing up." Aiden stands and glares at him.

"You're done here. Come on, Ivy." Thorne beckons for me to get up with the crook of his finger and I seethe.

He is the only person on this earth who can make me go from hot to frigid to infernal raging within nanoseconds.

I stand and pack my books away in my bookbag.

"Wow, don't you trust your girl around me?"

"I trust her. It's your ass I don't trust."

"Seriously?"

"Yes. Seriously."

"Do you treat all your girls like property?" Aiden squares his shoulders. "When last I checked, women weren't property."

Thorne walks around to him and steps into his personal space. Then he gets right up in his face, attracting the attention of the entire class.

Isabelle looks at me, her eyes wide. I'd caught her looking at me before but I ignored her, not wanting to encourage whatever thoughts she might have about the situation.

But now Thorne has made us the center of attention.

"Don't push me, Sabioni. Don't do it." Thorne shakes his head. "I like this classroom. The windows over there and the cleanliness of the floor. The janitors do a remarkable job making the place look nice for us. Say one more word to me and I'll ram your head through the window and cover the floor with your disgusting blood."

Oh my God. My stomach flips at the gory image Thorne just painted for the class, and I pray Aiden shuts up.

Thankfully, he does.

When I grab my bag Thorne takes my arm and ushers me out of the room.

I just manage to glance back at Isabelle and mouth an apology to her before we disappear through the door.

Isabelle and I were supposed to go to the pastry shop during the break between classes. Now I don't know where Thorne is taking me.

"What is the matter with you?" I try to shake my arm free from Thorne's grasp when we get into the hallway but he tightens his grip on me.

"Nothing is wrong with me."

"Are you serious? What are you even doing here? You do know you've threatened Aiden twice now. Where I come from that's enough to get you arrested."

He laughs. "I've been arrested many times. The cops have a nice room reserved for me. In any event, this is not L.A. We're at Raventhorn, and I hate that guy."

I can't believe what I'm hearing. "Aiden didn't do anything."

"I didn't like the way he was looking at you."

"But he wasn't looking at me in any kind of way."

"Yes, he was. You don't know him."

"Why do you hate him so much?"

I'm met with silence and we continue walking with no destination in mind. At least not one that I know of. I almost think Thorne isn't going to answer when he glances back at me.

"I grew up with him. For a long time he was taller and bigger than me." Thorne's voice sounds far away. "If Aiden wasn't kicking the crap out of me and threatening to kill me in my sleep, he was teasing me about being an orphan. That motherfucker was fascinated with my sister and always talked about raping her if she were still alive. That last fight we had happened because I stopped him from forcing himself on our maid. That is why I don't fucking want him anywhere near you."

My eyes snap wide and my blood runs cold. "Oh my God. That's awful."

"The only reason that asshole is at Raventhorn is because he's scheming with my uncle. They're trying to stop me from getting into my family's company, so I won't get the position that's rightfully mine."

This is the first time he's said anything against his uncle. I always thought he had a good relationship with him because he's so close to Caspian, but this sounds terrible.

"Really?"

"Yes. You didn't think it was weird for someone to transfer *here* from MIT in their third year?"

"It didn't really cross my mind but yes, that is weird."

"Not that Raventhorn isn't good, but MIT is MIT. It's the best for certain careers, and no one can replace that. That's where I wanted to go."

It feels like we're continuing that conversation from the other week when I told him about Juilliard and Berklee.

"You got in, didn't you?"

He glances at me again. "I did. At sixteen."

And he didn't get to go because he had to become a Knight. I stare back at him with new understanding, seeing more similarities between us than I knew existed.

"Try not to be alone with Aiden, okay? If I even suspect he's touched you, he's dead. You hear me?"

"Yes. I hear you." He takes me around a corner and I remember I don't know where we're going. "Thorne, where are you taking me?"

"Janitor's closet."

I snap my gaze back to him but he keeps his gaze dead set ahead.

"Why are we going to the janitor's closet?"

"I need to fuck you."

A rush of fire pulls at my insides. "I was at your place only a few hours ago."

"Yeah, exactly. *Hours.*"

"Thorne. We can't do this now. Not here."

"Remember, little deer. I *own* you. That means I get to fuck you whenever I want. *Wherever* I want." A devilish look creeps into his eyes, stealing my resistance away.

I should argue some more. Or something. But the lure of desire has wrapped invisible ropes around my brain, holding it hostage.

God. I'm so messed up. He's only doing this because he owns me.

If he didn't, I would have fought him and raised the alarm of harassment. But… would I?

Would I truly do that?

Shamefully, all I can think of is having him inside me again so soon.

And thinking about how good his cock feels makes my mouth water like a ravenous wild dog who's just discovered a fresh carcass.

We reach the janitor's closet and hurry inside. It smells of pine and disinfectant. Thorne closes the door and places a heavy box in front of it, then he continues with me to the far corner where there are more boxes.

He takes off his jacket and tugs on my T-shirt. "Take this off. Take everything off. I want to see all of you."

I set my bag down and my fingers tremble as I take my clothes off.

The moment I'm naked he picks me up and places me on the table that holds a box of cleaning supplies.

His mouth closes over my left breast and he sucks while he slides his fingers into my pussy.

"You're fucking perfect, Ivy." He kisses over the swell of my breasts while I moan from the pleasure he gives me.

The combination of his hot mouth and his fast fingers sends me over the edge.

"Tell me you want me," he husks in my ear.

"I want you." I moan back, appallingly meaning every word.

"You're mine. *Mine.*"

He takes out his cock and drives into me, imprinting those words deep into my soul.

Mine.

CHAPTER 22

Thorne

"The guys are ready." Lucian hands me the latest report. "They've stepped things up so I think we can go ahead and prep for the Reckoning."

"Good." I mull over the report, satisfied by what I see.

The two of us are sitting in the office space we share at Erebus House. It's good to hear that the guys are ready because this is the last week of training before things get next-level serious. It will be the survival of the strongest from here onwards.

Lucian leans forward, resting his elbows on his knees. "Do you have any idea of who you're going to choose?"

I raise my brows and give him a side-eye stare. "You know you can't ask me that, right?"

"I'm asking anyway."

"Alek has a good chance." That's all I'm telling him. I know he's concerned about Alek because they're cousins.

"That's good to hear. I promised his parents I'd look out for him. Of all the people in our family, they've been the most accepting of my mother and me."

"I know."

Like Ivy, Lucian is a stepchild. And his real father is in prison.

Lucian always caught flak from everyone because his stepfather is a high-ranking judge on the Knights' council and his mother used to be a stripper. She stripped to take care of Lucian when he was a kid. They're also Italian, not Russian like most of the families in the leadership.

"Alek is a hothead." He smirks.

"So are you."

"Yeah, but there's trouble and there's trouble. I'll worry about him when I head out to Russia for my placement."

Lucian's family are in tech, too. But tech in relations to sophisticated heavy duty weapons and aircraft. He's doing a yearlong placement at their branch in Russia before he returns here to finish his degree.

"Alek can handle himself." I set the report down and stare at him. "And if he's chosen for the unit, there's even less to worry about."

"I appreciate that." He gives me a curt nod. "What's going to happen when I'm gone? You and Caspian haven't said anything about a replacement to fill my spot."

"Because we're not getting one."

Lucian looks thoroughly surprised at my answer. "Really?"

"We still have you for a few months, and once you're gone we'll have to manage. You won't be gone forever."

"A year is a long time, though."

"Yeah, but this unit is for life. It's about trust. Trust is more important than ever now."

"It always was." He looks me over and I can see he's got questions. "What's going on with you, Thorne? First you save a freshman from certain expulsion, then act like a madman in her English class."

I smile briefly. "I'm good."

Everyone heard about how I threatened Aiden, and because Raventhorn is Raventhorn the whispers about Ivy and me began trickling across campus starting the night of the pool party.

Admittedly I did act like a psycho the other day but Aiden deserved it. People don't know the real him. Under that cool mask he's a sick motherfucker, so I end up looking like I'm the one in the wrong when we clash.

"And is the girl good, too?"

"She is." And I still have the taste of her in my mouth. In fact, it feels more like she's sunken under my skin and is now flowing through the fibers of my mind. "What about *your* girl? Don't tell me you won't miss Eilish when you're gone."

Normally he makes some comment to shoot me down and throw me off the topic of Eilish, but he doesn't look like he's going to do that today.

"It's going to be the first time I will be away from her for so long. At first I didn't want to go, but my stepfather insisted."

"We've all had to do a lot of things we didn't want to do."

"We have. Please take care of my girl for me while I'm away." I've never heard him sound so sentimental. And he finally—*after all these long years*—called Eilish his girl.

"Of course I will."

"Thanks, bro. Girls like her only come around once in a millennium. When you see them you know you'll never meet anyone quite like them again."

His words sink in and I nod, thinking of my own girl.

Ivy is a once-in-a-lifetime girl, too.

That's why I'm so fucking obsessed with her.

Tick. Tock.

It feels like there's an annoying clock in my head reminding me that time is my enemy.

I'm in my computer science class. I would have skipped it but I had to show my face today. Professor Kane is used to my absences, but he's also used to me pulling it together the night before exams and scoring higher than everyone.

I showed up today because we're doing practical work and I created the algorithm the class will be using for their project. If shit happens I need to be here to fix it.

Not being here makes me look bad.

Aiden is here, too, so I know if I were absent and the professor needed me that fucker wouldn't hesitate to taint my name.

I have two minutes left until the class ends. It feels like the longest fucking two minutes ever.

I'm only agitated with time because Ivy is at my apartment waiting for me.

I can't wait to have her again. She's all I've been thinking about all day. Since talking with Lucian earlier I've been salivating for her body like she's my last meal.

I plan to eat her the instant I see her.

Finally the two minutes are up. Heather, the girl I hooked up with over the summer, makes her way over to me. Painted on her face is the same sassy smile she's been using since the semester began to try to win me over.

She knows that hookup was just a one-time thing, so there's little point chasing me.

I spare her the embarrassment of the rejection I would have given her and move the opposite way.

Once I'm through the door I'm almost tripping over my feet in my haste to get to Ivy.

Several people try to stop me to make small talk but I keep going, my head straight and my dick harder the closer I get.

Within five minutes I'm at Erebus, climbing the stairs to reach my apartment.

I all but yank the door open and head to the bedroom. That's where I told Ivy to wait for me, and that's where I find her standing by the wardrobe, dressed in the yellow lingerie I bought for her. She looks like she just stepped out of a porn magazine.

The bra is tight and too small, so her voluptuous breasts are barely contained.

The thong—if you can call it that—is nothing but a string holding together a small triangle that covers the slit of her pussy.

Fuck me. This girl is fucking magic. Every other girl I've been with has been a poor substitute for her. Ivy Yegorov is the real deal.

And she's pissed at me. Clearly because of what I've dressed her in.

Or maybe she's just pissed to see me. I don't really care. She's fucking beautiful.

"You were supposed to be lying on the bed waiting for me." I grin at her and tilt my head to look her up and down.

"You are an asshole. I don't want to wear this."

"And yet you are."

"As if I had a damn choice."

"You always have a choice, Bambi. It's just that your particular choices are limited. And the alternative to defiance doesn't look that great for you. This, on the other hand…" I wave my hand up and down as if I'm touching her, caressing her body from head to toe.

"It makes me look like a slut." Her voice is stiff.

I grin back at her and hold my hands out wide. "But you're my slut. My good little slut."

"I'm *not* a slut."

I walk up to her and scan her beautiful, tempting body. She was fucking made for me.

Her throat works as she swallows and watches me. The other week she was scared of me, now she looks like she's scared of herself. Scared of what she's starting to feel for me.

She wants me, too. It's in her eyes all the time now, and it makes me savor how much I've broken her.

I catch her face and lift her chin. "Bambi, if I want you to be my slut then that is what you'll be."

"You bastard." Her hands fist at her sides.

"Yeah, I am. Now get on the bed."

She stares up at me. "I've changed my mind. I want to go home."

"Changed your mind about what exactly?"

"I don't want to be with you tonight."

I laugh and stroke the hollow of her throat. "Why's that?"

"You're not going to humiliate me."

"Oh, I see. Well, sorry, my little *slut* but that's not for you to decide. Neither is going or staying. Once again I have to remind you that I own your beautiful ass. So get on the goddamned bed."

Her confidence vanishes but the rage is still there, racing with the rapid beat of the pulse in her throat.

I release her and she glares up at me but she does as she's told, padding across the room to crawl onto the bed.

I don't know what it is with this girl. She stirs an uncontrollable havoc inside me that can't be contained.

"Lie on your back and open your legs for me." My voice is low and hoarse.

She lies on her back and opens her legs.

"Now move the thong aside and show me your pussy."

Her cheeks color, reminding me of roses. It's fascinating that she can look like an erotic goddess yet still capture the innocence of an angel.

She shifts the thong aside and I gaze at her little pink pussy with the lips parted. Then, like a feral animal, I lower my body and lick her gorgeous slit, worshiping the taste of her.

I move my gaze back to hers. My poor little deer is doing her best not to like what I'm doing to her.

"Wider. Open your legs wider for me and touch yourself." My voice is raw and filled with lust.

Ivy obeys and my dick becomes instantly harder at the sight of her fingers rubbing her clit.

I don't speak. I just watch.

Watch her body beneath mine coming undone at my command.

She watches me watching her touching herself, and her nipples turn into hard points pushing against the thin fabric of the bra. Her pussy grows wet and I push my finger inside, stroking too.

She moans.

"You like that."

"No."

"Don't lie to me." I stroke harder.

"I'm not lying."

"You fucking are." I bring my mouth to her clit and circle it, then I suck hard, making her cry out in pleasure.

I eat her pussy like it truly is the very last meal I will taste in the world of the living. Greed takes me and I slide my tongue to her asshole, licking that, too, around and around in a circle.

"Oh, my God."

"See, liar. You like what I do to you, how I corrupt you, how I make you want me."

Sliding my thumb to her asshole, I push into that tight little hole, and she comes. Ivy comes so hard, her body bucks and thrashes, shuddering with pleasure.

But most of all, she's shocked at herself.

I keep my finger at her back hole and play with it. "I will fuck your ass someday. Someday soon."

I draw back and strip off my clothes. She looks at my hard cock.

I'm wearing my piercing today. I opted not to wear it since we started having sex because I knew she was worried about it. I thought I'd ease her in gently. Now I want to give her more pleasure.

Her eyes grow and I rub the tip of my dick over her wet folds. Then I get on the bed and pick her up so she can straddle me. "I want you to ride me."

Ivy's eyes widen even more. I've never given her any control before.

Taking a little breath she slides down onto my cock. We've been fucking for days, but she's still so tight. My length stretches her pretty cunt and soon I'm buried to the hilt.

I can see the sweet pleasure spreading over her beautiful face. The pleasure is different from how she normally looks. That's because of my piercing—*mission accomplished.*

She closes her eyes like she's savoring every ounce of it but I hold her face again. "Open your eyes and look at me."

She opens her eyes.

"Good girl."

I kiss her and guide her to move her hips over me.

She kisses me back, and then we're fucking. I'm starved for her and I can't stop kissing her, or pounding into her. My fingers tangle in her hair and hers in mine. Her touch is like balm on my soul. Something I never knew I needed until her.

I lied to myself when I thought I could ever be done with her.

Now I can't see that happening.

And that's a problem for me.

Music fills the empty auditorium, touching every corner with the possession of a forbidden lover.

When you first hear the melody it sounds like something composed by Debussy, but when you listen carefully you realize it's something else. Something different. Something from someone with the same sort of talent that is yet to leave their mark on the world.

Ivy comes in here to practice sometimes, late at night when she's not with me, or the early hours of the morning.

I got used to her patterns long before I owned her.

I'm in my usual spot on the second-floor balcony, absorbed by the shadows like the Phantom of the Opera.

Ivy has never been aware of me watching her. I'm good at being stealthy, but it's easy when she's always so caught up in her music that she loses herself.

I'm almost jealous. I want her to lose herself like that when she's with me. I want her to touch me the way she caresses the keys of her piano, and I want her to obsess over me the way she does when she creates music.

I could go down there and talk to her but I wanted to observe her from afar and watch her in her element. I wanted to see her in a state where she can be herself.

During these moments she's not Ivy Yegorov or my little deer. She's Annika Bershov.

She plays the piano like her father did. I'm sure it was he who taught her to play.

When he came to Raventhorn he also studied music, but as a minor. He majored in cyber security intelligence because his family had always served the elite unit of the Knights.

His skills made him perfect to betray those who trusted him. I always wondered if my father ever knew him. I'm sure their paths would have crossed.

Ivy and I have the night off from each other because I had to train the guys. We have tomorrow night off, too.

Tonight I took the guys to the forest for the rough terrain. It will be similar to where they'll be for the Reckoning.

My Reckoning took place in Russia. It was arranged by three Pakhans in our alliance along with Aleksander. We had to complete one hell of a survival mission, so I more than earned my stripes as a Knight.

Sometimes I wonder how I keep my humanity.

Moments like these help.

Listening to Ivy's music reminds me of days gone by and memories of the past with my family. Our world was always dark, but our home had love.

That's how it started, with love, and how I remember it until everything ended in disaster.

I know my father did something to cause it, and I wish I knew what that something was. I guess I take after him in those ways because no one knows my secrets.

The girl I'm watching right now is another secret of mine. One that's fast becoming something else.

My phone buzzes in my pocket. I pull it out, believing it's a text from Caspian or Lucian, but it's not. It's a notification.

Last year when I was trying to find dirt on my uncle I set up alerts on all the phone numbers linked to him.

He uses a lot of burners and what we call ghost lines. Those are numbers that are untraceable. Unless the person tracking you is me.

The notification is coming from one of those numbers. It's a text.

I open the message and click on the link, hacking into his phone within nanoseconds.

The message says:

> I got the stuff ordered for you and bypassed the registration. It will take three months to create but after that you're good to go.

Aleksander messages back instantly:

> Well done, Claudio, I'll send payment right away.

I keep my tracker on his phone and witness five million dollars being wired to an offshore account. Because it's quicker, I then track where the phone message came from to find out which Claudio my uncle is speaking to.

My search comes up with none other than Claudio Hernandez, a black-market dealer who is banned from association with the Knights.

This again, Uncle.

This isn't the first time I've found him liaising with people he's not supposed to have any relations with. It was only last year that I found out he was trying to get a seat on the Camorra's high council.

The Camorra is the only group that the Knights don't ally themselves with. That's because of a long-standing feud, an unresolved murder we blame them for, and the clash of power.

I used the intel I found on Aleksander to help Caspian. Aleksander never knew it was me who found it because Caspian kept my name out of it, but I'm sure he had his suspicions. He would have known that Caspian wouldn't have been able to find out that sort of dirt without the help of someone like me.

Now there's this. Fresh dirt.

This text is good enough shit to get Aleksander in trouble, but I don't want to simply get him in trouble. I want him gone.

So I need the whole story.

What did he order from Claudio?

What's going to take three months to create?

What is worth five million dollars?

A wicked smile stretches across my face and Ivy's music drops to her signature death notes, perfectly in tandem with my thoughts.

Finally, I have something to work with that will enable me to play my uncle's game.

Am I crazy to think that if I win I might still get to keep the girl?

My malen'kiy olen'.

CHAPTER 23

THE CRISP MORNING BREEZE KISSES MY CHEEKS AS I STARE AT THE family of swans paddling down the river.

It's super early, but I was too restless to stay in, so I decided to go outside and enjoy my morning coffee by the river.

There's a serenity about the place that's soothing. It's just what I need to balance me, if only for the time I'm out here. It's a break. A moment of much-needed respite to regroup with myself.

I didn't see Thorne last night. He was busy, and so was I. I was practicing for my piano recital next week.

Professor Grimfrost thought it would be a great idea for us to have a small event to get some practical experience.

I've done a million of this type of recital in the past, but I'm nervous for this one. Not because of the incredibly talented students in the class who I consider better than me, but because I'm not myself.

Being with Thorne makes me feel like the girl with the borrowed life again.

I know I didn't exactly stop being her. But because everything about us is so reckless and volatile, I don't know what to feel.

The logical part of me remembers our arrangement and is scared to death.

The *other* part of me loses sight of the logical side when I'm around him.

I just stop thinking the way a normal person should.

It can't be a good thing to be so precarious around a guy who's blackmailing you.

And what's going to happen to us?

What's going to happen to me?

I've even lost sight of my idea to get into the Knights' database.

As it stands now, I've accepted that there's no way for me to get into the system without asking someone for help. At the moment, that person is nonexistent.

The only thing I can actually do is keep my eyes open for an opportunity to present itself, whatever shape or form that might take.

The crunch of leaves behind me pulls me out of my tumultuous thoughts.

It's Isabelle. She's carrying a little box from the pastry shop.

We haven't seen each other since my dramatic exit from English class on Monday with Thorne.

She gives me a little smile before she reaches me but I can see a ton of questions lurking in her eyes.

"Morning." She holds up the box and smiles brighter. "I come bearing sweet, tasty gifts."

"You're the best. I'm in need of a sweet, tasty gift."

"Perfect. I got deluxe strawberry and vanilla cupcakes with that pretty frosting we all love."

"Thank you." I move my coffee cup so she can sit next to me.

"Any time. I love that you love cupcakes as much as I do." Isabelle sits and places the pastry box between us and opens it, revealing the deliciousness. "Mackenzie is always on some sort of weird diet. This week she's not having refined sugar or anything brown."

I laugh. "Anything brown?"

"Yeah. I keep telling her most girls would kill to look like her, but she never listens. She's trying to lose weight for the Halloween gala. So she won't be joining us for any treats until after. She wants to fit into her costume."

"I wish that were all I had to worry about."

"Is that your way of warming me up to talk about Thorne Ivanov? You knew I was going to ask about him, right?"

I nod slowly. "I'm sure there are a ton of people who want to ask me about him."

"Actually, there are. You're seeing him, aren't you?" She's looking right at me, staring with that gentleness I first liked about her.

I can't tell her the whole truth, but I can give her a piece of it. "Yes, in some sort of way."

She bites back a smile. "I guess that's why you didn't want to do anything with Aiden."

"Yes and no. Thorne and I aren't exactly official." Talking about Aiden makes my stomach squeeze. I've been thinking about what Thorne told me about him. It made me realize that you really can't tell what a person is like just from looking at them. I'll be careful around him and make sure our meetings take place around people, just in case something happens.

"Don't worry, I'm not going to say anything. I'm sorry I warned you away from him."

"No need to apologize. You were right. It's just complicated. Thorne and I are an enigma I can't wrap my head around." And things have only become more complicated since we started sleeping together.

"Maybe it doesn't need to be complicated. I won't profess to know the inner workings of Thorne Ivanov's crazy mind and his wild ways, but he seems really into you."

God help my stupid heart. It's fluttering at the thought of being that one special girl at Raventhorn who managed to win over the campus god.

But I'm not her. Isabelle doesn't know the external circumstances.

"We'll see what happens," I say, giving her a hopeful smile.

"Yeah, maybe he will surprise you."

"Maybe."

I'm not sure if that would be a good or bad surprise, but I know that my feelings toward Thorne are changing in ways I never anticipated.

"You were absolutely amazing, sweetheart." Mom hugs me hard. I sink into her warmth, unable to believe that she's really here.

She and Levgen surprised me at my piano recital.

We're in the music theater on campus. I went on stage to play my piece and when I looked into the audience, there they were, sitting in the front row.

I couldn't believe it. I still don't know how I managed to contain my excitement and restrain myself from flying off the stage and into their arms.

Seeing them inspired me to play my heart out. The moment the event ended I rushed toward them.

There was no way I would have guessed they would have even thought to attend. When I met Isabelle's dad last week, I wished my parents could visit me, too. And here they are.

The event was hardly worth telling anyone about because it was so small. But Mom and Levgen flew across the country to surprise me because they knew how nervous I was.

"Ivy is always amazing." Levgen gives me a hug when Mom and I pull apart.

"Thank you so much. I can't believe you guys came to see me. Thank you for coming."

"I'm glad this was a nice surprise." Mom cups my face.

"It's the best." I hug her again, feeling close to tears. If only they knew what I've been through in the time I've been away.

"Come on, let's grab something to eat." Levgen taps my head. "There's a bistro in the city that I used to go to when I went to Raventhorn."

"That sounds perfect."

The three of us head toward the exit of the music building.

Mom links her arm with mine when we walk through the doors. "We thought we could take you shopping tomorrow and spend the weekend doing some sightseeing. That's if you don't have plans." She gives me a suspicious smile.

"Nope, I have no plans except spending time with you." Thorne will have to understand. I already messaged him to let him know I had to spend time with my parents.

"Are you sure?"

"Absolutely."

She and Levgen exchange a secret smile.

Mom thinks I have a boyfriend and I'm keeping him secret. Of course she's right, but Thorne is a secret I can never share with them.

We head to the restaurant, where we catch up on what's been happening in each other's lives.

As we speak, I think about my father. My desire to help him is so desperate that I'm tempted to ask Levgen about accessing the Knights' database. But I know I can't ask him anything without telling him my reasons why. It would be so inappropriate if I brought up that topic now and it would upset Mom.

Worse of all, I know neither of them will help me. In their eyes everything to do with my father needs to stay buried with the past. Neither of them would want to do anything risky, no matter how small to draw attention to themselves.

I keep going around and around in a circle with my thoughts on the matter. Everything I think of is a no-go. Including Thorne.

Things are weird enough between us without me mentioning my father to him.

Levgen starts talking about the anniversary trip to Dubai he's planning to take Mom on, and I push my thoughts about my father away.

I won't give up on him. I never will. Hope is still in my heart, even after all these years. Sometimes I just feel like if I keep wishing hard enough something will come up.

Right now I just have to be present in my mind and body. Mom and Levgen flew all this way to be with me. I need to enjoy the time with them to show that I'm grateful they're here. And that's what I do.

The meal we consume is so fantastic that Mom and I order another vegetable cannelloni to share between us, while Levgen gets a side of ribs.

"This place was everything back in my day," Levgen says with a deep chuckle. "I can't believe the food is the same."

"This was a great choice. The food here tastes amazing." Mom gives him a quick kiss.

"I'll have to come back here," I say, taking a sip of my soda.

"Yes, maybe someone special could bring you back for dinner," Mom replies playfully.

"Mom, please."

"Don't you *Mom, please* me. I can tell you're acting strange."

I roll my eyes at her. "You haven't seen me in weeks."

"I don't have to. I can tell from the way you sound on the phone, and you're always busy."

"Because I'm busy." I'm not going to fool my mother tonight or any other night. She knows me too well.

"I think it would be wonderful if you had a boyfriend."

"Just be sure he's someone worthy of my little girl," Levgen cuts in.

"I will bear that in mind when I decide to get a boyfriend." I humor them with a half-truth and my heart shies away when I think of how freaked out they would be if they knew I got myself mixed up with Thorne Ivanov.

Not even just mixed up. I'm officially sleeping with him.

I feel like one of those people who have Stockholm syndrome. The only difference between me and them is that I haven't been physically kidnapped.

The extra food arrives and we tuck in. Then I receive a text.

It's nine o'clock at night. There's only one person who would message me at this hour. My entire body goes rigid.

I retrieve my phone to check the message and see it's from that one person I thought of. Thorne.

The message says.

Come out back to the alley and see me.

My stomach squeezes and I narrow my eyes, staring at the words as if I'm glaring at him. There's no way he's here. Right? How did he even know where we were?

"Everything okay, sweetheart?" Mom asks.

"Yes. It's just my friend. They have a question about class."

"Oh, okay." She gives me a curious little smile.

I text back quickly:

What do you want?

The blue dots jump on the phone screen instantly, and he messages back:

I want your wet pussy riding my face.

I move the phone away quickly just as Mom is trying to get a peek, and the blue dots start jumping again.

If you don't come out, I'll go in and say hi to your family.

Oh my God, no. I couldn't even lie about who Thorne is if that happened. Levgen would know who he is right away. Mom would think I've gone insane for dating an Ivanov when I know the gravity of our situation. Then I'd have double the stress drilling away at my nerves.

"I just have to make a quick call," I say to Mom and Levgen, praying they can't hear the angst in my tone. "I'll be right back."

"No worries, sweetie. Go speak to your friend."

Speak. That's just the problem. I don't think Thorne wants to speak. "Thanks. I'll be right back."

I grab my little purse with my phone and rush out of the restaurant.

There's only one alley on the left of the building, so I head down it. It's dark and scary but since this is the good part of town, I thank my lucky stars it's not dirty and dangerous.

There are a few dumpsters lining the walls but other than that the path is clean. I search for Thorne but don't see him.

When I reach the very end of the alley a dark figure steps out from the shadows.

It's him. He has the hood up on his sweatshirt, and he's smoking again.

As he gets closer I'm reminded that this guy scares me and mesmerizes me in equal parts.

Sometimes I forget how dangerous he is. In the same breath I'm aware there's very little I know about him while he knows so much about me.

He even knew where I'd be tonight.

Thorne slips his hood back, revealing his handsome face in the faint moonlight. It takes me back to the night we first met. We've come so far since that night.

"Hello, Bambi." An easy, sexy grin slides across his face.

"What are you doing here?"

"I told you."

"How did you know where I was?"

"I tracked your phone."

My body goes rigid and anger slithers into my lungs. "You what?"

"You heard me."

"That is an invasion of my privacy."

"Listen to you trying to hand me my ass again. I told you you're mine. Meaning you have no privacy."

"Thorne, that is ridiculous. My parents are here, and you—"

He pulls me in for a kiss, crushing the words on my lips away with his. Thorne nibbles at my neck and feels up my breasts then, I don't know how he does it, but his kiss and his touch dissolve my anger to nothing but desire.

His kiss and his touch are all I'm aware of. I know I should have better control of myself, but the part of me that craves him forbids me.

He cups my sex and the jolt of pleasure at last triggers my awareness, reminding me we're in the alleyway. A place where anyone could catch us.

"Thorne, we can't do this here."

"I don't care where we are. I want to fuck you."

"But someone could see us." I press against his hard chest to loosen his grip on me but he pulls me closer.

"Either I fuck you here up against the wall or you come back to my car and have to explain to your parents why you took so, so long." The cunning smile he gives me tells me he already knows which option I'm going to choose.

Obviously I don't want to take too long.

"You asshole," I mutter. His smile turns wider.

"That comeback is getting tired. Newsflash: you like me just like this. You wouldn't want me any other way."

"I don't like assholes."

"Yes, you do. You like the darkness, little deer." He nibbles on my neck again. "That's why you like me. You like that I'm dangerous, and my disregard for everyone else's rules. And you like that I'm bold enough to do this."

Thorne pulls my top down under my breasts, exposing them to the air, then he lowers to suck. His mouth on my skin ends the argument.

He swirls his tongue around my nipples, hardening them, and the sensation shoots down to my core, leaving me wanting more.

With that sinful I-have-you-where-I-want-you grin, he ushers me into a corner alcove where we're secluded enough so people can't see us. Or rather, not from the road. Someone could still catch us if they chose to come down the path. The staff from the restaurant, or just some random person using the alleyway as a shortcut.

But right now, I kind of don't care.

Thorne unzips his pants and takes out his cock, then he turns me to face the wall and bunches up my skirt. He bends me over and slides my panties aside, then he slides his cock into me from behind.

I like this position. I always feel him deeper and it feels even better tonight. Maybe because we're outside and the possibility of getting caught makes it feel that much sweeter.

He starts pumping into me and we both moan from the sweet pleasure.

"Jesus, Ivy… you feel so fucking good," Thorne groans. "How the fuck were we supposed to skip tonight?"

He's right. It feels too good. So good that I allow myself to get lost in the wildness of this moment and stop thinking about where we are, who's waiting for me, and what we're doing.

Thorne grabs my hips and fucks me up against the wall, pounding into my body relentlessly with rough, hard strokes.

My moans come faster with every thrust into my throbbing pussy.

Anyone passing by would definitely be able to hear me but, again, I don't care.

Thorne speeds up and I try to grasp the wall to take the impact, as if I can sink my fingers into the bricks. I know I can't, but I need something to balance me so I don't fade away.

I can't believe we're outside fucking in an alleyway while my parents are waiting for me to return to dinner.

And I can't believe how good this feels.

How many lies have I told tonight?

No, I don't have a boyfriend, Mom, but look at me.

No, we can't do this here, but this is wild, and I'd do it again.

No, I don't like assholes, Thorne, but I like you.

My God. I like him, but didn't I know that all along? Of course I did, and I don't just like him.

When he took my virginity he didn't force me. I gave it to him. I gave myself to him.

I wouldn't be here now if I simply liked him.

He pounds harder, shaking the thoughts from my mind then he comes, and I join him when I feel his cum inside me.

Thorne pulls out but then he turns me around and slips his hand behind my head to guide me to his lips. We kiss and stay out here for far too long.

When he stops, I don't want him to.

I don't want him to leave either, which makes me realize that I'm in trouble.

Then he kisses me again.

CHAPTER 24

I stayed out in that alleyway with Thorne for nearly forty minutes. We made out and had sex again.

I had to tell Mom and Levgen that my so-called 'friend' had trouble with her coursework and needed my help to access the course files.

The friend I made up was based on Isabelle. In fact, I gave her name, so I'll have to remember that for future reference. My excuse was given in the spur of the moment. I always forget important details when I do that.

Of course, Mom didn't believe me because she was happy to think I might have a boyfriend I was speaking to, so neither she nor Levgen were mad at me. I also think Mom was happy to finish off the cannelloni by herself.

The craziness actually worked out.

My parents stayed for the weekend and we had a great time together.

We met for breakfast this morning and said our goodbyes before they left Boston at midday. I won't see them again until Christmas break.

I hope by then I might have my head screwed on. Except I don't have a plan for that.

Such a plan won't just magically appear anytime soon while I keep thinking about Thorne the way I am.

God. I even found myself missing him over the weekend.

And now.

It's nearly nine o'clock. It's already late and I'm supposed to see him later because he's busy training with the guys. But I've found myself shamefully counting down the time.

To fill the time I came outside to sit on the bench by the river and finish my composition. I had dinner with Isabelle and Mackenzie, who also invited me to go to the movies with them, but I declined because I needed time to myself to think.

I've been out here for over an hour now, but my mind is no more settled than it was when I first got here.

There's just so much going on.

Seeing my parents was nice. So was having that reckless moment in the alley with Thorne, but it makes me think hard about the situation I've found myself in.

I always thought that when I got serious about someone I'd be able to introduce them to my family, but this relationship—*if I can call it that*—is not anything of the sort. I'm not even supposed to like Thorne.

The circumstances of us being together are so fucked up. If I claim to want him—*and I do*—what does that say about me?

The wind blows, lifting my hair about my face. It causes a ripple on the surface of the river that makes the moonlight sparkle like specks of diamonds tossed over it.

The mixture of silver against shadows brings my composition back to my mind. I've almost finished creating it. When I first thought of the melody I knew it was one I would take my time enjoying.

I'm not even going to use it in my course. Pieces like these will be saved up for when I make it big. I want to preserve the inspiration behind them without the influence of anyone else's opinion.

Music is like art to me. I write what I hear and see, turning it into something beautiful. At least that's the goal.

"You haven't seen it yet, have you?" says the voice of the man I can't bleed from my mind.

I turn to find Thorne standing by the tree, watching me. As usual, I didn't hear him. He's also dressed in black again, so I can barely make him out in the shadows.

Thorne steps away from the tree like a creature of the night, his eyes glistening, focused on me as if I'm the only person in this world. It's almost scary to have someone look at you like that.

"What am I supposed to see?" I ask, keeping my gaze trained on him as he approaches.

"Weeks ago I told you to get closer to the river."

"Isn't this close? I am sitting next to the bank."

"No, it's not close enough. Come on, I'll show you." He grins and extends his hand for me to take.

I do, and he doesn't let me go. We hold hands as we walk along the riverbank.

His hand feels large and dominant around mine. Just like him.

"You're early." I glance up at him.

"We finished on time, so I came to find you. I knew you'd be wandering around campus somewhere, *Bambi*."

"I was working on my piece."

"The one from the library."

"How'd you know?"

"It's the way you look at the river. Like you're seeing the notes."

He never ceases to amaze me. "I was."

"Did you try the notes I suggested?"

"I did. And it worked."

He smiles and glances at me out of the corner of his eye. "Did you like it, though?"

"Yes. Clearly you play the piano."

He raises his brows. "Do I?"

"Yes, and you can create music." I feel like I'm trying to pick him apart. It's difficult because he's so closed off. He only allows you to see what he wants you to see. "Who taught you? You didn't just pick that up."

"My mother." He looks away but I catch the sadness dulling his eyes.

I feel sad, too, at the mention of his mother.

"Everyone in her family could play the piano. It was a skill they all learned from way back. We lived in Russia when I was little. I learned to play the piano before I could even speak properly. It was my second language."

"I'd love to hear you play sometime."

"Yeah, maybe. I haven't done it in a while."

"How long?"

"Over ten years. I found it difficult after my family… died."

"I'm sorry. I shouldn't have asked."

He gives my hand a gentle squeeze. "I wanted you to."

We stare at each other for a moment before we look back ahead of us at the shadowy path.

"Where did the name Ivy come from? You look more like an Annika."

"It was my grandmother's name. It's funny, I never stopped thinking as Annika. Sometimes when people call me Ivy I don't know who they're talking about." It feels strangely freeing to talk to him like this, probably because I don't have anyone else I can share these things with.

"I think of you as both, little deer." He holds my gaze, and I realize this is a new side of him I haven't seen. It's a tamer side that I don't think many get to discover.

We continue down a path that's different to where I've been before. It's older with a gathering of giant oak trees that look like they've been there since the beginning of time.

"We're here." Thorne points to the thickest tree which has a set of wooden steps going around the trunk.

I suck in a breath. How could I have missed this?

"It's beautiful. This was here the whole time?"

"Yes. The whole time. All your exploring, and you never found this place?"

"No."

"It's called Freyja's Grove, after the Norse goddess."

"Wow." I look around and he studies me as I take it all in.

"Come on. Wait until you see everything else."

"There's more?"

"So much more." He tugs on my hand, beckoning me to follow.

We take the steps all the way to the top of the tree. Being so high up in the air feels amazing. It's at least forty feet.

Right at the top is a little platform you can't see from the ground below us. The expanse of branches and leaves from the trees hides it, but it pushes right out to the middle of the river. The intricate vines wrapping around the structure have the same medieval Gothic design as the rest of the campus. I feel like I just stepped into a fantasy.

Thorne leads me across the platform. "Look down."

I do, and when I stare down into the water and see a colossal statue of a woman with a shield and a sphere under the water, the air leaves my body.

The moonlight casts its silver glow down on it, but there's a set of underwater lights that illuminate the statue, bringing it to life.

It's more than a masterpiece. It's art and music and the essence of everything in this world that was ever touched by inspiration.

"Oh my God." I breathe out the words on the edge of a whisper. I almost feel like I shouldn't speak. As if the magnificence demands the same reverence you'd show in a church. "This is so beautiful."

"This is one of my favorite statues on campus. I love all the others, but this is something else."

He's absolutely right.

Giant-sized statues of the original Knights of Raventhorn guard the entrance of the campus. The statues take up the whole length of the enormous drive up to the main building, where it ends with Raventhorn himself with the raven on his shoulder and his sword in his hands.

All those statues have a powerful, godly look, but this one we're staring at is everything.

I feel so silly now that I never heeded Thorne's advice to take a closer look at the river. Everyone else has probably seen this a hundred times.

I never got a proper tour of the campus. Now I realize that I really missed out.

Over the last few weeks I've familiarized myself with all the places I needed to be. Most of my spare time has either been spent with Thorne, cleaning Myrridin House, or studying.

"I've never seen anything like this before," I say.

"Neither have I. The man who led the Knights when the school was built got his wife to build all the statues you see on campus."

"Really?"

"Yes. It was so she could share a piece of the legacy. He wanted her to build this one and the angels on the rooftops because all the statues around were so masculine. He wanted his wife to be remembered as the person who supported him most. This statue was their favorite, so they were buried together at the base."

I'm so impressed with him and the story I have goosebumps. "Who is she, Thorne? The statue."

"This is Freyja. Goddess of love, beauty, youth and fertility. But she also has another side, so she was also the goddess of war. Two sides but the same brilliant person. Just like you."

I look back at him and find him already staring at me. Something in his eyes seems less guarded. Less defensive. Less unhinged.

At first, I stare, processing the beautiful words he just said about me.

Then I find myself biting back a smile, until I'm actually smiling.

Thorne catches my face and searches my eyes. "You're smiling at me."

"I always smile."

"Not for me."

"Well, I guess I am now. You just compared me to a goddess. It's a massive upgrade from a Disney animal." I sound like I'm joking but the warmth of his words is swelling my heart.

He leans in and brushes his nose along mine. "You were always a goddess. I don't have to tell you that."

He tilts his head but he's a breath away from my lips.

Filled with the magnetism of his charm, I move in to kiss him. I press my lips to his like I'm tasting him, then I actually kiss him.

It feels like we've kissed a million times over but this is the first time I've initiated a kiss.

Slipping his hand behind my head, he takes control and sweeps his tongue into my mouth, claiming me with the taste of his power.

He makes me feel alive and like I can be me. Like I don't have to hide.

When I'm with him I feel free.

That's what I crave about Thorne Ivanov.

"I'm meeting you at the English building then I'm taking you to lunch," Thorne whispers into my ear.

We're lying in his bed and I'm cocooned in his arms.

It's been one of those nights again when we didn't sleep. Now it's morning and nearly time to leave for class.

I turn to face him, giving him a questioning stare. "Really? You're taking *me* to lunch?"

"Yes, I'll be waiting at the door in case that prick has any more wise ideas."

He's talking about Aiden. I have another tutorial session with him.

Thorne releases me and slides off the bed, dragging on his boxers.

I sit up, pulling the sheets over my breasts so I can watch him. Part of me likes seeing him act all possessive over me, even if it gets a little crazy.

"What?" He smirks, and his messy just-got-out-of-bed hair falls over his eye, making him look like a forbidden fantasy.

"I have lunch with Isabelle and Mackenzie today. The two of them have been annoyed at me for ditching them over the last few weeks."

"Well, I'm sure Izzy and Mack won't mind if I join you."

I give him a narrowed stare and laugh. "*Izzy and Mack*? Since when are they Izzy and Mack?"

"I've always called them that."

"Seriously?"

"It stuck in high school. They love me."

"They're scared of you."

He chuckles. "Believe me, I'm the big brother they never knew they had."

"Maybe you should tell them that."

"Nah. I like having people scared of me."

I shake my head at him. "Also, aren't people going to start talking even more if they see you with us? With…me?"

"Since when do I care what people think?" He grabs a cigarette and lights up.

"I just thought that maybe…"

"Fuck maybe. I'm joining you for lunch." He tugs on the sheet and I pull back. "Join me in the shower."

"Let me message Isabelle and I'll be there."

"Okay."

He backs away, watching me. When he walks into the ensuite I release the breath I'm holding.

This is how we've been since the night of the alleyway. That was two weeks ago.

I'm starting to feel less like a hostage and more like his… *girlfriend*.

Except I'm not.

Thorne doesn't seem to think about us like that. He just does what he wants.

I'm finding it hard to be like that.

I get off the bed with the sheet wrapped around me and go into the living room. I left my bag out here last night with my phone inside.

I pad across the room to get it but I stop when the glare from Thorne's computer screen comes on. It must have detected my movements. He has one of those new tech computers.

This, however, is the first time he's left it unlocked.

Usually when I'm here, it's off.

A desperate idea whispers to me, compelling me to check if he might have access to the Knights' database.

This could very well be the opportunity that I needed to keep my eyes open to see.

I hear the shower turn on. He'll expect me to join him soon. It doesn't take that long to message Isabelle, but I have to look at the computer.

I rush over to the computer, which brightens even more when I get closer.

I don't even know what I'm looking for but the task becomes a million times easier when I see the Raventhorn crest icon on the home screen with the label *Knights' Database* underneath it.

Oh my God. This is it.

My instincts were right. It makes sense that Thorne has access to the database because of who he is.

I grab the mouse and click on the icon, but of course it needs a password.

I wouldn't even know where to begin to figure that out and I don't have the time.

"Looking for something?" Thornes voice makes me jump but I'm quick to save myself by clicking off the screen so he can't see that I was in the database.

I whirl around to face him, trying not to look guilty. "I was looking at the time. My phone battery died," I lie.

"Oh. Alright. There's a charger in the room you can use."

"Thanks."

Trying to act as normal as possible, I continue to my bag and get my phone.

I walk to him and think of what I could do now that I know Thorne can access the database right here in his living room.

I stare at him and I know that no matter how close we've gotten, fact is still fact.

I want to access the database to see if I can find the man who's responsible for the crimes my father is in prison for. But to Thorne, my father *is* that man.

To him, my father took his family away from him.

So why would he help me find the scar-faced man?

CHAPTER 25

Thorne

I VY TRIED TO ACCESS THE KNIGHTS' DATABASE.

I knew she was lying the moment she looked at me, but I played along.

She left just now and I went back to my computer to check the history to see

what she was trying to find.

There's no way she was looking for the standard stuff I'd use the database for. It's something else. If it weren't, she would have asked me.

I'm aware Levgen kept a lot from her, and she's new to what most of us are used to here, but I suspect this is about her father.

Understandably, we don't talk about him. *Ever.*

It's a touchy subject for me. Just as much as it must be for her.

Except my family is dead. Her parents are still alive.

Essentially I'm sleeping with my enemy's daughter. I just haven't thought of Ivy as such.

In the beginning she fascinated me and I couldn't stop thinking with my dick. I wanted to own her. Now I'm thinking with something more.

I don't even know when the fuck that changed, but it did.

Usually I don't care about anything, but I care enough to find out what she wanted from the database. Even if it's to do with her father.

She'll lie if I ask her about what she was doing, but I have my ways of getting information from people. And I have just the thing in mind for my little deer.

Until then, I have my uncle to worry about.

I switch off the computer and make my way into the kitchen to brew a strong cup of coffee.

Today will be another long day. First I have to make sure Aiden keeps his hands to himself and doesn't fuck around with Ivy. Then I'm going to the docks later tonight.

I haven't been able to get information on what Aleksander is up to with Claudio Hernandez, but I think I might have a lead of sorts.

I'm taking Caspian with me. It didn't sit well with me to investigate his father in this way without telling him. Whatever is happening is serious if it involves Claudio Hernandez. So it was only fair I let Caspian know.

It seems Aleksander and Claudio are most likely meeting in person and trying to do things off the record as much as possible. Meaning they can't be tracked and people like me can't figure out what they're doing.

That's fine. I'll find a way to work around it. I always do. It's just a matter of putting the pieces of the puzzle together.

I just hope it doesn't take me too long because time isn't on my side.

The next shit Aleksander will throw my way is his list of potential brides. That's going to make things difficult for Ivy and me. Especially because she doesn't know anything about it.

It won't be fair to her to continue this… thing we have when I'm engaged.

Fuck. I don't even want to think of that word.

Hopefully I'll find the first puzzle piece tonight. All being well, Caspian and I will be talking to a guy my uncle has worked with in the past. His name is Kai. He's with the Yakuza. He's gotten his hands dirty for my uncle on more than one occasion.

He should have some information for us about what Aleksander is buying or making.

It cost me a hundred G's to get Kai's help and buy his silence—for the moment.

The bad thing about people like him is that he gives his allegiance to the man who can pay him the most. Today that might be me. Tomorrow it could be my uncle.

I just have to work smarter and faster at figuring out what's going on before Aleksander catches on that I know he's up to shady shit again.

I make my coffee and head out, preparing my mind to take on the day.

"Heard you went to lunch with Ivy Yegorov today." Caspian casts a curious glance my way.

"I did. What of it?" I keep my focus straight ahead as we walk along the docks. We're heading to an underground boxing club on the south side. That's where we'll link up with Kai.

Caspian chuckles. "Are you serious? Weeks ago, when I asked you about her, you said she was just a girl. Since then I've been hearing a lot about you and *this girl*."

I glance at him but say nothing.

"She's also the only girl you haven't spoken about and the one you've been linked to the longest." He nods as if that should give his deduction more weight. "Clearly you like her."

"Yes."

At first he gives me an amused smile, but then the smile fades and morphs into his usual serious expression. "What are you going to do? My father will be arranging your marriage contract any day now."

"I know. And… I don't know what I'm going to do."

"I fought my father tooth and nail to be with Willow," he says with reflection, and I remember all he went through.

Caspian impressed the hell out of me. I didn't know he could love anybody the way he loves Willow.

Aleksander hated her because she knew his wife was cheating on him with her father and kept it a secret. She could hardly be blamed because she was ten years old when she found out. Aleksander made it his duty to make her life hell, including forbidding Caspian to see her.

He only allowed Caspian to marry Willow because he was interested in getting the Raventhorn fortune. As the sole heir she got everything after her parents died. Caspian's marriage to her took our wealth way above what we could achieve in this lifetime, but Aleksander still did all manner of things to screw with her.

"You've come a long way," I say, looking him over.

"So have you."

"My situation is different." I can't even tell him all the ways it is.

"There may come a time when it won't be."

"I'm not sure I have a choice. At least not yet."

"Let's see what happens."

I give him a curt nod. Five minutes later we arrive at the club.

There's a big match going on. The place is packed with a roaring crowd cheering for the fighters in the ring who are both giving all they have.

I spot Kai across the room, standing by the bar talking to one of his workers.

He's a tall, wiry man with a shaved head and a tattoo of a panther inked on the right side of his face. His head and neck have more tattoos of swords and Japanese symbols.

He sees Caspian and I and waves us over.

We approach him and he greets us with a cunning grin. He's the kind of fucker you know not to trust or mess with.

"Hello, Ivanovs, arms out," Kai instructs in his cultured Japanese accent. "I hope you don't take offense to a quick search."

"Of course not." I give him a thin smile and glance at Caspian before I lift my arms.

Two bulky guards who look like Sumo wrestlers step forward and search us for weapons. We don't have anything on us but that doesn't mean we came unprepared.

You never can tell when meetings like these might go south. That's why our guards are hidden away outside just in case we need them.

In any event, if shit went down in here we'd use *their* weapons. My patience is already non-existent, so if Kai fucks with us, I would personally fuck him up so bad he'd need to be identified by his dental records.

"All clear," the biggest guard says once he's finished checking us.

Kai's smile widens. "Follow me."

He leads us through a set of wooden doors which takes us away from the noise of the crowd. Then we walk into a washitsu room. Decorated with the traditional Japanese sliding doors and bonsai trees, it looks completely out of place with the rest of the club.

"Please take a seat." He points to the tatami mats on the floor with a rattan table and handwoven futons on either side of it for us to sit on.

Caspian and I sit next to each other, while Kai sits in front of us.

"You certainly keep a man like me in business."

"What have you got for me?" I don't have time for chit-chat or his riddles tonight.

"Not a lot, I'm afraid. Your uncle is a very secretive man. I guess that's what makes him so fitting for his line of work."

I raise my brows. "For a hundred thousand you better have something *useful* to tell me."

The tick in his jaw tells me he doesn't like what I said, and if I were anyone else I wouldn't live long enough to take my next breath. "Aleksander is making a special blend of fentanyl."

"Fentanyl?" Caspian looks from Kai to me, narrowing his eyes. "That makes no sense."

It doesn't make any sense whatsoever. "Are you sure?"

"Positive."

Fentanyl is a synthetic opioid that's similar to morphine but a hundred times stronger. People use it to manage pain but it sells for a pretty penny on the streets. Especially when it's mixed with other street drugs.

"How did you find this out?" Caspian asks.

"I have sources from the logistics company he's used before. They're expecting a shipment of this fentanyl in three months' time. Aleksander made the order yesterday."

"The Knights already have an alliance with the Ramirez cartel, who produce fentanyl," I cut in. Aleksander has the world's finest at his beck and call. That's why this makes no sense.

"Perhaps Aleksander has his reasons for getting it somewhere else," Kai surmises. His expression holds the same air of mischief as before. I can never tell if he's being completely open and honest, or if he's holding things back.

"You sound like you might know more than you're saying." I level him a hard stare.

"That is all I know, young one. Men like your uncle are good at hiding secrets, so what you need to ask yourself is what is he hiding from you this time? What might he not want you to find out?"

I've asked myself those questions already. But as simple as they are, he's right. Men like Aleksander are good at hiding secrets.

And now we know he's cooking up some special blend of fentanyl.

What for?

"Keep an eye on this for me. I'll pay you more. More than him if he finds out we've been around here."

Kai dips his head. "You know where my allegiance lies."

"Of course." *Bastard.* He's trying to tell me that if Aleksander pays him more than he thinks I can pay, he'll screw me over.

I stand, signaling the meeting is over, and Caspian follows.

We let ourselves out and wait until we're outside the club before we speak.

"My father is a man of many mysteries." Caspian shakes his head. "Why would he need to get fentanyl supplied by a black-market dealer who's banned from associating with the Knights?"

"It's something he wants to hide from us. I'm going to keep my eyes on Claudio."

"What can I do?"

"Keep an eye on your father. It's easier for you to do it."

"Sure."

I hate vague shit like this. It leads you to that make-or-break moment where most people are stumped.

One wrong move and you either miss what you're supposed to find, or your enemy catches on that you're onto them.

I can't let that happen. This information is all I've managed to gather in the last two months of Aleksander playing me like a bitch.

It must mean something.

Something useful to me.

CHAPTER 26

I SPREAD POLISH OVER THE WOODEN CUPBOARD AND BUFF THE SURFACE until it shines.

Tiffany wants the function room spotless. She's hosting a luncheon tomorrow with the presidents of the other sorority houses.

I'm still on cleaning duty for another few weeks, so the job of preparing the place went to me and Isabelle.

Isabelle will be joining me in a little while. She had a late class.

The two of us will be the only students on campus tonight—Friday night—who'll be doing the most boring job ever.

I'll be seeing Thorne later, so I'm using the time to myself to think about how I might get access to the database on his computer.

Maybe I could hire a hacker to hack into Thorne's computer.

How much would that cost?

A few hundred? A thousand dollars?

More.

What am I even thinking?

Anything I could ever come up with in that regard is crazy.

Thorne is a world-class tech god who got into MIT when he was sixteen and has the same IQ as Einstein.

It was a miracle that his computer was left on for me to peruse for the time I did. His password for something so important as the database is probably going to be some outlandish craziness with a thousand characters. It would cost me an arm and a leg to find someone with the skill level to hack it, and I don't know if that someone would want to hack Thorne Ivanov's computer.

Since I've been here, the only person bold enough to argue with him has been Aiden. And look how that turned out.

God, where is the *Mission Impossible* crew when you need them.

All things impossible aside… could I really do that to Thorne?

Pay someone to hack him?

Doing so is a different sort of betrayal. There were several times over the last few weeks when he could have betrayed me. But he didn't.

He's also changed. True to his word, he met me for lunch yesterday and sat with me and the girls. Everyone was staring at us. Even the staff who work in the café.

When I told Isabelle and Mackenzie that Thorne was joining us, they were intrigued. It was awkward when he first got there but they loosened up and we all had a great time. It was normal.

He was normal for me and I felt like the girlfriend again. The girl with a different sort of borrowed life. Not the dead one masking herself with the skin of the living.

If I did hire a hacker and he found out, I would be no different than my father in his eyes.

That doesn't mean I can drop this idea.

I haven't stopped thinking about my father rotting away in the Hallows. I'm never far from tears when I think of him.

I keep remembering the night of the attack on the palace. How he got me safely to Mom before he went back to try and save the others.

I keep thinking if only I'd tried to stop him. If only he'd just come with us, that might not have happened. But then, maybe they would have still found him guilty because there was evidence that linked him to the attack.

I've never known what that evidence was specifically but I heard there were links to the plot and the setup of the attack. Over the years I've tried not to think about those parts because none of that sounded like something my father would do.

I can only imagine what his life must have been like at the Hallows for the last nine years. It will be ten in January.

So I'll have to find a way back into Thorne's computer.

Me. I have to physically do it myself.

Maybe Thorne will leave the computer on again.

Maybe I can watch and wait for him to use the database and hope he'll leave that open, too. People make mistakes like that all the time.

He did, just by leaving his computer on while I was there. So maybe I'll get another opportunity.

The door opens and a flustered Isabelle walks through. She looks like she's been crying, so I stop what I'm doing.

"What happened to you?" I look her over, realizing that I'm right when she gets closer and throws her bag down.

"I'm so mad, Ivy. I'm so fucking mad." She grabs the duster and joins me.

"What the hell happened? Is it Tiffany?" She's been busy with her entourage of stylists getting her ready for her date with Warner Sluskia, the president of the Zeta Kappas. I don't think she had a run-in with Isabelle, but it's not impossible.

"It's Kade."

"Oh no. What did he do now?"

"I just found out he's been ruining all my dates on purpose and threatening anyone who wants to date me."

My mouth drops and nearly hits the floor. "What the hell? Are you serious?"

"Yes. Remember Ryan? Remember how great everything was going then suddenly everything went to hell?"

"That was Kade's doing?"

"Yes. What an asshole."

"How the hell did you find out?"

"Morty, from Lapetus, told me. He asked me out and said he wasn't afraid of Kade. I reckon Kade wouldn't be bothered with him because Morty dresses like Dr. Seuss."

I groan, feeling my stomach scrunch from the mean-spirited nature of Kade's cruelty. Bad things have happened to me since coming here, but they don't know me. I'm the new girl. New to their world and their school.

Isabelle is new to the school, but she's so nice. And Kade knows her.

"He's got to be doing this for a reason. And what is this, high school? We're supposed to be adults in college."

"He's trying to ruin me. Maybe he's even done other things I don't know about."

"I wouldn't put it past him at this point. Isabelle, I don't think this is to do with whatever happened with your mother. This feels like something else. Something more vindictive."

She dips her head and nods slowly. "It was easier to have a reason to explain why he hates me. But he really just hates me."

"What the hell is going on in here?" Tiffany's voice fills the room. Her

Valley Girl accent grates on my nerves but I school my expression when I look at her.

She walks in, her heels clicking against the floor.

Dressed in a black bodycon, studded Louboutins, and her hair in loose beach waves, Tiffany looks ready for the red carpet. But the scowl on her face makes her look like an old sea hag.

"You two are supposed to be cleaning not conferencing about shit. This place better be ready for tomorrow or I'm adding another month to your punishment."

"Another couple of hours and the room will be done." I glare at her, doing my best to keep my temper under control.

"I want it done within an hour!" she screams in my face. "So clean the fucking place, bitch. You think you're above the rest of us because you're with Thorne Ivanov?"

She looks like she's been dying to ask me that question. Like someone who just got something off their chest which has been weighing them down for eons.

I've caught her giving me filthy, evil looks since the whispers about Thorne and I started spreading. I knew she was jealous. Mackenzie told me that Thorne has been turning Tiffany down since high school.

I'm about to answer her when the loud exaggerated sound of someone clearing their throat pierces through the heated tension between us.

When I see Thorne standing in the doorway looking like he's about to incinerate Tiffany, my spirits lift. But guilt twists my heart when I remember my previous thoughts about hacking his computer.

This is the first time he's been here with anyone around, least of all Tiffany.

"Thorne. What a pleasant surprise." She sets her shoulders back and pastes on a phony-as-hell smile.

"Cut the shit, Tiffany. We both know it's never pleasant to see me." He walks in, right up to me.

His eyes lock on mine for a brief moment before he takes the cleaning cloth from me and walks over to Isabelle to take the duster from her.

Isabelle and I exchange surprised glances.

"What's this business?" He holds up the cloth and the duster, staring at Tiffany.

"They're cleaning." Tiffany speaks in a firm tone but her eyes betray her fear and wariness of him.

"We have staff for that."

"This is a punishment they both deserved."

"Here." Thorne hands her the cloth and duster. She takes them grudgingly and stares at him wide-eyed.

"You do it," Thorne adds in a voice filled with venom.

"What?"

"You heard me. You fucking clean and have it done within the hour."

Isabelle's eyes nearly pop out of her head, while my back goes ramrod straight.

"I have a date with Warner." Tiffany glares back at him, as if her answer is enough to excuse her from his demand.

"He can wait."

"But he's already been waiting for me."

"Your lord just gave you an order." Thorne lifts his chin and glares down at her. "You dare defy me?"

"No, my lord."

I'm so shocked I feel like I fell asleep and dreamt this.

"Good, now get it done. And don't you ever dare expect any of these girls to clean shit ever again. Is that understood?"

Tiffany's face reddens and I can tell she wants to give him a mouthful but holds her tongue. "Yes."

"Yes, what?"

"Yes, my lord."

"Ivy, Izzy, come on." He looks at us and cocks his head toward the door for us to follow him.

Isabelle picks up her bag, and the two of us leave the room with Thorne. Leaving behind a furious-as-hell Tiffany.

We stop in the hallway and I smile at him. "Thank you so much."

"Yes, thank you," Isabelle says, hugging her bag to her chest.

"No worries." Thorne looks from Isabelle to me. "How long has this been going on?"

"Pretty much since we started." I bite the inside of my lip.

Thorne's brows snap together. "Why the hell didn't you say something?"

I shake my head. "I didn't want to cause trouble."

He looks at Isabelle, who shakes her head like me.

"I don't have anyone like you to turn to," she speaks in a lowly voice.

"That's never been true, *Lolita*." He looks at her little dress and gives her a kind smile. It's strange seeing him be the hero.

It pulls on my heart when Isabelle looks like she's about to burst into tears. I know that's to do with the whole thing with Kade. Tiffany talking to us like we're shit didn't help. But this has.

"Thank you, Thorne." She smiles at him, then looks at me.

"You're welcome, Izzy."

"I'll leave you guys to enjoy your evening."

She nods at us both then heads down the corridor.

Thorne's already looking at me when I return my focus to him.

"Wrong move, Bambi. Wrong move. The last time Tiffany did shit to you, you got in trouble."

"I know."

"Make sure you tell me if she does anything else. You hear me?"

"Yes… *my lord*," I tease, giving him a playful smile. He smirks. "How come you're here. I thought I was going to meet you."

"Change of plan. I have a surprise for you."

My hopes rise with excitement of what this surprise could be. "What is it?"

"It wouldn't be a surprise if I told you, would it?"

"Not so much."

He grins and tugs on the hem of my shirt. "Pack a bag. You're going to be away for two nights."

"We're going away?"

"We're going away."

CHAPTER 27

THORNE TOOK ME TO AMHERST.

We got in his car—a Ferrari. It was the first time I'd seen it and had him drive me anywhere.

When we drove off campus it felt like we were leaving all our troubles behind and venturing off to a new world. And when I spotted the *Welcome to Amherst* sign excitement overwhelmed me.

Weeks ago, when I missed out on the trip, I was so disappointed.

I've always wanted to visit Amherst to learn more about Emily Dickinson's life and the inspiration behind her work. She's always been one of those writers from the past who left a mark on me. She loved to use nature and landscapes, too, to spark her creativity.

What she did with words, I try to do with music.

Thorne booked us at the Inn on Boltwood, a stylish boutique inn with the ambiance of the old world.

We got their best room and Thorne had me in bed the moment we stepped through the door.

We woke up early today and started the day off with a gourmet breakfast, then we spent the day at the Emily Dickinson Museum and sightseeing.

I could tell Thorne was bored for most of the time but he didn't show it.

Today was the best day I've had in a long time, and I experienced it with him.

Now we're at dinner, eating a fine meal of Wagyu beef tagliolini. We can't have wine in here, so we're drinking mocktails, but we have some wine back in our hotel room we saved for later.

I feel like we've exited time and space today, but there are moments when I'm pulled back to think of reality. The reality where we're not really what we appear to be, and I'm still the daughter of a disgraced Knight.

A Knight who sits in prison for something I know in my heart he didn't do.

Thorne and I don't talk about my father at all. Sometimes my answers verge on the truth to him, but I have to think fast to be mindful of his feelings.

And then there's that little voice in the back of my mind telling me I still need to be careful because Thorne knows my secret.

He stares at me while I allow my pasta to dangle from my fork.

"What's going on in that head of yours, little deer?" He takes a sip of his drink.

"Just stuff."

"What stuff?" He gives me a toothy grin and rolls his sleeves up his thick forearms, exposing his tattoos and muscle. I swear he's gotten bigger over the last few weeks.

"Everything," I confess. I guess my answer could mean every and anything.

"Thinking of music? There were a few times today when I thought you were going to burst into song."

I laugh and he smiles at me the way he does whenever I find myself laughing around him. Sometimes I think he says things just to hear me laugh.

"I can't sing. At least not well. I hum when I need to sound out my notes but I promise you'll never hear me bursting into song."

"I suppose your music isn't exactly the like burst-into-song kind, is it?"

"Not really."

"It's darker."

"Yes."

Thorne is the first person to truly notice that aspect of my music. He once said that it sounded like death. There's a reason for that. The answer lies with the nine-year-old girl I was who saw the hallways littered with the bodies of the people she once knew. Losing my father—even though he's still alive—felt like death. So did losing who I used to be.

"Why is it so dark?" he asks, keeping his gaze on me.

"My…past."

He nods, understanding. "Would you ever consider creating something lighter?"

"Maybe. There's a lot of lightness here. Thank you for this trip. It meant a lot to me."

"You're welcome. I'm sure you had a better time with me than *Aiden*."

"Of course. Also I wouldn't have been hanging out with Aiden on the trip. Isabelle and Mackenzie were there. So were Sawyer and Eilish."

"Believe me that asshole would have found a way to hang out with you. Just remember what I said about him."

"I remember."

"I'm trying to get you a different tutor."

I blink at him several times. "That's not necessary."

"Yes, it fucking well is."

"We're always in the library or around people."

"I would feel better if he weren't anywhere near you."

There's that protectiveness again. It makes me crazy, but he also makes me feel safe.

His expression turns more pensive and I think of what he told me weeks ago about his uncle and Aiden. I haven't asked about that since because the time wasn't right, but I've wanted to. Now that we're talking about it, I feel I have an opening.

"How are things with your uncle and Aiden?"

Thorne tilts his head and chews briefly on the inside of his lip before he straightens again.

"Absolute shit. I'll be lucky to get my legacy after graduation. Aiden has basically replaced me."

"Can your uncle do that?"

He sighs with the frustration of a man who's thought of every idea and failed. "Yes, he can."

"Why would he do that to you? That makes no sense."

"Because he can. Because… he thinks I'm just like my father, and that means I'll be a threat to him."

This is the most Thorne has ever said to me about himself and the things that worry him. He doesn't talk about his father either, or his family for that matter. Like me when I talk about my father, I know he's being mindful of my feelings.

"Why would your uncle think that?"

"He's right. A man like my uncle has secrets he wants to keep close to his heart. I have a penchant for finding out things like that. I take after my father in every way. That makes me as dangerous to my uncle as he considered my father to be." He pauses for a moment. "Aiden can't do what I can do. He has skill, but I'm something else. He'll also be the mindless automaton my uncle wants him to be. Aiden and his family want to climb the ladder of power so he'll do whatever he's told. I won't."

"I'm sorry."

"Don't be. You know what I'm sorry about?"

"What?"

"Wasting my breath on those fuckers when I could be tasting you." The salacious look he gives me sends streaks of liquid heat flowing through my body from my head and down into my core. "Come, let's go back to the room. Time to play with you again, little deer."

His voice is like a dirty lullaby. Soothing and tantalizing in the most decadent of ways. It makes me feel sexy and excited that this seriously hot guy wants me.

I take his hand when he extends it to me and allow him to lead me back to our room.

He pulls me to his hard body when we're inside, pressing his erection into my belly as he crushes his lips to mine.

"Feel me, *Annika*." The use of my real name speaks to that part of me deep inside who longs to be her—Annika. The part of me I had to suppress to live.

He takes my hand and guides it to his cock. I grip his steel-hard length through his pants, and he returns to my lips.

"See what you do to me, little deer. Only you."

I pull away to stare into his bright blue eyes, my mind fragmenting from his words. "Me?"

"Fucking always."

He kisses me again, giving me a glorious, breathless kiss that makes the world blur around us and my nerves sizzle with pleasure.

Our bodies crash into the wall and he consumes my mouth. It feels like I've been waiting for this moment forever.

He kisses me until my lips feel like they're on fire. Then he drags his mouth away from mine to pull my top over my head and tugs on my skirt. "Clothes off. Now."

We pause for a few seconds to take off our clothes. I squeal, laughing when he scoops me up and throws me on the bed.

A breath later he's covering me with his gorgeous, muscular body, kissing me again.

Leaving my lips, he kisses his way across my face and down to my neck, then he lifts me so that I'm on top of him. But he doesn't stop there. He flips me around so my pussy is in his face and his cock is in mine.

"You know what to do. Don't you?" He takes his cock and strokes the side of my breast.

"I do."

"Then please me with your hot little mouth, and I'll please you, too."

I take his cock into my mouth and suck.

"Good girl." His voice is low and warm on my skin.

Running his tongue across my pussy lips, he leaves a streak of hot fire.

The juxtaposition is maddening, leaving me wetter than I've ever been in my life. When he starts licking into my pussy I moan, wanting to come.

While I suck him, taking him into my mouth as deeply as I can, he does the same to me.

He laps at my clit, knowing exactly what to do to make me grind against his face.

It feels so good that soon my orgasm takes me and I come in shivering gasps.

Thorne drinks me, allowing me to climb down from the sexual high before he slides out from under me and positions me on my hands and knees so he can slam into my pussy from behind. Then he's moving, his hard cock owning me again in a wild animalistic way.

My entire body is tight with arousal and filled with him forcing more and more pleasure into me.

My pussy spasms around his cock and he squeezes my ass cheeks in response.

"You like when I fuck you, don't you, little deer?"

"Yes," I cry out.

"Do you want me to fuck you harder?"

"Yesss. Fuck me harder, Thorne."

He does and I come instantly. Waves of red-hot pleasure ripple through me like wild electrical currents.

He fucks me into the mattress, every thrust of his cock sending me deeper into the realms of wild pleasure, and I'm utterly lost in the sensation because this is sheer possession.

Thorne drives into my G-spot and it feels like I don't stop coming.

He, on the other hand, is still rock hard.

He pulls out of me, slides off the bed, and retrieves a set of chains from his bag. I gasp when I see them.

They look like something you'd see in a BDSM club. Of course, the closest I've ever been to a club like that is watching TV, so seeing this toy in real life has my head spinning.

The only time Thorne had me bound was the night he discovered who I really was.

"Don't be scared, *malen'kiy olen'*." He smiles. "I just want you like this."

"You want me chained up?"

"Yes. Captive and bound to my mercy."

I almost ask him if I'm not already like that, but I don't. Instead I allow him to guide me to the top of the bed where he secures the chains around my wrists then around the rails on the headboard. The metal feels cool and tight around my wrists.

I won't be able to escape these without him.

"I won't hurt you. Unless you want me to. Pain can be pleasurable sometimes." He speaks in a sing-song voice and grins, then he nibbles on my breasts. "Do you want me to hurt you, Annika?"

"No. Don't hurt me. Not yet."

"Not yet. I like that answer. Okay, I won't hurt you yet, baby." That's the first time he's ever called me that. My body liked it. "Let's do this first. I need to come inside you."

He spreads my legs wide and plunges back into my body.

The restraints somehow amplify the pleasure coursing through me. I don't know how it's possible, but it is.

Maybe it's because I feel more like I'm giving myself to him. Whatever it is, it's unreal.

He pounds into me and the rush of energy devours me. It's so potent that I scream.

Thorne gives me a victor's smile. The kind you'd see on a conqueror when they've taken everything and left nothing behind.

With that smile set on his face, he pulls out of me. Then he flips me again so that I'm on my hands and knees. My restrained hands are crisscrossed, but the chains are just long enough for me to place my hands on the mattress to balance myself.

I glance over my shoulder, trying to see what Thorne is up to.

"This ass is mine," he speaks in a low growl, pressing his thumb over the tight rosette of my asshole. "Mine to fuck."

I gasp and clench. He promised he would fuck my ass one day. I'd forgotten. I'd gotten lost in everything else and got comfortable with our routine. I should have known better than to make that mistake.

The chains around my wrist should have told me things would be changing tonight.

"Will it hurt?" My voice trembles.

"It will sting at first, but then it will feel just as amazing as everything else we do. Maybe even better. It depends on how freaky you want to be with me. Ready?"

"Yes… I'm ready." I'm not, but I'm wrapped around Thorne's fingers again.

The conqueror's smile returns to his face and he grabs my hips. I turn to face the headboard and my hair falls over my face like a veil.

Thorne smears my juices into my asshole, then I feel the head of his cock pressing into me. It's the weirdest sensation ever.

He pushes his cock into me, stretching me to take him. And that's when it hurts and my ass feels like it's burning from the outside in.

I grab at the sheets as if they can help me and try to steady my breathing. That doesn't work. "It hurts Thorne."

"Stay with me. You'll feel good soon."

I listen and quickly find that he's right. Once he's stretched me and he's sliding in and out of my asshole, it feels good.

It actually feels good. Too good.

I lose my mind to pleasure again. And so does he. Thorne speeds up, pounding into my body hard and fast. Then we both move against each other until his climax fills me.

I can barely breathe by the time he's done with me. Feeling like the life has drained from my body, I slump down into the mattress.

Thorne pulls out and gently eases me on to my back again, then he stares at me, watching me catch my breath.

He lowers his head to plant kisses on my lips, then all along my thighs.

When he lifts his head, we gaze at each other for a long tender moment before he gets off the bed and pulls his boxers and pants back on.

Thorne returns to me and brushes another kiss along my lips. "Do you feel good, little deer?"

"Yes… that was unreal."

"We'll do it again soon." He tugs on my wrists and I think he's going to undo my chains, but he doesn't. "Next time will be even better. Now let's play another game."

"What are we doing this time?" We've done everything now. He's had me everywhere. There are no more virgin parts left on me.

"A game of truth. You're going to tell me what you wanted to find on the Knights' database."

CHAPTER 28

Ivy

He knows…

The blood drains from my body and all the pleasure I felt only moments ago evaporates into the thin air.

As Thorne stares down at me waiting for an answer, I'm reminded of just how crazy he is.

Damn it. He knew. He fucking knew this whole time—*for days*.

He probably knew I was trying to access the Knights database right from when I was still standing by his computer. And he allowed me to believe…

Believe what, Ivy?

That he *didn't* know?

"Please don't deny it. I checked the history on the files when you left that day. I know you tried to access it."

"So you played me by bringing me here?" I feel foolish again.

"You know that part wasn't a game. This is, though."

Like *this*—naked and chained to the bed with his cum leaking down my thighs from my ass—I feel vulnerable as hell.

And I'm embarrassed. I'm embarrassed by my situation and embarrassed he caught me and called me out.

"Undo the chains now, Thorne."

"No. Not until you tell me what you wanted. It's to do with your father, isn't it?"

"Undo the chains."

"Tell me."

"Or what, you'll leave me like this and get your uncle?"

"Like fuck. You're mine. No one gets to see you like this but me." He looks infuriated that I would even suggest such a thing. "Tell me what you wanted."

I weigh my options and realize I don't have any.

I never did. Besides, isn't it easier to tell him what I need from the database now that he knows what I was trying to do?

This is not about me. It's about my father.

"Undo my chains and I'll tell you. I don't want to talk to you like this. It's serious."

Thorne stares at me for a moment, contemplating.

Relief washes over me when he lowers to undo my chains. I'm even more relieved when he allows me to get off the bed and go to the bathroom to clean myself off.

I return to the room moments later and pull on my nightshirt. Thorne watches me with the keenness of a fox, his eyes following me as I pad back over to the bed.

I sit on the edge and he pulls up the chair next to it so he's sitting in front of me.

"I'm waiting, little deer."

I blow out a ragged breath. "I wanted to check the database because I'm looking for someone."

He sits straighter and narrows his eyes. "Who would you be looking for?"

"It's a man. I was at the palace on the night of the attack with my father."

Thorne's eyes widen. "What?"

"My mother was a surgeon. She had to go back to the hospital to work that night, so my father took me to work with him."

"You saw what happened?"

"Not enough to do anything to save my father. He left me in a room to sleep. The sound of gunfire woke me, so I hid in the secret passage. A man came into the room…" My breath catches as my mind fills with the haunting memory of the scar-faced man. It's been almost ten years since I had to tell this story so it's hard.

"The man had a deep scar on his face." I pause for a beat and blink past the painful memories. "My father's friend, another guard, came in after him, and the man with the scar killed him. He said he was going to kill everyone, then he carved out his heart."

Thorne stands but there's something more than shock on his face. It looks like… recognition.

"Did he say anything when he took the guard's heart? The man with the scar on his face."

"Yes, some strange foreign words. *Valin mortilum dohaliues.*"

"Jesus." Thorne touches his cheek and stares at me, searching my eyes. "Say those words again."

"*Valin mortilum dohaliues.* I don't know if I'm saying it right. That's what it sounded like to me."

"Yes. Those are the words." He's speaking to himself. He moves over to the window and stares out at the night. "*Valin… mortilum dohaliues…*"

"Thorne…"

He turns back to face me. "You thought the scar-faced was a Knight?"

"He had the tattoos. I *know* he was a Knight." I didn't know it was possible for Thorne to turn pale, but he has.

"You're absolutely sure?"

"I'm positive. I remember everything I saw that night." My breath catches as my lungs constrict from the angst wrapping around them. "That man was a Knight, and he was responsible for the attack. That's why I believe my father is innocent. He was set up."

"If that's true… then your father really had nothing to do with the massacre at the palace or the plot to kill my family two years before."

"No. He didn't."

His head drops for a moment, then his gaze climbs back up to meet mine. "I've seen the scar-faced man, too."

I stand now and stare at him, shock slamming into my body. "You have? Where?"

"He was at my home in Russia on the night of the attack. I hid in the closet and watched him carve out the hearts of my guards. But I didn't see his tattoos. So I never knew he was a Knight."

"Oh my God." My body feels like lead. Like it might topple over from the weight of this revelation and never move again.

"It's the same guy, Ivy. He said those same words. *Valin mortilum dohaliues.*"

CHAPTER 29

Thorne

SHOCK TANGLES WITH THE TRUTH, ELECTRIFYING THE SPACE BETWEEN us.

Ivy stares back at me and I at her. She's right there, paces away, but it feels like she's on the other side of the moon.

I'd thought that perhaps she wanted to look at the database to see what evidence it held against her father.

No way would I have ever imagined this. That she saw the scar-faced man, too. And she didn't just see him. She's provided some of the missing pieces that has mystified many, including me, for years.

The scar-faced man is a Knight, and those words…

Those words *valin mortilum dohaliues* are the ones I couldn't remember.

It feels strange to hear them now and cast my mind back to my eight-year-old self.

I forgot the words—or whatever the hell they are—but now I'm sure of them.

I'm *sure* those were the same words the scar-faced man spoke as he carved out the hearts of my guards.

Hearing those words flow from Ivy's lips was like remembering an old tune that was locked away in my memory but always remained a part of me.

Ivy is like the missing piece of my brain. She held memories that I don't have yet.

I share too many coincidences with this girl. This is one more thing.

Although she may not remember the words exactly, when you know what something sounds like you can always try to find out what it is.

Over the years I couldn't even do that.

How did she remember and I didn't?

Maybe the answer is as simple as that. She did and I did not.

She was also able to see the guy's Knight tattoos.

I never saw those.

I was more terrified than I want to admit because I've grown up to be this strong person everyone sees. But I was eight years old. The weakest I'd ever been in my life.

I'd just watched Caspian get taken away. I thought the men were going to kill him, and I knew my family had been taken, too. People around me I'd known from birth were all dead. It was a nightmare.

"Thorne…" Her voice, soft, searching and gentle, seeps into my soul. I want to answer her but all I can do is stare.

Earlier, when I asked her why her music sounded like death, she said it was because of her past. I understand now.

"Those words: *valin mortilum dohaliues*. I never remembered what they were. I just couldn't." My voice sounds hoarse, as if I haven't spoken for a hundred years.

"Do you know what they mean?"

"No."

She looks disheartened. "I've tried looking them up but I don't even know what language it is. At one point I thought it was Old Norse, but when Levgen started teaching me how to speak it I knew those words were something else."

"Maybe it's something old, or just a language we don't know." I try to focus but my mind is all over the place. "Do you remember anything else about that night?"

"That's all I saw. Remembering that scar-faced man terrified me for years. I'd never seen anyone die before, so when he killed my father's friend it was awful."

"I'm sorry."

"Thank you… No one believed my father when he told them about him. No one could identify anyone like him, but I guess the description is too vague. I knew if I saw him again I would know who he was, with the scar or without it. That's why I wanted to look at the database."

"I've searched it before. He's not there. My uncle searched too."

Her shoulders slump. "Oh." With that simple word I can see just how much she wants to help her father. I would be the same if I were her.

"When the attack happened my uncle searched high and low for that man. He checked everything available to him. That included the Knights' database. The moment I became a Knight and got access to the database I searched for him, too."

Ivy looks even more despondent.

"When things don't add up in our world the answer is always that it was an inside job." So many things are. "Apart from me, no one else had seen the scar-faced man. There was no mention of him until two years after my family's attack when your father spoke of seeing him at the palace. That's the only reason your father was allowed to live."

Ivy's breath catches and her pulse leaps against the pale skin of her throat. "That's why?"

"Yes. My family's deaths are an anomaly that no one has been able to resolve. With all our resources, the Knights have had to file their deaths away as a mystery." I take a measured breath. "My uncle is an asshole but he wanted justice for his brother's murder. He was willing to keep *anything* that would help get that, so when he thought your father was linked to the plot he kept him alive at the Hallows. He hoped that one day something else would come up and your father would be able to identify him. But nothing else has."

"My father didn't do anything, Thorne. He took his job as seriously as he took being a father to me. I know that in my heart. I might have been young, but I know that."

I believe her.

I actually believe her. But belief in this situation is nothing without proof. We still need proof, still need answers, still need so much *more*.

"I will keep that in mind."

She looks grateful to hear that. This girl will make me do anything for her. I wish I could tell her I believe her just to see that look of gratitude again.

But I'm not there yet. There's too much pain in my soul. It's too raw and right now, all we have are words and memories.

I have to figure out what all of this means before I can say anything like that to her.

"I don't think your father knew the scar-faced man was a Knight. Tonight is the first I'm hearing that. Who else knows?"

"Just my mom."

I narrow my eyes. "Not even Levgen?"

"No. He doesn't know the man was a Knight or anything about the strange words he spoke."

That's odd. "Why wouldn't your mom want you to tell him that? That might have helped your father's investigation." *It could have helped me.*

"My mom was terrified. She was so scared we were going to die. The Knights were going to kill us, Thorne. *Death by firing squad.*" A tear runs down her cheek. "When Levgen saved us my mom barely wanted me to mention my father's name. Every time I spoke about the scar-faced man she shut me down. She thought I would say whatever I needed to to help my father. She didn't believe me. No one believed me. They thought I made it up to help him."

"I was hardly believed, either. People thought I made up a monster to explain the disaster and the loss of my family."

She sniffles and nods. "Over the years I hated that my mom didn't want to hear anything about that horrible night. But as I got older I understood her. I was her little girl and she didn't want to watch me die like that. She wasn't even thinking about herself. In her mind my father was guilty and she was going to do whatever she could to protect me, and Levgen. He didn't need to help us."

I nod, understanding her, too. "He risked a lot."

"He did. But sometimes… I feel like I really died. I imagine feeling those bullets piercing through me. I can see myself being ripped apart, and I see my mother, too. The two of us as dead as those people were at the palace."

She pauses and wipes her tears. I walk over to her and rest my hands on her shoulders.

"It didn't happen."

"But it could have and nearly did."

"It didn't. I'm not going to let anything happen to you or your family."

"Really, Thorne?"

"I promise."

"Thank you. You'll never know how much that means to me."

"I think I do." I give her a faint smile, showing I understand. "Is there anything else you need to tell me?"

She shakes her head slowly. "No. You know everything about me now. *Everything.*"

"Then leave this with me." I pull her closer, holding her to my heart. "I will look into it further."

"What are you going to do if you've already searched the database before?"

"The two of us can start by looking through it together." I think that will make her feel better in some ways, even though it's pointless. "I don't think we'll find him but we can look. Maybe you'll see something I didn't see."

"I would really like that." She seems hopeful, then thinks for a moment. "Thorne, I thought all Knights had to be on the database. If he's not there and he's a Knight, isn't that against some law?"

"Yes, but some Knights aren't on there. There are various reasons for them to stay hidden but, oftentimes, there are some we refer to as rogue Knights. I suspect this guy is like that."

Her eyes darken with a mixture of fear and curiosity. "I don't think he was working by himself."

"Neither do I." I cup the side of her face and she places the flat of her palm to my chest. "I think someone hired him. But now that I know he's a Knight it narrows my search." Even though I still feel like I'm swimming in the ocean trying to pull the drops of water apart.

I'll need help.

Not Caspian, though. As much as I would like to tell him what I've learned tonight, and as much as he deserves to know, I can't say a word. *Not yet.*

I can't tell him because of her.

Ivy.

The moment I say one word about this he'll want to know where I got my information. I'd have to tell him her secret. Telling him her secret puts him in that position of conflict. He's supposed to be the next leader of the Knights and the next Pakhan of the Komarovski.

He'd be bound to kill her just for avoiding the death sentence.

Kill first, ask questions later.

I can't let that happen to her, so I'll say nothing to him.

The only person I can trust to help me now, and trust with Ivy's secret, is Lucian.

I just hope that maybe, maybe we can get to the bottom of this.

Finally…

CHAPTER 30

I REST AGAINST THORNE'S CHEST.

We're lying in his bed wrapped within the warmth of his sheets and each other.

It's just past three in the morning. I fell asleep in his arms and woke up over an hour ago. I haven't been able to sleep since.

I'm already an insomniac but the last two weeks have been particularly bad.

It was two weeks ago that I stood in that hotel room in Amherst with Thorne, spilling the rest of my secrets about the scar-faced man.

It was two weeks ago that we realized we both knew the man, and Thorne has been looking into the situation since.

It was another strange twist of events but on this occasion, it's left me more restless than ever because for once I have hope.

That sounds incongruent and doesn't make sense. Hope is supposed to set you at ease and make you feel positive, but I feel none of those things.

I won't feel anything of the sort until my father is free. And that still feels like a faraway dream for the lost little girl inside me.

All I have right now is the knowledge that I'm not alone anymore. Thorne knows everything, and he's done everything he could to give me that closure I wanted when Isabelle first told me about the Knights' database.

Thorne and I searched it together, even though he knew we'd find nothing, and he even showed me stuff about my father. Recent updates and pictures that were taken a few years ago.

They'd shaved Dad's head and battered him. But the worst thing was, Dad was missing an eye. I cried and cried and cried when I saw that.

Thorne did his best to comfort me, but there's only so much anyone can do. There will only be so much he can do going forward. Telling him the truth doesn't mean we fixed things. So I'm still in limbo.

I shuffle to face Thorne. My movements don't wake him. He's still out cold.

I stare at him, fascinated that even like this, in this sleep state, he projects that air of danger.

Most people, even animals, look softer, less harsh and more vulnerable in their sleep. He doesn't.

Thorne still looks like the vengeful god lying in wait to wreak havoc on anything that stands in his way or takes what belongs to him.

I never felt more like I belonged to him than in those moments back in Amherst when he held me. Something happened between us that night that felt like more than the sharing of truths and memories of darkness.

Every time I've questioned myself about my feelings for Thorne I always put up that wall in my mind to stop myself from falling for him.

I can't even see that wall now. There's not a single brick in sight, and I don't think I've been able to see the wall for a while now.

I don't even know when it came down, but I know I fell for Thorne a long time ago.

Now, as I look at him, I know I love him.

I love him.

He stirs and a shudder runs through me. It's like he heard my thoughts. I hope he didn't, because falling for him was never part of the plan.

He looks at me and caresses the top of my head.

"Bambi, you're awake." His voice is thick with sleep and sex.

"I was just thinking."

"Too much thinking again, little deer. Come here to me." He guides me to his lips and kisses me.

Thorne shuffles on top of me, then he's inside me again, pounding into my body.

I fall asleep after we come and he's kissing my neck, whispering sweet nothings in Russian to me. I drift into a dream where there's grayness and silence, then I stir when I hear voices.

The voices sound angry and rushed.

I open my eyes and am momentarily disoriented when I realize it's morning.

The bright sun is spilling through the windows onto me.

Now that I'm awake I can hear the voices better.

It's Thorne and…

Tiffany?

That can't be right.

Why would she be here in Thorne's apartment?

And what the hell could they be arguing about?

I glance at the clock on the wall. It's ten.

"This isn't fucking happening." That's Thorne. He's shouting at her.

I have to know what's going on. It's definitely not anything good.

Quickly, I get off the bed and put on my clothes. I wrap my hair in a messy bun, then take a deep breath and make my way out of the room.

As soon as I turn the corner I see Tiffany.

It's actually her.

As usual, she's dressed to the nines. Like she needs to be picture ready to sign that modeling contract from Chanel she hopes to get.

What the hell is she doing here?

I see Thorne next. He's shirtless and looks like a model, too, with his abs on show and those muscular thighs pressing against his sweatpants.

Tiffany spots me and scowls. "Good God. Look what the cat dragged in. Is that seriously what you like to fuck, Thorne?"

"Shut the fuck up," Thorne shouts at her.

"What's going on? Why are you here, Tiffany?" I glare at her. She can disrespect me all she wants at the sorority house where she's queen bee, but not here. Not in front of Thorne. "I'm sure you're not here to question Thorne's sexual preferences."

She smiles at me as if my words mean nothing. "Bitch, I am still your president. And I don't think that's any way to speak to the future Mrs. Ivanov."

My lungs collapse, trapping my next breath. Her words grip my heart like a wrench and twist. Twist until it stops beating inside my chest.

What did she just say?

"Tiffany. Get. Out." Thorne's voice is drill-sergeant stern, but I notice he didn't correct her.

"What does she mean by the future Mrs. Ivanov?" Although my voice trembles I keep my gaze fixed on him now.

"Oh, you didn't tell her, Thorne?" Tiffany laughs heartily as if she just heard the funniest joke in the world. "He's supposed to get married. To me."

I snap my gaze back to her.

"Sorry, Bambi." Tiffany gives me a condescending smirk and I see now what's so funny. The joke is me.

"I said get the fuck out. Fucking get out now." Thorne points at the door. "And don't you dare speak to her."

"Of course, my lord." The sarcasm in her voice is so lethal it's suffocating, even though she hasn't touched me. The answer is a play on the other week when Thorne told her to clean the function hall. I can tell she's absolutely loving every second of getting us both back.

But what is *this*?

What madness is this?

Tiffany turns on her heels and leaves, slamming the door behind her.

I turn back to Thorne, searching his eyes, my heart praying that she was lying.

"Is it true?" My voice is slow and muddled, as if I just made a sound without speaking any coherent words.

Thorne dips his head, breathes out a ragged sigh, and slowly looks back at me. "Yes. It's true."

Tiffany just said her piece and the truth, but I'm still just as shocked to hear it from him. The confirmation hurts me deep to my soul.

"You knew this whole time that you had to marry Tiffany?"

"No. I didn't know I had to marry her. But I knew I had to get married. My… uncle. He's forcing me to get married in order to get my position in the company after I graduate."

Tears pull at my eyes. I blink, willing them away, but I know I won't be able to hold them back. "Why didn't you tell me?"

His lips part and he attempts an answer, but then he shakes his head. "I'm sorry. I should have told you."

Humiliation builds in my chest like hot steam but instead of rising, it sinks in my stomach and freezes into a giant ball of despair.

Thorne has to marry Tiffany to take his position in a multibillion dollar company. Of course he wouldn't choose me.

Choosing me would mean he gets nothing.

"I guess you're done with me now."

"No." He steps forward.

"Yes. It's over, Thorne."

I turn to leave but he rushes forward and grabs me. "It's not fucking over. You're mine."

"Stop it. I was never yours. This was never real to you if you knew you could never keep me." My words hit the mark. His eyes fill with a sadness I'd never known he could possibly feel. "Let me go."

"Ivy." His grip tightens, hurting me.

"Let me go, Thorne. At least give me the dignity of leaving. I just found out my boyfriend is marrying someone else." I don't even know why I called him that if we were never real, but I'm glad when his fingers loosen.

The tears fall when he releases me, and I follow in the wake of Tiffany's trail. *Leaving.*

When I walk through the door my heart sinks further. My heart is aching so much I can't breathe.

It was only hours ago that I accepted that I loved Thorne. *Hours.*

How could that be and now this has happened?

I've lost him.

He has to marry Tiffany.

What's worse is everything we never spoke about.

I'm still a secret. I'm still a dead girl walking. I still have to trust Thorne to keep his silence.

According to our agreement I have no right to release myself from his ownership, but I just did.

What the hell is going to happen now?

And how did things get worse?

CHAPTER 31

Thorne

SEVERAL MINUTES HAVE PASSED SINCE IVY LEFT, BUT I'M STILL STANDING in the same spot.

The sound of the door closing as she left still echoes through my mind. The sight of her tears glistening in her beautiful eyes still pulls on my soul. The deep hurt laced within each word she spoke still pains me.

And once again I'm at that place. At the crossroads, not knowing which way to go.

Left or right. Backwards or forwards.

No matter what I choose, I'll still lose. And Ivy was right. I never had the option to keep her.

My fucking uncle struck again and, like always, he dealt his hand before I could even see what was coming.

I got the message about Tiffany from Aleksander an hour ago. He said she was such a suitable choice he didn't bother with anyone else on his list of potentials.

Tiffany found out she was to be my bride at the same time I did and was on my doorstep before the hour was up.

I didn't have time to prepare or talk to Ivy. Now I'm stuck.

Tiffany and I aren't supposed to be getting married until we graduate, but in a few weeks' time we'll officially be engaged, so Ivy was right. It's over.

It's over, and it felt like we just began. This is a fucking nightmare.

Ivy was everything to me. She *is* fucking everything.

I have to figure this out. I can't let her go.

I just can't.

She's *still* mine.

Before nightfall the whole campus knew I was to be engaged to Tiffany.

People might be scared of me but there's nothing you can do to stop the world from talking. Not even I have that power.

I didn't care about myself. Words are just words to me. Who I cared about was Ivy.

I found myself outside her window, watching her cry and willing myself not to go in and comfort her.

Resuming stalker mode, I did the same thing for the rest of the week. Watching and waiting, but I don't know what I'm waiting for. At this point I just want to be near her.

I stopped myself from going tonight because Lucian and I stumbled across some stuff to do with the scar-faced man.

We're in my apartment sitting in the living room, working through the documents we've gathered.

When he agreed to help me the first thing we sought to do was try to identify him with what we knew.

Because so much time has gone by it was harder to go through the list of people who wanted to hurt my family and set up Ivy's father. All this time the focus has been on the former.

The first thing Aleksander did when my family was killed was go through the list of all my father's enemies. Old and new at the time.

Everyone he could think of was questioned and investigated thoroughly, then he kept a keen eye on them for years. He still keeps his eyes on them.

Focusing on the scar-faced man is a new angle because we know more about him now.

Lucian and I think that those words the man spoke are some sort of a death ritual. So is the whole cutting out the hearts thing. Now we're trying to narrow down what the words mean, where they came from, and possibly what group the man might have belonged to.

"This is what I found last night." Lucian hands me a document with some Armenian and Persian words. "These are all synonymous with death. I think *valin mortilum dohaliues* is a made-up language of both those languages."

"What does it mean?" I ask, setting the document on my lap.

"I could be wrong, but it seems to translate to mean the same thing as the Knights' Oath."

And this is why I needed his help. I would have never figured that out, even if my mind were free of the shit that's happening.

"Given that we know this guy is a Knight, I think that sounds like you *are* on the right track. So, we're looking for groups that love the Armenian and Persian language?"

"Or a dead language they came from." Lucian looks like he has an idea. He moves to my computer and taps away at the keyboard.

I walk over to him. "What are you thinking?"

"There was something I came across some time ago. An incident in Uzbekistan that involved the murder of a Knight. There it is."

I see he's accessed the top secret files on the database. They talk about a mercenary group called The Hand who killed a senior Knight and his family. The Knight was an oligarch who'd just inherited some land, but there was conflict over the land's ownership. When he was killed the land went to the Mongolians.

The record states two mercenaries were killed in the attack on the Knight, and they were both Knights.

"This group—The Hand—is known to use dead languages to keep themselves secret. Kind of like how we use runes and speak Old Norse," Lucian explains. "I know it's a long shot but this could be a lead."

"We need to look into them. I guess we'll know sooner or later if we're right or wrong."

He nods. "There are some people I need to speak to."

"I'll come with you."

"No. And no offense, but some people don't take too kindly to the Ivanovs."

I raise my hands. "No offense taken. Who are these people?"

A look of discomfort washes over his face. "People my real father knew from the Italian mafia. The ones who aren't exactly allies with the Knights, but they're not enemies either. They know stuff, and they know people."

"I'll do whatever you think will work."

"Great. Then I'll take this to them and see what happens. If they de-cide to help me, it will be on the basis of who wants to speak out against this group, or not. When these people kill they're not supposed to leave any traces. That's why no one talks about them."

"I'm sure it's not going to look good on my scar-faced friend that he left witnesses behind. He would have known about me, but not Ivy."

"Yeah, but that won't stop him from coming after you. You were both safe because people thought you made him up. Now that we know he's not made up, you especially will have a target on your back. If you don't *already* have one."

"I know. I've been speaking to my own sources in the underground. Since no one is truly trustworthy, I knew from the moment I opened my mouth I'd have a target on my back. But I need to get to the bottom of this, Lucian. For myself, but more so for her. My family is dead. All I can get is justice, but she might be able to get her father back."

Lucian studies my face, analyzing me with the attention of a heart surgeon trying to save his patient. He's silent for a moment, just looking at me, then he shakes his head. "Are you seriously going to marry Tiffany?"

"Lucian. Don't ask me about that."

"How the hell do you expect me not to ask you about it?"

He's asked me before and I didn't want to talk about it. Instead I steered him to help me with the shit I found on Aleksander and my mission to find the scar-faced man.

"It looks like you've chosen Tiffany over Ivy," he points out.

"Fuck you Lucian. You know I haven't. And it's not that simple. If it were I would choose Ivy a million times." I seethe at him. "This is about the fucking company."

"I get that but your uncle had no motherfucking right to change the rules on you the way he did."

I swallow past the lump in my throat and try to think beyond the block in my mind. I know the answer to my conundrum lies with the connection I still have with the past.

"That company was the only thing my father had. If I don't fight for it, it feels like I'm letting go of the only thing he put his heart and soul into creating. That was his legacy. Aleksander is trying to take that away from me."

"I never knew your father, but when you talk about him it's always with great respect. You always say you had a home full of love."

I smirk without humor. "Didn't know you were paying attention to that."

"People like me listen because I didn't have that kind of home until my stepfather came along. I might not always get along with him but I know he loves my mother and me. If you can talk about your father with such honor, and you were only eight when he died, it means you and your family were his priority. *You* were his legacy. Not the company."

His words sink in, clearing the fog of conflict from my mind. It gives me the freedom to truly think.

I think of my father and the way he was with my mother, my sister and me. We were inseparable but my father was the glue that held us together. He spent time with our family, creating those unforgettable memories.

That is my legacy.

"I don't think your father would be happy with your uncle forcing stipulations on you, or you trying to meet them." Lucian raises a brow.

I stand, suddenly knowing what I need to do. I still have nothing to work with but Aleksander doesn't have me cornered yet.

If this were a game of chess I'd still have to make my move and keep playing to the end, even if my best pieces had been taken away from me.

The game isn't over until I'm checkmate.

That means I can still win, but I have to keep moving and find a way.

I grab my jacket.

"Where are you going?" Lucian looks me over.

"To see my uncle. We need to talk."

Lucian smiles.

It's late, so I already expected my asshole uncle to be pissed to see me at his home. The thing is, he would have been pissed at my presence anyway.

He's sitting in the living room wearing his dressing gown, watching TV.

When I walk in, the scowl on his face deepens. It's the kind of unwelcome expression you'd find on a person who's shooing away a dog with mange.

"What the hell do you want at this hour?"

"I'm not marrying Tiffany." Those words feel like a release of my soul.

Aleksander looks taken aback but there's a look of triumph lurking in the corners of his eyes.

"Did I just hear you right?"

"You did. I'm not marrying her, so you can tell her father that whatever deal you made is off the table."

"Think carefully about what you're passing up, nephew."

"I know what I'm doing."

"So you know what this means. Don't you?"

"Oh, yes, uncle. I'm well aware."

"Such a sacrifice for fresh pussy."

"Watch your words." I walk up to him and he winces, trying not to show he's afraid of me. I could kick the shit out of him right now. The way he used to beat me when I was a kid. I only hold back because of Caspian. "Don't let me kill you."

"Looks like I was right about you and Ivy Yegorov."

"Yes, you were."

"Okay, well, declining the stipulation of marriage to the girl I have chosen for you violates my terms. So, if I were to allow you to work at *my* company, all you would ever be is an errand boy." The smile he gives me is sickening.

"I will never be your fucking errand boy. And don't think this is over, or that I don't know what you're up to."

The triumphant look on his face fades. "I'm not up to anything."

"Something is always going on with you. Something's going on *now*. By trying to get rid of me, you've only attracted my attention even more. I can't wait to find out what you're hiding. Whatever it is you never wanted me to know."

He half lunges at me. "I am still your fucking leader. You will have respect."

"Of course, my lord." I borrow Tiffany's words and smile.

The asshole doesn't like my comeback one bit. *Good.* He and I are just getting started.

I'm done talking, so I leave him to stew on my defiance.

I march outside, jump on my motorcycle, and ride away from Aleksander and his miserable schemes like I have hellfire on my ass.

There are so many obstacles in the air and the tension is high now that I've declared war on my uncle.

As my leader, Aleksander will always have power over me, and the secrets I hold about Ivy could still get me killed.

I've placed myself open for attack in more ways than one. And I just gave up my chance to get my share of the company for a girl I blackmailed into being mine.

I'm such an idiot. I always had the answer. I could have ended this days ago. Maybe weeks.

This was never just about obsession or addiction.

I know myself.

I loved Ivy from the first moment I saw her.

She was always mine.

CHAPTER 32

I WALK ACROSS THE STONE PATH LEADING TO THE AUDITORIUM, FEELING like a shell of my former self.

The moon is clear and high in the sky, beaming down on the arched rooftops of the buildings around me. The clouds gather around like warships hungry for the taste of blood.

Everything feels like it's on edge. Just like me.

I remember when I first started here at Raventhorn and met Thorne.

I was so freaked out by him, but that was also because he mesmerized me, and I didn't know what to do with myself.

We've been on this roller coaster of a relationship with all sorts of things thrown at us, and now that he's out of the picture I feel lost.

Lost like I was before I got here and met him.

This has been such a difficult week.

Of course, Tiffany broadcasted the news of her upcoming engagement to Thorne. The whole campus knew from day one and everywhere I went people were looking at me. Some were laughing, some gave me looks of sympathy, some just stared at me.

I've had to sit through various social gatherings with Tiffany and her minions sniggering behind my back.

I guess that was the price I paid for being foolish and dropping evidence of who I was in the tunnel for him to find.

But more than anything, my accident was the price I paid for falling for Thorne Ivanov.

I never knew that when my mother told me to avoid anyone with the surname Ivanov, I was going to fall for one.

Surprisingly, although it feels like the world knows about Thorne and me, Mom and Levgen are none the wiser. The only times when I had to hide my relationship from them was when they were physically here, and the few times when Mom called and Thorne was with me.

I guess it doesn't matter anymore.

The only thing I should be worried about now is the whole situation with the scar-faced man. When it comes to that, I have nothing. Just Thorne. And I haven't seen him since I walked out of his apartment on Monday morning.

It's not something I can leave alone, but it's going to be hurtful to see him and not have him touch me or kiss me.

It's going to be hurtful knowing he's not mine anymore.

Pushing aside my sorrow, I enter the auditorium using the side entrance. The dim automatic lights are already on in the main section, so I assume the janitor must be here.

Oftentimes when I come by at this hour, it's just me. The place is usually silent and dark until I start playing my music.

I walk down the little hallway when, suddenly, the melodious music of my composition comes to life, playing all around me.

Someone is playing my music on the piano.

My actual composition.

I rush down the hall and into the main section of the auditorium where the grand piano sits on the elaborate stage. Behind it is Thorne, playing my music as if he composed it himself.

I stop short, staring in shock as he plays each note with elegance, grace and confidence. As if he's played my song every minute of every hour of the day.

The shock consumes me, warming my heart.

He told me it was over ten years ago that he last played and that he found it hard because it reminded him of his losses.

Hearing him play now for me lifts my soul.

Thorne looks across and stares at me with a deep fervency that makes me feel alive again.

I continue my pursuit toward him, taking the little steps that lead up to the stage.

He finishes off the piece and his fingers linger on the keys of the piano before he looks at me again.

"You're here." I speak in a whisper-soft voice.

"Yes, Bambi. I'm here."

I went through moments this past week when I would have given anything to hear him call me Bambi.

"And you know my song like you practiced it."

"That's what comes from hours of stalking you."

A shiver of heat rushes over me. You're not supposed to get turned on by
hearing that someone stalked you, but this guy is the antithesis to every rule.

The normal rules of society don't apply to him.

"You were here, watching me." I speak the words more to myself than
as a question to him.

"I was here."

"And you're here now. Should I be worried?" The dark thought crosses
my mind that he could be here about my secret.

Thorne gets up, walks over to me, and touches my face. "Your secret
dies with me." He lifts my chin and holds my gaze, staring into my eyes as
if he wants me to see into his soul and know my secrets are safe with him.

"Really?"

"Yes. I'm here to get my *girlfriend* back." Thorne gives me a brief smile
while I stare up at him and not quite believing I heard him right.

"Your girlfriend?"

"My girlfriend. I foolishly made her believe I didn't choose her when I
did. I was just conflicted. You will always come first in my life."

"But your company—"

"No. You. Just you. Only you. I love you."

My heart stops beating for a few seconds and my mind stills, trying to
take in the magical words he just spoke.

"I love you, Annika." Thorne speaks again with more conviction in his
tone, calling me by my real name. The smile that always mesmerizes me
dances across his face.

"I love you, too." The words are so easy to say. There's no confusion, no
worries, no fear. Just love. Pure love.

His smile brightens. "Then forgive me. Forgive me for making you feel
that you aren't everything to me."

I answer him with a kiss and when he kisses me back, I feel like I'm
home.

Thorne pulls me closer, slipping his hand behind my head to deepen
the kiss. Then he picks me up and sets me on top of the piano.

The malice that lights up in his eyes as he rolls my skirt up to my hips tells me he's back to his usual sexiness. And I'm about to get reacquainted with him.

"I missed this pussy." He bends and buries his face between my thighs, moving aside my panties so he can suck on my pussy lips.

My breath is already going short, seizing in my lungs from the pleasure.

"And the taste of you." He lifts his head, stares at me, and licks his lips as if I really am delicious to him.

The sight of him savoring me builds that desire low in my core.

"Thorne—"

"Shhhh. Feel this, little deer." He licks me again, then sucks hard on my clit, pulling pleasure through my body right down to the tips of my toes.

I moan out loud and my voice carries around the hall, echoing off the walls.

Thank God it's just the two of us in here, because everyone would hear me.

He sucks my clit then slides two fingers into my slick, wet opening to finger-fuck me.

Mindless moans fall from my lips and I come on his fingers. "Oh my God…"

"That's my girl."

He takes off my panties, then he shoves his pants down his hips, unleashing his cock.

Seconds later he's inside me.

God, I missed this.

I missed us.

Thorne pushes inside and I wrap my legs around his hips, locking him against me.

We both groan, then he smiles down at me and starts to fuck me.

Pleasure shatters my body. I'm already so sensitive, but my body soaks up what he gives me as if I didn't just orgasm.

Heat races across my skin and I can feel the pleasure building again.

I moan from the intensity, pressing my heels into his ass as he pounds harder into me.

"I'm going to fuck you harder, baby," he whispers over my skin, then he makes good on his word and I lose myself.

We keep going just like this for the rest of the night, taking our passion from the auditorium to his place.

We miss the next day of class, then time fizzles out and I lose track of the days as we make up for lost time.

I once heard of a crazy story about a couple who fucked each other to death.

I never believed that such a thing was possible until Thorne Ivanov.

Suddenly, it's Wednesday. Because the emails and text messages started flowing in asking where we were, we had to tear ourselves away from each other to get back to the real world.

It felt like stepping back into an alternate reality. The one good thing about it was that the campus now knew we were back together and Thorne wasn't marrying Tiffany.

The effect of that news was vastly more satisfying for me than for Tiffany when the campus thought she was going to be with Thorne.

Isabelle told me that Tiffany was so embarrassed she's retreated to Switzerland for the next two weeks.

Thorne and I meet up again for dinner. We're sitting in a booth in a quiet area of the Italian restaurant on campus. We're enjoying pizza, but we're also talking business.

There've been some new developments with Thorne's search for the scar-faced man. He'd previously told me his findings on the mercenary group called the Hand, and before we got back together, he'd been talking to a few people.

He leans on the table and plays with the end of his fork. "I found two reports with the same MO as the crimes we saw, where witnesses state they heard the killers chanting some foreign words."

"When did these incidents happen?"

"Over the last five years, and the witnesses all died mysterious deaths. One of them disappeared for three years, and their body was found in a river."

Chills rush down my spine. I'm aware that what we're delving into is dangerous. The kind of dangerous you leave alone.

"You will be careful, Thorne. Won't you?"

"Don't worry about me. I can take care of myself. You know as a Knight, I'm not exactly like most guys my age."

Because he was trained to kill.

"I know. Still, I worry."

"I'll be careful. Providing I'm on the right track with the mercenary group, the next step would be to find out who hired them."

I bring my hands together. They're sweating from nerves. This is my least favorite subject, but it's something we need to discuss. "That sounds like it might be incredibly difficult."

"It will be, but even if I only find one person they've worked with in the past, that might give me more leads." Thorne sounds optimistic. I'm using that to encourage myself. "Someone would have referred them. I just have to take things back as far as I can and hope that I get the answers we need."

"Do you think we'll really get them?"

"I have to believe we will. This is a lot further than I've ever gotten but I have to bear in mind that this is a new direction. It will present its own obstacles. I'm waiting to hear back from one of my sources."

I press my lips and my thumbs together at the same time. "I keep thinking about my father at the Hallows." I feel like I can talk a little more freely about my father now that the scar-faced man is in the picture.

Thorne reaches across the table and touches my cheek, his eyes softening. "I promise I will do everything I can to find this guy. I hope finding him will exonerate your father."

Moisture gathers in my eyes. "You sound like you believe he had nothing to do with your family's deaths."

"Yes. I don't believe he had a part in that." He nods slowly, and my heart soars.

For years I waited to hear those words. The person who could have said them to me was Mom, but she wouldn't even entertain any other truth but the one she was told.

"Thank you. That means a lot, Thorne."

"I know."

How strange that I was to stay away from anyone with the Ivanov surname, but I met the one who mattered most. He ended up believing me to the point where he's willing to help me.

"Come on, let's go back to my place. I need you again."

I smile back at him, looking forward to spending the night with him.

"I'm just gonna wash my pizza hands and I'll be right with you."

"Hurry back." He gives me a quick kiss before I get up.

I head to the ladies' restroom and wash my hands.

I thought I was alone in here, so when I hear a rustling sound at the end of the cubicle it makes me jump.

God, I'm so paranoid. I need to get ahold of myself. I'm in the bathroom, so there's nothing to worry about. I walk down the mirrored aisle to dry my hands and check my hair.

I look down at the dryer and wave my hands under it to activate it, then I look back in the mirror. And my lungs seize when I see a man standing in the far corner behind me. A closer look causes my body to turn to ice when I realize it's the scar-faced man staring back at me.

He smiles, and it's the most gruesome sight.

I'm momentarily frozen, but I'm compelled to turn around and check that what I'm seeing is real.

In the split second it takes for me to turn my head and look, he's gone.

Literally gone. Like I imagined him being there.

But I know I didn't.

I saw him. And he saw me.

Oh my God… *he knows me.*

CHAPTER 33

Thorne

I HAVE LUCIAN AND THE CAMPUS SECURITY SCOURING THE GROUNDS for that motherfucking fuck.

If he's here I'll find him, but I know in my heart that monster is gone.

I won't even bother to question how he got on campus without anyone seeing him. All Knights know about the secret tunnels. And if you're tech savvy, you'd know how to rig the cameras to your advantage.

I want to join the men but right now I have to take care of Ivy. She's a nervous mess.

We've just arrived back at my place. I'm in the kitchen making her some herbal tea that Caspian's mom used to make for us to calm us down.

When I'm done, I take it out to the living room to Ivy.

She looks worse in the few minutes that I've been gone.

"Drink this. It will help with the shock." I hand the tea to her and she takes it with trembling hands. Her hands are shaking so much I fear the tea might spill in her lap.

It nearly does, so she sets the cup down on the coffee table.

"I'm sorry. I just need… a moment," her voice rattles out in a stammer.

"Of course. Drink it in a few minutes." I sit next to her and pull her into my chest.

"I can't believe it, Thorne. I can't believe it. He knows me."

"This is my fault."

"Don't say that."

"It has to be. Someone must have reported back to the man that I'm looking for him." And he came after her because of me.

But does he actually *know* her?

I've never told her secret to anyone except Lucian. She doesn't even know that he knows. I didn't tell her because I didn't want her to worry. She doesn't know Lucian like I do, so there's no basis for trust.

Outside of him, I've been careful with my words.

"I wish I could say I imagined that man, but I didn't. He was right there in the bathroom with me. Then he was gone."

It seems that he used the side door. I checked the bathroom myself after Ivy told me she saw him.

"He was on campus, Thorne. Right here on campus."

"That means I smoked him out and he's in Boston. We can find him and get to the bottom of everything."

Terror fills her eyes, but I also read hope. She knows I'm right, and as bad as this incident was, it means I'm on the right track.

The motherfucker *is* part of that mercenary group, and now he's on my turf.

"What are you going to do?"

"Don't worry about me. Drink the tea, then I want you to get some sleep. You hear me?"

She nods and picks up the cup again to drink the tea.

An hour later, I get her to sleep, and I talk with Lucian. He and the men found evidence that someone had been in the secret tunnels and the cameras were tampered with, but the trail has run cold.

No surprise there. That's okay. I won't stop looking for him.

Now that the scar-faced man has presented himself, vengeance is rippling through me.

I just have to backtrack my activities over the past week to who I spoke to. One of them alerted the scar-faced man about me.

When I get off the phone with Lucian I fire off a message to Kai.

Although I have him watching Aleksander, I talked to him about the scar-faced man, too. He was helpful in giving me intel about the mercenary group, as were Lucian's people. It was them who found the reports of the other incidents.

Kai messages back confirming he'll look into this on his side, then another message comes through from an unknown number.

Thinking it's campus security, I open it and my blood heats when I read the words:

If you don't stop searching for the scar-faced man death will follow.

My entire body goes rigid. I stare at the message for a few seconds until it disappears from the screen.

The fucking message is gone. I search the phone's inbox and deleted files, but it's not there. It's vanished.

"The fucking message was sent in vanish mode," I explain to Lucian as we walk across the docks.

We're heading to Kai's. He might have some information for us. The sort we needed to meet in person to get. He called me a few hours after the cryptic message came through.

"Did they just send it as a text to your number, or was it in an app?"

"It was a text. Whoever sent it has some elaborate encryption wrapped around the source code so I can't track the number. Every time I unlock the encryption it recreates another code that's harder to unlock."

Lucian frowns and bites the inside of his lip. "Let me have a go at it. It sounds like you need to find a way to isolate the encryption with a virus or something."

"I fucking tried that. It didn't work. Their code also has some sophisticated antivirus code protecting it."

"I might still be able to find a way around it. My viruses are a little more whacked up than yours. Also, you're not yourself."

I don't argue because I'm not myself at all and I'm thinking straight at all. Right now, I feel like shit run over by a speeding rocket. Of course I'm not thinking straight. Everything is all over the place in a colossal mess, so I'm taking longer than I usually would to accomplish things.

"Okay, see what you can do." I nod.

"Did you tell Ivy about the message?"

"No. She was still asleep when I left." My guards are with her. I have men inside and outside the apartment. "I'm not telling her."

"That's perhaps for the best."

"I want to see if I can wrap this up without involving her. Today was too much, and now that I have whoever this person is warning me, I feel like I need to find that fucker even faster."

Lucian casts me a wary glance. "This has gotten crazy, Thorne. Obviously I'll help you with whatever you need, but are you sure you shouldn't tell Caspian? And maybe take precautions because of the warning?"

I'm already shaking my head before he can finish the sentence. "Not yet.

Not until I absolutely have to. Caspian mustn't know Ivy's secret. And as for the warning…" My voice trails off as I think about it. "I might be a fool for not heeding it, but I need the truth."

"Okay, I just wanted to check."

"Finding this guy means retribution for me. He'll lead me to whoever hired him to kill my family, and I'll be able to free Ivy's dad, too. But I can't just involve Caspian right now because things are too complicated."

"Okay. We also have to figure out who sent the message, because they know what we're up to, which means we're being watched."

"I know." The hard truth that I had eyes on me hit the moment Ivy told me she saw the man in the bathroom.

We continue down the path to Kai's club. Everything is like it was weeks ago when I brought Caspian here.

Kai's men search us and when they're done, Kai smiles.

"You owe me, Ivanov. I have a little treat for you. My little bird found a spider in the garden."

"You found a spy."

"I certainly did." He nods. "Follow me."

I glance at Lucian, feeling hopeful.

Kai leads us through the doors. Instead of heading to the room he took us to last time, we descend a set of stairs into a dungeon.

There's a man tied to a lone chair in the middle of the room. The man is beaten so badly blood has turned his shirt red.

His face is a battered mess and there are bald spots on his head where his hair has been ripped out.

"This is a spy for The Hand." Kai points to the man. "The cameras picked him up in here the other day when you came by. My allies also found footage of him at other places you'd visited. We realized the culprit who told The Hand you were looking for one of their assassins had to be him."

Kai, Lucian and I walk around to face the man. He lifts his head to stare at us. When his eyes lock on mine, he smiles, revealing missing teeth.

Yes, this is definitely the motherfucker who ratted me out.

"What the fuck are you smiling at?" I get up in his face.

"You being here. You don't even realize that you've already lost."

I throw a fist in his face and he howls with pain. "Don't stop there. Why don't you tell me just how I've lost."

"We'll kill you and turn your little girlfriend into a whore. We'll pass her around so the men can take turns fucking her."

I knock the rest of his front teeth down his throat. The man spits blood and shouts from the pain. I ball my fist to punch him again but Lucian grabs my arm. Had he not done so, the man would be dead.

"We need him alive, Thorne." Lucian tightens his grip on my arm.

"You won't get shit from me." The man laughs.

I try to calm the fuck down so I can ask him my questions. "Who is the man with the scar? And where is he?"

"Fuck you."

"Wrong answer." Another punch lands in his face, but it's nowhere as hard as it could have been.

"Perhaps this will give him some encouragement." Kai taps my shoulder and presents me with my gun. I had to hand it over when we were searched. I take it and nod my thanks. "You may also want this. This is our guest's father." He shows me a picture of an elderly man in a wheelchair.

On seeing the picture the man's eyes bulge like they might leap out of his head. "No. Please. Not my father."

"Not so cocky now, are you?" I give him a maddening smile. "Ready to tell me what I want to know?"

"They'll kill me."

"I'll kill you *and* your father. How about that?"

"Okay, okay. But please don't hurt my father."

"Start talking, motherfucker." I slap his face with the back of my gun, making him shout out again.

"The man with the scar is called Salvatore. I don't know where he is, but I last saw him at the Grunge Club. He knows the owner. It's possible he's staying there."

"How the fuck did he know I was looking for him?"

"The Hand gets an alert when people start digging around for them. It could have been something as simple as a Google search notification. They know even if you have firewalls up."

So, they knew from the moment Lucian and I started searching, but it would have been easy to narrow things down because they would have known about me. Maybe they always had their eye on me.

"How many men does our scar-faced friend have with him?"

"I don't know information like that."

"How do you contact him?"

"I don't. He contacts me when he needs me." He coughs.

"Where does he think you are now?"

"My hotel. I told him I was going to be there all night."

"Perfect, so he doesn't know you're here." I raise a brow, and the man stares back at me, his eyes pleading.

"No… he doesn't."

"All the better." I flip my gun and shoot him between his eyes just as he's taking a breath. Now he will never take another. I never promised to spare his life. If I'd let him go he'd only raise the alarm again.

"We can get a head start without the scar-face knowing now." I stand straighter and wipe blood off me.

"The Hand are not people to mess with, young one," Kai warns, looking from me to the dead man in the chair.

"Neither am I." I shove my gun back in my pocket. "Keep your eyes open for me and I'll make sure you get whatever you want. This is a big deal."

"Of course."

I pray I've bought us some time. Anything is better than not knowing where to turn next. Now we have a lead.

Or not…

The Grunge Club is closed and cleared out by the time we get there. Someone must have been watching our dead friend back at Kai's.

I can tell people must have left in a hurry. There are half-empty beer bottles and half-eaten food on the tables in the restaurant section.

I head back to my apartment with a heavy heart. Thankfully, Ivy is still asleep and sleeps through the night.

I wake up before her the next morning and make her breakfast. When she walks into the kitchen wearing my miles-too-big shirt, she looks like a little forest creature. She has that doe-eyed look when she stares at me that makes her appear more vulnerable.

She smiles at me and the color returns to her cheeks when she notices the food on the table.

"Oh, wow. This looks delicious."

"I hope it tastes as good as it looks." I pull her into my arms and kiss her. "How are you feeling?"

"Just… I'm still shaken. I slept through the night, though, so I guess your tea must have worked."

"Good. Get something to eat and I'll take you out. I thought we could drive into the city and go for a walk in the park." I'm trying to take her mind off the situation, but truthfully, I need the distraction, too.

I'm supposed to be in a computer science class in an hour but there's no way I can deal with seeing Aiden today. Since I removed myself as his competition in the company he hasn't bothered me, but he still reminds me of the messy situation with my uncle.

Caspian was livid about the whole thing. Not because I chose Ivy but because I essentially allowed his father to win. I assured him that I hadn't given up and choosing Ivy *was* my win.

Ivy gives me a weak smile and stands on her tiptoes to kiss my chin. "I'd love to go to the park. Are you sure we can?"

"Yes. We just need to be back for later. I'm meeting Lucian." He's working on finding out where the warning message came from. I'll join him later. Hopefully he'll crack the code. It will be one less thing to solve and possibly another lead. "We can leave as soon as we're done here."

"Great. A walk in the park is just the thing I need."

"Perfect."

We eat breakfast, get ready, and leave.

Within the hour we're walking through the public gardens hand in hand. Like this, we feel like a normal couple. A couple like the others here enjoying the day.

My mind, however, is a battlefield. Last night's disaster has left me in a state of flux. The only information I got from last night was the scar-faced man's name.

I glance at Ivy and take in the trouble in her expression. She looks like she's doing her best not to be terrified.

"I'd like us to join Caspian and Willow for Thanksgiving." The holiday is three weeks away.

Ivy snaps her attention to me with her eyes wide. "You would?"

"Yeah. It would be fun. Don't worry, my uncle won't be there. He's going to be away." Her parents are going to be away, too, which is why I thought I'd ask her to join us.

"I'll join you. I've hung out with Willow a few times with Eilish and the girls. She seems cool. Not that Caspian isn't. I just mean—"

"I know what you mean." I chuckle.

"I want to tell my parents about us. But my mom… she's…"

"Wary of the Ivanovs," I fill in.

"How did you know?"

"I just did." I remember when I first met Ivy and told her my name she was more scared than most people to hear it. When I learned the truth about her, I figured her mother would have warned her about my family.

The sound of a speeding car turns my attention to the path across from us. This is part of the park so there aren't supposed to be any cars down here, but a black Ferrari is speeding toward us as if it's competing in the Grand Prix.

My senses kick into overdrive, so I pull Ivy closer to me as we continue walking.

The car gets close and the blacked-out window of the driver's side rolls down, then all I see is a gun pointing at us.

As the spray of bullets flies I grab Ivy. She screams and the sound fuels the terror in my soul.

A bullet rips through my arm, but I hold on to her as I propel us over the side of the bridge.

There are screams from the people around us as we land in the water. Then we're going down.

I don't know how deep the water goes, but I manage to gain control of our momentum and swim back up to the surface.

As Ivy and I emerge, I realize she's unconscious.

"Ivy." I frantically check her to see if any of the bullets hit her, and that's when I find the blood trickling down the side of her head.

CHAPTER 34

Thorne

IVY HIT HER HEAD…

It could have been worse.

She could have died, and it's all my fucking fault.

I don't even know if I was already too late to heed the warning from the message. The guy last night told me I'd already lost.

So maybe I was already too late.

Maybe I'd lost the game the moment I stirred the nest and started looking for the scar-faced guy—*Salvatore.*

Clearly I'm way in over my head again.

I'm sitting next to Ivy's hospital bed. We've been here for the last four hours. She woke up briefly and spoke to me before she fell asleep again.

The doctors have been running tests to check for any more damage.

Ivy has a concussion. She hit her head badly, so the doctors want to keep her overnight for observation. I don't know when it happened but it must have been as we were going over the bridge.

When I looked at her in the water, I thought she was dead. I thought she got shot, and my world ended. It wasn't until I got her out of the water that I realized she had a head wound.

A bullet grazed my arm. I was lucky, too, but I'm not worried about myself. I've been shot before. This is nothing in comparison to the past.

Right now, I just want Ivy to be okay.

I told Lucian what happened. And I had to call Ivy's parents, too. They got on the first available flight so they're on the way here now. I don't know how I'm going to face them.

The doctors wanted to call them, but I felt it was more appropriate for me to do it.

It was strange speaking to her mom. All the guilt in the world rested on my soul as she cried. I never imagined that my first words to Ivy's mother would be: *'Sorry, your daughter is in the hospital. She got caught in a drive-by shooting.'*

Fuck my life. Nothing is going right. Even the good things are a struggle.

I don't know where to begin, but I'm going to fix this.

Things have just become more dangerous than I ever imagined. I always know what to do but I feel like my wings have been clipped.

Ivy wakes up an hour later. She looks more alive in her face but the terror is back in her eyes. I don't have to explain to her what happened. She remembers.

She bursts into tears when she looks at the bandage wrapped around my arm.

"This is all my fault," she chokes out. "I shouldn't have told you anything."

I touch her cheek. "Don't you dare say that."

"It's true. I should have known how dangerous this could be and kept my mouth shut."

"I would have found a way to make you talk."

"It's still my fault. I feel like I should never have gone to Raventhorn."

"I wouldn't have met you." I stroke the side of her cheek.

"Maybe that would have been better."

"No. It wouldn't have." I shake my head and give her a small smile. "You're mine, remember that. Now I'm going to keep you safe."

"I need to keep you safe, too."

"It's not your job to do that." I smirk. "Stop worrying. Your parents are on the way."

Her breath catches. "I have to tell them the truth. I have to."

"It's probably best. Try to get some rest."

She relaxes against her pillows. The lost look in her eyes tugs on my insides.

Her parents arrive just before nightfall, and it's awkward as fuck.

Ivy's mom walks in first, catching me just as I kiss her daughter. I was about to go out to get Ivy some chocolate.

Ivy's mom looks surprised while Levgen casts me a knowing look. The kind that says he knows his daughter is in the hospital because of me.

I decide to give them some privacy and wait outside. I'm not leaving, though.

I head to the waiting room nearby.

Half an hour later Levgen comes in to find me.

His face shows the same stern expression as before, but there's also wariness in his eyes. I don't know if that's because of who I am or because Ivy must have told him I know their secret.

I stand when he gets close.

"How's your arm?" He glances at my wound.

"I'll live."

"Ivy told me what happened. She told me everything. And I'm aware of what you know."

"I see."

"Thank you for keeping her secret. Given who your uncle is, I would have never expected that of you."

"I love her." I would have said something safer, like I care about her or something along those lines, but now isn't the time to tread softly. I want him to understand that I didn't mean for anything to happen to Ivy.

Levgen looks surprised by my confession but his prior sternness returns. "If that's true, then you can't put her in danger ever again."

"I didn't mean to."

"This was a drive-by shooting, Thorne. You both could have been killed. I could have been flying here to identify my daughter's body in the morgue. Please think about that."

The image of Ivy lying on a morgue slab devastates my soul. "I won't put her in danger again."

"Ivy told me about the man with the scar on his face. She said you're investigating him. If he truly belongs to the group she told me about, then it won't end here." He swallows and his jaw clenches. "They will keep coming for you. So you cannot keep going as you are. This is above you."

"But I have to do something."

"Let me take over. Send me everything you have. I'll get my team to look into it. My guards are here and I'm here. I won't let anything happen to my little girl."

I want to resolve this situation myself. But... maybe I should listen this time, to keep Ivy safe. I remember the moment when I thought she was dead.

Her body was limp in my arms and she'd gone ghostly pale. I can't allow that to happen again.

"Okay. I'll send you what I have tonight." I nod, feeling defeated.

"Good. We have to do whatever we can now to find this guy. I know what finding him means to you, too. Is Ivy's secret still safe?"

"It's safe."

"We owe you for that, Thorne Ivanov. You have given us a lead we never thought we'd find. We may even be able to get Ivy's father out of prison. We owe you for everything."

I dip my head respectfully to acknowledge his gratitude, but I feel like a failure.

CHAPTER 35

"CONCUSSIONS CAN MAKE YOU FEEL REALLY SICK." THE NURSE GIVES Mom and me a sympathetic smile. "If you feel any nausea or discomfort, please let us know."

"Thank you. I will," I answer.

"Get some rest. You're going to need it. I'll come back to check on you later."

I nod and instantly regret it. My head still feels like it's going to fall off. I've been given mild painkillers but all they did was take the edge off.

It's better to feel the pain than being dead. Nothing can describe the terror I felt when I saw that gun and heard the bullets flying. I didn't see the shooter but I guessed it was someone to do with the scar-faced man.

That was the second time in my life I'd been in danger. This time Thorne saved me.

Mom and I watch the nurse leave.

I gaze out the door when she walks through it, hoping I can catch a glimpse of Thorne and Levgen.

Levgen went outside to speak to Thorne before the nurse came in. He hasn't been gone long, but it feels like forever.

Visiting hours will be over soon. Thorne has been with me the whole time but I hope to see him again. And I want to know what Levgen said to him.

I told my parents everything, so all the secrets are laid out on the table.

The door swings shut and I look back at my mother.

I know she's mad at me. Of course she would be. I did everything she told me not to do. I awakened an assassin, put myself and our family in serious danger by exposing our secret, and I lied. I lied terribly.

I'm mad at myself, and I'm also embarrassed that Mom got the confirmation that Thorne is my boyfriend when she walked in on us kissing. As if things weren't bad enough.

I saw the way she looked at his tattoos. Especially the dragon on his neck. Then there were the ones all over his left arm. The arm that got grazed by a bullet.

She's used to the two little Knight tattoos Levgen has on the underside of his wrist, but to her, Thorne must have looked like the rebel.

My mother is not showing her true emotions only because I'm lying in a hospital bed. She's glad I didn't die.

"I'm sorry," I mumble, keeping my gaze on her.

She's looking at me, too, her eyes filled with so many emotions it hurts me. I see worry, terror, grief and disappointment. That last one really hits hard.

"I wish you'd told me what was going on. Now that I know you've been dating Thorne Ivanov I understand why you were so secretive."

"I didn't mean to be." I try to sit up, even though my head is protesting in pain. It feels too awkward to talk to her about something so serious while I'm lying down.

"I don't know him."

"But I do."

"Sweetheart, you are young."

"Maybe so, but I know what my heart tells me."

"Thorne's uncle is the man who sentenced us to death. How can you think that we are safe now?"

I have to believe what my heart whispers to me. That Thorne would never expose us. "It's been months since he found out about us. He could have told his uncle who we really were, but he didn't. He put himself in danger to find that man who set Dad up."

"You don't know what men can be like. Your father…" Her voice trails off and her breath hitches. She looks close to tears but I know she'll do everything she can to hold back like she always does.

"Dad didn't do what you think he did, Mom. He didn't."

"He hurt me deeply. Every time I think of him I remember him running back to the palace, leaving me all alone to protect you. I loved him so much. And… I never stopped." Her voice drops to that low whisper I'm used to when she talks about my father.

It's like she's scared the walls will hear her. The only person the walls could tell her secrets to is Levgen. So I understand why she sounds like that. It's because she doesn't want to be disrespectful to the man who risked his life to save us.

"Your father wasn't there when I needed him most. He chose to go back and leave us. For his loyalty, we lost him, and we could have died."

I search the gloom in her eyes and try to find light, but there's none. "Mom, I understand you. I understand how you feel but I don't think Dad meant for any of this to happen. That's why he made sure we were safe before he went back."

She stares back at me for a moment before giving me a clipped nod, and it feels like a eureka moment. This is the first time ever that I've gotten something so positive out of her toward my father.

"Let's stop talking about this now." She sniffles. "It can't be good for you. You need to rest."

"I can't rest when so much is going on."

"You should try."

The door opens and Thorne and Levgen enter the room. My spirits lift and I wish I could run into Thorne's arms.

Mom watches him carefully when he walks to my side, then she watches both of us.

"Visiting hours are over, so I'll be back first thing in the morning." Thorne touches my cheek.

"Are you going to be okay?"

"Of course. Don't worry about me."

I glance at the bandage around his arm, my heart shrinking away when I think that bullet could have hit his heart.

I don't care how badly my head hurts or who's watching me, I throw my arms around him and hug him hard.

"Thank you for saving me," I whisper into his ear.

"Anytime, Bambi."

We pull apart and he gives my mother a curt nod. "Mrs. Yegorov."

"Take care." I'm glad Mom speaks, even though her tone wreaks of caution.

Thorne and Levgen exchange glances, as if they are in silent agreement over something I'm not privy to, and then he's gone.

The moment he leaves, I feel lost again.

I worry whether he'll be safe.

I have my parents, but Thorne doesn't have anyone like that to look out for him.

I see Thorne for a little while the next day.

Like he promised, he's here first thing in the morning. But then it's time to leave the hospital.

Levgen booked us into a little cottage in Charlestown to stay for the week. I don't need to be out of college for such a long time, but Levgen and Mom are worried about my health and safety.

They have a doctor on call and the cottage is heavily guarded.

The story we're going with is that we had a family emergency. No one knows Thorne and I were involved in the incident yesterday, and we're keeping it that way.

Levgen told me that he's taken over the investigation of the scar-faced man.

Although I feel better knowing that he'll be looking into the matter from here on, and Thorne would be safer handing everything over to Levgen, it's still unsettling.

I spend most of the day in bed. Having a concussion is no fun at all. I have moments of extreme dizziness in which I feel like I'm going to fall and fall and don't stop falling. Then there's the pain in my head from the actual wound.

It feels like there's a hole there.

By nightfall, I feel slightly better, so I decide to sit by the window and do some composing.

I miss Thorne. He's called and sent messages but I miss seeing him.

I hate that I'll be stuck here for the next week and I'll only see him when he comes by. I miss my friends, too.

I messaged Isabelle and Mackenzie to let them know about my *family emergency* so they wouldn't worry.

I stare out the window, look at the guards by the trees in the garden and the full moon high in the sky.

I'm safe, but why do I still feel that spine-tingling sensation that I'm being watched?

Watched by the scar-faced man.

I can't see him but I feel like he's out there somewhere.

I feel like it's just a matter of time before I see him again.

CHAPTER 36

Thorne

THE MOON SHINES BRIGHTLY IN THE SKY TONIGHT, AND THERE'S NOT a cloud in sight.

Maybe the heavens wanted to witness the ritual of the Reckoning for themselves. The original Knights believed the gods would look down from Valhalla during this trial and handpick their chosen ones.

I'm standing on the peak of the Saddle Ball Mountains with Caspian and Lucian. The three of us are dressed in our Knights tunics, but we're wearing a black sash on our shoulders. The mark that's worn to represent life and death. Apart from the ritual of the Reckoning, it's also worn by executioners.

The Reckoning represents the true birth of a Knight and the death of the old self.

I put all my worries and the events of the last few days aside to be in top form tonight.

Of the eight pledges who were sent into the rough terrain for tonight's trial, four stand before me. The four I was confident would succeed from the get-go:

Kade, Dmitri, Logan and Alek.

Tonight they were pitted against the Bratva task force and a pack of ravenous wolves while they attempted to catch two prisoners.

Blood must be spilt in this ritual, so we were given Bratva prisoners who were sentenced to death for murdering an orphanage full of children.

Our pledges retrieved the prisoners, and now they have them bound and gagged at my feet, ready for me to give the final command to complete the mission. To kill.

I look at them—Kade, Dmitri, Logan and Alek—raw-faced and bloodied. I thought my Reckoning in Russia was fucked up, but what I did to them for the last six hours will forever leave a mark.

To me, the other four might have tried, but they didn't make the cut because they didn't want it as much as these four did.

Tonight was the only night where no one was assigned to a group, but these four found each other and worked together to make sure they all got here.

Put simply, they understood the assignment of life and death, and it will bond them for the rest of their lives.

The other four are yet to make it back. As they have failed, I am no longer responsible for the condition they return to us, dead or alive.

"*V etu noch' vy stanovites' muzhchinami. Zapechatay yego svoyey zhertvoy,*" I speak in Old Norse, which translates to 'On this night, you become men. Seal it with your sacrifice.'

I look at Kade, who reminds me so much of myself and stares at me as he slashes the throat of the prisoner at his feet.

Alek has been given the task of killing the second prisoner. The group assigned him with that task, not me. They think they decided this to distribute the tasks evenly, but I know they did it to make sure he's on par with them. They've been a pack for years and have only just accepted him into their fold, so watching him kill will test him.

The group doesn't realize that Alek knows exactly what they're up to, and he's potentially more deadly alone than they are together as a group. He's the kind of man who will do whatever he needs to do to get what he wants.

That's why he doesn't just slice his prisoner's throat from ear to ear the way Kade did. Alek uses the sword on his back and rams it straight through the prisoner's throat. And he does it with a sadistic smile on his face.

"Well done, men." Caspian steps forward. "You've worked hard and I am happy to select the four of you to be part of my elite. From this night onward we are brothers in arms bounded by the Oath. Take the bodies away. I will see you back on campus."

"Yes, my Lord." They speak in unison, bowing their heads.

They proceed to take the bodies away, and Caspian, Lucian and I look at each other.

It's over.

We picked our elite, and now we have the task of being the elite.

"Any thoughts, guys?" Caspian looks from me to Lucian.

"Not from me," Lucian replies. "I'll go pack up the stuff."

"I'll join you," I say, falling in step with him.

Lucian wanted to talk about the warning message. He has a contact from Markov Tech checking it out. They're a company within our alliance. I might have given Levgen everything to investigate himself, but that doesn't stop me from finding out where that message came from.

"Actually, cousin, I'd like a word," Caspian calls out to me.

I stop in my tracks. Lucian glances back at me, offering a look of support. We both knew Caspian would want to speak to me at some point. I've been dodging him for days.

It was three days ago that the incident occurred. Prior to that, I'd seen him just after Ivy and I got back together. That's a long absence for us.

I turn back to face him.

His expression is stern with that no-nonsense look he sports when he knows I'm keeping something from him.

It's particularly bad tonight because I've never kept anything from him for this long.

"Hey, what's going on?" I try to make my voice sound like my usual jovial self. The carefree guy who thought he had the world at his fingertips.

"How about you tell me?"

"Nothing to tell."

"Don't insult me with that bullshit." His voice rises and his face hardens, showing the depth of his frustration. "Thorne, I take you for a brother. You and I have been closer than I was with Zak."

His words are like a punch to my gut and I feel like shit. Because he's right.

Zak was his older brother. When he was alive he was the best brother anyone could ask for, but he and Caspian never shared the closeness that we have.

"You haven't been the same since you've been with Ivy. I know something's going on with you and I wish to God you would tell me."

I stare back at him, wanting to share it all with him, but everything goes back to keeping Ivy's secret.

It's not that I don't trust him, but it's not as simple as that.

"There is something going on." I swallow past the rocks in my throat.

"What is it?"

"I can't tell you right now."

His brows snap together. "What the fuck does that mean?"

"It means what I said. I can't tell you right now."

"But—"

"Caspian. There are some things I can't give you, and I'm asking you to trust me to tell you when I can. Please. Do this for me. I swear to you, on the Oath, that I will tell you the first chance I get."

He sets his shoulders back, lifts his chin, and stares me down like he's going to fight, but then his jaw loosens and he nods. It's with reluctance, but he nods.

"By the Oath, you swear."

"By the Oath, *I* swear."

"I'll remember that. I'm not happy about it, though."

"I know."

We walk back to the cars in silence and pack up our stuff before we head back to campus.

It's only nine. Not that the time matters these days. But now that I'm by myself, I think of Ivy.

Today was the first since she left the hospital that I didn't see her.

I wanted to give her parents a break from me. Her mother in particular is very uncomfortable around me.

I'd head to the Verge and get a drink, but I can't bear it tonight. I'd either have some girl trying to rub her tits in my face, or I'd run into the new elite partying.

My phone rings, piercing through the silence of my apartment.

It's Lucian.

We didn't get to talk earlier because Caspian was around. I tried calling him when I first got back but his phone was switched off, so I sent him a text.

I grab my phone from the coffee table and answer. "Hey, man."

"Where are you?" There's a serious edge to his voice that piques my attention.

"My apartment. What's going on?"

"I found a whole bunch of stuff for you. It's…not good, Thorne. None of it."

My scalp tightens with the trepidation of what he could have found. "What did you find, Lucian?"

"Answers to everything. It's Levgen, Thorne. The message came from him. But he's behind it all, and he might have put Ivy and her mother in danger. He was the one who hired the scar-faced man for both attacks. He had your family killed."

CHAPTER 37

M Y FINGERS RACE ACROSS THE PIANO KEYS, STIRRING THE MUSIC TO life.

Mom and Levgen wanted me to play my latest composition, so they've gathered here in the living room to listen to me.

Even though fear clings to the air, in the quaint little cottage the music sounds homey and the warmth of love surrounds us.

I finish my piece and they applaud.

"That was beautiful," Levgen says.

"Absolutely beautiful." Mom agrees with tears glistening in her eyes. "I don't know what I did to get such a talented daughter."

"Oh, Mom, thank you. It's not finished yet."

"But it sounded like something from heaven." She moves toward me and hugs me, then plants a kiss on my forehead.

"How about I get us some chocolate cake before we head to bed?" Levgen suggests, smiling proudly at both of us. "It's been a long day."

"Sure thing." Mom lets out a light chuckle.

She seems more at ease today. I don't want to think it's because Thorne didn't come by. She's still wary of him, which is understandable, but at least she hasn't tried to stop me from seeing him. I wouldn't stop, but it gives me hope that she'll warm up to him someday.

Levgen leaves us and Mom sits on the stool next to me.

She's barely left my side since we've been staying here.

Today she took me shopping and when we got back Levgen took us sailing on the river. I was feeling a lot better, so they wanted to make the most of the time they had with me. It was nice but there were moments when I just wanted to lie down.

"How are you feeling?" Mom asks.

"I'm still the same as five minutes ago when you asked." I giggle.

"It wasn't five minutes ago. It was more like ten." Mom's eyes twinkle with humor. "Okay, I see your point."

"I'm fine, Mom. Just tired now."

"Yeah, me too. I think we overdid it today."

"It was great spending time with you, though."

"And you. It was nice to hear you play your new piece, too. When we found this cottage and saw the piano we couldn't help but take it. The cottage is actually going on the market. We were thinking of buying it so we could be close to you."

"Mom, you don't have to do that."

"We wouldn't move from L.A. as such, but it would be nice to visit more often and have a place of our own to come to. You could also use it as a getaway whenever you want."

"Okay. Whatever makes you worry less about me."

The distress I've witnessed over the last few days returns to her eyes. "I will always worry about you. Now more than ever. I don't want you to go back to Raventhorn, or *anywhere*, but I know I can't keep you locked away in a tower forever."

I wish I could tell her I'll be safe, but I can't. I can't promise her such a thing when I don't know what's happening. Levgen hasn't told me anything more since we got here, so I feel clueless.

"Please try not to worry. Levgen is looking into everything. He knows what he's doing." At least my reassurance seems to calm her.

The doorbell rings, interrupting her next words. We look at each other, both of us wondering who that could be at this time of night.

It's nearly eleven.

"I'll get it." I push to my feet.

"Wait, maybe let Levgen answer the door. We don't know who it is."

"Mom, there are fifteen guards outside. And I don't think anyone who wants to harm me would ring the bell."

"Okay… I guess you're right."

I saunter away and answer the door. When I open it, I'm so glad that I insisted on getting the door. It's Thorne.

I'm so excited to see him that I throw my arms around him. "Oh my gosh, you're here."

"I'm here, Bambi." He holds me as if this is the first time we've seen each other in centuries.

When he releases me he cups my face and I notice the deeply troubled look in his eyes straight away. He's also carrying a big envelope.

"Are you okay?"

"Where are your mom and Levgen?"

I notice that he didn't answer the question, but he doesn't look okay. "They're out back."

"I need to speak to them. I need you there, too."

"What's going on, Thorne?"

"I'll tell you in a minute."

"Okay. Come with me."

I lead him to the living room where Mom is. Levgen walks in after us carrying a tray holding several slices of cake.

The venomous look Thorne gives Levgen sends a cold shiver through me. I've never seen him look at anyone like that. Not even Aiden when he threatened to kill him.

The look is so potent that Levgen sets down the tray.

"Is everything okay, Thorne?" He looks him up and down. "It's late—"

"Fourteen years ago my father commissioned you for business on a hedge fund. The two of you worked together for years before that."

I glance at Levgen. I wasn't aware that he knew Thorne's father.

"I work with many members of the Knights' council."

"Yeah, you did. Except my father was the one who put your company on the map. Your wealth grew exponentially after that. Sure we all want a piece of the pie, but what my father didn't know was that you were working your way up to become a senior Knight. To do that you needed to possess a certain net worth."

"Where's this going, son?"

Thorne shakes his head. "Don't do that. Don't call me son."

"Thorne, what's this about?" I cut in, curiosity getting the better of me.

His eyes soften for a fleeting moment when he looks at me but quickly return to their previous hardness.

"When my parents found out Levgen was stealing from his clients they threatened to expose him, so he hired an assassin to have them killed. He wanted the entire family dead."

"What is he saying?" Mom steps forward and looks at Levgen, then at Thorne. "Thorne, Levgen would never do that."

"It's the truth."

"This is nonsense," Levgen speaks up.

"Levgen, don't fucking deny the truth. I have all the proof right here." Thorne holds up the envelope and pulls out a few documents. "These are encrypted emails between you and the mercenary group." He throws the documents on the floor at Levgen's feet.

"This is the contract for thirty million that you signed with them to kill my family." Thorne throws more paperwork down. "This is the fucking contract you signed with them for fifteen million to plant false evidence at the palace when you set up Ivy's father. And this is a fucking picture of you and the scar-faced man."

My lungs lock and the fibers of reality slip from my grasp leaving the air around me thick like tar.

Levgen set Dad up. It was him all along.

Him.

Thorne holds up the picture and the contract for us all to see and Mom looks like she might fade away to nothing.

Defeat has stolen the strength from Levgen's expression and he looks cornered.

Cornered and trapped in shock that Thorne could have found out his dark, dirty secrets.

"The only reason I haven't killed you yet is because I'm not going to do that in front of your wife and daughter." The calm mask cloaking Thorne's tone speaks of his danger. "With my father out of the way, you took his place in the auxiliary leadership. He'd referred you before, so they were all too accepting of you when he died. But that is just the top of the shit. All of that was done for one single reason."

"What reason?" Mom asks, but she's glaring at Levgen.

"To marry you," Thorne replies.

Mom and I both look at Thorne now.

"What do you mean?" Mom's voice is so weak I can barely hear it.

"He killed his first wife. She didn't die of an illness. She was poisoned. He poisoned her and made it look like she died of natural causes." Thorne continues staring at Levgen with that murderous expression in his eyes. "Why don't you tell the family you stole from your best friend what you did to get them."

My legs turn to water, and I feel like I might wither away. I look at Levgen, my brain struggling to comprehend what Thorne is saying. And yet something sinister whispers to me that I knew things were off. Not exactly about the way he helped us, but about *him*.

I was too young to really understand, but it was strange how he married Mom with ease and then they were a couple. I remember her looking awkward around him for years, but he was never like that. He fell into the role of the husband from day one.

"I saw you first," Levgen says to Mom in a tight voice. "I met you before him."

The him he's referring to is my father.

"But you introduced us." Mom's voice trembles.

"I did, but I didn't know you were going to fall for him. I couldn't marry you because I was promised to Susana. I married her anyway but I always planned to kill her. When she died, my next step was to get you back from my thieving best friend." When he blinks it's like that mask of the savior slips off his face and I see him for who he really is. "First, I had to get in with the senior Knights so I would be allowed to marry you. My family inheritance rules are strict and I would always be bound to have an arranged marriage with anyone who was of age in Susana's family. Unless I was a senior Knight. Nicholai Ivanov was in the process of helping me accomplish that goal when his wife and daughter discovered what I did to my clients. That's why I had them killed, but I left a loose end."

"Me." Thorne gives him a mirthless grin.

"I wasn't worried about a child but it turns out I should have been. For years I plotted to get rid of Gustave. The opportunity came about at the palace two years after I was rid of Nicholai's family. I set him up to take the fall for the murders but I left another loose end." Now he looks at me.

"You put me in danger," I choke out.

"You weren't supposed to be there. Your mother was called in to work at the hospital and your father had to take care of you."

"I can't believe this is really true." Mom swallows, shaking her head. "You did this?"

"I'm sorry my love." Levgen stares back at her. "I've always been in love with you and all I wanted was to be with you. You should have always been my wife, and Ivy should have been my daughter."

"So you took me away from Gustave? You put me and my daughter in the worst kind of danger."

"I set things up so the only thing you could do was turn to me. I thought staging your deaths would have taken care of everything. It did. Until now."

"Nobody ever suspected you of anything, but you were the puppet master," Thorne grates out. His free hand is balled into a tight fist at his side. "You hired mercenaries who pride themselves on working under the radar to do your dirty work. But you slipped up."

"Ivy was the wild card." Again he looks at me. "You weren't supposed to be at the palace with your father that night, so you saw things you shouldn't have seen. I didn't know until days ago that you'd identified the scar-faced man as a Knight, and I didn't know you heard his death chant."

"Those two little details put everything together the moment I told Thorne." I stare at my stepfather, not wanting to believe that he's really this monster, but he is. "Nothing made sense until we spoke and realized we'd seen the same man."

"Yes."

"Then our search for the scar-faced man got you in trouble because you'd hired him for the jobs," Thorne fills in. "You sent me the message warning me away from finding him because he was in touch with you."

I wasn't even aware of such a message.

"Had you listened to my warning, none of this would have happened. But you had to go and kill his spy. That's why he tried to kill you. He will keep trying because you know too much."

"This is madness. You have to stop him, Levgen," Mom blurts.

"I'm afraid it's too late for that," comes a cold, raspy voice from the corner of the room.

We all turn around to look and my soul fractures at the sight of the scar-faced man standing in the doorway.

My God. He's here. Inside the house with us. How did he get in without the guards noticing him?

He steps forward with a psychotic smile that belongs in a horror movie. "Sorry, Mrs. Yegorov, you can't stop me and there's no one to help you. My men have surrounded the place and all your guards are dead." His voice is emotionless and raspy, matching the gruesome appearance of his face.

"I told you I would take care of the situation." Levgen steps forward.

"And yet the boy is here." The man looks at Thorne. "Here with all the evidence and probably more shit to expose me and mine."

"You motherfucking bastard. You killed my family." Thorne squares his shoulders. The man holds his hand up.

"I wouldn't move if I were you." He wiggles his fingers, and two men carrying guns enter from behind him.

One points a gun at Thorne and the other at Mom. The guns have red laser pointers shining on Mom and Thorne's foreheads.

Terror closes my throat, and I dare not breathe. My nerves are amplified when the man approaches me and yanks me toward him.

My body is already weakened from the situation, but having him touch me makes me feel sick to my core. But that becomes the least of my worries when he places the cold metal barrel of his gun against my head.

I go still in his arms, my eyes on Thorne who looks frozen in fear for me.

"Let her go," he barks.

"No. I don't think so. Here's what I want, Thorne Ivanov. You can give me everything you have on me." He glares at Thorne, then switches his gaze to Levgen. "And you, old friend, you can give me fifty million for my troubles. And you get to pick which of your girls lives. Your wife or your stepdaughter."

This is an absolute nightmare. I can't believe this is really happening.

Dark terror spreads across Levgen's face like a rash. "Let them both go and I'll give you everything."

"No. You've crossed me one too many times with your *loose ends*. I demand a heart from one of the people you love."

"Just take mine. Please don't hurt them," Levgen begs. "Kill me and let them go."

The man laughs out loud, and I feel the rattle of his laughter pulsating through my being. "No. Choose now."

The sound of gunshots outside cuts through the moment.

Gunfire rips through the air again and Levgen takes the chance to lunge for Mom. He pushes her out of the way of the laser focused on her head. The two tumble to the ground but one of the guards fires a shot and hits Levgen.

I barely register what's happening before Thorne moves into action and pulls out his gun to shoot the guard. He also shoots the scar-faced man in the arm.

Yelping in pain, the man releases me and I rush toward the corner to take cover behind the piano.

At that moment, Caspian rushes out of the kitchen and shoots the scar-faced man in the chest. Lucian is behind him with some of the guards I've seen at Raventhorn.

"Obviously, I didn't come alone either," Thorne snarls, pointing his gun at the scar-faced man. "I knew you were watching me and waiting for the right moment to attack, but you wanted to see what shit I had on you first. That's why you came out tonight."

The scar-faced man falls to his knees, dropping his gun and grabbing his chest. "End me then, Knight."

"This is for my family." Thorne shoots him in the head and the monster from my nightmares slumps to the ground in a pool of blood, vanquished.

Thorne fires another two shots.

Three bullets in total. One bullet for each member of his family. He fires two more times while looking across at me.

One bullet for each of us. Him and me.

For the pain we both suffered.

Then Thorne hurries to me and takes me into his arms.

I look across at Mom and Levgen. Mom is crying and shaking as she stares at Levgen lying lifeless on the ground before her.

She's covered in blood, and Levgen has a bullet wound in his head.

His eyes are wide open, but he's not with us anymore.

He's dead.

He died protecting my mother. The woman he loved.

CHAPTER 38

MOM IS IN A COMPLETE MESS OF DISTRESS AND DESPAIR. She's sitting in the chair in the corner of my bedroom. She didn't want to go back to hers. Memories of Levgen haunt us both like a bad dream that you can't wake up from.

It's strange to think that just hours ago he was alive and still the stepfather I loved. Now he's dead and we know he was the real monster in the dark.

Fresh tears stream down Mom's cheeks when she sees me.

I walk up to her and hand her a steaming cup of chamomile tea.

I went downstairs to make it for her. In light of what happened tonight my efforts are futile, but it's something. I had to do something to make her feel better no matter how small, or pointless.

She uses the cup to warm her hands although it's not cold in here.

Tired eyes stare back at me when her gaze climbs up to meet mine. "Is everyone still here?"

"Yes, but I think they're nearly done."

Thorne is downstairs with Caspian and Lucian. They contacted a cleanup team who are removing the bodies. Including Levgen's.

"Thorne booked us into a guest house near campus." If it weren't so late, Mom and I would have left already. Being surrounded by death, disappointment, and grief is making it harder to leave the nightmare behind.

"Please thank Thorne for me. Thank him for everything. God knows what would have happened if he hadn't come by…." She starts crying again, breaking down like she did before.

I take the cup from her and set it on the dresser so she doesn't burn herself, then I sit next to her and put my arm around her shoulders.

"Mom."

"I'm sorry. I'm so sorry. There's so much to take in and I don't know if I'll ever be strong again."

"You will."

"I don't know how to feel."

"You're in shock." I'm in shock too, yet I'm surprisingly holding it together. But I think that's because I know Mom needs me. We can't both fall apart.

"I'm in the deepest shock. Levgen ruined our lives. Your father has been in prison this whole time because of him and I had to give up everything to save us." Her breath catches as she dries her tears. "I should have believed you. I *should* have believed you, but I never wanted to hear anything that could put us in danger."

"I understand. What Levgen did was just… despicable. Dad thinks we're dead." Tears pull at my eyes and I can't control the few that slide down my cheeks.

Mom sees me crying and takes my hand. "I have to fix this."

"I think we can now."

She pulls me in for a hug and holds me. We stay like that until a knock sounds at the door.

I get up to answer it and find Thorne standing on the other side.

Sympathy fills his eyes when he looks at Mom who has her head in her hands, weeping.

I step out of the room so Thorne and I can speak in private.

"She's in a bad way." I release a haggard breath that feels like it's been fighting to break free of the compression in my lungs.

"I'm so sorry for everything."

"I'm sorry for you too. I'm still linked to someone who hurt you deeply." I bring my hands together. "It was bad enough when I felt like your enemy's daughter, but when we realized that my father was set up I felt better. Only to realize now that my stepfather was the orchestrator of this disaster."

"That's on him. Not you. Never you."

"Thank you for thinking like that."

"Of course. Ivy, you are a victim. Just like me. You hear me?"

I nod. "Thank you for everything."

"You are welcome."

"How did you find out all that stuff? There was a lot there. It was everything."

"Before the shooting I got a message from an unknown number warning me away from searching for the scar-faced man. I had someone look into it to find out who it came from. As soon as they were able to identify Levgen they found everything else."

"I'm glad you were still looking after he told you to hand him everything."

"Honestly I'd stopped because I didn't want to put you in danger, but I wanted to know who sent me the message."

"I can't believe it was really him."

"Monsters are often the people you know who hide behind the mask of kindness and love. You would never imagine that Levgen was responsible for any of this because he loved you. He loved you and your mother in a sick, selfish way."

I nod, agreeing. "What happens now?"

"I'm heading back to campus. There's some stuff I need to do for your father."

My heart lifts as if carried up by wings. "My father?"

"Yeah. I think he's been in prison long enough. I don't want him to wait a minute longer."

I move into him, hugging him hard. "Oh Thorne. Thank you so much."

"It's over now…*Annika*." He says my name as if he's trying it out for the first time. "It's over. You don't have to be afraid anymore."

I look up at him. "Thanks to you."

Four days later Mom, Thorne, and I wait outside the Knights' central office.

My father was flown here from the Hallows two days ago.

Dad spent the last two days being processed, whatever that means. No one has ever made it back from the Hallows alive, so I guess it had something to do with that.

We weren't allowed to see him until today. It's like waiting for someone to come out of a courthouse.

Any minute now my father should walk through those sliding doors as a free man.

It will be the first time he'll see us in almost a decade.

Mom links her arm with mine. She looks brighter than days ago but still drained. I have every emotion still running through me

The two of us stare directly at the doors as if we're scared he'll come out and we'll miss him.

We've been watching officials go in and out for the half hour that we've stood here waiting.

All sorts of crazy things are running through my mind and I keep worrying that something will go wrong.

This is too good to be true, so something may happen and we won't see him. *What if they send him back?*

As if sensing my thoughts Thorne takes my hand and gives it a gentle squeeze.

The doors slide open, and I wait with my breath swelling in my chest, hoping that this time it will be my father.

And it is.

Dad walks out dressed in the same black clothes he would have worn at the Hallows. But he's carrying a duffel bag.

Unlike the picture I saw of him weeks ago, his hair has grown back. It's still cropped but at least it's not shaved. And he has a patch covering his lost eye.

When he sees us he stops and stares, tears streaming down his cheeks.

"Go," Thorne mutters, and we do.

Mom and I run toward my father, who pulls us into his arms.

The last time the three of us were together like this we were at the helm of danger, fleeing for our lives. Now we have a fresh start.

Dad cups my face and smiles down at me. "Annika," he whispers, pressing his forehead to mine. "It's really you?"

It sounds so good to hear his voice. "Yes Papa, it's me."

He touches my cheek and I no longer feel like the lost little girl.

Dad focuses on Mom next and tries to speak, but he's so caught up in emotion it breaks him. It breaks her, too.

While they hug I look at Thorne and find him staring at us.

I owe him everything.

He did this for me. He gave me my father back.

I feel sad that I can't bring his family back too.

But I promise to give him all my love.

CHAPTER 39

"Everything good?" Caspian asks as I walk through the door and close it behind me.

"Yeah." I sit and rest against the sofa.

We're in the office at the frat house. I just got back from seeing Ivy. I was helping her parents get settled into the new home the Knights gave them, by way of apology.

This is the first time in history that they were proven to have sent an innocent man to the Hallows. Because Gustave Bershov was the senior guard and not just any old innocent man, I imagine the compensation will be more than over the top.

It will never be enough though to make up for what he went through.

Gustave received a full pardon and because of the evidence I provided on Levgen, the whole set up to stage Ivy and her mother's deaths were excused.

"Are you sure you don't have any more secrets up your sleeves?" Caspian smirks.

I spread my arms out wide for show. "Nothing at all."

It was only the day after the showdown at the cottage that I told him everything. When he came to my aid it was without any knowledge of what was happening. He just knew I needed his help.

He brought the Bratva task force with him, which is how we were able to overpower the men the scar-faced man brought with him. And the man himself.

"Don't ever do that to me again. I understand why you did it but I felt like you didn't trust me."

"You know it wasn't that."

"Yes. I know, but that's what it felt like. Remember, I was the one who was taken captive. I deserved to know what was going on."

I nod, agreeing. "Yes, you are absolutely right, but I couldn't put you in the position of conflict."

"And you love Ivy so much that you even protected her from me." He gives me a knowing smile.

"Yes. I guess that's what happened."

"For the record, I would have kept your girl's secret."

"Thank you." I make a fist and place it at my heart, showing my appreciation for his allegiance.

"No worries."

"Now I can go back to my original shit problems."

"Actually, you might not." He picks up an envelope and hands it to me.

"What's this?"

"It's from Kai. About my father. He sent one of his men with it. He left a few minutes before you arrived."

"Have you looked inside?"

"No. I left that for you. Shows you can trust me." He taps his chest. "Kai said all the answers you need are inside. He says he did it for free because it will get my father off his back if we make the right choice."

Now I'm more than curious. I tear open the envelope and pull out the first document. It's Aleksander's medical records.

I see exactly what I need to see at the top of the page and immediately stand.

"What is it?" Caspian asks with a hint of dread in his tone.

"Kai's right. This is the answer. We have to go to Ivanov Tech now."

"What's going on?"

"I'll tell you on the way."

We arrive at Ivanov Tech within the hour.

Aleksander is sitting in his office going through paperwork when we walk in.

The door was open but Caspian closes it behind us. His face is a stony mask.

Aleksander looks furious to see us. "What the hell are the two of you doing here? I did everything I was supposed to, to free Gustave Bershov."

If I'd allowed this asshole to handle Gustave's release he would still be at the Hallows. The new year would come and he'd *still* be there.

Aleksander wasn't even impressed with my work to uncover the mystery of my family's deaths.

The asshole is bitter because *he* didn't do it. I got the justice we sought for so many years, and the glory will go to me for solving his brother's murder. Not him.

Once I presented him with the paperwork and got his clearance, I went to one of the judges to do the rest. Aleksander was fucking around, taking his own sweet time and talking shit about running it through the council as a trial.

Nothing of the sort needed to be done. It's times like this when I'm grateful for my defiance.

I walk up to him and rest the copy of his medical records before him.

He gazes down at the document and his eyes stay there, glued to what I unearthed.

If anyone were to search for this they'd find a dupe that shows a healthy man.

But I have the original. I have the truth.

"You're dying," I state, saying the words carefully. I can be a motherfucker, but I'm not about to taunt a dying man.

The records show that Aleksander has an inoperable brain tumor. He's been receiving treatment for the last year and has been given a year to eighteen months to live.

Under the law of the Knights, he's supposed to step down as leader because when you have such an illness it is believed that you won't be able to fulfill your duties.

Under the law of succession that my father and him agreed to, Aleksander is supposed to hand over the company to Caspian and me for the same reasons. It was an agreement which they signed in blood.

This secret is what he didn't want me to find out. Having me working at the company would have left him open for me to do so, because I've discovered many of his secrets before. And he doesn't know how to hide from me.

This is a big one I shouldn't have found out. It signifies the end of him.

The shipment he's supposed to receive is part of some new age treatment he's been trying, because his tumor is no longer responding to conventional treatment.

Finally, Aleksander lifts his head and looks at me, then he looks at Caspian.

Neither of us knows what to feel. Aleksander has been horrible to us our entire lives.

But Caspian will remember him as the man who moved heaven and earth to rescue him when he was taken.

I will remember him as the man who provided me with a home.

"Come to gloat?" He tries to keep his usual cynical expression but fails.

"That's something you'd do," Caspian replies.

"Yeah, you're right, son. That is something I would do. What about you, Thorne? You have every reason to gloat. You said you couldn't fucking wait to find out what I was hiding."

"Yeah. I did say that and I still feel the same."

"Why didn't you just tell us?" Caspian asks.

"Really? So I'd lose the leadership to *you*." Aleksander gives him an incredulous glare. "But I guess you're here to take it, aren't you?"

"We should be."

"*Should?* Don't tell me you're here out of the goodness of your heart."

"No. You killed my heart a long time ago."

"Then what? What the fuck are you going to do? Broadcast it so the Knights Council can shove me through the door and kick me to the curb?"

"I've handed that decision to Thorne to deal with."

Now I smile because the look of fury and defeat on Aleksander's face is priceless.

I've wanted to kill his ass for so long for the way he's screwed with me, but my decision is so much better.

I straighten and stare him down. "I will allow you to keep your leadership in the Knights until your death. We won't say anything."

Aleksander looks shocked that I would allow him to keep his leadership. I have a reason for that and it's not because Caspian and I aren't ready to take charge now. We are and we'd do it today if we needed to.

I'm using the position as leverage and allowing Aleksander to keep it because he could force the Knights' law on me and still demand that I marry someone of his choice. If he did so and I refused him again the way I did with Tiffany, I would lose my Knighthood.

Although Ivy's father is a Knight, her mother is not of Knight descent. That would be enough for him to force a marriage contract on me because our family is part of the leadership. The rules are different for us, but as leader Aleksander can change them. Regardless of his sickness.

The other reason I'm allowing him to keep the position is that the women in our lives aren't ready for us to lead the Knights yet.

Ivy is still eighteen and Willow is nineteen. They need time to adjust.

I guess we do too, now that we have them.

Caspian made the same decision last year, so it appears that Aleksander is getting away with murder twice. But this is all for our benefit.

Aleksander quirks a brow. "What else is there? You want more don't you?"

"Yes I do. You will step down from the company with immediate effect and *we* will take over. *With immediate effect.* There will be no *internship* for me, and no fucking marriage contract. Under no circumstance will you choose a wife for me. I get to be with whoever I want and have my birthright. Refuse my offer and you lose every motherfucking thing."

Silence passes between us. It's so tense and thick you could touch it. I expect it to take on a life of its own and suffocate me.

Of course he doesn't want to lose the company or the leadership of the Knights. He put his life into this company, but he'd lose so much more if he weren't the leader of the Knights.

Lifetimes seem to pass between us as he contemplates his decision, then finally he nods.

"Okay. You win, but you already knew that, didn't you?"

I give him a thin smile. "Pleasure doing business with you, Uncle."

He seethes, throwing back a steely stare.

Caspian and I walk out, leaving him.

Once we're outside we look at each other but we don't say anything.

No words need to be said because we just got control of a multibillion dollar empire.

We both won.

Now to secure the next item on my list.

Ivy.

I want the world to know she's mine and I'm never letting her go ever again.

CHAPTER 40

I'M BACK AT RAVENTHORN AND EVERYTHING LOOKS AND FEELS AMAZING to me.

I arrived half an hour ago and decided to go for a walk by the river. I'm seeing Thorne later, but I wanted to get reacquainted with the campus.

I've been away for a total of two weeks. The bulk of that time was spent with my mother and father.

The Knights gave Dad a two-story mansion in Lexington and released all his assets so he has access to everything he previously owned.

He's been given that part of his life back, but my parents have a lot to figure out for themselves.

I have no doubt that they'll get back together, though. Mom is talking about relocating here in Boston, so that's a good step. I want them to get back together.

I know we won't forget Levgen's' treachery anytime soon, but focusing on him taints the goodness we have received in getting Dad back. It also prevents us from moving on.

With my parents taken care of, I now step back into the shoes of my life here, but I don't feel like the same person I was when I left.

For the first time since coming here, I feel like I belong.

I'm not a stepchild anymore, who has to be careful with her secrets. I'm here as the daughter of a Knight who is no longer disgraced.

That's why everything feels so different.

I walk along the river and spot Isabelle and Mackenzie crossing over the bridge. The two see me, too, and start running toward me.

No one knows the truth yet. It will be announced next week as part of the protocol to clear my father's name, but I want to tell them.

Especially because I'm going back to my old name—*Annika*.

I never really stopped being her so it won't be hard.

"Oh my gosh, you're actually back." Isabelle hugs me.

"I'm back."

"We missed you, girl." Mackenzie gives me a hug too. "I hope everything is okay at home."

"Yeah, how are your parents?" Isabelle stares at me with concern.

"There's ... some stuff I have to tell you. Can we grab a coffee?"

"Of course," Isabelle says and Mackenzie nods, then the two exchange worried glances. "Come on. It will be our treat."

"Thanks."

We head down the path. I look at them and feel grateful to have them as my friends. That feels good, too.

Thorne is standing by my living room window when I return to my room.

My heart lifts at the sight of him.

Talking with Isabelle and Mackenzie was quite emotional, but I did it. I feel better for getting everything off my chest and my life feels more real now.

I'm no longer a secret shared by a handful of people.

Thorne turns to face me. An easy, sexy grin slides across his handsome face as he looks me up and down. "A word of advice, Bambi. It's not good to keep your lord waiting for you when he can't wait to feast on your body."

"Sorry, my lord, I was talking to my friends."

"How did that go?"

"Good. They know I'm Annika Bershov now."

His smile widens. "That's good, *Annika*. I'll bet your father is happy about that."

"He is. My mom is too. I finally feel like I can be myself and not hide in someone else's body."

"You were never in someone else's body. You were always Annika to me, and I like this body." He gives me a scandalous look that has my body temperature rising.

"Do you now?"

A cheeky grin dances on his firm lips. "Come here to me, Annika."

I love the way he says my name and the ravenous look in his eyes. I walk over to him, and he pulls me in for a kiss.

"I have something for you," he whispers across my lips.

"What is it?"

Thorne reaches into his pocket. He pulls out my ring. The ring my father made for me. The ring that sent me on this wild, crazy path with Thorne Ivanov and led me here.

He holds it up to the light, then hands it to me. "You can wear this with pride now."

I beam back at him, then I look at the inscription engraved on the inside of the band. "Thank you. You're right. I *can* wear it with pride now."

"You can wear it until we're engaged. Then you'll *only* wear my ring."

A tremor shoots through me, then my blood drains from my face and I know I'm pale. Fire rushes back to my skin when I truly process what he said and suddenly I'm so hot I can't breathe. "What did you say?"

"You heard me. I told you, you're mine. I meant it, so I'll never be done with you. Not even death can keep me away from you, *Annika Bershov*."

His words leave me breathless, as if the air has deserted my lungs. But my mind and body are filled with him.

"Me too. It's the same for me too."

"I love you." He smiles again and brushes his nose over mine.

"I love you, too."

We fall into a kiss that's filled with promises and all my dreams come true.

It turned out that Thorne Ivanov was my Knight in shining armor, and I can't wait to be with him for the rest of forever.

EPILOGUE

Thorne

Six weeks later

BLUE IS DEFINITELY MY LITTLE DEER'S COLOR.

She looks like she's ready to walk down the runway of a Victoria's Secret fashion show.

I gaze at her standing by my bed dressed in the lingerie I bought for her. It's similar to the yellow set I got months ago, but this is blue and it looks like it was made for her.

My dick is practically on the verge of exploding, so I don't know how I'm managing to control myself.

Earlier, I was in a Knights' meeting for hours and all I could think about was her. And getting back here to her so I could own her body again and again and all over a-fucking-gain.

By the time I got here I just wanted to consume her, but when I saw her like this I needed a moment to savor her and commit her body to memory. This is the kind of image a man needs in his head always, so when he takes his last breath he knows he lived a good life.

It's the little deer's birthday today and I have all kinds of plans for her, starting now.

Annika sets her hands on her hips and pretends to pout.

I've had six weeks to get used to thinking of her and calling her by that name. It wasn't that hard for me because I've known it for so long.

"Tell me again how pleasing you is supposed to be a good birthday present for *me*." She folds her arms under her breasts, drawing attention to her deep cleavage.

"Oh no, little deer. You got this the wrong way around." I walk up to her and grip a good handful of her lush ass. "It's me who's going to be pleasing you. You're just wearing the uniform I picked out for you."

She giggles and glances down at herself. "Uniform?"

"Uniform number one."

"There's more?"

"Just one more. The best thing about dressing you like this is taking it off and seeing what's underneath." I slide the straps of her bra down her shoulders and undo the butterfly clasp holding it together.

Her gorgeous breasts fall out and I'm harder for seeing her pink puckered nipples.

"You've seen me like this many times."

"And yet, it's always like the first time." I give her a sinful smile and crouch down to pull her panties off with my teeth. I slide them down her legs and take pleasure in adoring her perfect body.

"You are so crazy."

"I hope you remember that when we fly off to the Bahamas tomorrow."

Her mouth falls open. "What?"

"Birthday present number two."

Annika's eyes light up with excitement. "You're serious."

"Of course I am." I lick over the silky skin of her legs.

"Thank you so much. I've always wanted to go there."

"I know, that's why we'll be there for the next ten days." I waited for the perfect time to take her.

She celebrated Christmas in Russia last week with her parents, but they allowed me to have her for her birthday and New Year's.

"You're the best, Thorne."

"So are you." I slide up between her thighs and lick over the smooth mound of her pussy. "For tonight, let's focus on birthday present number one, where you get to tell me to do whatever you want me to do to you."

Her eyes light up again but there's a hint of sexy mischief in the depths of the gray hues. "Really?"

"Yes, Bambi, *really*. Tonight your wish is my command. So, what do you want your lord to do to you?"

She bites back a delicious smile, then gives me a full-blown one. "I want you three times."

"Is that so?"

"Yes. Once in the bed, then in the shower, then in the hot tub."

"Jesus woman. Looks like we're going to be up all night again."

"I hope you're not tired."

"You know I'm not." I laugh and pick her up then set her on the bed.

She watches me take my clothes off and I love the desire in her eyes and the rosy stain of her cheeks.

I bend down to get a good taste of her pretty, pink pussy, before I bury my cock deep inside her, granting her first wish.

I land a fist in the punching bag and it bounces from the fierce impact.

I'm downstairs in the training room at the frat house.

Snow is blanketing outside so I can't do my usual workout. I've been down here for three hours using the equipment.

This area is set up for serious training. I'm entering the UFC tournament in a few weeks, so I need to make sure I'm on my game.

My little deer and I got back from the Bahamas yesterday. We had such a blast it was hard coming back. I've had the best time of my life with her. Now we're back for the second semester of college.

The time has flown by so fast I don't know where it went. At least only good things are happening.

Caspian and I took over Ivanov Tech with ease. We'd been training to take over the company all our lives so we simply slipped into the shoes of the men we were meant to be.

The first thing I did when I got into that office was get rid of Aiden and his father. The two kicked up a stink but I quickly silenced them with the dirt I found on them being involved with smuggling shit into the country.

With them out of the way I could breathe.

Aleksander, on the other hand, is a shadow of his former self, but now when I see him I notice the effects of his illness.

Whatever he's doing is helping to prolong his life, but since I've been keeping tabs on his progress I know the clock is still ticking over his head. The doctors still believe he only has a year to eighteen months to live, so his various treatments will only help until they stop.

Until then, I imagine he'll continue being the dictator he is, but he'll know that he's on my time. Every time he looks at me he'll be worried about what I could still take away from him.

And most of all, he'll know I *allowed* him to keep his position.

For him that is the same as pity, the worst thing to an Ivanov man.

The door opens but I don't break focus as I throw another series of punches at the bag and pivot into a perfect roundhouse kick.

It's only then that I look around that I see Kade standing by the platform watching me.

He's proven to be even better than I thought he'd be, but I think that's because of the demons that still haunt him.

"Morning, boss." He smirks. "If that bag were a man you would have destroyed him ten times over."

"Something like that." I nod at him and fix the support wrapping on my hands. "Whatever you want, you better talk fast. My girl should be here any minute."

"Okay." He chuckles. "I want you to train me."

I give him a narrowed stare and grab my bottle of water from my side. "I already trained you, and you are part of my elite."

"I know, but I don't mean like that. Not like for the Reckoning. I know you were holding back, Thorne."

I continue looking at him. He's right. I was holding back. Most people don't know that about me, unless I want them six feet under.

"What's this about?"

"I need to get better. When I fight you I don't need to hold back, but knowing *you're* holding back means I'm not as good as I'd like to think I am."

Now he's got me curious. "What do you need to get better for?"

"I'd rather not talk about that." Unease creeps into his face.

"Then I'm not going to help you."

He thinks for a moment, then the tension in his face eases. "I got some intel about my family. The people responsible for their deaths."

"And what kind of people are they?"

"A mixture. But the ones I need to worry about aren't the good kind."

"Don't tell me I picked you to join my elite and months from now you'll wash up dead somewhere." I smirk.

"With your help, that might not happen." He draws in a breath. "You got your retribution by getting the man responsible for killing your family. I just want mine. I want justice too. From all of them. From the weakest to the strongest."

There's something psychotic about the way he speaks that grips me. Once again, he sounds like me, reminding me of myself.

I feel inclined to agree to whatever this is, just to keep an eye on him.

The ritual of the Reckoning dictates that I'm supposed to have his back from now on anyway.

"Okay. Training starts tomorrow at five a.m. Don't be late."

"Thank you." He dips his head and grins. "I appreciate it."

Just then the door opens and Annika walks through.

Her expression dims when she notices Kade. I know she doesn't like him. She's never told me but I know and I have a feeling it's to do with Isabelle.

Isabelle has crushed on Kade for years but nothing has come of it.

To be honest, I wouldn't want him anywhere near her.

"Annika." Kade bows his head when Annika gets closer.

"Hi." She gives him a polite smile.

"Enjoy the rest of your day." He looks at both of us before he leaves.

When Annika looks back at me I jump off the platform and grab her for a kiss.

"You don't like my friends." I nibble her cheek and she giggles.

"I never said that."

"You don't have to. Anyway, I missed you."

"You just saw me hours ago."

"Like fuck, exactly. *Hours.* I need you again."

"Then take me." She rubs her nose over mine.

"With pleasure."

I pull her back in for another kiss and hope no one comes down here. I plan to take her right here and if anyone disturbs me, they're dead.

EPILOGUE

Annika

One month later

ISABELLE AND I ARE ON OUR WAY TO EILISH'S OFFICE TO TRY TO convince her to go to the party with us.

Myrridin House is throwing its first party of the year. Since we're in the heart of winter, we decide on a snow and ice theme.

Everyone has been looking forward to it. Everyone except Eilish, because Lucian is heading to Russia tonight.

Eilish has been putting on her game face and acting like she'll be okay, but she's not. I saw her crying in the garden this morning.

She was there for me a lot when I was going through hell and couldn't tell anyone. She has been there for Isabelle too.

"I think Eilish will love this. No one can say no to a little sugar." Isabelle holds up the pastry box full of cupcakes she got and gives me an uncertain smile. "These are her favorite."

"Then this was a good idea."

"I hope so, and I hope she got to see Lucian before he left." Isabelle grimaces. "She was talking about not saying goodbye to him because it's so hard.".

"I hope she changed her mind. I felt guilty this morning when I saw her. I was with Thorne. When she saw us together it was clear she was missing Lucian." Thorne and I were kissing in the snow. Since we're the only two people on this planet when we're together, we didn't notice her straightaway.

Isabelle giggles. "Don't feel bad about that. Eilish and Lucian have been so-called best friends forever. They've had time to get it on. You and Thorne didn't waste time."

I smile back at her. "No, we didn't."

"Does he have another surprise for you tonight?"

I blush. Since we got back from the Bahamas for the holiday of a lifetime, Thorne has been on this quest to shower me with gifts and surprise getaways.

"I think he will."

"You lucky girl."

"Hey, you'll be lucky too, soon."

"I don't know, but we'll see, right?" Her tone is flat. "I guess I'd have to date first wouldn't I?"

"Yes you would." I place emphasis on my words to show my intense agreement. She hasn't attempted to date anyone since she found out that asshole Kade was screwing with any guy interested in her.

"I'll think about it."

"Or just do it. I saw Curt Matthews looking at you earlier."

"I noticed him, too, but since he has his own teeth, is under the age of sixty-five, doesn't dress like Dr. Seuss, and is good looking I doubt he'll be *allowed* to slip through the net."

"I'm sure Kade isn't still playing that game. That was several months ago."

"I don't know for sure, but it would certainly explain why every guy who is remotely interested in me changes course like the wind and backs away from coming near me."

"Do you want me to talk to Thorne?" I've asked her that before.

"No. It's silly and I need to deal with it myself in whatever way I can." She nods.

My shoulders slump. "Okay. Let me know if I can help."

"Of course."

We reach Eilish's office and knock on the door. There's no answer but I'm sure she's in there. I can hear muffled sounds.

Isabelle and I glance at each other when she knocks again and there's still no answer.

I'd hate for Eilish to be in there crying again so I brave the task of opening the door and hope she won't be mad at me. People say it's better to ask for forgiveness than permission.

When the door swings open my mouth drops, so does Isabelle's and the two of us stand frozen to the spot as we stare at Eilish and Lucian kissing against the wall.

They're so engrossed in each other that they haven't even noticed our intrusion. And I'm so happy for them I can't stop staring.

Thank God, my common sense kicks in and I realize they'll be bound to notice us if we stay any longer.

I grab Isabelle who is so entranced by the sight of them she hasn't thought to move.

It's only when I ease the door shut that she snaps out of the trance.

On seeing that she looks like she might scream I tug her away and wait until we get a very safe distance before I stop.

She shrieks and jumps up and down, nearly dropping the pastry box. "Holy shit. This is such good news."

"I know and there we were thinking she was depressed."

Isabelle laughs. "I feel like shouting the news from the rooftop. But oh my God no, I would never do that." She covers her mouth and giggles. "But you know what I mean."

"I know what you mean." I smile.

"I thought he'd left campus already."

"Looks like he stayed a little longer for her."

"Yes, but damn it, he's going away for a year. Let's hope we don't have to wait that long to find out what happens next."

"Let's hope so. Come on, let's go to the party."

"Yes," she answers in an over-excited voice.

We share the cupcakes and finish them before we reach the hall, then we notice the absolutely beautiful ice sculptures on the terrace. And it's just started to snow.

It looks like something pulled from a fairytale.

"Oh my, look at that," Isabelle gasps.

We head outside, away from the music and dancing students to walk around the sculptures and admire their beauty.

We walk the entire length of the terrace, getting lost in the artwork. They make me hear music. Happy music.

Since my father was released from prison my music doesn't sound so much like death anymore. I can be versatile whereas before I couldn't.

"These are so gorgeous." I mull over the sculpture of the ballerina at the end of the platform.

Isabelle joins me and twirls around it as if she's the ballerina, then she spins me around and we laugh as if we've been drinking all night.

"Maybe I should be a dancer." She continues twirling.

"It would suit you." I scan her little dress. It's not as doll-like as some of her others but she still looks like a doll.

She's about to say something but then stops abruptly. The smile on her face cracks and falls as if someone smashed it, and she stares ahead at the snow-covered garden below.

I follow her gaze and my smile fades too when I find Kade standing there watching us.

No. Not *us*.

He's watching her.

He's standing by the willow tree with his hands in his coat pockets clearly watching *her*.

Kade isn't even bothering to hide it. And the look on his face…

In the moonlight it's haunting. He looks like an otherworldly creature sent to kill.

Kill.

That's how he's looking at Isabelle. As if he wants to kill her.

She sees it too and her pale skin becomes paler. It's also as if the realization has rooted her to the spot and she looks like she can't move.

My spine tingles with that get-the-hell-out-of-here sensation that tells me to take her and run. The last time I saw anyone look so demented was when I encountered the scar-faced man.

Just the thought of him sends icicles racing over my lungs and I have to remind myself that he's dead.

"Bambi."

Thorne's voice snaps me from my daze.

The moment I look at him, I feel safe again. I glance back at Kade but he's gone. Isabelle is still staring ahead though, as if she can still see him.

Thorne comes up to me and slips an arm around my waist. "Hey."

"Hi. We were just admiring the sculptures," I explain, trying to keep the wariness out of my voice.

"They just started serving those strawberry cocktails you like. Thought I'd come and get you."

"Thanks."

He glances at Isabelle. "You okay Izzy?"

"Yeah. I'm fine." Isabelle looks at him and tries to smile but the smile doesn't quite reach her lips.

"It's freezing out here. Come on let's go inside."

"Sure."

She follows us when Thorne ushers me ahead but I keep my eye on her. I see the nervousness still in her as she looks over her shoulder at the spot where Kade previously stood.

When we get to the door and Thorne opens it, Isabelle schools her expression and tries to look like her usual sunshine self but I can see she's not okay.

I feel like she needs to be careful of Kade. I don't know why or what his problem is but that's how I feel deep down.

Mackenzie and the other girls join us once we're inside.

After a few minutes of talking with them Isabelle looks better and more relaxed, so I don't feel too bad when Thorne pulls me away from the group.

He leads me back outside to the winter wonderland where we walk through the woods and over to the river. We're alone now, and the moment and surroundings are so beautiful that I make myself forget about the unpleasant encounter with Kade.

Instead I think of the gorgeous amazing man I'm with as we walk along the river.

"I'm going to marry you in snow like this," Thorne says, speaking against the silence.

From time to time he says things like that. We're not officially engaged yet but he keeps dropping hints as if it's coming. He also acts like we're already married. The other day he called me his wife. It would have been a swoon worthy moment if he hadn't said it to my father.

It was still nice to hear him say it. Dad smiled at me, then he looked at Mom who couldn't stop herself from laughing. My parents are back together now. Thorne and I were visiting them for Sunday dinner.

"A wedding in the snow? Not a hot summer day?" I glance up at Thorne.

"No, that's not us. It will look just like this and we'll take our vows under the moonlight. This reminds me of you." He picks up a platinum lock of my hair and allows it to coil around his finger. "What do you think?"

"I'd like that."

"Good, because I can't wait."

"Me neither."

He grins back at me. "Come here, Bambi."

I move into him and he kisses me. Like with all his kisses, I get lost in him.

EPILOGUE

Kade

I STARE THROUGH THE STAINED-GLASS WINDOWS OF THE HALL.

Isabelle can't see me watching her but she knows I'm still out here.

She's talking to her little group of friends. Mackenzie is standing next to her, probably making a joke about someone or spreading some kind of gossip. Whatever it is has the group laughing.

Isabelle barely smiles. She still looks shaken from seeing me earlier.

Now that Thorne and Annika are gone she's lost and vulnerable again.

Just the way I like her.

I've watched her for years but back then I wasn't sure what part she played.

Now I'm *sure*.

Now I know what the sweet little Lolita doll did.

And I have her just where I want her.

Everyone who's not me is my enemy.

And she is enemy number one.

She and I are just beginning.

I can't wait to see how we'll end.

Run and hide, Lolita. The wolf is coming for you.

WHAT'S NEXT?

Thank you so much for reading *Vicious Knight.* xx
If you liked it, please leave a review. Your support means everything to me.

If you want a little more of Thorne and Annika's wild romance, click here
to read about their trip to the Bahamas.

Next up is the following book in Sins and Saint series, *Devious Knight* where
you get to see Kade and Isabelle's story.

To those who have been following my Raventhorn world and waiting for
Lucian and Eilish's story, don't worry it's coming. It will be in this series.
Thank you for staying with me. xx

You can also check out Caspian and Willow's story by reading the Cruel
Secrets Duet.

If you want to see more of the Knights in action start with Devil's Kiss and
Arranged marriage romance. Please note the events of this series takes place
after the Sins and Saints Series.

If you want to keep updated on my books and this series join the Facebook
group, Dark Odyssey, Faith Summers' Reader Group.

ABOUT THE AUTHOR

Faith Summers is a *USA Today* bestselling author of gripping contemporary, new adult, and dark mafia romance.

She is renowned for writing alluring, fast-paced stories filled with angst, relatable characters that capture the hearts of readers, and unforgettable happily ever afters.

With a rich academic background in law and psychology, Faith skillfully weaves elements of mystery and suspense into her narratives to enrich her stories.

Faith lives in England with her husband and two sons. When she isn't creating her stories, you can find her in a ballet class or ice skating, where she finds additional inspiration and balance.

Faith also pens contemporary and fantasy romance as Khardine Gray.

Author Links

Email: Faithsummers@blissromancepublishing.com
Website: www.faithsummers.com
Amazon: www.amazon.com/author/faithsummers
Instagram : www.instagram.com/faith_summers_books
Facebook: www.facebook.com/FaithSummersBooks